CW00376947

TRUE BLUE

BY

William Henry Giles Kingston

TRUE BLUE

Published by Epic House Publishers

New York City, NY

First published circa 1880

Copyright © Epic House Publishers, 2015

All rights reserved

Except in the United States of America, this book is sold subject to the condition that it shall not, by way of trade or otherwise, be lent, re-sold, hired out, or otherwise circulated without the publisher's prior consent in any form of binding or cover other than that in which it is published and without a similar condition including this condition being imposed on the subsequent purchaser.

ABOUT EPIC HOUSE PUBLISHERS

Few things get the adrenaline going like fast-paced action, and with that in mind, **Epic House Publishers** can give readers the world's best action and adventure novels and stories in the click of a button, whether it's Tarzan on land or Moby Dick in the sea.

Chapter One.

The old Terrible, 74, was ploughing her way across the waters of the Atlantic, now rolling and leaping, dark and angry, with white-crested seas which dashed against her bows and flew in masses of foam over her decks. She was under her three topsails, closely reefed; but even thus her tall masts bent, and twisted, and writhed, as if striving to leap out of her, while every timber and bulkhead fore and aft creaked and groaned, and the blocks rattled, and the wind roared and whistled through the rigging in chorus; and the wild waves rolled and tumbled the big ship about, making her their sport, as if she was a mere cock-boat.

Stronger and stronger blew the gale; darkness came on and covered the world of waters, and through that darkness the ship had to force her way amid the foaming, hissing seas. Darker and darker it grew, till the lookout men declared that they might as well have shut their eyes, for they could scarcely make out their own hands when held at arm's length before their noses.

Suddenly, however, the darkness was dispelled by the vivid flashes of lightning, which, darting from the low hanging clouds, circled about their heads, throwing a lurid glare on the countenances of all on deck. Once more all was dark; then again the forked lightning burst forth hissing and crackling through the air, leaping along the waves and playing round the quivering masts. Now the big ship plunged into the trough of the sea with a force which made it seem as if she was never going to rise again; but up the next watery height she climbed, and when she got to the top, she stopped as if to look about her, while the lightning flashed brighter than ever; and then, rolling and pitching, and cutting numerous other antics, she lifted up her stern as if she was going to give a vicious fling out with her heels, and downwards she plunged into the dark obscurity, amid the high foam-topped seas, which hissed and roared high above her bulwarks. Her crew walked her deck with but little anxiety, although they saw that the gale was likely to increase into a hurricane; for they had long served together, they knew what each other was made of, and they had confidence in their officers and in the stout ship they manned.

The watch below had hitherto remained in their hammocks, and most of them, in spite of the gale, slept as soundly as ever. What cared they that the ship was rolling and tumbling about? They knew that she was watertight and strong, that she had plenty of sea-room, and that they would be roused up quickly enough if they were wanted. There was one person, however, who did not sleep soundly—that was her Captain, Josiah Penrose. He could not forget that he had the lives of some eight hundred beings committed to his charge, and he knew well that, even on board a stout ship with plenty of sea-room, an accident might occur which would require his immediate presence on deck. He was therefore sitting up in his cabin, holding on as best he could, and attempting to read—a task under all circumstances, considering that he had lost an eye, and was not a very bright scholar, more difficult of accomplishment than may be supposed. He had lost an arm, too, which made it difficult for him to hold a book; besides, his book was large, and the printing was not over clear, a fault common in those days; and the paper was a good deal stained and injured from the effects of damp and hot climates. He was aroused from his studies by a signal at the door, and the entrance of one of the quartermasters.

"What is it, Pringle?" asked the Captain, looking up.

"Why, sir, Molly Freeborn is taken very bad, and the doctor says that he thought you would like to know," was the answer. "He doesn't think as how she'll get over it. Maybe, sir, you'd wish to see the poor woman?"

"Certainly, yes; I'll go below and see her," answered the Captain in a kind tone. "Poor Molly! But where is her husband—where is Freeborn? It will be a great blow to him."

"It is his watch on deck, sir. No one liked to go and tell him. He could do no good, and the best chance, the doctor said, was to keep Molly quiet. But I suppose that they'll let him know now," answered the quartermaster.

"Yes; do you go and find him, and take him below to his wife, and just break her state gently to him, Pringle," said the Captain.

Captain Penrose stopped a moment to slip on his greatcoat, and to jam a sou'wester tightly down over his head, before he left the cabin on his errand of kindness, when a terrific clap was heard, louder than one of thunder, and the ship seemed to quiver in every timber fore and aft. The Captain sprang on deck, for the moment, in his anxiety for the safety of his ship, forgetting his intention with regard to Molly Freeborn.

Poor Molly! There she lay in the sick-bay, which had been appropriated to her use, gasping out her life amid the tumult and disturbance of that terrific storm. She was one of three women allowed, in those days, under certain circumstances, to be on board ship for the purpose of acting as nurses to the sick, and of washing for the officers and men. Her husband was captain of the maintop, and as gallant and fine a seaman as ever stepped. Everybody liked and respected him.

But Molly was even a greater favourite. There was not a kinder-hearted, more gentle, sensible, and judicious person in existence. No one had a greater variety of receipts for all sorts of ailments, and no one could more artistically cook dishes better suited to the taste of the sick. Most of the officers, who had from time to time been ill and wounded, acknowledged and prized her talents and excellencies; and the Captain declared that he considered he owed his life, under Providence, entirely to the care with which she nursed him through an attack of fever when the doctor despaired of his life.

"All hands on deck!" was the order given as soon as the Captain saw what had occurred. The main-topsail had been blown from the boltropes, and the tattered remnants were now lashing and slashing about in the gale, twisting into inextricable knots, and winding and wriggling round the main-topsail yard, rendering it a work of great danger to go out on it. The boatswain's whistle sounded shrilly through the storm a well-known note. "All hands shorten sail!" was echoed along the decks. "Rouse out there—rouse out—idlers and all on deck!" Everybody knew that there was work to be done; indeed, the clap made by the parting of the sail had awakened even the soundest sleepers. Among the first aloft, who endeavoured to clear the yard of the fragments of the sail, was William Freeborn, the captain of the maintop. With knives and hands they worked away in spite of the lashing they got, now being almost strangled, and now dragged off the yard.

The Captain resolved to heave the ship to. The wind had shifted, and if they ran on even under bare poles, they would be carried on too much out of their course. It was a delicate and difficult operation. A new main-topsail had first to be bent. It took the united strength of the crew to hoist it to the yard. At length the sail was got up and closely reefed, hauled out, strengthened in every possible way to resist the fury of the gale. It was an operation which occupied some time. The fore-topsail had to be taken in. The helm was put down, and, as she came slowly up to the wind, the after-sail being taken off also, she lay to, gallantly riding over the still rising seas. Though she did not tumble about, perhaps, quite as much as she had been doing, her movements were far from easy. She did not roll as before, as she was kept pressed down on one side; still every now and then she gave a pitch as she glided down into the trough of the sea, which made every timber and mast creak and quiver, and few on board would have been inclined to sing:

At length William Freeborn was relieved from his post aloft, and came down on deck. Paul Pringle, his old friend and messmate, who had been hunting for him through the darkness, found him at last. Paul grieved sincerely for the news he had to communicate, and, not liking the task imposed on him, scarcely knew how to begin.

"Bill," said he with a sigh, "you and I, boy and man, have sailed together a good score of years, and never had a fall-out about nothing all that time, and it goes to my heart, Bill, to say any thing that you won't like; but it must be done—that I sees—so it's no use to have no circumbendibus. Your missus was took very bad—very bad indeed—just in the middle of the gale, and there was no one to send for you—and so, do you see—"

"My wife—Molly!—oh, what has happened, Paul?" exclaimed Freeborn, not waiting for an answer; but springing below, he rushed to the sick-bay, as the hospital is called. The faint cry of an infant reached his ears as he opened the door. Betty Snell, one of the other nurses, was so busily employed with something on her knees, that she did not see him enter. The dim light of a lantern, hanging from a beam overhead, fell on it. He saw that it was a newborn infant. He guessed what had happened, but he did not stop to caress it, for beyond was the cot occupied by his wife. There she lay, all still and silent. His heart sank within him; he gazed at her with a feeling of terror and anguish which he had never before experienced. He took her hand. It fell heavily by her side. He gasped for breath. "Molly!" he exclaimed at length, "speak to me, girl— what has happened?"

There was no answer. Then he knew that his honest, true-hearted wife was snatched from him in this world for ever. The big drops of salt spray, which still clung to his hair and bushy beard, dropped on the kind face of her he had loved so well, but not a tear escaped his eyes. He gladly would have wept, but he had not for so many a long year done such a thing, and he felt too stunned and bewildered to do so now. He had stood as a sailor alone could stand on so unstable a foothold, gazing on those now placid and pale unchanging features for a long time,—how long he could not tell,—when Paul Pringle, who had followed him to the door of the sick-bay, came up, and, gently taking him by the shoulders, said:

"Come along, Bill; there's no use mourning: we all loved her, and we all feel for you, from the Captain downwards. That's a fact. But just do you come and have a look at the younker. Betty Snell vows that he's the very image of you, all except the beard and pigtail."

The latter appendage in those days was worn by most sailors, and Bill Freeborn had reason to pride himself on his. The mention of it just then, however, sent a pang through his heart, for Molly had the morning before the gale dressed it for him.

Freeborn at first shook his head and would not move; but at last his shipmate got him to turn round, and then Betty Snell held up the poor little helpless infant to him, and the father's heart felt a touch of tenderness of a nature it had never before experienced, and he stooped down and bestowed a kiss on the brow of his newborn motherless child. He did not, however, venture to take it in his arms.

"You'll look after it, Betty, and be kind to it?" said he in a husky voice. "I'm sure you will, for her sake who lies there?"

"Yes, yes, Bill; no fear," answered Betty, who was a good-natured creature in her way, though it was a rough way, by the bye.

She was the wife of one of the boatswain's mates. Her companion, Nancy Bolton, who was the wife of the sergeant of marines, was much the same sort of person; indeed, it would not have done for the style of life they had to lead, to have had too refined characters on board.

"Bless you, Freeborn—take care of the baby, of course we will!" added Nancy, looking up from some occupation about which she had been engaged. "We'll both be mothers to him, and all the ship's company will act the part of a father to him. Never you fear that. As long as the old ship holds together, he'll not want friends; nor after it, if there's one of us alive. Set your mind at rest now."

"Yes, that we will, old ship," exclaimed Paul Pringle, taking Freeborn's hand and wringing it warmly. "That's to say, if the little chap wants more looking after than you can manage. But come along now. There's no use staying here. Bet and Nancy will look after the child better than we can, and you must turn in. Your hammock is the best place for you now."

The gale at length ceased; the ship was put on her proper course for the West Indies, whither she was bound; the sea went down, the clouds cleared away, and the glorious sun came out and shone brightly over the blue ocean. All the officers and men assembled on the upper deck, and then near one of the middle ports was placed a coffin, covered with the Union-Jack. There ought to have been a chaplain, but there was none; and so the Captain came forward with a Prayer-book, and in an impressive, feeling way, though not without difficulty, read the beautiful burial service to be used at sea for a departed sister; and the two women stood near the coffin, one holding a small infant; and there stood William Freeborn, supported by Paul Pringle, for by himself he could scarcely stand; and then slowly and carefully the coffin was lowered into the waves, and as they closed over it, in the impulse of the moment, the bereaved widower would have thrown himself after it, not knowing what he was about, had not Paul Pringle held him back. Down sank the coffin rapidly, and was hid to sight by the blue ocean—the grave of many a brave sailor, and of thousands of the young, and fair, and brave, and joyous, and of the proud and rich also, but never of a more kind-hearted honest woman than was Molly Freeborn. So all on board the Terrible declared, and assuredly they spoke the truth.

Chapter Two.

Onward across the Atlantic, as fast as her broad spread of white canvas filled by the wind could force her, glided the staunch old "seventy-four," which bore our hero and his fortunes, though at that time they did not look very prosperous; nor was he himself, it must be acknowledged, held in much consideration except by his own father and his two worthy nurses. His fare, too, was not of the most luxurious, nor suited to his delicate appetite. Milk there was none; and the purser, not expecting so juvenile an addition to the ship's company, had not provided any in a preserved state,—indeed, in those days, it may be doubted whether such an invention had been thought of,—while a round-shot had carried off the head of the cow in the last action in which the Terrible had been engaged. As she furnished fresh beef to the ship's company, they would not have objected to a similar accident happening again.

Poor Molly's child had, therefore, to be fed on flour and water, and such slops as the doctor and the nurses could think of. They could not have been unsuitable, for it throve wonderfully, and was pronounced by all the ship's company as fine a child as ever was seen.

"Have you been and had a look at Molly Freeborn's baby?" asked Dick Tarbrush of his messmate, Tom Buntline. "Do now, then. Such a pretty young squeaker. Bless you, it'll do your heart good. He's quite a hangel."

Similar remarks were made, one to the other, by the men; and one by one, or sometimes a dozen of them together, would come into the women's cabin to have a look at the baby, and then they would stand in a circle round him, with their hands on their hips or behind them, afraid to touch it, their pigtails stuck out as they bent down, their huge beards, and whiskers, and pendent lovelocks forming a strong contrast to the diminutive, delicate features of the infant, who might, notwithstanding, one day be expected to grow up similar in all respects to one of them.

After the gale, the Terrible encountered head winds, and light winds, and calms, and baffling winds of every description, so that her passage to the station was long delayed. It gave time, however, for the baby to grow, and for the discussion of several knotty points connected with him. The most knotty of them was the matter of his christening. Now, the crew held very much the same opinion with regard to their Captain that a certain captain held of himself, when one day he took it into his head to make his chaplain a bishop, that of his own sovereign will he could do all things. They knew that when there was no chaplain on board, he could bury a grownup person, and so they thought that he surely could christen a little infant. They accordingly, after due deliberation, resolved to send a deputation to him, requesting him to perform the ceremony.

After some discussion, it was agreed that it would be advisable to carry the baby itself with them, to strengthen the force of their appeal. It was thought better that the women should not appear; and Paul Pringle was selected unanimously to be the bearer of the child. Now honest Paul was a bachelor, and had literally never handled a baby in his life. He, therefore, felt an uncommon awe and trepidation, as half unwillingly and half proudly he undertook the office. However, at last, when coyly led forward, with his head all on one side and a beaming smile on his honest countenance, he found that his big paws, stretched out, made a first-rate cradle; though, not being aware of the excessive lightness of the little creature, he very nearly chucked it over his shoulders. Betty and Nancy, after arranging the child's clothes, bestowing sundry kisses, and giving several important cautions, let the party of honest Jacks proceed on their errand.

"Well, my lads, what is it you want?" asked the Captain in a good-natured voice, as the seamen, being announced by the sentry, made their appearance at the door of the cabin.

Paul Pringle cleared his voice before speaking, and then he said, very nearly choking the baby in his mechanical attempt to pull a lock of his hair as he spoke:

"We be come for to ax your honour to make a Christian of this here squeaker."

The good Captain looked up with his one eye, and now perceived the small creature that Paul held in his hands.

"Ah, you mean that you want him christened, I suppose," answered the Captain, smiling. "Well, I must see about that. Let me have a look at the poor little fellow. He thrives well. See, he smiles already. He'll be a credit to the ship, I hope. I'll do what I can, my lads. I don't think that there's anything about it in the articles of war. Still, what can be done I'll do, most assuredly."

While Captain Penrose was speaking, he was looking kindly at the infant and playing his finger round its mouth. He had had children of his own, and he felt as a father, though little indeed had he seen of them, and they had all long since been taken from him.

"Now you may go, my lads, and I'll let you know what I can do for you," he said after some time.

On this the deputation withdrew, well pleased with their interview.

As soon as the men were gone, Captain Penrose turned to the articles of war, and all the rules and regulations of the service with which he had been furnished, and hunted them through, and turned them over and over again, but could find nothing whatever about the baptism of infants. Most assiduously he looked through his Prayer-Book: not a word could he discover authorising captains in the navy to perform the rite. He pulled down all the books on his shelves and hunted them over; there were not many, certainly, but they made up by their quality and toughness for their want of number: not a word on the subject in question could he find. For many an hour and for many a day did he search, for he was not a man to be baffled by a knotty point or by an enemy for want of exertion on his part, though at last he had to confess that in this matter he was beaten. He therefore sent for Paul Pringle, and told him that though he could bury all the ship's company, and could hang a mutineer at the yardarm, or could shoot him on the quarterdeck, he had no authority, that he could find, for christening a baby. Much disappointed, Paul returned to his shipmates. In full conclave, therefore, it was settled, with poor Will Freeborn's consent, that as soon as the ship reached Port Royal harbour, in Jamaica, the little fellow should be taken on shore to be christened all shipshape and properly. When the Captain heard of this, he gave his full consent to the arrangement, and promised to assist in its execution.

The flag of the gallant Sir Peter Parker was flying in the harbour of Port Royal when, after a long passage, the Terrible fired the usual salute on entering, and dropped her anchor there. Two or three days elapsed before the duty of the ship would allow any of the crew to go on shore. On the first Sunday morning, however, it was notified that a hundred of them might have six hours' leave, and that if the infant was presented, after morning service, before the minister of one of the parish churches, he would perform the wished-for ceremony. Great were the preparations which had been made. Betty Snell and Nancy Bolton were dressed out with shawls, and furbelows, and ribbons of the gayest colours and patterns, and looked and thought themselves very fine. Nothing could surpass the magnificence of the child's robe. All the knowledge of embroidery possessed by the whole ship's company had been expended on it, and every chest and bag had been ransacked to find coloured beads and bits of silk and worsted and cotton of different hues to work on it. The devices were curious. There were anchors and cables twisting about all over it, and stars and guns, and there was a full-rigged ship in front; while a little straw hat, which had been plaited and well lined, was stuck on the child's head in the most knowing of ways, with the name of the Terrible worked in gold letters on a ribbon round it. Certainly, however, nothing could be more inappropriate than the name to the little smiling infant thus adorned. Never had such a dress been worn before by any baby ashore or afloat.

Then his shipmates took care that Will Freeborn himself should be in unusually good trim, and they got him to let Nancy Bolton dress his pigtail, while Sergeant Bolton stood by, and got him into conversation; and as for Paul Pringle, he turned out in first-rate style, and so did two of Freeborn's messmates and especial chums, Peter Ogle and Abel Bush, both first-rate seamen. All the men who had leave, indeed, rigged out in their best, and adorned themselves to the utmost of their power. The boatswain, also, got them a dozen flags, which they hoisted on boathooks and other small spars; and they had on board, besides, a one-legged black fiddler, and a sort of amateur band, all of whom were allowed to accompany them.

On shore early on Sunday morning they went, and marshalled as they landed from the boats which conveyed them on the quays of Kingston. The one-legged black fiddler, Sam, being the only professional, and the rated musician on board, claimed the honour of leading the way, followed by the rest of the band with their musical instruments. Then came the father of the baby, Will Freeborn, supported on either side by Paul Pringle and Peter Ogle, who each bore a flag on a staff; and next, Betty Snell, to whom had been awarded the honour of carrying the important personage of the day; and on one side of her walked Nancy Bolton, and on the other Abel Bush, one of the three proposed godfathers, with another flag. In consequence of the numberless chances of war, it had been agreed that the child should have three godfathers and two godmothers; besides which, each of the godfathers was to have a mate who was to take his place in case of his death, and to assist Freeborn in looking after his son, so that there was every probability of poor Molly's son being well taken care of. These, then, came next, bearing aloft an ensign and a Union-Jack, while the rest of the crew, with more flags, rolling along, made up the remainder of the procession.

But the person who created the greatest sensation among the spectators, especially of his own colour, was Sam Smatch, the one-legged fiddler; nor did he deem himself to be the least in importance. No one was in higher feather. He felt himself at home in the country—the hot climate suited him; he saw numbers of his own race and hue, inclined, like himself, to be merry and idle. How he grinned and rolled his eyes about on every side—how he scraped away with his bow—how he kicked up his wooden leg and cut capers which few people, even with two, could have performed as well! As to the rest of the band, he beat them hollow. In vain they tried to play. If they played fast, he played faster; when they played loud, he played louder; for, as he used to boast, his instrument was a very wonderful one, and there were not many which could come up to it. The crowd of negroes who collected from every side to stare at the procession, admired him amazingly, and cheered, and shrieked, and laughed, and clapped their hands in gleeful approbation of his performance.

Thus the procession advanced through the streets of Kingston till it reached the church door, it wanted still some time to the commencement of service, so the men were enabled to take their seats at one end of the building without creating any disturbance. There was plenty of room for them, for unhappily the proprietors, merchants and attorneys, the managers of estates and other residents, were very irregular attendants at places of worship. The few people who did collect for worship stared with surprise at seeing so unusual a number of sailors collected together; and more so when the service was over, to see Paul Pringle, acting as best man, lead his friend Freeborn, and the two nurses, and the rest of his shipmates, up to the font.

The clergyman had been warned by the clerk what to expect, or he would have been equally astonished.

"What is it you want, my good people?" he asked.

"Why, bless your honour, we wants this here young chap, as belongs, I may say, to the old Terrible, seeing as how he was born aboard of her, made into a regular shipshape Christian."

"Oh, I see," said the minister, smiling; "I will gladly do as you wish. You have got godfathers and a godmother, I suppose?"

"Oh, Lord bless your honour, there are plenty on us!" answered Paul, feeling his bashfulness wear off in consequence of the minister's kind manner. "There's myself, Paul Pringle, quartermaster, at your honour's service; and there's Peter Ogle, captain of the foretop, and Abel Bush, he's captain of the fo'castle; and then, d'ye see, we've each of us our mates to take command if any of us loses the number of our mess; and then as there's the two godmothers Nancy and Betty, right honest good women, the little chap won't fare badly, d'ye see, your honour."

"Indeed, you come rather over-well provided in that respect," observed the minister, having no little difficulty in refraining from laughing. "However, I should think that you would find two godfathers and one godmother, the usual number, sufficient to watch over the religious education of the child."

"No, your honour," answered Paul quietly; "I'll just ax you what you thinks the life of any one of us is worth, when you reflexes on the round-shot and bullets of the enemy, the fever,— 'Yellow Jack,' as we calls him,—and the hurricanes of these here seas? Who can say that one-half of us standing here may be alive this time next year? We sailors hold our lives riding at single anchor. We know at any moment we may have to slip our cable and be off."

The clergyman looked grave and bowed his head.

"You speak too sad a truth," he answered. "Now tell me, what name do you propose giving to the child?"

"Billy, your honour," answered Paul at once.

"William?—oh, I understand," observed the clergyman.

"No, Billy, your honour," persisted Paul. "Billy True Blue, that's the name we've concluded to give him. It's the properest, and rightest, and most convenient, and it's the name he must have," he added firmly.

"But what is the father's name? What is your name, my man?" asked the clergyman, turning to Freeborn.

Will told him.

"Oh, then I understand Billy True Blue is to be his Christian name?" said the clergyman.

"Yes, your honour," answered Paul. "D'ye see, he'd always be called Billy. That would be but natural-like. Then where's the use of calling him William? And True Blue he is, for he was born at sea aboard a man-o'-war, and he'll be brought up at sea among men-o'-war's men; and he'll be a right true blue seaman himself one of these days, if he lives, so there's an end on the matter."

The last remark was intended as a clincher to settle the affair. The clergyman had no further objections to offer to the arguments brought forward, and accordingly the child was then and there christened "Billy True Blue," to the infinite satisfaction of all his friends.

On leaving the church, the party adjourned to various houses of entertainment to drink their young shipmate's health. Much to their credit, at the time appointed they reappeared on board, returning to the quay in the style they had come, none of them the worse for liquor. Captain Penrose had reason to be satisfied with his system of managing his ship's company.

Chapter Three.

The Terrible was not allowed to remain long idle, for those were stirring times, as there were Frenchmen and Spaniards, and the Dutch and Americans to fight; indeed, all the great maritime countries of the world were leagued against Old England to deprive her, as they hoped, of the supremacy of the sea. Again the Terrible was under weigh, standing for the Leeward Islands to join the squadron of Sir George Brydges Rodney. A day or two after she sailed, the surgeon came to the Captain with an unusually long face.

"What is the matter, Doctor Macbride?" asked Captain Penrose.

"I'm sorry to say, sir, that we have two cases of yellow fever on board," was the answer.

"What, Yellow Jack—my old enemy?" exclaimed the Captain, trying to look less concerned than he felt. "Turn him out then—kick him away—get rid of him as fast as possible, that's all I can say."

"More easily said than done, I fear, sir," answered the surgeon, who was well aware that his Captain was more anxious than he would allow; for, from sad experience, he well knew that when once that scourge of the West Indies attacks the crew of a ship, it is impossible to say how many may be the victims, and when it may disappear.

"You are right, doctor. We must do our best, though, and put our trust in Providence," answered the Captain gravely. "Let the men be on deck as much as possible. We will have their provisions carefully looked to, and we must have their minds amused. Let Sam Smatch keep his fiddle going. Fear of the foe kills many, I believe. Now if we could meet an enemy, and have a good warm engagement, we should soon put Yellow Jack and him to flight together. And I say, doctor, don't let the men see that you are concerned any more than I am."

After a little further conversation, the doctor took his departure.

The ship continued her course across the Caribbean Sea, with light winds and under the hottest of suns; and the fever, instead of disappearing, stealthily crept on, attacking one man after another, till fifty or sixty of the crew were down with it. Death came, too, and carried off one fine fellow, and then another and another, sometimes five or six in one day. At last there was a cessation, and the spirits of the sick as well as of the healthy revived; and Sam Smatch set to work and fiddled away most lustily, and the crew danced and sang, and tried to forget that there was such a thing as Yellow Jack on board. Several of the sick got better, and even the doctor's and the Captain's spirits revived. Once more it fell calm, and, as the Captain was walking the quarterdeck, Dr Macbride came up to him with a grave face.

"What is the matter now, doctor?" he asked in as cheerful a voice as he could command; for whatever he felt in private, he would not allow himself to appear out of spirits before his officers or crew. "What! not driven the yellow demon overboard yet? Kick him—trounce him—get rid of him somehow!"

"I am sorry to say, sir, that he has attacked the women," answered the doctor. "Betty Snell is very ill, and Mrs Bolton is evidently sickening. What the motherless baby will do, I cannot say. Probably that will die too, and so be provided for."

"Heaven forbid!" said the Captain, "for the honest father's sake. The child will have plenty of nurses. We must not forget poor Molly—how nobly she braved Yellow Jack himself when the sick wanted her aid! We all are bound to look after the baby. The sooner it is taken away from the poor woman the better. Let me see. Tell Paul Pringle to go and get the baby and bring it up to my cabin. That is the most airy and healthy place for the little chap. We must rig out a cot for it there. Freeborn himself would feel bashful at taking his child there. Either he or Pringle must act as nurse, though. I have no fancy for having one of the ship's boys making the attempt. They would be feeding him with salt beef and duff, or smothering him; and as for waking when he cries at night, there would be little chance of their hearing him. But I will go below with you, doctor, and visit the poor people. Come along."

Saying this, the good Captain descended to the lower-deck with the surgeon. The weather side of the ship forward had been screened off and appropriated to the sick. As he appeared, those who were conscious lifted up their heads and welcomed him with a look of pleasure; but many were raving and shrieking in the delirium of fever, and others, worn out by its attacks, were sunk in stupor from which they were not to awake. Then the Captain visited the berth of the two women. Mrs Bolton was still struggling in a vain attempt to ward off the disease, and endeavouring to nurse poor little Billy; but she could scarcely lift her hand to feed him, and evidently a sickness and faintness was stealing over her.

The Captain said nothing, but going out, sent a boy to call Paul Pringle. He soon returned with Paul, who, stooping down, said quietly, "Here, Mrs Bolton, you feels sick and tired, I know you does. You've had hard times looking after Betty Snell, and I'll just dandle the youngster for you a bit. You know you can have him again when you feels better and rested like."

Thus appealed to, poor Nancy gave up the baby to Paul, who dandled it about before her for a minute; then as she was casting an affectionate glance at it, he disappeared along the deck with his charge. It was the last look she ever took of the infant she had nursed with almost a mother's care. Her husband was sent for. In a short time she was raving, and before that hour the next day both she and Betty were no longer among the living. Their loss was severely felt, not only by their husbands, but by all the crew. They and forty of the men were committed to the deep before the termination of the passage.

At last the Terrible reached Gros Islet Bay, in the Island of Saint Lucia, that island having been captured by the English from the French. In a short time a considerable fleet collected there, under Admiral Sir George Rodney and Rear-Admiral Hyde Parker. Still the fever continued on board the Terrible and several other ships.

"Nothing but the fire of the enemy will cure us, Sir George, I fear," observed Captain Penrose when paying a visit one day on board the flagship.

"Then, my dear Penrose, I hope that we shall not have long to wait, for they are collecting in force, I hear, round the Island of Martinique; and the moment the fleet is ready for sea, we'll go out and have a brush with them," was the Admiral's answer.

This news was received with joy by every man in the fleet, and all exerted themselves more than ever to hasten its equipment. The Captain had some idea of leaving little Billy on shore, but both Freeborn and Pringle begged so hard that he might be allowed to remain that the Captain gave up the point.

"I don't know how long I may be with the little chap," observed poor Will. "It would break my heart to be separated from him; and if we go into action, we'll stow him away safe in the hold, and he'll be better off there than among foreign strangers on shore who don't care a bit for him."

There was much truth in this remark, and so little True Blue still continued under charge of his rough-looking protectors. It is extraordinary how well and tenderly they managed to nurse him and feed him, and how carefully they washed him and put on his tiny garments. Paul Pringle was even a greater adept than his own father; and more than once the Captain could scarcely refrain from laughing as he saw the big, huge-whiskered quartermaster in a side cabin, seated on one bucket, with another full of salt water before him, an apron, made out of a piece of canvas, round his waist, and a large sponge, with a piece of soap in his hand, washing away at the little fellow. The baby seemed to enjoy the cold water amazingly, and kicked and splashed about, and spluttered and cooed with abundant glee, greatly to Paul's delight.

"Ah, I knowed it. He'll be a regular salt from truck to kelson!" he exclaimed, looking at the little fellow affectionately, and holding him up so as to let his head just float above water. "He'll astonish them some of these days. Depend on't, Will," he added, turning to Freeborn, who had come in to have a look at his child.

The Captain had directed the hammocks of the two men to be slung in this cabin, and little True Blue had a cot slung along close to the deck; so that if by chance he had tumbled out, he would not have been much the worse for it. As the father and his friend were in different watches, they were able, under ordinary circumstances, to relieve each other in nursing the baby; but when any heavy work was to be done, and the services of both of them were required on deck, Sam Smatch, who was not fit even for ordinary idlers' work, was called in to act nurse.

This was an employment in which Sam especially delighted, and he would have bargained for a gale of wind any day in the week for the sake of having to take care of little True Blue. Billy, from the first, never objected to his black face, but cooed and smiled, and was greatly delighted whenever he appeared. Sam altogether took wonderfully to the baby, and used to declare that he loved it as much as he did his own fiddle, if not more. He would not say positively—both were his delight—both squeaked; but his fiddle was his older friend. Billy, indeed, never wanted nurses, and there was not a man on board who was not happy to get him to look after. The greatest risk he ran was from over-kindness, or from having a tumble among the numerous candidates for the pleasure of dandling him when once they got him among them on the maindeck; and no set of schoolgirls could make a more eager rush to snatch up the little child left among them, than did the big-bearded, whiskered, and pig-tailed tars to catch hold of Billy True Blue.

Among the other candidates for the pleasure of nursing little Billy was a young midshipman, known generally as Natty Garland. He had been seized with the fever, and been carried, for better nursing, into the Captain's cabin. This was his first voyage away from home, where he had left many brothers and sisters. It was nearly proving his last. Although he looked so slight and delicate, however, he did recover; but it was some time before he was fit for duty.

Devoted to his profession, Natty Garland, in spite of his delicate appearance, became a first-rate, bold, and intelligent seaman, liked by his Captain, respected by his superior officers and his messmates, and an especial favourite with the men.

Just before Sir George Rodney had entered Gros Islet Bay, the French fleet, consisting of twenty-five sail of line-of-battle ships and eight frigates, under Admiral Count de Guichen, had been haughtily parading before the island, trying to draw out the then small and unprepared squadron of Rear-Admiral Hyde Parker. The British officers and men fumed and growled at the insult, longing for an opportunity of paying off the vapouring Frenchmen. Never, therefore, were anchors weighed with greater alacrity than when the signal was seen from Admiral Rodney's ship for the fleet to make sail and stand out to sea. A course was steered for Fort Royal Bay, in the Island of Martinique, where the French fleet was then supposed to be. The English fleet consisted in all only of twenty line-of-battle ships and two frigates, but their inferiority in point of numbers in no way made the British seamen less eager to encounter the enemy.

Now the former order of things was reversed; the smaller fleet was blockading the larger, which was equally prepared for battle. It was a beautiful sight to see the stout ships, with their white canvas set alow and aloft, as they glided over the blue sea in front of the harbour containing their vaunting enemy. In vain they tacked and wore, and stood backwards and forwards, never losing sight of the harbour's mouth. Every opportunity of fighting was offered, but the Frenchmen dared not come out.

At length Admiral Rodney, disgusted with the pusillanimity of the enemy, returned to his anchorage in Gros Islet Bay with most of the line-of-battle ships, leaving only a squadron of the faster sailing copper-bottomed ships and frigates to watch the enemy's motions, and to give him notice should they attempt to escape. The seamen little doubted that they would soon have a brush with the enemy. Among all, none seemed to anticipate a battle with greater satisfaction than Will Freeborn. His spirits rose higher by far than they had done since the death of his wife; and that evening, when Sam Smatch struck up a hornpipe on the forecastle, no one footed it more merrily than did he.

"All right," observed Paul, "I'm glad Will's himself again. Poor Molly, she'd be pleased to see him happy—that I know she would, good soul."

Whether Will's heart was as light as his feet might be doubted. Several days passed, and the Frenchmen kept snug at their anchors. "They'll move some day or other, and then we'll be at them," was the general remark. Still there they lay. None of the English crews was allowed to go on shore; but the ships were kept ready to weigh at a moment's notice. Daylight had just broken on the 16th of April 1780, when a frigate under a press of sail was seen approaching the bay. A signal was flying from her masthead. It was one which made the British tars shout with satisfaction; it was, "The French have put to sea!"

Round went the capstans, up came the anchors, the broad folds of white canvas were let fall from the yards and sheeted home, and in the course of a few minutes the whole fleet was under weigh and standing out to sea. No one fiddled more lustily than did Sam Smatch, and a right merry tune he played, while the crew of the Terrible with sturdy tramp pressed round the bars of the capstan; and never was a topsail more speedily set than that under charge of Will Freeborn.

No sooner was the fleet clear of the harbour than the enemy was discovered in the north-west. Instantly the signal was made from the flagship, the Sandwich, for a general chase. How shrilly the boatswains sounded their pipes, how rapidly the men flew aloft or tramped along the decks, while sail after sail was set, till every ship was carrying as much canvas as could by any art or contrivance be spread on her yards! Beautiful and inspiriting was the sight. The enemy saw them coming, but did not heave-to in order to meet them, endeavouring rather to escape.

All day long the chase continued, and it was not until towards the evening that, from the British ships, it could be discovered that the Frenchmen's force consisted of no less than twenty-three sail of the line, a fifty gun ship, three frigates, a lugger, and a cutter. Darkness came on, however, before the British could get up with them; but sharp eyes all night long were eagerly watching their movements, and few on board any of the ships could bring themselves to turn in to their hammocks.

During the night the wind came round to the southward and east, greatly to the satisfaction of all on board the English fleet, and when morning broke the Frenchmen were seen close-hauled under their lee.

"What can them chaps be about now?" asked Will Freeborn of Paul Pringle as they stood near each other before going to their respective stations. "They are not going to sneak away after all, I hope."

"I'm not quite so sure but that they are going to try it on, though," answered Paul, eyeing the distant fleet of the French with no friendly eye. "But I'll tell you what: Admiral Rodney is not the chap to let 'em off so easily. Ah, look! they are tacking again; they see it won't do. Hurrah! lads, we'll be at them now before long."

The cheer was taken up by others, and ran along the decks, and was echoed from ship to ship along the British line. Every preparation was now made for immediate action. The magazines were opened, the powder and shot were got up, the bulkheads had long been down, the small-arms were served out, the men bound their heads with their handkerchiefs, threw off their jackets and shirts, buckled on their cutlasses, and stuck pistols in their belts. Meantime, as it had been arranged, Sam Smatch was sent to look after Billy True Blue, and to carry him down into the hold as soon as the ship was getting within range of the enemy's fire.

"Let me just have a look at my boy!" exclaimed Will, as Sam brought him out on deck, as he said, to show him the enemy whom he would one day learn to thrash.

Will took the child in his arms, and he gave a glance of affection; then, giving little Billy back to Sam, he urged him not to delay too long in taking him below, and sprang aloft to his post in the top, to be ready to make any alterations that might be required in the sails while the ship was going into action.

Some hours from sunrise passed away, during which time the fleet was slowly approaching the reluctant enemy. It wanted but ten minutes to noon, when the signal flew out from the masthead of the Admiral for the fleet to bear down on the French, each ship to steer for and closely engage the one nearest to her in the enemy's line. The order was received with a hearty huzza. It was promptly and exactly obeyed. Still, from the lightness of the wind, it was nearly one before the engagement became general. And now along the whole line arose dense volumes of smoke— bright flashes were seen, and the roar of the guns, and the shouts and shrieks of the combatants were heard. Thickly flew the round-shot—the gallant Admiral in the Sandwich was engaged with two big Frenchmen, who seemed to have singled her out for destruction, but right nobly and boldly did she bear the brunt of the action. Shot after shot struck her, many between wind and water, and some in her masts and spars, which in consequence threatened to go overboard. The Terrible, too, was hotly engaged with an opponent worthy of her. What her name was could not be discovered.

"Never mind!" was the cry; "we'll soon learn when we make her haul down her flag!"

Hotter and hotter grew the action. Many were falling on both sides. Nearly all the English ships had lost both officers and men, killed and wounded; while, especially, they were dreadfully cut up in their rigging. Freeborn had come below to serve a gun.

"I see, mate, how it is!" cried Pringle to him. "Those Frenchmen are fighting to run away. It's strange not one of our fellows on deck have been hit yet. They've aimed all their shot at our spars."

"Hurrah! lads, then," answered Will in a high state of excitement, which Pringle could not help remarking. "Fire away, lads. We'll stop them if we can from running away, at all events."

As he spoke he applied his match to his gun. At the moment it sent forth its missile of death he tottered back, and before Paul Pringle could catch him had fallen on the deck. Paul stooped down and raised up his head.

"It's all over with me, Paul," he said in a low voice; "feel here."

There was a dreadful wound in his side, which made it appear too probable that his prognostication would prove true. The rest of the men near turned round with glances of sorrow, for he was a general favourite; but they had to attend to the working of their guns.

"Paul," he continued, "you and the ship's company will, I know, look after my motherless child. I leave Billy to the care of you all. Bring him up as a sailor—a true British tar, mind. There isn't a nobler life a man can lead. I would not have him anything else. The Captain's very kind, and will, I know, do his best for him. But I don't want him to be an officer—that's very well for them that's born to it; but all I'd have liked to have seen him, if I had lived, is an open-hearted, open-handed, honest seaman." Poor Will was speaking with great difficulty. His words came forth low and slowly.

"Yes, yes, Will," answered Paul, pressing his friend's hand. "We'll look after him. There's not a man of the Terrible who would not look at little True Blue as his own son; and as to making him a seaman, we none on us would dream of anything else. It would be utterly impossible and unnatural like. Set your mind at rest, mate, about that. But I say, Will, wouldn't it do your heart good to have a look at the younker?"

"Not up here; a shot might hit him, remember," answered the poor father. "And if they was to move me, I don't think that I should ever be got below alive. No, no, Paul; I'll stay here. It's the best place for a sailor to die."

Just then there was a cry that the enemy's ships were retreating. First the Count de Guichen's own ship, the huge Couronne, was seen standing out of the action, followed by the Triomphant and Fendant, leaving the Sandwich in so battered a condition that she could not follow. The other ships imitated their leader's example. One after another, the British ships found themselves without opponents. They endeavoured to make sail and follow; but their running rigging was so cut up that few could set their sails, while the masts of many went over their sides. All they could do, therefore, was to send their shot rapidly after the flying enemy, and give vent to their feelings in loud hurrahs and shouts of contempt. The Frenchmen little thought how well this same running away was teaching the English to beat them, as they did in many a subsequent combat, until, learning to respect each other's bravery, they became firm friends and allies, and such, it is to be hoped, they may remain till the end of time.

The sound of the shouts seemed to revive poor Will Freeborn.

"Now, mate, you'll see Billy, won't you?" said Paul. "It'll do your heart good."

Will smiled his assent. He was feeling no pain then. A boy was sent to summon Sam and the baby. Meantime the doctor came on deck.

"Let him lie here," said he after a short examination; "his moments are numbered."

Sam soon appeared. Paul took Billy from him, and, kneeling down, held the baby to the lips of the dying father. The men, no longer required to work the guns, clustered round the group. Will kissed his child and held him for a moment in his grasp.

"Shipmates," said he, raising his voice, "you'll all of you be kind to little True Blue—I know you will; there's no use asking you. And God will look after him—I know He will, and forgive me my sins. Here, Paul, take the child—I'm slipping my cable, shipmates!"

He turned his eyes on the infant, and, pointing towards him, fell back into the arms of Abel Bush and Peter Ogle, who had come to have a last look at their old friend.

He was dead, and little True Blue was left an orphan.

Chapter Four.

Poor Billy True Blue little knew the loss he had experienced, when, as usual, he kicked and frisked about, and spluttered and cooed, as that evening Paul Pringle, with a sad heart, was dipping him in a tub, preparatory to putting him into his cot. Paul had soon to send for Sam Smatch to take his place, as he had plenty of work on deck in repairing damages. Besides being much cut up in hull and rigging, the fleet had suffered greatly, and had had six officers and one hundred and fourteen men killed, and nine officers and one hundred and forty-five men wounded. The Admiral's ship, the Sandwich, had suffered the most severely; and it was only by the united exertions of her own and other ships' companies that she was kept afloat during the night and all the next day, till she could be got back again into Gros Islet Bay. There every possible exertion was made to repair damages, so as to be in a state to go in search of the enemy.

It was not, however, till the 6th of May that Sir George Rodney received intelligence that the French fleet had left the Island of Guadaloupe, where they had been repairing their damages, and were approaching to windward of Martinique.

Once more the English fleet was ordered by signal to put to sea; and with no less zest than before the anchors were run up, and under a crowd of sail they stood out of the bay. The wind, however, was contrary, and for several days the ships had to continue beating against it through the passage between Martinique and Saint Lucia till the 10th, when, as the morning broke, the Frenchmen were seen mustering the same number as before, about three leagues to windward.

"Hurrah! we'll have them now; they'll not demean themselves by running away!" was the general shout on board the British ships.

Nearer the English approached. The French formed in line of battle and bore down upon them. The hearts of the British tars beat high. They thought the time they were looking for had assuredly come; but when scarcely within so much as random shot, the Frenchmen were seen to haul their wind, and being much faster sailers than the English, they quickly got again beyond speaking distance. The English seamen stamped with rage and disappointment, as well they might, and hurled no very complimentary epithets on the enemy.

"The time will come when we get up to you, Monsieur, and then we'll give it you, won't we?" they exclaimed, shaking their fists at the enemy.

Several times the French came down in the same style, as Paul Pringle remarked, "like so many dancing-masters skipping along, and then whisking round and scampering off again."

Words will not describe the utter contempt and hatred the British tars felt in consequence of this for their enemies. Had the French mustered twice their numbers, and could they have got fairly alongside of them, yardarm to yardarm, they supposed that they could have thrashed them, and probably would have done so.

At last Admiral Rodney himself, in the hope of deceiving the enemy, made the signal for the fleet to bear away under all sail. The manoeuvre had the desired effect, making the French fancy that the English had taken to flight; and now growing bold, like yelping hounds, they came after them in full cry. The English captains guessed what was expected of them, and did their best to impede the progress of their ships, so as to let the enemy gain as much as possible on them. On the Frenchmen boldly came, till their van was nearly abreast of the centre of the English, who had luffed up till they had almost brought the fleet again on a bowline.

Now, to their great satisfaction, there was a shift of wind, which gave them the weather-gage. That was all Admiral Rodney wanted, and once more the hearts of the British seamen beat proudly with the anticipation of battle and victory.

The signal was made to engage. The British ships bore down on the enemy. It seemed no longer possible that he would decline to fight. On board the Terrible all stood ready at their guns, eyeing the foe. Sam Smatch had been despatched with his little charge into the hold, and ordered, unless he would incur the most dreadful pains and penalties, not to return on deck.

Sam grinned on receiving the order. He had not the slightest intention of infringing it. He was not a coward; but he was a philosopher. He had had fighting enough in his day. He had lost a leg fighting, and been otherwise sorely knocked about; and he had vowed, from that time forward, never to fight if he could help it. He had no king nor country, so to speak, to fight for; for though he had become a British subject, he had not appreciated the privileges he had thereby gained; and, at all events, they had failed to arouse any especial patriotic feelings within his bosom. Nothing, therefore, could please him better than his present occupation; and tucking his fiddle under one arm, and making a seat for the baby with the other, he descended with the most unfeigned satisfaction into the dusky depths of the bottom of the ship.

How intense was the indignation of the British seamen, when, just as they were within long range of the French, they saw ship after ship wear, and, under a crowd of sail, take to an ignominious flight! What showers of abuse were hurled after them, as were numerous random shots, though neither were much calculated to do them any harm. However, by seven in the evening, Captain Bowyer, in the Albion, who led the van, was seen to reach the centre of the enemy's line. In the most gallant style he opened fire, supported by the Conqueror and the other ships of the van. In vain the ships of the British centre endeavoured to get into action. Every manoeuvre that could be thought of was tried, every sail was set. The brave old Captain Penrose walked his deck with hasty strides and unusual excitement.

"Oh, how I envy that fellow Bowyer!" he exclaimed. "How rapidly his men work their guns! We would be doing the same if we were there. However, the time will come when I shall have another stand-up fight with them before I die. It may be soon, or it may be some time hence; but the time will come, that I feel assured of."

"I hope, sir, when it does arrive, you, and all with you, will come off victorious," observed the second lieutenant, who was in no way inclined to enter into what he called the Captain's fancies.

"No doubt about it," answered the Captain. "I trust that I may never live to see the day when a British fleet is worsted by our old enemies, the French, or by any others who have ships afloat."

In spite of the partial engagement taking place, the remainder of the French fleet continued its flight under a press of sail. Right gallantly the Albion and Conqueror continued the cannonade; but, again, the quicker heels of the French enabled them to keep out of the reach of the remainder of the British fleet, and finally carried them free of their pursuers.

Still, although night had closed in, Admiral Rodney persevered in following them up; but the wind had shifted, and given the French the weather-gage, an advantage which they employed in keeping out of action. Day after day passed, and then they were to be seen spreading over the blue sea in the far distance, but not daring to come nearer. Either they were waiting for reinforcements, or for some accident which might give them such a vast superiority that they would no longer have any fear of the result of a general engagement.

Great, therefore, was the delight of the British, when, on the morning of the 19th, the wind shifted suddenly, and enabled them to bear down under a press of sail on the enemy. The Count de Guichen could no longer, it was hoped, avoid an action; but, ere the English could get their guns to bear, the fickle wind again shifted and left the enemy the choice of engaging or not. Although the van of the French was to windward, their rear was still to leeward of the British van, now led by the gallant Commodore Hotham. Immediately he bore down upon them and opened his fire.

The Terrible was in this division, and took a leading part in the fray. Several ships on both sides were now hotly engaged. The French Admiral, seeing this, seemed to have made up his mind to risk a general action; and as soon as his van had weathered the British, which the shift of wind enabled him to do, he bore away along their line to windward and commenced a heavy cannonade, but at so cautious a distance that his shot did little damage. The Terrible's opponent soon sheered off, and, having more speed than pluck, quickly got out of the range of her guns, greatly to the disgust of all the crew.

"Look here, mates; is this what those frog-eating Johnny Crapauds call fighting?" exclaimed Paul Pringle, pointing to de Guichen's distant line, firing away at the main body of the British fleet. "Unless fellows are inclined to lay alongside each other, yardarm to yardarm, and have it out like brave men, to my mind they had better stay ashore and leave fighting alone."

The sentiment was echoed heartily by all his hearers, and more particularly so, when in a short time the whole French fleet was seen fairly to take to flight, and, under a press of sail, to stand to the northward. The British fleet continued all the next day in chase; but, on the morning of the 21st, not a Frenchman was to be seen; and as many of the ships had suffered severely in these partial actions, and were much knocked about by long service, Admiral Rodney stood for Barbadoes, where they might undergo the required repairs. They arrived on the 22nd in Carlisle Bay.

It was not for some time that the crew of the Terrible had a moment to think of anything but the stern calls of duty. At last, however, the old ship was once more ready for sea, and then one spoke to the other about little Billy True Blue, and their promise to Will Freeborn; and it was agreed that an assemblage of the whole ship's company should be held, to decide the course to be pursued for his rearing and education. The forecastle, or, as seamen call it, "the fo'c's'l," was the place selected for the meeting. Tom Snell, the boatswain's mate, Sergeant Bolton, Peter Ogle, Abel Bush, Paul Pringle, of course, the three godfathers' mates, and most of the petty officers, spoke on this important occasion. Sam Smatch would have been there, but he had to look after the baby in the cabin; he had, however, explained his opinion, and claimed the right of voting by proxy; which claim was fully allowed, seeing that he was absent on the public service. The warrant-officers were not present—not that they did not take a warm interest in the matter, but they did not wish to interfere with the free discussion in which the men might wish to indulge. Sergeant Bolton, however, came, and it was understood that he knew their feelings in all the important points likely to be broached. His rank might have kept him away, but he was present, because, as he said, "I ham, de ye see, the hinconsolable widower of Nancy Bolton, the hintfant's nurse, and how do ye think hany one can have more hinterest in the hangel than I?"

Tom Snell was looked upon as a great orator; not the less so that he often enforced his arguments with a rope's end.

"Mates," said he, rising, when all the men were assembled, perched about in every available spot and in every possible attitude, and he brought one clenched fist down on the other open palm, with a sound which echoed along the decks, "this is how the case stands, d'ye see. There's a baby born aboard this here ship, and that baby had a mother, a good real shipshape woman, who was as kind a nurse to all on us as was sick as could be. Well, I won't talk on her; she dies, and two other women acts as nurses to the baby; they were good women too, but I won't talk on them." Tom passed the hairy back of his rough hand across his eyes, and continued: "Now the baby fell to the natural care like of his daddy, a true-hearted honest sailor as ever stepped. He'd have done honestly by him, and brought him up as a right real seaman, there's no doubt; but, d'ye see, as ye know, mates all, a sneaking Frenchman's round-shot comes aboard us and strikes him between wind and water, so to speak, and pretty nigh cuts him in two. Before he slipped his cable, many on you who stood near knows what he said to us. He told us that he gave the baby to the ship's company—to look after—to be brought up as a seaman should be brought up. One and all on us would do the same and much more, as I know, for little True Blue, seeing as how he naturally-like belongs to us—ay, mates, and we would be ready to fight for him to the last; and if there was one thing would make us keep our colours flying to the last, it would be to prevent him falling into the enemy's hands, to be brought up as a capering, frog-eating Frenchman. But, mates, d'ye see, this would be very well if we could all stick together aboard the same ship, and for his sake I knows we'd try to do it; but, as you knows, there are the chances of war—we may be separated—one may go to one ship, one may go to another, and who is he to go with, I should like to know? Now I don't want that any on us should lose the pleasure and honour of looking after him, that I don't—I'd scorn to be so unjust to any one; but we wants to settle when the evil time arrives when we, who has served together so long, and fought together, and stuck together like brothers and true seamen should, comes to be scattered, who the little chap, Billy True Blue, is to go with—that's the point, mates, d'ye see? He can't go with us all. He must be with some one on us, the primest seaman, too, who'll teach him to knot and splice, to hand-reef and steer, and all the ways of a seaman. That's what we has to do. We can't teach him much yet, you'll all allow, and the Captain says as how he'll give nine dozen to any man as puts a quid of baccy in the younker's mouth; so we can't even learn him to chaw yet, which to my mind he'd do better nor anything else, as he's most practice with his jaws just yet; but the time will come when he can use his fists, too, and the sooner he gets 'em into the tar-bucket the better, says I." This opinion was loudly applauded by all present.

Tom made some further remarks to the same effect. "And now," he concluded, "any one on you who has got anything for to say for or again' what I've been a-saying, let him stand up on his legs and say it out like a man."

Bill Tompion, one of the gunner's crew, thereon arose with a sudden spring, and, having squirted a stream of tobacco juice through a port, exclaimed:

"What Tom says is all very true. No one here nor there will want to deny it; but what I axes is, who's to have charge of the younker? That's what I see we wants to settle. When I fires my gun, I doesn't blaze away at the air, but looks along it and sees what I'm going to fire at, and takes my aim; and, d'ye see, if it's an enemy's ship not far off, I generally hits, too. Now that's just as I was saying, mates, what we have to do. We wants to fix on fit and proper persons to look after our little chap aboard here,—the ship's own child, I may say,—to see that he gets into no mischief, and to bring him up as a seaman should be brought up. Now I'd like to be one on those to look after him, and Tom would like to be one, and many on us would like to have the work, and most of us, ay, and all of us," (there was a general cheer); "but, mates, it isn't the men who'd like it most, but the men who is most fit, d'ye see, we are bound to choose. Now I speak for myself. I'm a thoughtless, careless sailor—I've run my head into more scrapes than I'd like to own. I'm very well afloat, but ashore I wouldn't like to have on my conscience to have charge of that young chap, d'ye see; and as for Tom Snell, he'll speak for himself. Betty Snell kept him straight, there's no doubt of it; but now she's gone, poor Tom's all adrift again, and it's just a chance if he goes for to splice once more, what sort of a wife he'll pick up. Therefore, says I, neither Tom nor I'm the best man to look after Billy True Blue. But, mates," (here Tompion stopped and struck his hands together), "I does say that I thinks I knows who is a good man, a fit man, and a friend and messmate of Will Freeborn, and that man is Paul Pringle. He's what the parsons calls a godfather, and so I take it he's a sort of a guardian like already, and he's had charge of the little chap ever since poor Betty and Nancy lost the number of their mess; and if Paul will take charge, and I'm sure he will, I says, 'Let him be one of the guardians.'"

Paul rose. "Mates all," said he, giving a hitch to his waistband, "I thanks ye. Don't you think as long as body and soul keep together I'd look after little Billy True Blue, who was born aboard this ship, whose father and mother was my friends, and who, I may say, is just like a son to me? I know you all sees this; but, mates, I may any day slip my cable, as you and all of us may do, but still one man's life is not so good as three, and therefore, I says, let me have his father's friends and messmates, Peter Ogle and Abel Bush, two good men and thorough seamen, to help me; and I can say that I believe one and all of us will do our duty by the boy—we'll not fail to do our best to make him an honest man and a true sailor."

There were no dissentient voices to Paul's proposal. Never was a meeting for any subject held with so much unanimity. The three godfathers' mates were chosen as their assistant-guardians, and thus, as far as numbers could ensure care, little True Blue had every chance of being well looked after.

Chapter Five.

Captain Penrose was very well pleased when he heard of the arrangements the seamen had made with regard to little Billy. More than once, however, he spoke to Dr Macbride and some of his officers about him in whom he had most confidence.

"As you know," he remarked, "I am now childless, and have no kith or kin depending on me; and if the boy turns out well, when old enough, I think of getting him placed on the quarterdeck. The son of many a seaman before the mast has risen to the top of his profession. My wife's grandfather was a boatswain; my father-in-law, his son, was an Admiral and a K.C.B. He won't have interest; but if he's a good seaman, and is always on the watch to do his duty,—to run after it, not to let duty come to him,—he'll get on well enough, depend on that."

The fleet of Sir George Rodney was now divided. While he despatched a portion, under Josias Rowley, to reinforce Sir Peter Parker at Jamaica, threatened by a powerful French squadron, he sailed with the greater part of the remainder for New York. It must be remembered that the American War of Independence was then going on, and that the French had promised to aid the insurgent colonists.

The old Terrible was still on the Jamaica station; but it was understood that she would soon be sent to join the squadron off New York. She and the gallant old Thunderer, 74, which had so long braved the battle and the breeze, were together, the crews of both eagerly looking out for an enemy.

There was an enemy approaching they little dreamed of. Cape Tiburon, at the west end of the Island of Hispaniola, or San Domingo, the name by which it is now better known, had been sighted the day before, so that all knew well whereabouts they were. There was a perfect calm, and the water was as smooth as the most polished glass—not a ripple was to be seen on it; but yet it was not a plain, for huge undulations came swelling up from the southern part of the Caribbean Sea, which made the big ships roll till their lower yards almost dipped into the water.

Captain Walsingham and several of the officers of the Thunderer, taking advantage of the calm, had come on board the Terrible to visit Captain Penrose and his officers. They were a merry party; they had done their duty nobly, and they were anticipating opportunities of doing it again, not to speak of gaining prize-money and promotion.

"Walsingham, my dear fellow," said Captain Penrose to his younger brother Captain as they were taking a turn on the quarterdeck after dinner, "I do not altogether like the look of the weather. I have, as you know, been in these seas a good deal. These perfect calms are often succeeded by sudden and violent storms, often by hurricanes; and though we may have sea-room and stout craft, in such a commotion as I have more than once witnessed, it will require all our seamanship to keep afloat."

"No fear," answered the younger Captain, smiling, "the Thunderer is not likely to fear the fiercest hurricane that ever blew;" and he looked with all a true seaman's pride on the noble ship, which floated so gallantly at the distance of a few hundred fathoms.

"At all events, take an old man's counsel," said Captain Penrose, stopping in his walk. "I would not be so rude as unnecessarily to urge you to leave my ship; but, my dear fellow, get on board as fast as you can, and make her ready to encounter whatever may occur. If the threatenings pass off, no harm is done. I must prepare the Terrible for a gale."

Thus urged, the younger Captain could no longer decline to take the proffered advice, but calling his officers, their boats were manned, and they returned on board the Thunderer. In the meantime, everything that could be done was done to prepare the Terrible for a fierce contest with the elements. Royal and topgallant-yards were sent down—topmasts were struck, rolling tackles were made fast to all the lower yards, and all the guns, and everything below that could move, were secured. A thin mist pervaded the atmosphere; the heat grew excessive; both sky and sea became the colour of lead; and an oppressive gloom hung over the waste of waters. Still the wind did not stir, and even the swell appeared to be going down. Hour after hour passed away.

"Our skipper is a good officer, there's no doubt about it," observed some of the younger men as they walked the forecastle. "But he's sometimes overmuch on the safe side, and if a moderate breeze were to spring up, and an enemy appear in sight, she'd slip away long before we could be in a fit state to go after her."

"You are very wise, mate, I daresay," said Abel Bush, who heard the remark. "But just suppose the Captain is right and you wrong, how should we look if the squall caught us with all our light sticks aloft and our canvas spread? Old Harry Cane, when you meet with him in these parts, is not a chap to be trifled with, let me tell you."

The younger seaman might have replied, but the force of Abel's argument was considerably strengthened by a loud roaring sound which broke on their ears. Far, too, as the eye could reach, the ocean appeared torn up into a vast mass of foam, which rolled on with fearful rapidity, preceded by still higher undulations than before, which made the ship roll, and pitch, and tumble about in a way most unusual and alarming. The officers, speaking trumpet in hand, were issuing the necessary orders to try and get the ship's head away from the coming blast; but the little wind there yet was refused to fill the head sails, and only made them beat and flap against the masts.

"I told you so, mates," said Abel Bush as he passed Ned Marline, the young seaman who had been criticising the Captain's arrangements; "never do you fancy that you know better than your elders till you've had as much experience as they."

Paul Pringle had been watching the Thunderer. He had served on board her; he had many old shipmates now belonging to her; and he naturally took a deep interest in all concerning her.

"She's a fine old ship, that she is!" he exclaimed as he cast a last glance at the gallant seventy-four, before turning to attend to his duty.

She was then not a quarter of a mile to leeward. Now down came the fury of the hurricane; with a roar like that of a wild beast when it springs on its prey, the tempest struck the Terrible. The headsails, which alone were set, in an instant were blown from the boltropes, and flew like fleecy clouds far away down to leeward. The helm was put up, but the ship refused to answer it. The tempest struck her on the side. The stout masts bent and quivered in spite of all the shrouds and stays which supported them, and then over she heeled, till the yardarms touched the seething ocean. Fore and aft she was covered with a mass of foam, while the waters rushed exultantly into her ports, threatening to carry her instantly to the bottom. The crew hurried to secure the ports. Many poor fellows were carried off while making the attempt. In vain Captain Penrose and his officers exerted themselves to wear the ship. Like a helpless log she lay on the foaming ocean. While still hoping to avoid the last extreme resource of cutting away the masts, the carpenter appeared on the quarterdeck with an expression of consternation on his countenance.

"What has happened below, Chips?" asked Captain Penrose.

"Twelve feet water in the hold, and rapidly gaining on us," was the answer.

"It is probably the water which has got in through the ports; but man the pumps: we must get it out again as fast as we can," answered the Captain.

"They'll not work while the ship is in this position, sir," said the carpenter.

"Oh, well, then, we must get her out of it!" cried Captain Penrose in a cheerful voice, though his heart was heavy. "All hands stand by to cut away the masts."

The order was repeated from mouth to mouth, for no voice could have been heard along the deck. The carpenter once more went below to sound the well. He shortly returned with even a worse report than the first. The order was therefore given to cut away the masts. He sprang to his post at the mizen-mast, which was to go first; but, just as he was about to cut, the ship righted with a sudden jerk, which well-nigh sent everybody off his legs. All believed that the dreaded resource would not be required, but still the helm was useless, and therefore the ship could not be got before the wind. Not a minute had passed before she was once more struck on the opposite side with a still more furious blast of the hurricane. Over the big ship heeled to it, till first the foremast went by the head, carrying all the topmast rigging over the bows; the mainmast followed, going by the board, and the mizen-mast was quickly dragged after it, the falling masts wounding and killing many of the crew, and carrying several overboard. Not a moment, however, was lost, before, led by the officers, all were engaged with axes and knives in clearing the wreck. But now the seas leaped up furiously round the labouring ship, tossing her huge hull wildly here and there, as if she had been merely some small boat left helplessly to become their sport.

Now, for the first time, Paul Pringle and others bethought them of looking for the Thunderer. So full of salt spray was the air that they could scarcely make her out, near as she was to them; then on a sudden they saw her dark hull surrounded by the seething foam, but her stout masts were not visible. She, as they had been, was on her beam-ends. Suddenly she, too, righted; up rose the masts, in all their height and symmetry it seemed.

"She has come off scatheless!" cried one or two.

"No, no, mates!" cried Paul Pringle in a tone of anguish. "See! see! heaven have mercy on their souls!"

Down, down, sank the big hull; gradually tier after tier disappeared; the foaming waters leaped over the decks—the tall masts followed—down—down—down—and in another instant the spot where the brave old Thunderer had floated was vacant, and seven hundred human beings were hurried at once into eternity. In vain could the crew of the Terrible hope to render them assistance—the same fate at any moment might be theirs. No one had even time to mourn the loss of their countrymen and friends. Every nerve must be strained to keep their own ship afloat. Still the water rushed in.

The opinion became general that a butt had been started, (that is, the end of a plank), and that the ship must go down. Even Captain Penrose could no longer conceal from himself that such was too probably the case. He, however, and his officers exerted themselves to the utmost to maintain discipline—no easy task under such circumstances in those days, when men who had braved death over and over again in battle with the greatest coolness and intrepidity, have been known to break open the spirit stores with the object of stupefying their minds with liquor to avoid facing the king of terrors.

Fiercer and fiercer raged the hurricane, and now all hopes of saving the ship, or of preserving their own lives, were almost abandoned. Paul Pringle, with Abel Bush and Peter Ogle, were seen to be very busy. They were collecting such shattered spars and small ropes, and casks and other articles, as they could most easily lay hands on. These they quickly converted into a small but very strong raft, with a sort of bulwark all round it. In one of the casks they stowed a keg of water, and some biscuits and beef; and in another they stuffed the bedding of a hammock and some blankets; and they stepped a mast on the little raft, and secured a flag to it. The raft might, probably, have borne four or five men, but there was only sitting room for one just alongside the cask which had the bedding in it. When all was ready, Paul Pringle disappeared into the Captain's cabin, and returned carrying in his arms Billy True Blue, followed by Sam Smatch, who had his fiddle and bow tucked under his arm.

"Now, Sam," said Paul, pointing to the raft, "you see that. You didn't enter to do a seaman's duty; so you, if any one ought, may quit the ship. Now, you see, none on us knows what moment she may be going down; and so, Sam, just jump into this raft and make yourself fast, so that no sea can wash you off, and take Billy True Blue with you. Though he's on the ship's books, he isn't entered to do duty; so he may quit her without any shame or disgrace, d'ye see. Bear a hand now, Sam."

The black did as he was bid; and having secured his beloved fiddle in one of the casks, held out his arms to receive little True Blue. Paul for some instants could not bring himself to part with the child. He pressed his lips to its little mouth as a fond mother might do; and then Peter and Abel followed his example with no less signs of affection; but a cry which ascended from below, that the ship was settling down fast, hurried their proceedings.

"There, Sam, take him," said Paul with a tone of deep feeling, giving up the child to the black. "Watch over him, Sam, for he's a jewel, mind that. You may be driven ashore on that island out there, and as you know the lingo of the people, you may do bravely among them. Your fiddle will stand you in good stead wherever you go, and you may play them into good humour. But mind you, Sam, as soon as you can, you are to get to a British port, and to go aboard a man-of-war, and say who the boy is, and what he is, and how he's to be brought up; and try and find out any old shipmates of mine, or Peter's, or Abel's, or the Captain's—for I know he'll join us—and say that it was our last dying message, just before the waters closed over us, that they would stand in our shoes and look after the boy. We trust you, Sam. You loves the boy. I knows you do.

You'll be faithful, lad?"

"Yes, Paul; so help me, I will," answered Sam with much feeling, pressing his shipmate's hand held out to him.

"Stay," said Paul suddenly, "you shall not go alone, Sam. There's another who loves little True Blue, and as he's one of the youngest in the ship, no one will complain that he has a chance of his life given him. It's Natty Garland. Has any one seen Natty Garland?"

The young midshipman was nowhere to be found. The Captain highly approved of Paul's proposals, and men hurried off in every direction to look for the lad.

The Captain retired to his cabin to write a hasty despatch, describing the condition of his ship. He expected that it would be the last he should ever indite. "I will entrust this with the young boy," he said to himself. "I am sure the explanations it will give will exonerate me for the loss of the ship."

When he returned on deck, the midshipman had not been found. The Captain was about to give his despatch to Sam, when two men returned, bringing young Garland with them. They found him between two of the guns on the middle deck almost stunned from a fall. Had they not arrived when they did, he very likely would have been washed through a port and drowned. He soon recovered in the air, and was told what was proposed.

"To leave the ship while others stay?" he exclaimed. "No, no. I am an officer, and it is my duty to stick by the ship to the last."

"Right, Garland," said the Captain, taking his hand warmly. "But I do not propose that you should leave the ship till she will no longer float; and then I have to entrust you with a despatch, which you must deliver to the Admiral, and explain how the ship was lost."

"I will obey your orders, sir," cried the boy, bursting into tears; "but I would rather stick to the ship like the rest and go down in her, if go she must."

"Maybe the ship won't go down, though," said Sam.

As Sam spoke, the fury of the hurricane seemed slightly to decrease. The Captain and officers again felt some hopes of saving the ship, by heaving overboard the upper deck guns which could be most easily got at. It was a desperate resource, as the ship would thus be left utterly helpless and a prey to the meanest enemy; still it was better than allowing her to go to the bottom. As she rolled, now one gun, now another, was cast loose, run out, and let slip through the ports. It was difficult work, for one gun slipping on board and getting loose might create the most desperate havoc and confusion. Several guns had been sent plunging into the ocean, when the Captain gave the order to hold fast. Suddenly, as the hurricane began, it ceased. The ship rolled and tumbled about as violently as ever, having no masts to steady her; but some minutes passed and she had not sunk lower in the water; her pumps were got to work steadily; all hands which could be spared were sent with buckets to the lower-deck to bale away; and though at first the impression they made did not appear on so large a bulk of water, it was soon evident they assisted the pumps in gaining on the leaks.

No one, with but one exception, was idle. Everybody was straining every nerve to keep the ship afloat, and to clear her of the wreck of her masts. The only exception was Sam Smatch. Not aware that the state of affairs had much improved, he sat, as ordered, on the raft, holding little True Blue, and expecting every moment to feel the ship sinking from under him.

Bravely and energetically the men laboured on. Once more the ship floated nearly at her usual level; but the continued clank of the pumps showed that it was only while they were kept going constantly that she would do so. The hurricane, with loud mutterings in the distance, died away, and the jury-masts being got up, a light wind from the eastward enabled a course to be steered for Jamaica. Paul had come and released Sam, and sent him with the child into the cabin.

"Gentlemen," said the Captain to his officers assembled round him, "a merciful Providence has preserved our lives. Every man has done his duty; but let us not boast that it is owing to our own strength or exertions that our ship is still afloat. Our fate might have been that which I fear has overtaken the Thunderer. Alas! we shall have a sad account to give of her." Captain Penrose surmised too truly what had happened. Neither the Thunderer nor a single man of her crew was ever heard of again.

Chapter Six.

The Terrible was with difficulty kept afloat while jury-masts were being got up, and sails were made to carry her to Jamaica. Never had her brave crew felt so unwilling to meet a foe; but, as Tom Snell, the boatswain's mate, observed:

"What is sauce to the goose is sauce to the gander, d'ye see, mates; and the chances are that all ships afloat are likely to be pretty evenly tarred with the same brush."

So it proved. The French suffered as severely as the English. Many vessels of each nation, both men-of-war and merchantmen, were cast away; in some cases the whole of the crew perishing, in others a few only escaping.

Little True Blue had, therefore, at a very early age, to encounter "the battle and the breeze."

"He was just beginning to get the use of his sea-legs," as Paul observed; and it was his great amusement and that of the boy's other guardians, as well as of Sam Smatch, and occasionally of the other men, to teach him to employ them. They would sit on the deck in a circle, and, stretching out their arms, let him run about between them. First he began by merely crawling, and that he did at a very rapid rate; then he got up by degrees and worked his way along their legs, and in a week or two afterwards he could move about between them; but great was the delight of the honest Jacks when he discarded even this support, and toddled boldly from one to the other with a true nautical roll. What shouts of laughter—what applause was elicited at his performances! and Billy was almost smothered by their beards as they kissed him as a reward for his success. Even at this early age, Billy showed, as most children do, a strong inclination to have his own way; but, loving him heartily as they did, they had been too well disciplined themselves to allow him to have it, and no one kept him more strictly in order than did Paul Pringle himself.

Sam Smatch would have done his best to spoil him; but he got for his pains several severe pulls by the ears, boxes on the cheek, and kicks on the shins, so at last he fortunately was compelled to exert his authority and to report him to his head guardians. Billy was a noble little fellow; but he no more nearly approached perfection than does any child of Adam. Billy was destined to experience, before long, more of the ups and downs of a naval career.

It was on the 25th of August 1781, that the Terrible, forming one of Rear-Admiral Sir Samuel Hood's squadron, arrived off the Chesapeake, and then proceeded to Sandy Hook, where they joined Rear-Admiral Graves, who, being senior officer, became commander-in-chief and sailed in quest of the enemy. Paul Pringle and the rest of the crew of the Terrible were eager once more to meet the foe.

"Here we've been a-cruising up and down these two years, and never once been able to get alongside them Frenchmen, to have a regular-built stand-up fight!" exclaimed Paul as he and Abel Bush and one or two others were stretching their legs on the forecastle.

"I should just like to show a Monsieur to Billy, and tell him all about them," observed Abel. "We can't begin too soon to teach him how he ought to feel for them. I knows well enough that we mustn't make him hate them, because, d'ye see, they are our enemies; but we may show him how he must try and give them a sound drubbing whenever he can catch them, because that's his duty to his country, and it's good for them to pull down their pride, d'ye see."

Abel's opinion was loudly echoed by all his hearers. There soon appeared every probability of the wishes of the old Terribles being accomplished. Early on the morning of the 6th of September, the French fleet was discovered at anchor across the Chesapeake, extending in a long line from Cape Henry to the Middle Ground.

The British ships were cleared for action, and stood towards the enemy. When the French perceived them, they also got under weigh and stood to sea, their line being formed as the ships drew from under the land. It was a fine sight to see the two fleets thus approaching each other in battle array. The hearts of the British tars warmed at it—their courage rose.

"We must have Billy up and show it to him!" exclaimed Paul Pringle to Peter Ogle. "Here, boy, you just run below and tell Sam Smatch to come up with the child. The Monsieurs won't begin to open fire yet, and it will do his heart good to see the sight—that it will."

Sam in a short time appeared with Billy in his arms on the forecastle.

"You don't want to keep a baby up here while de enemy is firing at us, Paul?" said Sam, with his teeth giving signs of an inclination to chatter.

"No fear, Sam," answered Paul with a quizzical look at the black. "We'll take care that no harm comes to you and the baby."

He called him the baby; but little True Blue was now able to understand much that was said to him, while he could talk in a fashion of his own. Though his sentences were not very long, his friends understood well enough what he meant to say; and, judging by their shouts of laughter, it might be supposed that his remarks were witty in the extreme.

Paul now lifted him up in his arms, and pointed to the French fleet.

"See here, Billy," said he, "look out there at the Monsieurs. You must learn to drub them some day, mind you, if we don't do it just now. You knows what I mean?"

"Ay, ay," answered Billy, doubling his little fists; "Billy fight en'y—fight Fen!"

The sentiment was received with the loudest applause by the crew. On the Captain inquiring what had occurred, "It's little Billy True Blue, sir, standing up and a-swearin' as how he'll drub the Frenchmen," was the answer.

Even Captain Penrose at such a moment, which must be awful to all thinking men when about to engage in deadly combat with an enemy, could not help smiling at the account, however much he might be inclined to doubt the correctness of the assertion.

"Let him get a little bigger before we try his metal," he replied. "Take him below at once. We are nearing the enemy's line, and shall soon have their shot come rattling aboard us."

The day had drawn on before the two hostile fleets could approach each other; but the rear ships, from want of wind, were far astern when the Princessa, Shrewsbury, Intrepid, and Montague, leading, followed closely by the Terrible and Ajax, got into action and bore the whole fire of the van and centre of the French fleet. Right gallantly did the English tars stand to their guns; and seldom have they had more need of their boasted courage. Round-shot and chain-shot and langridge came showering thickly down upon them. The English line was to windward, and might easily have got out of the fight; but this the Captains disdained to do, though anxiously looking for the assistance of their friends. The wind more than once shifted, and each time that it did so, it enabled the French to bring more of their ships down on the English centre, especially on the Terrible. She looked like some noble monster brought to bay. Although with one opponent abeam, and two others on her bows, and another on her quarter, pouring their shot in upon her, not a man flinched from his gun. Numbers fell, killed or wounded, but their places were instantly supplied by their shipmates. Several guns were dismounted, but others were got over from the opposite side, and fought with the most determined spirit. The brave old Captain walked the quarterdeck as coolly as if no enemy was in sight, casting an eye aloft every now and then, to assure himself that the flag, which he had resolved should fly to the last, was still untouched.

Paul Pringle was one of the quartermasters at the helm. Several shipmates and friends had fallen around him. He saw the enemy's shot striking the ship's sides between wind and water, and he could not help feeling the very perilous position in which the old ship was placed. In spite, however, of the tumult, the death and havoc which raged around him, his thoughts turned anxiously towards his little charge down in the distant hold. "Well, if the Captain goes, and I go, and we all go who have charge of him, there is One above who will look after him and tend him better than we can," he said more than once to himself. "Still I wish he were safe out of this. For myself, I'd as lief go down with my colours flying as strike them; but that would be hard for him, and yet the old ship seems very uneasy. Heaven watch over him and protect him!"

As Paul said this to himself, a shot came flying from the ship on the Terrible's quarter. Suddenly Paul was torn from his hold of the wheel, and, with two other men, was seen struggling on the other side of the deck. Captain Penrose had at that moment faced aft and seen what had occurred.

"Paul Pringle gone!" he said sadly to himself. "A better seaman never died fighting for his country."

Scarcely had the well-merited eulogium passed his lips, than, from among the mangled forms of his shipmates, and covered from head to foot with their still warm blood, up sprang Paul himself, and with a bound returned to the wheel, the spokes of which he grasped firmly, singing out with stentorian voice and a prolonged cadence, "Steady!" as he passed them rapidly round.

The man who had been ordered to take his place stopped when he saw him, with a look of amazement, uncertain whether it was his ghost or not.

"It's myself, Jack," said he; "but it was a near touch and go, and for some moments never did I expect to be on my legs again, let me tell you, lad."

Still hotter and hotter grew the fight; but the firing sent down the little air that there had been, and it fell so that no more of the British ships could get up to the support of those engaged. Still the van and centre bravely supported the unequal fight. The carpenter came and reported to the Captain that he had sounded the well, and that the water was gaining rapidly on the ship.

"Man the pumps, then, Mr Chips, and try and clear her," was the answer.

Some men were at once told off for that purpose, ill as they could be spared from the guns, and sent below.

Scarcely had they set to work when a shot came in, carrying off the heads of several of them; another shortly followed and destroyed the pumps. Mr Chips and the survivors, with some of his crew whom he collected, strenuously exerted themselves to repair the damage; but it was a long time before they could get the pumps to work.

All this time little Billy remained with Sam in the hold. Billy, it must be confessed, began to cry at the din and uproar, for he could not make out what it all meant; and the teeth of the poor black, who knew too well, began to chatter in right earnest, and his heart to quake. It was, in truth, a very trying time for Sam. He had a lantern with him, but it gave a very dim, uncertain light; and from the crashing just above his head, and the rushing sound close to his ear, he knew that the shots were finding their way in between wind and water, and that the latter element was gaining a rapid entrance into the ship. Every now and then the splinters, and occasionally also a shot, which fell through the hatchways, showed him that death was being dealt rapidly around just above him; and he dared not therefore move, as he wished to do, to the orlop-deck, into which the shot of an enemy does not often find its way. Then, again, the sound of the water washing about below his feet alarmed him. He began to anticipate the most dreadful of fates.

"De poor little Billy and I will be drowned down here in dis dark hole, and no one come to look for us. What me do? Oh dear! oh dear! Poor little Billy!"

Then he wrung his hands bitterly, while Billy stood between his knees, looking up inquiringly into his face, and wondering what made him so unhappy. Then Billy cried himself, not exactly knowing why. Then he stopped and endeavoured, as far as his knowledge of language would carry him, to ask Sam what was the matter.

"No ask, Billy—no ask," answered Sam, shaking his head mournfully. "De old ship very ill— hear how she groan and cry!"

Indeed, the sounds which reached their ears were very appalling. The ship herself groaned and moaned as the water rushed through her, and the pent-up air made its escape, and the bulkheads creaked loudly, and then from above came the saddest shrieks and cries. They were from the cockpit, where the poor mangled fellows who had been brought below were placed under the hands of the surgeons. Besides all this, there was the unceasing roar and reverberation of the guns, shaking the ship's sides as if they were about to fall to pieces; while there was the rattle of shot, and the crash and tearing of planks, and the rending asunder of stout timber.

In time Billy got accustomed to the sounds, and did not seem to connect them with any especial danger to himself and his friends. Not so poor Sam, who grew more and more alarmed, and not without reason; for although he was unable to ascertain how the battle itself might terminate, he saw too evidently that unless it was shortly brought to an end, and the crew were able to exert themselves in keeping her afloat, the ship would go down with all on board still fighting on her decks. Anxiously he waited. There seemed to be no cessation of firing. Then, taking Billy in his arms, he exclaimed, "Better be shot than stay and drown here!" and rushed frantically up the hatchway ladders.

"Down, Sam—down! Is the boy mad?" exclaimed several who saw him. "You'll be having little Billy hit if you don't take care, Sam."

"No, Sam not mad; but de ship is sinking!" he cried out. "De ship is sinking, I say!"

These sounds very soon reached the ears of the Captain.

"Then we'll sink with her, my boys!" he exclaimed; "for strike that glorious flag of ours while I'm alive, I will not. Fight to the last, my lads, say I; and let us show the boasting Frenchmen what they are to expect from every ship they attack before they can hope to take her."

The officers and men who stood near echoed the sentiment, and from gun to gun along the decks it flew, till the whole ship's company broke forth into one loud enthusiastic cheer.

Probably the Frenchmen heard it; but they continued firing with effect, till suddenly their helms were put up, and, their rigging being in far better condition than that of the English, away they stood before the wind towards the mouth of the Chesapeake; and as the shades of night were rapidly closing down on the world of waters, they were soon hid from sight. The English seamen, as they receded into obscurity, looked at the enemy with hatred and contempt. Forbidden by the Admiral to follow, and in truth unable to do so, they felt like chained mastiffs bearded in their kennels by a pack of yelping hounds, who have carried off their bones and pretty severely handled them at the same time. It must be confessed, indeed, that although the French could not claim a victory, they decidedly had the best of it in the fight, their ships having suffered much less than those of the English.

The Count de Grasse, in the Ville de Paris, commanded, and he gained his object of landing a body of troops to assist the Americans, which contributed so much to their success over Lord Cornwallis.

Once more the British ships were left alone, the enemy having, to all appearance, vanished into thin air. The reports brought from time to time to Captain Penrose were truly disheartening. With many men killed, and still greater numbers wounded, and the rest pretty well knocked up with their exertions, it was difficult work to keep the pumps going, by which alone the ship could be saved from going down. There was to be no slumber or rest for any one during all that night; and the Captain and officers could only feel thankful that a gale did not spring up, or that the enemy did not come out and have a brush with them.

When morning broke, the signal for the fleet to get more to windward and to repair damages was flying at the masthead of the flagship. The order was obeyed, and all the day was spent in plugging shot-holes, and in bending new sails or mending rent ones, and in reeving fresh running rigging. Captain Penrose, with an excusable feeling, could not bring himself to reveal the condition of the old Terrible to the Admiral.

"If we must go down, let us first get alongside the enemy, and then, yardarm to yardarm, let us both go down together, or carry her by boarding, and win a new ship for ourselves!" he exclaimed while talking the matter over with his officers.

The idea was approved of by all of them, and they all expressed a hope that the opportunity might be allowed them of carrying it into execution. As was intended, it was repeated to the men, and soon passed along the decks, all joining heartily in the wish that, they might thus have the chance of punishing the enemy.

"But what is to be done with little Billy True Blue?" inquired Sam Smatch. "He can't board with the rest, I guess."

"No, Sam; but we will have a bodyguard for him," observed Peter Ogle. "When Paul Pringle comes for'ard, we'll ax him what he says to it. When we board and drive the Frenchmen before us, the bodyguard, with Billy in the middle, must follow closely after; and then, d'ye see, we shall win a prize, take care of Billy, and lick the Frenchmen all under one."

When Paul Pringle heard of the plan, he highly approved of it, at the same time that he put the question, "Who's to take care of Billy, mates, and form this same bodyguard you speak of?"

Now, of course, everybody would wish to do the fighting part, and to be among the first on board the enemy's ship. Who would form the bodyguard? That was a poser. Of course Sam Smatch would be one; but then by himself he would not be of much use, as his wooden leg might chance to stick in a hole and stop his progress. At last they agreed to refer the matter to the Captain, and to get him to tell off a body of men for that purpose.

Paul Pringle was selected to be the bearer of the message. Hat in hand, he stood before his Captain.

"What is it, Pringle?" asked the old man.

"Why, sir, please you, I be come about the business of the ship's child, sir, Billy True Blue," began Paul. "We hear as how we are to get alongside an enemy and to take her, and we've been thinking how we are to get little Billy safe aboard if the Terrible, bless her old ribs! was for to take it into her head to go down; and we thinks as how if he was to have a bodyguard, whose business was to keep round him and look after him, seeing as how Sam Smatch can't do that same by himself, that it would be the best thing for the youngster we can arrange."

Much more to the same effect Paul explained; and the Captain finally promised that if there was a chance of getting alongside an enemy, he would appoint some men to the duty.

"And what is more, I will place the party under command of Mr Garland," said the Captain. "Billy is such a pet with him, that I am sure he will do his best to defend him."

"That I know he will, sir!" exclaimed Paul. "That will just do, sir. None on 'em will fight the worse for knowing how kind you've been to us—that they won't;" and honest Paul scraped his way out of the cabin.

The enemy, however, showed no inclination to give them the chance they wished for. Although Admiral Graves kept his fleet sailing up and down in front of them, they continued to leeward, without any attempt to approach. The Count de Grasse was more intent on carrying out his immediate object of effecting the safe debarkation of the troops than in sustaining the honour of his nation. He was a wise man, for by risking an action he might have been defeated and lost the attainment of both objects.

In spite of the battered condition of the Terrible, she maintained her position in the line; but she was only kept afloat by the most strenuous and unremitting exertions of her brave crew. Another night and day passed, and each hour the difficulty of keeping her afloat became more apparent. Her masts and spars, too, were much wounded, and it became a question how she would be able to weather even a moderate gale. Still the ship's company worked on cheerfully, in hopes that they might have the chance of gaining a ship for themselves. At length the wind fell very light, and the Admiral, ordering the fleet to lay to, sent an officer on board each ship which had been engaged, to inquire into her condition and the state of the wounded. It was a trying time when the Captain of the flagship himself came on board the Terrible. Half the men were lying about between the guns, overcome with fatigue, while the remainder were working away at the pumps in a way which showed that they knew their lives depended on their exertions. He examined the ship below, and when he went on deck he cast his eye on the masts and spars. He then took Captain Penrose aside, and, after talking with him, went back to the flagship. He soon returned, and a few more words passed between him and the Captain.

Captain Penrose then appeared on the quarterdeck with a sorrowful countenance.

"Gentlemen," said he with a voice almost choked with emotion, turning to his officers, "and you, my gallant fellows, who have served with me so long and so faithfully, I have sad news to tell you. It is the opinion of those competent to judge, that we cannot hope to keep the old ship afloat much longer. If we could put her on shore, we might save her to carry us yet longer through the 'battle and the breeze;' but we have only a hostile shore under our lee, with an enemy's fleet in sight, far superior to ours, and which has lately been reinforced by five ships-of-the-line; and therefore, my friends, it has been decided that we must abandon and destroy her."

The old man could scarcely speak for some minutes, while a general groan ran through the ship's company. Paul Pringle turned his eyes towards the distant fleet of the enemy, and thought, "But why can't we get alongside some of them Monsieurs and take a ship for ourselves? We'd do it—we knows we could, if the Captain would give the word."

The men were mistaken; but the expressions to which they gave vent showed the spirit which animated them.

"Now, my lads," continued the Captain, "the boats of the squadron will soon be alongside. Each man will have ready his bag and hammock; the officers their clothes, nautical instruments, and desks. One thing I promise you,—and that's a satisfaction to all, I know, boys, as it is to me,—that, come what may, our stout old ship, which has carried us so long through the tempest and the fight, will never fall into the hands of our enemies."

The last remark was received with a loud shout, which seemed, as it was intended to do, to relieve the spirits of the men.

"Well, lads," the Captain went on, "I wish that I had nothing more painful to say; but another bad part of the business is, that I must be separated from the larger number of you who have served with me so bravely and faithfully. I am appointed to the Fame, whose Captain has been badly wounded, and will go home; and I may take with me one hundred and ten men—the rest will be distributed among the ships of the fleet short of their complement. The first lieutenant will call over the names of those selected to go with me; but, lads,—my dear lads, who are to be parted from me,—don't suppose that I would not gladly have you also—ay, every one of you; and wherever you go, you will, I am sure, prove a credit to the ship you have served in, and the Captain you have served under."

The Captain could not go on, and many a rough seaman passed the collar of his jacket across his eyes; and then, led by Tom Snell, they gave three thundering cheers for the Captain and officers of the dear old ship they were going to leave for ever.

In a short time the boats of the squadron came alongside. The intermediate period had been spent in getting their bags and bedding ready, and now all stood prepared for the word to step into the boats. Of course the Captain had chosen Paul Pringle; so he had Abel Bush, and Peter Ogle, and Tom Snell, and the other assistant-guardians of little Billy, while Sergeant Bolton with some of his marines were drafted into his new ship, and Sam Smatch was thrown in to the bargain.

Captain Penrose had chosen Natty Garland to be among the officers to accompany him. He had called him up before the ship was abandoned.

"Most of your messmates and friends are appointed to other ships, Garland," he said; "I can probably get you a berth on board nearly any you may like to name, or, if you like to follow your old Captain's fortunes, I will take you with me."

"Oh, sir, I will go with you without a moment's doubt!" answered the young midshipman warmly. "I am sure, wherever you are, I shall find the right sort of work to be done."

"I trust you may, my lad," answered the old man, smiling and putting out his hand. From that time he became a greater friend than ever of the brave boy.

The Fame now bore down to receive her new Captain and the addition to her ship's company. Three of the Terrible's officers accompanied their Captain; the rest were distributed among the vacancies in the fleet. There floated the old Terrible, with her well-riddled and torn sails furled, but her pendant, and ensign, and Union-Jack still flying at her peak and mastheads. She was deserted. The lieutenants, with the master-at-arms and the quartermasters, had gone round her decks to assure themselves that no human being remained in her. The shot, too, had been withdrawn from all the guns; and such things belonging to her as could be more easily removed had been carried away. Now the four lieutenants in as many boats returned. Accompanied by picked men, they went to different parts of the ship. As they walked along her silent decks, the groans and sighs which rose from below made their hearts feel sad. They descended to different parts of the hold, and, each collecting such combustible materials as they could find, set fire to them and hastily retreated. Once more they returned to the boats and pulled away for the Fame. Night was coming rapidly on. Scarcely had they reached the deck of the Fame before flames burst forth from every part of the Terrible, Brighter and fiercer they grew. Now they found their way through the hatchways and climbed up the masts and rigging; they twisted and turned along the bowsprit and out to the taffrail. Still by their glare could be seen the victorious flag of England waving proudly in the breeze.

Now, fore and aft, the old Terrible was one mass of flame,—a huge pyramid of fire,—which shed a lurid glare on the clouds above, on the surrounding water, and on the white sails and dark hulls of the ships. Suddenly there was a concussion which shook the very atmosphere, and made the ships roll and shiver as if struck with an ague. Now up in one mass of fire rose the upper deck, and masts, and spars, high into the air, where for an instant they hung suspended, and then, bursting into millions of burning fragments, down they came, scattered far and wide, hissing into the ocean. Here and there, for a few minutes, some shining flames could be seen scattered about; but they quickly disappeared, the hull itself sank, and now but a very few charred fragments remained of the fine old Terrible. A groan burst from the bosoms of the gallant tars who had lately manned her, joined in equally by her Captain; and Billy True Blue, breaking into a flood of tears, was carried still inconsolable to his hammock.

Chapter Seven.

Sir George Rodney remained, from ill health, for some time in England, and the British squadrons on the West India and American stations were engaged chiefly during that time in guarding the Island of Jamaica from the contemplated attacks of the French. Captain Penrose soon taught his new ship's company to love and trust him as much as the old one had done. The Fame was constantly and actively engaged, and he took good care, as usual, that the weeds should not grow under her bottom.

Billy True Blue was all this time rapidly growing in size and strength, and in knowledge of affairs in general.

Time passed on. Sir George Rodney returned from England and took command of the West India fleet. The French still intended to take Jamaica, but had not, and he resolved, if some thousand brave British sailors in stout ships could prevent them, that they should not. With this object in view, he assembled all his ships at the Island of Saint Lucia, where, having provisioned and watered them, he lay ready to attack the Count de Grasse as soon as he, with his fleet, should venture forth from Fort Royal Bay, where they had been refitting.

Paul Pringle and his shipmates were as eager as ever for the battle.

"I do wish little True Blue was big enough to join in the fight—that I do, even if it were only as a powder-monkey. He'd take to it so kindly—that he would, I know," said Peter Ogle to Paul.

"I've no doubt about that, Peter," answered his shipmate. "But we'll wait a bit. He'll be big enough by and by, and we mustn't let him run any risk yet. We'll send him down below, as we used to do in the old Terrible, with Sam Smatch. Sam will have more difficulty in keeping him quiet than he had then."

"But I wonder when we shall get at these Frenchmen?" said Abel Bush. "They seem to me just as slippery as eels. When you think you've got them, there they are gliding past your nose, and safe and sound at anchor under their batteries, or in some snug harbour where you can't get at them. Well, Paul, night and morning, I do thank heaven that I wasn't born a Frenchman—that I do."

"Right, Abel; so do I," said Paul. "Ah, here comes little True Blue. Now, I'll warrant, about the whole French fleet they haven't got such a youngster as he is—no, nor nothing like him."

"Like him! I should think not!" cried Peter Ogle in a tone of voice which showed that the very supposition made him indignant. "No more like him than a frog is like an albatross. No, no; search the world round, I don't care in what country, ashore or afloat, black, or brown, or white, you won't find such another little chap for his age as Billy True Blue."

The child, as he walked along the deck with a slight roll, which he had learned as soon as he put his feet to the planks, seemed well deserving of the eulogium passed on him. He was a noble child, with a broad chest and shoulders, a fair complexion, though somewhat bronzed already, and a large, laughing blue eye, with a good honest, wide mouth, and teeth which showed that he could give a good account of the beef and biscuit which he put into it.

"Sam says I no big enough to fight de French," said Billy, pouting his lips, as he came up to his old friends, followed closely by the black. "I put match to gun—fire—bang. Why no I fight?"

"Huzza, Billy!" cried Peter Ogle. "That's the spirit. You'd stand to your gun as well as the best of us, I know you would. But we can't let you just yet, boy. Make haste and grow big, and then if there are any Frenchmen left to fight, with any ships to fight in, you shall fight them, boy."

This promise did not seem at all to satisfy Billy. He evidently understood that the ship was likely to go into action; and though it was a long time since he had been sent into the hold with Sam, he had a dim recollection of the horrors of the place, and fancied that he would much rather be with his friends on deck. Of course Sam was ordered to take charge of the little boy, as before.

The British had not long to wait for the expected meeting with the enemy. At daylight on the 8th of April 1782, the Andromache frigate, commanded by Captain Byron, appeared off Gros Islet Bay, with the signal flying that the enemy's fleet, with a large convoy, was coming out of Fort Royal Bay and standing to the north-west. Instantly Sir George Rodney made the signal to weigh, and by noon the whole fleet was clear of the bay. The Admiral stretched over to Fort Royal, but finding none of the French ships there, or at Saint Pierre's, he made the signal for a general chase. Night came on, but still a sharp lookout was kept ahead.

Paul Pringle and Abel Bush walked the forecastle, where the second lieutenant of the ship was stationed with his night-glass. The Fame was one of the leading ships. It was the middle watch. Paul put his hand on Abel's shoulder. "Look out now there, mate; what do you see now?"

"Ten, fifteen, twenty lights at least. Huzza! That's the enemy's fleet. We shall be up to them in the morning."

The lieutenant was of the same opinion, and went to make his report to the Captain. The men now clustered thickly on the forecastle to watch the Jack o' Lantern-looking lights, which they hoped proceeded from the ships with which they expected in the morning to contend. As the mists of night cleared away on the morning of the 9th, the French were discovered in the passage between Dominique and Guadaloupe. A signal was seen flying, too, at the masthead of Sir George Rodney's ship, to prepare for battle and to form the line. The French convoy was made out under Dominique, but the ships of war appeared forming their line to windward and standing over to Guadaloupe.

Unfortunately, however, the British fleet got becalmed for some time under the high lands of Dominique, and unable to get into their stations. The instant, however, that the welcome breeze at length reached the van division under Sir Samuel Hood, he stood in in gallant style and closed with the enemy's centre. By noon the action had commenced in earnest, and was maintained by this division alone for upwards of an hour without any support from the rest of the squadron, the gallant Barfleur being for most of the time hotly engaged with three ships firing their broadsides at her. At length the leading ships of the centre got the breeze, and were able to come to the support of the van. Many of the French ships even fought well and gallantly, but, in spite of their superiority in numbers, were very roughly handled. In consequence of this, when the Count de Grasse saw the rear of the British fleet coming fast up, having the weather-gage, he hauled his wind and withdrew out of shot. Two of the French ships were, however, so much cut up in hull and rigging that they were compelled to leave the fleet and put into Guadaloupe.

Nothing could exceed the disappointment and rage of the British seamen at this proceeding. They had made sure of victory, and now to have the enemy run away and leave them in the lurch was provoking beyond all bearing.

Several British ships had suffered—the Royal and the Montague, and the Alfred especially, Captain Bayne, who commanded her, being killed. Still the crews entreated that they might not be sent into port, and, with the true spirit of British seamen, undertook to repair damages at sea, in which request they were seconded by their officers. For two days they were at work without cessation, making sail, however, whenever they could, and beating to windward in the direction the French fleet had gone.

The enemy were carrying all the sail they could press on their ships; and by the evening of the 10th they had weathered the Saintes, a group of rocks and islets between Dominique and Guadaloupe, and were nearly hull down.

Towards noon of next day the officers were seen to have their glasses more frequently and intently fixed on them; and by degrees, while the main body grew less and less distinct in the blue haze of the tropics, two ships, with their topmasts down, were perceived standing out in bold relief, and therefore known to be considerably to leeward of the rest, and much nearer the British. The breeze since the morning had been increasing to a fresh and steady gale.

With unbounded satisfaction the seamen saw the signal thrown out from the flagship for a general chase. The gallant Agamemnon, now beginning to earn her well-merited renown, with the noble Fame, and other ships forming Admiral Drake's division, were ahead of the rest of the fleet. Crowding all sail with eager haste, they dashed on to secure their hoped-for prey. They saw the disabled Frenchmen making signals, calling their countrymen to their relief.

It was a period of intense anxiety; for the doubt was whether the Count de Grasse would abandon his ships to their fate or bear down to their relief, and thus lessen the distance between the enemy and himself. Eagerly they were watched. There remained no doubt that the English would cut off the two disabled Frenchmen, when gradually the bows of the distant ships of the enemy were seen to come round, and the Count de Grasse, adopting the nobler course, came bearing down under a press of sail to attempt the rescue of his friends.

"Now, gentlemen, we shall have them!" exclaimed Captain Penrose in a cheerful voice as he walked the quarterdeck with some of his officers. "Before this time to-morrow we shall have fought an action which will, I trust, be for ever celebrated in the annals of English history."

Down came the Frenchmen in gallant style, faster than they expected; and the more experienced saw, from the scattered positions of the British ships, that the result of an action at that moment would have been very doubtful. Intense, however, was the disappointment of the greater number, when, towards evening, the leading ships of the two fleets being not a mile apart, they saw the signal of recall made.

Captain Penrose smiled at the impatience of his officers and men.

"I know Rodney pretty well by this time," he remarked. "He is as eager for the fight as any of us, but he is no less anxious for the victory, and knows that will best be obtained by forming a compact line. See! what do those signals he is now making mean?"

"To form the line of battle," answered the signal-officer.

"All right, master. Place us as soon as possible in our proper position," said the Captain. "What's that signal now?"

"Ships to work to windward under all sail," was the answer.

It soon became too dark to make out any further signals, so the fleet continued, as last directed, to beat up in the direction of the enemy all night. When dawn broke on the 12th, a French ship of the line was discovered in a disabled condition, towed by a frigate, a considerable distance to leeward of the main body of the French fleet.

Directly a signal could be seen, Admiral Rodney made one for the four leading ships of the fleet to chase, in order to capture the two Frenchmen. It was the same drama enacted as on the previous day. It would have been a stain on the white lilies of France had the Count de Grasse allowed his two ships to be captured; and therefore, once more, to the great delight of the British, he bore up with his whole fleet for their protection.

There seemed no longer a possibility of a general action being avoided. The signal was made, ordering the British ships to their stations, and a close line ahead was formed on the starboard tack, the enemy being on the larboard. Rear-Admiral Drake, in the Princessa, 70 guns, commanded the Blue Division; the van, which was led by the noble Marlborough, followed closely by the Arrogant, Conqueror, Fame, Russell, Norwich, and other ships, which, with their brave Captains, were destined to become famous in story.

At half-past seven in the morning, Rear-Admiral Drake's division, which led, got within range of the long-sought-for enemy, and soon from van to rear the British ships were sending forth their terrific broadsides. The French replied boldly; and now the two hostile fleets were wrapped in flames and smoke, while round-shot and missiles of all descriptions were passing between one and the other. Both appeared to be suffering alike, and many a brave seaman was laid low. The Fame had got early into action, and gallantly taken up her position opposite an opponent worthy of her. Her brave old Captain walked the quarterdeck, calm as usual, watching with eagle eye the progress of the engagement, and waiting for any opportunity to alter to advantage the position of his ship.

It was just such a fight as Paul Pringle and the crew generally had long wished for; and fierce and bloody enough it was, too. Of course little Billy was down below, as secure from harm as his friends could make him. Few of those present had ever been in a hotter or better contested fight. The officers, at all events, knew how much depended on the result—the safety, probably, of all the British possessions in the West Indies. All the seamen thought of was, how they best could thrash the Frenchmen; and they knew that all they had to do was to stick to their guns and blaze away till they were ordered to stop. Towards noon the wind shifted, and enabled the British fleet to fetch to windward of the enemy.

"See what that gallant fellow Gardner is about with the Duke," observed Captain Penrose to the master, who was near him.

Putting the Duke's helm up, he was standing down under all sail in a bold attempt to break the enemy's line. There was a groan of disappointment given by all who saw him when his maintopmast fell over his side, and, unable to keep his position, he dropped to leeward.

Sir George Rodney in the Formidable, however, supported by the Namur and Canada, was more successful. Keeping up a terrific fire, he dashed through the French line about three ships off from the Ville de Paris, followed by all those in his rear; then, immediately wearing, he doubled on the enemy again, pouring in on them his crashing broadsides. By this bold manoeuvre the French line was broken and thrown into the utmost confusion: their van bore away and endeavoured to reform to leeward; but, too hotly pressed by the British ships, there seemed little probability of their accomplishing this.

Still the Frenchmen, though evidently losing the day, fought with the most desperate courage and resolution. For a short time, while still the battle was raging between many ships, the crew of the Fame ceased firing; for one opponent had sheered off whom they were unable to follow, and another was approaching. Whether the cessation of the roar of the guns made Sam Smatch careless, is uncertain; but just as a ninety-gun ship was bearing down on the gallant Fame, who should appear on the quarterdeck but little Billy True Blue! At that moment the Frenchmen let fly a crashing broadside, speedily returned by the crew of the Fame. Round-shot and bullets were flying about like hail, blocks and yards and splinters were rattling down from aloft, and blood and brains and mangled limbs were being scattered here and there. Unharmed and undaunted, the little fellow stood amid the wild uproar and the havoc and destruction and the scenes of horror taking place on every side.

The Captain at length turned round and saw the child standing near him.

"Oh, go below, boy! go below! You may be hurt, my child!" he exclaimed in a voice of the deepest concern. He turned to young Garland, who was near him, repeating, "Take him below instantly out of harm's way."

Billy had never disobeyed the Captain's commands before; but he struggled violently in the midshipman's arms and cried out, "No, no! Billy stay on deck and fight French!"

The fine old Captain was raising his hand as a sign that he must be obeyed, when he was seen to stagger. Nat Garland let go the child and ran to catch him; but before he could get up, he had sunk on the deck, just raising himself on one arm; but that slowly gave way, and he lay still on the deck.

Billy True Blue flew up to him with a cry of grief.

"Oh, Captain, Captain, what is the matter?" he exclaimed. Young Garland and those who stood near with deep grief thought that their gallant chief was dead.

"Captain, Captain, do speak—tell Billy what is the matter?" said the child.

At length the old man opened his eyes and smiled as he saw that innocent infantine face looking down upon him.

"Alfred—Edgar," he whispered slowly. "Yes, dears, I know you; but I am going—going to another world of peace and quiet, where we shall all meet. I have had a rough life away from you; but duty, dears, duty kept me from home—always follow duty wherever it leads."

Billy could not make out what the Captain was talking about, and others thought that he was speaking to him. In a little time he came more to himself, and they were about to take him below, but he insisted on being left on deck.

"I am shot through and through," he said. "I will breathe the open air and see how the fight goes as long as I live. But take that little boy below out of danger."

Soon after he had spoken, he again became partly delirious, and Billy shrieked and struggled so violently that the midshipman, who had a fellow-feeling for him, again set him down, and he ran back to his dying friend.

Captain Penrose now cried out for something to drink; but when it was brought, he would take it from no hands but those of Billy. Unconscious or regardless of the danger which surrounded him, the child sat himself down composedly on the deck, and continued to moisten the lips of the old man. Now a loud, true British hurrah ran along the decks of the Fame. Another English ship was coming up, and the crew of their opponent, unwilling to encounter the fire of a fresh antagonist, were hauling down her colours. The Captain raised himself up on one arm, and his eye fell on the white flag of France coming down from the masthead of the enemy.

"Hurrah! hurrah! hurrah!" he feebly exclaimed.

"Hurrah! hurrah! hurrah!" shouted Billy in a shrill tone, waving his little hat. Then the fine old seaman fell back, and when they got up to him he had ceased to breathe.

Hitherto Sir Samuel Hood's division had been becalmed, but now getting the breeze, it came up in gallant style to take part in the action. Still many of the French crews fought on with the most heroic bravery. The Glorieux especially, commanded by the Vicomte D'Escar, made a most noble defence. Her masts and bowsprits were shot away by the board, but her colours were not struck till all her consorts were taken or put to flight. Her brave commander fell in the action. Monsieur de Marigny in the Caesar displayed equal bravery. Having sustained the fire of several ships, he was, when almost a wreck, closely and vigorously attacked by the Centaur. His colours, it appeared, were nailed to the mast; and though his men were falling thickly around him, and he himself mortally wounded, he would not yield.

At length, several other British ships coming up, one of the French officers cried out that the ship had surrendered, and at that moment her brave Captain was said to have breathed his last. No sooner did the Caesar surrender than her masts fell over the side. The Ardent, which was in the midst of the British fleet, struck to the Belliqueux, an English ship with a French name, and the Hector, 74, to the Canada, 74, commanded by Captain Cornwallis. He, however, left his prize to be taken possession of by the Alcide, and made sail after the French Admiral in the Ville de Paris, who, with his seconds, was endeavouring to rejoin his scattered and flying ships.

Boldly the brave Cornwallis approached the huge Ville de Paris, and right gallantly opened his fire; and so ably did he hang on her, and cut up her sails and rigging, some other ships coming up to his support, that it was impossible for her to escape. Still the Comte de Grasse, although his fine ship was almost cut to pieces and multitudes of her crew killed, seemed determined rather to sink than to yield to any ship under that of an Admiral's flag. At length Sir Samuel Hood came up in the Barfleur, and poured in a tremendous broadside. Even then the gallant Frenchman held out, firing away from both sides of his ship on his numerous opponents for a quarter of an hour longer; when at length, seeing that all his own ships had deserted him, and that night was coming on, just as the sun set he hauled down his flag.

The enemy's fleet continued going off before the wind in small detached squadrons and single ships under all the sail they could crowd, closely pursued by the British ships, which were consequently much dispersed.

Sir George Rodney, on seeing this, made the signal to bring to, in order to collect his fleet and secure the prizes. The signal was seen from many of the ships, and obeyed; but Commodore Affleck, in the Bedford, with other ships which were ahead, not observing it, continued the chase, keeping up a hot fire on the flying enemy.

"Well, mates!" exclaimed Paul Pringle, as that evening, with little Billy on his knee, he sat at the mess-table between the guns which had been so well served, and had served their country so well, "we've had a great loss, for we have lost as brave a captain, and as true a man, as ever stepped aboard of a man-of-war; yet, mates, he died as he would have wished, in the hour of victory; and then, just think on't, we've had as glorious a day as I'd ever wish to see. Maybe few of us will ever live to see another such. But, mates, there's another thing we have to be grateful for—that is, that our little Billy here has escaped the Frenchmen's shot. What should we have done if he had been killed? It would have broken my heart, I know."

"Grappled with the first Frenchman we could have met, and blown her and ourselves up together—that's what I'd have been inclined to do!" cried Tom Snell, who was generally an advocate for desperate measures. "But how was it the little fellow got away from Sam? How was it, Billy?"

"I ran up, and leave Sam down dere," answered Billy.

"Has anybody seen Sam since then?" asked Abel Bush.

On comparing notes, it was discovered that no one had seen the black since the commencement of the battle. It was agreed, therefore, that instant search should be made for him. Paul having procured a lantern from the master-at-arms, the messmates went below with Billy. They reached the spot where the child said he had left him, but no Sam was there. They shouted his name through the hold, but no reply was made. They hunted about in every direction.

"He must have gone on deck and stowed himself away somewhere," observed Paul Pringle.

Just then Abel Bush said he heard a groan. Going towards the spot, there, coiled up, not far from one of the hatchways, was poor Sam. After calling to him several times and shaking him, he lifted up his head.

"Who dere? Oh dear, oh dear! What de matter?" he moaned out.

"How was it you let little Billy True Blue run away and nearly get killed, Sam?" asked Paul.

"Billy killed! Oh dear, oh dear! Den kill me!" cried poor Sam, trembling all over.

"But he isn't killed, and we don't want to kill you," answered Paul. "Get up, though, or we shall fancy you're in a fright or drunk."

"But I can't get up—'deed I can't!" cried Sam. "Leg shot away. I no walkee."

On hearing this, Paul and his companions lifted up the poor black, and sure enough a leg, but it was his wooden one, was shattered to fragments, and the stump to which it was secured considerably bruised. It then came out that Sam had really attempted to follow little True Blue when he ran on deck, but that, just as he was getting up the hatchway on the lower-deck, a shot had come through a port, and, striking his wooden leg, had tumbled him down again, when by some means or other he had rolled down into the hold, and there, suffering from pain and fear, he had ever since lain, unwilling and unable to rise, dreading lest harm should happen to his little charge, and fearing not a little, should such have been the case, the consequences to himself. He was half starved, too, for he had had nothing to eat all day, and was altogether in a very wretched plight. When, however, he was brought on deck, with some food put into his inside and the assistance of the carpenter, he was once more set on his legs. Many a day, however, passed before the sound of his once merry fiddle was heard on the forecastle of the Fame, for the crew loved their gallant commander too well to allow them to foot it as had been their constant custom during his lifetime.

Little rest had the crews of any of the ships that night after the battle. Not far from the Fame lay the Caesar, which had been so gallantly defended, now a prize to the Centaur. One of the lieutenants of the Centaur, with the boatswain and fifty of her men, were on board the prize, fully four hundred Frenchmen not having yet been removed.

Suddenly flames were seen to burst forth from the lower ports of the Caesar. How the fire originated no one could tell. In vain must have been the efforts of those on board to extinguish it. Boats put off from all the ships near to rescue the unfortunate people on board; but before they could reach her the fire had entered her magazine, and with a dreadful explosion she blew up, hurling every one on board to destruction. The English lieutenant and boatswain, with fifty men, and the four hundred Frenchmen remaining on board, all perished.

For this most important and gallant victory Sir George Rodney was created a peer of Great Britain, Sir Samuel Hood a peer of Ireland, and Admiral Drake and Commodore Affleck baronets of the United Kingdom.

Chapter Eight.

Among the ships forming the squadron under Admiral Graves, ordered to proceed to England, was the Hector, 74, captured from the French in the glorious battle of the 12th of April 1782. Captain Bouchier, who had commanded the Zebra sloop, had been appointed to her to take her home; and although her complement had been filled up chiefly by invalids, and French and American prisoners, who had volunteered to serve in her, it was necessary also to have a certain number of prime seamen on board. These were drafted from several ships, and, to the no small satisfaction of Paul Pringle, he with Abel Bush, Peter Ogle, and Tom Snell were taken from the Fame.

As the Fame had already a fiddler, and the Hector had none, they got leave for Sam Smatch to accompany them.

Paul was anxious to let Billy live a little more on shore than he had hitherto done. "D'ye see, Abel," he observed to his chum, "it's time, to my mind, that he should begin to get his ribs lined with true honest English beef, and sniff up some of the old country's fresh sharp air, and learn to slide and play snowballs, which he can't do out in these hot outlandish parts; for if he don't, he'll not be growing into the stout chap we wants him to be. You mind when we was little, how we used to tumble and roll about in the snow?"

"'Deed I do, mate," answered Abel. "There's nothing like a roll in the snow and a mouthful of good air to put strength into a fellow's back; besides, to my mind, Billy ought to be ashore a little to learn the ways and manners of people there—not but what I thinks our ways afloat are better, or just as good; but, d'ye see, as some day or other I suppose he will have to go on shore for a spell, he'd be just like a fish out of water if he has never been before—not know what to do with hisself any more than a bear in a china shop, or a ploughman aboard a ship."

At length, on the 15th of August, Admiral Graves, in the Ramillies, 74, with his convoy of merchantmen and prizes captured from the French, sailed for England.

The fleet continued its course without any occurrence worthy of note till the night of the 22nd of August, when Captain Bouchier, from the bad sailing qualities of the Hector, and from her comparatively small crew, unable to make or shorten sail as rapidly as was necessary, found that she was dropping astern. She was an old ship; when captured, many of her guns had been removed at Jamaica, fifty-two only remaining; and her masts had been replaced by others of smaller dimensions, while her crew, all mustered, amounted only to three hundred men.

"I didn't think things were so bad," observed Paul to Abel after they had been on board a few days. "Howsomever, Abel, we'll do our duty and trust in Providence."

The weather became very threatening, and soon very bad after they parted from the fleet; and the officers, as they went about their duty, could scarcely conceal their anxiety as to what might be the fate of the ship, should matters, as appeared too probable, grow worse than they were.

The Admiral's ship must be followed for a short time. On the 8th of September, the Caton, 64, and Pallas, frigate, sprung dangerous leaks. The Admiral, consequently ordered them to bear away for Halifax.

On the 16th, when the fleet was in latitude 42 degrees 15 minutes north and longitude 48 degrees 15 minutes west, the weather gave signs of changing, and a violent gale from the east-south-east sprung up and increased towards night. The crews of the ships did all that seamen could do under such circumstances; sails were furled or closely reefed, topmasts were struck, and everything secured to meet the rising tempest. Still it blew harder and harder, and the sea increased and ran mountains high, so that all knew, should one ship be driven against another, most probably both would go down together. With unabated fury it continued all night till three o'clock in the morning, when for a moment there was a lull, and many thought that the tempest was over; but sadly were they deceived. With a roar of thunder, down came the wind upon them in a terrific hurricane; and on board the ill-fated squadron the crashing of masts and spars told of the sad havoc it was committing, while numbers of the merchantmen were thrown on their beam-ends at the same instant, never to rise again.

The Ramillies had been carrying her mainsail, when, the squall striking her, she was taken aback, and before the clew-garnets could be manned and the sail clewed up, the mainmast went overboard, carrying with it in its fall the mizen-mast, the fore-topmast and foreyard; the tiller broke off at the head, and then in an instant the noble ship lay a helpless wreck on the tossing ocean. The carpenter sounded the well, and it was found that a leak had been sprung, and that there were six feet of water in the hold. The chain-pumps were manned; but great was the dismay when it was found that they were choked and would not work.

When the day broke, indescribable was the scene of horror and distress which the light disclosed. Nearly all the ships of war were dismasted and otherwise disabled. Many of the convoy had suffered in the same way, and others had actually foundered, while the tumultuous sea around was dotted thickly with wrecks. Numbers of unhappy beings, both men and women, were seen either lashed or clinging to them, or to shattered masts or spars, while the utter impossibility of lowering a boat in such a sea rendered their situation still more piteous. In vain they shrieked—in vain they waved for assistance. One by one they were torn from their holds, and, hopelessly struggling, sunk amid the waves. Some of the ships less disabled managed to steer near a few of the wrecks; and by means of ropes hove to them, a small number were thus saved, but small indeed compared to the many who were imploring assistance; and gradually the ships drove on before the gale, and they were left to their miserable fate.

Very soon all the ships of war parted company, and the Ramillies was left with a few merchantmen only around her. Her crew were exerting themselves to the utmost to save her. Some of her guns and her heavy stores were, during the course of the day, thrown overboard, in the hopes of easing her; but she still laboured violently, and the pumps could not be cleared. Two more anxious days passed, and, in spite of all their efforts, the leak increased till there were ten feet of water in the hold. The Admiral now began to despair of saving the ship. Happily the gale had abated, so he made a signal to the merchantmen still in his company to come down to his assistance, and to take on board his crew. Their boats thickly surrounded his flagship, and by four o'clock in the afternoon all the ship's company of the Ramillies were distributed among them. She had by this time fifteen feet of water in her hold.

The last sad act of the drama was to be performed. By the directions of the Admiral, her commander, Captain Moriarty, set her on fire fore and aft, and then, with his boat's crew, pulled on board the merchantman prepared to receive him. In a few minutes the fine old ship with a loud explosion blew up, and the merchantmen she had been convoying sailed on their way.

On the 4th of October, the Canada, 74, Captain Cornwallis, reached Spithead, and brought accounts of the hurricane and its dreadful effects. In vain those who had friends on board that large fleet waited to hear tidings of them. The Admiral and his scattered crew arrived, but no other man-of-war of all the number ever reached the shores of Old England.

After the Hector parted company from the fleet, she continued on her solitary voyage. Her leaky condition made it necessary to keep her pumps constantly going, a task which her weakened crew were ill able to perform. Had it not been for Paul Pringle and his shipmates from the Fame, the greater number would soon have flinched from the work.

Sam Smatch, too, aided not a little, and his fiddle was in constant requisition to keep up their spirits. When not engaged in playing for the amusement of the men, he employed himself in fiddling to little True Blue, whom Tom Snell had lately undertaken to instruct in dancing a hornpipe. No more apt scholar was ever found.

"Anybody would know that he was a true sailor's son by the way the little chap handles his feet!" exclaimed Tom with delight as he and his old shipmates stood round, with intense admiration depicted on their countenances, while Billy was performing in public for the first time. "Watch now there his double shuffle—how he slips his little feet about just as if they were on ice!—and hear what a crack he gives his fingers. It won't be long before he'll take the shine out of many a big fellow who fancies that he hasn't got an equal."

Similar remarks of approbation continued to be showered down on Billy, who certainly entered into the spirit of the dance with all the zest that his patrons could desire, while Sam Smatch fiddled away and grinned from ear to ear with delight.

They were thus engaged when, on the afternoon of the 24th of September, a cry was heard from the masthead that two sail were in sight. In a short time it was ascertained that the strangers were standing towards the Hector. Whether, however, they were friends or foes, she was not in a condition to avoid them. On they came, and towards evening it was seen that they were French frigates, of forty guns each. Captain Bouchier addressed his people, urging them to stand boldly to their guns, and promising them to fight the ship to the last. Paul Pringle backed the Captain with all his influence among the men; but his heart was very sad, for he felt that, from the great superiority of the enemy, they would very likely come off victorious; and if so, little Billy True Blue might be carried to France and brought up as a Frenchman. Such an idea had always been a horror to him, and the too great probability that it might now be realised made his heart sink lower than it had ever done before.

The only alternative seemed to be that of going down with their flag still flying; but the safety of little Billy, who would be involved in the catastrophe, made that too terrible to contemplate. So Paul talked to Abel, and Tom, and Peter, and his other friends, and they went round among the men and urged them to stand boldly to their guns, to blaze away as fast as they could, and to try and beat off the Frenchmen. Night came on before the enemy got up to them, and for some time the two frigates were seen hovering just beyond range of their guns, as if uncertain whether or not to attack them.

Of course Billy, in spite of his entreaties to be allowed to remain on deck, was sent below with Sam, who received the strictest charge under no pretence to allow him to escape. An hour or more passed, and then, through the thick gloom of night, the two strangers were seen drawing near. As they ranged up, after passing her quarters and pouring in a heavy fire, the Hector opened her broadsides in return. Now they sailed by, and first one and then the other crossed her bows, raking her as they did so. Broadside after broadside was poured into her. Many of her brave crew were struck down, some never to rise again. Still Captain Bouchier, ably seconded by Captain O'Brien Drury, who was on his passage to England, continued to defend the ship, though, from want of hands, a complete broadside could never be fired.

Still the few strong, able-bodied seamen made up in activity in a great measure for the paucity of their numbers, and for the weakness of the rest. Paul, Abel, Tom, and Peter, and the rest literally flew about the decks, and handled the guns as if they were quakers made of wood and not of heavy metal.

The officers laboured like the men; their example encouraged the sick and wounded, who slid out of their hammocks and seized the gun-tackles, hauling at them with an energy which no one would have supposed they possessed. Even the Americans and French, in the excitement of the moment, seemed to forget that they were helping their late enemies, and laboured like the rest, in spite of the showers of shot which came crashing in on them. Still, exert themselves as they would, they knew that the Frenchmen must have been aware, from their mode of firing, that they were short of guns, because, having approached while it was yet day, they had seen by her size that she was a seventy-four-gun ship.

The Captain and master stood by the helm, and frequently had to call the men from the guns to trim sails, in order to alter the position of the ship, and to avoid being raked by the French frigates, who, nimble in their movements, again and again attempted to cross her bows and stern. Frequently they succeeded, and their shot came tearing along her decks, and ripping them up fore and aft, wounding the beams and knocking some completely away. Still the British would not give in. Had there been more men on board the Hector, the slaughter would have been much greater. As it was, numbers were falling on every deck.

At length the discouraging cry arose that the Captain was desperately wounded. At that moment his voice was heard exclaiming, loud above the din of battle, "Never fear, my lads; my heart is unhurt, and that still beats for you!"

Just then the first lieutenant was standing not far from Paul Pringle when a shot struck him to the deck. Paul stooped to raise him.

"Let me remain here, my lads," he said in a low voice. "It's all over with me; but stick to your guns. Tell the men never to give in."

These were his last words, for his life was ebbing fast away. Now it was known that Captain Drury had taken command, and once more the courage of the crew, which had begun to sink at the loss of their two principal officers, revived as before. The Frenchmen must have been severe sufferers by the fire of the Hector, and must have felt the apparent hopelessness of compelling her to strike.

Suddenly there was a cry that the French frigates were ranging up alongside, with the evident intention of boarding. Their decks had been seen crowded with men, and there could be no doubt that they had troops on board.

"Boarders, prepare to receive boarders!" shouted Captain Drury through his speaking trumpet. Of course the most active and best men had been told off for the service. Crash came the two ships of the enemy, one on each quarter. Paul Pringle, with Abel Bush, were among the leading men of the party, headed by the second lieutenant, while several of their old shipmates were with them. The instant the Frenchmen's bows touched the Hector's sides, numbers of the enemy came swarming on board on the upper deck and through the ports on the main deck. Paul and Abel and their companions rushed aft, with cutlass in hand, to repel the Frenchmen who were attacking on the starboard side. Pistols were flashing, bullets whizzing, and swords were clashing, while a hot fire of musketry was kept up from the enemy's poops, and the great guns which could be brought to bear were playing away without cessation. There seemed, indeed, every probability that numbers would gain the day. Paul began to think so likewise. Still, amid the desperate fight, one idea was uppermost in his mind. It was about little True Blue. It was the dread, if the enemy gained the day, that he would be turned into a little frog-eating Frenchman.

"Remember our own little True Blue, mates!" he shouted. "Whatever we do, don't let the Crapauds have him. Huzza for our Billy! Huzza for little True Blue!" and he and his old shipmates, making a fresh and still more desperate onset against the enemy, cut them down right and left, and drove them back with prodigious slaughter, some on board the frigate and some into the water, where many sank to rise no more. Just then, either from accident or design, the frigate on that side sheered off; but the Frenchmen who had attacked on the larboard side had already gained a footing on the Hector's deck. Every inch of it was, however, being hotly disputed; and now Paul and his companions, with their newly-invented battle cry, rushed over on that side to the assistance of their shipmates. Their coming turned the tide of the fight. "Huzza for Billy True Blue! Huzza for our Billy!" shouted Paul, and Abel, and Tom, and Peter. Step by step, as they had advanced, only at a much greater speed, the Frenchmen were driven back,—though numbers never got back, being cut down as they stood,—till at last the rest, with desperate springs, endeavoured to regain their ship. Very few accomplished their intention, for most of them shared the fate of their friends in the other ship.

Many, indeed, had no friendly plank to step on, for the frigate fell away and left them deserted on the Hector's decks. No one thought of asking for quarter, and in the heat of that desperate fight no quarter was given. The instant the ship was free of her opponents, the crew flew back to their guns and began to blaze away with as much energy as before. Now the old seventy-four's yards and blocks, and rigging, came rattling down from aloft; her sails hung in tatters, and the water rushing in told of numerous shot-holes between wind and water, while scarcely a brace or a sheet remained to enable her to alter her position. Once again the Frenchmen ranged up alongside. Again the cry was heard, "Boarders, repel boarders!"

As before, two parties of seamen, and a few of the invalid soldiers and others, rushed to repel them. Neither party could tell how far success was attending the exertions of their friends. Paul's was very nearly overpowered; but again Billy True Blue's name was shouted to the rescue, and, with as much slaughter as before, the Frenchmen were driven back to their ships. On the larboard side the fight was even more obstinate; but British pluck gained the day, and tumbled most of the Frenchmen into the sea.

Again the Frenchmen drew off and opened their broadsides. Dawn was now breaking, and what a scene of wreck and havoc did the pure fresh light disclose! Captain Drury gazed with grief at the state of the ship, for he knew that the increasing light would exhibit it to the enemy and encourage them in persisting in the attack. Still he resolved to make them pay dear for their victory, if they were to gain it; and calling on the half-fainting crew to persevere to the last, he ordered them to pour their broadsides into the enemy, who were just then passing them abeam. The men with alacrity obeyed, and cheers, though often faint and feeble, from nearly dying men ran along the decks, and showed the enemy that the true British courage of the Hector's crew was still unabated. Again another broadside was loaded, and they were preparing to pour it in on the enemy, when what was their surprise to see both the frigates make all sail and stand away to the westward! Some parting shots and some hearty cheers were sent after them; and then numbers of the brave crew sank down exhausted on the decks, slippery with the gore of their shipmates.

Even Paul Pringle began to tremble like a child, and could scarcely drag his legs after him as he went below to assure himself of the safety of little Billy. Stout-hearted as he was, he could not help shuddering at the scenes of horror which met him on every side—at the shattered condition of the ship, and the shrieks and groans of the wounded, now in the hands of the surgeons. Many poor fellows lay about, too, apparently unhurt, but expiring through fatigue. Still, nothing stopped him till he reached the hold.

The water was finding its way down there from the shot-holes above, and all was dark and gloomy. He groped his way on, shouting out for Sam and Billy. At length little True Blue's voice was heard.

"Here I, Billy; but Sam no let me come."

"Yes, Billy, you go now—you go now," said Sam in reply. When Paul got up to them, he found by the dim light of the lantern which Sam had that he had made the child fast to a stanchion, evidently for fear of his again running away, and he was now busily engaged in casting him loose.

As soon as little Billy was free, he rushed up to Paul, who took him in his arms and hugged him and kissed him, as a fond mother would have done, while the child burst into tears, exclaiming:

"Billy so—so berry glad Paul not hurt. How Abel? how Peter? how Tom?"

"Not one of them hit, my boy, I believe," answered Paul, giving him another hug. "You've been thinking on us, then, have you? And we was thinking on you, that we was, bless your little heart; and we made the Frenchmen know that they shouldn't have you as long as we'd a plank to float you on, and an arm to strike for you. And now, Sam, just stump up out of this, and try and get Billy some breakfast. I must go and lend a hand in getting the ship to rights."

In the action one lieutenant and eight men had been killed, and thirty-two wounded—their brave captain among the number, having lost his arm, and being otherwise much injured, while from that day many other poor fellows sank under their hardships and privations.

The hope now of reaching England was abandoned, and the ship bore up for Halifax. Scarcely, however, was the helm shifted when a squall struck her, and in an instant, as if they had been mere willow wands, the already injured masts went with a crash over the sides. Now the tempest came on and roared louder and louder, and the sea got rapidly up and tossed the big ship helplessly about, and, before the slightest sail could be made to keep her before the wind and steady her, a sea struck her rudder and carried it away.

Thus like a log she lay, tossed about by the waves. The riven decks could ill keep out the water which washed aboard her, while many of the beams gave way, and those of the orlop-deck bent and cracked till several of them fell into the hold. Nothing now seemed to stop the entrance of the water. Paul and his old companions exerted themselves to the utmost. They did not like to believe for a moment that the ship would go down, and yet they could not help seeing that such a fate was too likely to befall her. Furiously raged the hurricane. Higher and higher rose the sea, and more and more the ship worked; and the leaks increased till the entire hold was flooded, and casks and provisions of all sorts were rolled helplessly about; the bread was spoiled, the water-casks were stove in, and the greater portion of the fresh water destroyed.

"Paul, what is to be done?" said Abel to his friend.

"Pump away, mates, and trust in Providence," was the answer. "Fresh hands to the pumps, ho!" he sang out with as cheerful a voice as he could command.

His shipmates followed his example and worked away with fresh energy; but pumping is exhausting work, and dry work, too, and there was scarcely any water left, and but a few casks of spirits could be got at. These were carried aft and kept under charge of a sentry. A small quantity only was served out at intervals to each man with a little biscuit; and this was all the crew had to sustain life and enable them to undergo the increasing exertions they were called on to make. Many of the invalids could no longer exert themselves in the slightest degree, and numbers died every day. The surgeons went among the poor fellows and did their utmost, but without sufficient or wholesome sustenance their efforts were unavailing; and one of the saddest labours of each morning was to commit to the deep those who had perished during the night.

At length the gale ceased, and jury-masts were rigged, and the officers thought that by getting a sail thrummed under the ship's bottom some of the leaks might be stopped. By great exertions they got the sail placed as was intended, but it had no effect whatever: the leaks continued to increase, and consternation and despair appeared on the countenances of nearly all. Some poor fellows actually sank down at the pumps and died; others refused to work at them any longer, declaring that it was utterly useless making the attempt to keep the ship afloat, and the officers had to use the greatest exertions to persuade them to remain at their duty.

"Come, come, mates!" exclaimed Paul Pringle when he saw several quitting the pumps, "there's not a man of you but what would be ready to stand to his guns and die at them gladly; then why not stand to the pumps to the last, and die like true men doing our duty? Hurrah! lads, who knows but what we may keep the old ship afloat till help of some sort comes to us? And never let it be said that we turned cowards and shrank from our duty."

Thus exhorted, the greater number again seized the pump-handles and buckets, and continued to work away as before. Still it was too evident that, spite of all their exertions, the leaks were gaining on them. Even the most hopeful began to despair that all their efforts would do no more than prolong their lives. Some few, indeed, went to their hammocks, and, lashing themselves in, declared their intention of remaining there, and thus going down with the ship.

"Oh, shame on you!" cried Paul Pringle when he saw some of them doing this. "Do you call yourselves British seamen, and yet afraid to face death at your quarters? The ship is still afloat, and may float for some hours longer for what you can tell. Think of your duty, lads—think of your duty, and never flinch from it to the last."

While Paul was saying this, however, his brave heart was very sad. In the cabin of the Captain's steward sat Sam Smatch, holding little True Blue on his knee. The child's countenance showed that he partook of the anxiety of all around, and, moreover, that he, too, was suffering from the want of proper sustenance; the colour had forsaken his cheeks, and he looked thin and weak. In vain his friends had foraged for him; they could find nothing but damaged biscuit and salt beef, uncooked. Paul often thought of making a raft; but out in the Atlantic what would be the use of that? It might only prolong the child's life for a few hours, and inflict on it greater sufferings. Still, he said nothing on the subject.

Again and again the carpenter sounded the well. Each time his report was more disheartening. The end of September arrived, and there was not a drop of spirits or water in the ship. Death in another dreadful form now stared the seamen in the face. Each day the poor feverish wretches cried out for water to moisten their lips, but none was to be had. Many died from that want alone, others from starvation.

Each morning the horizon was anxiously scanned, in the hope that some ship might be in sight to bring them relief. Even an enemy would have been welcomed, for their condition would have excited the compassion of their greatest foes.

Daylight, on the 3rd of October, broke. From the report of the carpenter, the officers knew that the ship could not float many hours longer; and, like brave men and Christians, they prepared to meet that death which now seemed inevitable. The day drew on—slight were the hopes that another would ever dawn on them. A few still refused to give way to despair. Paul Pringle was among the number. He climbed to the head of the jury-mast to have another look out. In vain he looked—still he lingered. Then his eye brightened. "A sail! a sail!" he shouted. With the most intense eagerness he watched her. "She sees us! she sees us! she is bearing down on us!" he cried, still remaining at his post to watch her.

In a short time her hull rose above the horizon, and those on deck could see her. Many burst into tears, and some fell on their knees on deck, and thanked Heaven that assistance had been sent them. Still their anxiety was great, for even before the stranger could get up to them the ship might go down.

"Well!" cried Paul Pringle, seizing little True Blue and holding him in his arms, "if she does, I'll have a swim for it, and save the most precious thing aboard—that I will." Paul had got a grating ready, into which he was prepared to spring should the catastrophe occur.

Still the Hector floated. The stranger proved to be the Snow Hawk, a letter of marque, belonging to Dartmouth, commanded by Captain John Hill, from Lisbon, bound to Saint John's, Newfoundland. No sooner did Captain Hill come on board and understand the miserable condition of the Hector, than, without bargain or agreement, he at once offered to render every assistance in his power. Some few of the wounded were at once removed, but darkness prevented the others leaving the ship. He therefore remained by them all night; but though the spirits of some revived, it was a night of fearful anxiety to many, who believed that at any moment the ship might go down. Paul was of opinion that she would float, but he never let go of Billy, and kept a sharp eye on his grating in case of accident. The next morning, as the men were told off into the boats, only two hundred out of the three which had left the West Indies were found to have survived. As most of the Hector's boats were damaged, it took a long time to remove the crew; and the greater part of the day had passed before all, with their wounded Captain, were on board the Hawk. Scarcely had the last boat left her than the Hector made one plunge and went down head first into the depths of the ocean. So crowded was the Hawk, that Captain Hill threw overboard a considerable quantity of his cargo to accommodate his passengers. The wind held fair, but all hands were put on a very limited allowance of provisions and water. The last cask of water was abroach on the very day the Hawk reached Saint John's. No man more deserved to have his name held in remembrance than Captain Hill for his generous and humane conduct on that occasion.

In time, Paul Pringle and his companions, with their young charge and most of the survivors of the Hector's crew, found their way to the shores of Old England, by which time peace was proclaimed, and men began to indulge in the fond fancy that wars were to cease for ever on the globe.

Chapter Nine.

The year 1793 had commenced, the French had cut off the head of their King, set up the red cap of freedom, proclaimed the age of reason, pronounced liberty, equality, and fraternity to be the rule of the world, and to illustrate their meaning were preparing the guillotines and the cannon to destroy the noblest, the fairest, and best in their own land, and to attack any people who might differ from them in opinion.

War had already broken out with Great Britain. The people of Old England were girding their loins for that gigantic struggle, when nearly all the powers of Europe were leagued with those enemies who strove to overwhelm her. Right noble was the struggle, and right brave and gallant were the soldiers and sailors who then fought for the safety and honour of their well-loved country. Busy preparations were going forward. All classes were exerting themselves, from the highest to the lowest. Ministers were planning and ordering, soldiers were drilling, ships were fitting out in every harbour.

Grass did not grow in the streets of Portsmouth in those days. A large party of seamen were proceeding down the High Street of that far-famed naval port one bright day in summer. There came first undoubted men-of-war's men, by their fearless bearing and independent air betokening a full consciousness of their value; a young and thorough sailor boy, stout, broad-shouldered, with a fair though somewhat sunburnt complexion, a row of teeth capable of grinding the hardest of biscuit, and a fine large joyous eye and pleasant mouth, exhibiting abundance of good humour and good nature, yet at the same time firmness and decision.

The seamen stopped not far from the Southsea Gate, opposite a large placard, on which it was announced that the thirty-six-gun frigate Ruby was fitting for sea with all possible despatch, and that she had lately been commissioned by a young enterprising commander, Captain Garland, and was in want of first-rate able seamen, as well as other hands, to whom no end of fighting, prize-money, liberty, and fun of every description was promised. The offers and promises thus liberally made were very similar to those put forth in the same way when other ships were fitting out; and seamen had already learned to look more to the character of the ship and captain than to any other inducements held out to them.

"That will just suit us, Paul," said one of the men after they had carefully spelt over the paper, not without some trouble.

"I'm thinking it will, Abel. But I say, mate, I wonder if Captain Garland is the youngster we had aboard the old Terrible?" answered Paul Pringle, for he was the person addressed. "He was a fine little chap then. Can he have grown into a Post-Captain already?"

"Why, just look at our Billy True Blue here," observed Peter Ogle, putting his hand on the shoulder of the lad who has just been described. "See, a few years has made a great change in him from the weak little baby he was when he was shipmate with the youngster."

The boy smiled as he looked at his own strong fists and arms, and then glanced at the countenances of his friends.

"To be sure—to be sure," said Paul Pringle. "He was a fine true-hearted boy, and there's no doubt he'll prove a brave, dashing, and a good captain. Let's hear what Tom Snell, Marline, and the rest say to the matter."

They waited till the other seamen came up. With the latter was a one-legged black man, with a fiddle-case under his arm. He was no other than Sam Smatch, who had, ever since the last war, followed the fortunes of Paul Pringle and his old shipmates. The whole party were now grouped together before the placard, with Billy True Blue in the centre. They were not left long to consult together without interruption, for the placard served the purpose for which a bait is hung up in a wood, or placed at the bottom of a pit, while the hunter stands by to watch for the appearance of the animals it may attract. In this case, the first lieutenant of the Ruby was acting the part of the hunter. He had taken a survey of the men from a shop window, and speedily made his appearance on the spot. They knew him by the single simple epaulette on his shoulder. He addressed them at once in a free, hearty tone.

"Well, my lads, you see what's wanted," said he. "If you wish to serve under one of the smartest, bravest officers in the Navy, you will join the Ruby. We want some prime hands like most of you. Come, which of you will join? Say the word and stick to it."

"Why, sir, d'ye see, we all goes together, or we doesn't go at all," said Paul Pringle, stepping forward. "We've been shipmates off and on for many years, and we wish to be so till we lays up in ordinary again."

"I may, perhaps, be able to arrange that matter," answered the lieutenant, not liking to show all the satisfaction he felt, or to yield too soon to the demands the men might make. "But that boy, now? Perhaps we may have boys enough on board already. I suppose you don't wish to take him to sea?"

"Not him, sir! If he doesn't go, none on us goes," answered Paul briskly.

"None on us," echoed all the other godfathers.

"He is your son, I conclude, my man?" said the lieutenant, addressing Paul.

"No, sir, not mine more than Abel Bush's or Peter Ogle's, or any of them astern there," answered Paul. "No, sir, he belongs to us all, d'ye see, sir? He's the son of an old shipmate, sir, killed out in the West Ingies, fighting with Lord Rodney; and his mother was an old shipmate too; and so the boy was left to the ship's company, and they chose us to look after him—and we have looked after him, and we intend to look after him; and we loves him just as if he was a son, and more nor some fathers do their sons, and that's the truth on't, sir; and so we all intends to ship with him, that we may have him among us, that's it, sir."

"That's it, sir," echoed the rest, to show that they were all of one mind.

"Well, if you all like to join provisionally, I will see what the Captain will consent to do," answered the lieutenant.

Now as none of the party had the slightest idea of what joining provisionally meant, they were very much inclined to declare off altogether, when just then a young active man, with an extremely pleasant expression of countenance, in the full-dress uniform of a Post-Captain, was seen coming up the High Street. He stopped when he got up to the group of seamen.

"Ah, Mr Brine, are any of these men going to join us?" he asked, glancing his keen eyes over them. His countenance brightened when he saw Paul Pringle.

"Why, I believe that I see an old shipmate whom I have not met for many a year; and not one only—two or three more of you I remember clearly. Am I not right?" said he. "We served together in the old Terrible, and afterwards in the Fame."

"I thought so, sir!" exclaimed Paul with a cheerful voice. "I remember you now, sir, that I do, though I shouldn't if you hadn't told me where we'd been together. Maybe, sir, you remember a little baby you used to be kind to, born aboard the ship. There he is, sir."

"What, Billy True Blue! Of course I do," answered the Captain in a pleasant tone. "Come here, my lad; and you still follow the sea, do you? You began pretty early."

"There's no other calling to my mind a man would wish to follow, sir," answered True Blue.

"All right, my men," said Captain Garland; "if you haven't got a ship, I shall be very glad if you will join the Ruby. I do not believe that there are many frigates in the service will beat her in any way, and I promise you it will not be my fault if she isn't a happy ship."

"Just one word, sir, with the rest and we'll tell you," said Paul.

"As many as you like," said the Captain; and he and his lieutenant stepped aside.

Scarcely a minute had passed before Paul Pringle came up to him.

"We'll all join you, sir, Billy and all," said he; "and I suppose, sir, you'll not object to take Sam Smatch in? He always goes with us; and though he's not wanted to nurse Billy now, there isn't a better hand with his fiddle to be found anywhere. He might get a good living on shore—that he might, sir; but he'd rather stick by us, as he's always done, in spite of all the ups and downs of a life at sea, sir."

"Sam Smatch? Of course we'll have him!" said the Captain, not trying to conceal how highly pleased he was at getting so fine a haul of good men at one time for his ship. "And now I wish you to accompany Mr Brine on board at once and enter. When it's known that we have a fair number of good men, others will join; and the faster we man the ship, the sooner we shall get to sea and be at the enemy."

A little more conversation passed. Paul and his companions went on board and entered; and Mr Brine, soon convinced that they might be trusted on shore, allowed them to go. They employed their time so well in singing the praises of their new Captain, that in a week or two the Ruby was fully manned. In those days the crew themselves were chiefly employed in fitting the ship for sea, and as they all worked with a will, in a very short time longer she had all her stores and provisions on board, and was ready to go out to Spithead. The remainder of the officers had joined; Blue Peter was hoisted, and, with a fair breeze, she stood out of Portsmouth Harbour. In two days more her powder was on board, and under all sail she was running out at the Needle Passage.

The frigate was on the home station; but there was plenty of work for her. The enemy's cruisers were very active; and they had some fine fast frigates, which committed a great deal of mischief among the merchant shipping, and carried off numbers of prizes.

Captain Garland determined to capture one or more of these, if he could, without delay. His ship soon showed her fast-sailing qualities by making prizes of a number of small fry, in the shape of French coasters, "chasse-marées," and two or three larger merchantmen, which were sent into either Plymouth or Portsmouth to be disposed of. This sort of work, however, did not satisfy the wishes of either the Captain or his officers or crew. Among those most eager for the fight was Billy True Blue Freeborn. That was the way in which his name had been entered in the ship's books. He recollected clearly what a battle was, though he had not been engaged in one since that fierce engagement when he lost his friend and chief, Captain Penrose.

Since then, he had been for the greater part of the time at sea, partly on board a man-of-war, but mostly in merchantmen and coasters, where Paul Pringle took him, that, as he said, he might not be afraid of rocks and shoals, or the look of a lee-shore in a gale of wind. Out of all that time he had only remained three years on shore, as his kind guardian remarked, "to get his education, and to larn manners."

Paul Pringle used to boast among his friends that Billy True Blue was already a perfect seaman, and that he would sooner trust him at the helm on a squally night, or on the lookout forward on a dark one, than he would most men twice his age; but he took care never to say this in True Blue's own hearing, lest, as he observed, "the lad should larn to think too much of hisself."

True Blue had not been long on board the Ruby before he became a favourite with most of his new shipmates. Had he not had watchful guardians about him, he would soon have been spoilt by them. To see him dance the hornpipe, while Sam Smatch played his old fiddle, was, as his admirers declared, "indeed a pleasure not to be met with any day in the week," except on board the Ruby. How he could shuffle and spring, and whirl, and whisk, and snap his fingers! He looked as if he was made of India-rubber, filled with quicksilver. And then he had a very good voice and a fair notion of singing, and right merrily he could troll forth some of those stirring sea-songs which have animated the gallant tars of Old England to perform deeds of the greatest heroism, and have served to beguile and soothe many an hour of their existence on the ocean, far away from home and all its softening influences.

There were several other boys on board the frigate, among whom, naturally, True Blue took the lead. He was good-natured to all of them. If they quarrelled with him, as some would, and would insist on having it out with him in a fight with fists, he generally managed to make them very cautious about trying the same experiment again.

There was one big fellow, Gregory Gipples by name, who set himself up as a sort of leader among the other boys as soon as he came on board, though he had never before been at sea. He was a big hulking fellow; and as he had a certain amount of cleverness about him, he tried to make it appear that he knew a great deal more about things than he really did. True Blue instinctively discovered that he was a braggart and inclined to be a bully.

Another boy was of a totally different character. At first sight, so delicate did he look that it seemed surprising that little Harry Hartland had been allowed to come to sea at all. But boys were wanted, and the officers who had to pass them were not very particular; besides, on further examination, Harry was stronger than he looked, and the bright expression of his countenance showed that he would probably make up by intelligence what he lacked in physical power. He had also been carefully and religiously educated, and his habits were very refined compared with those of most of the other boys. They soon learned to call him "Gentleman Harry," though he did not seem pleased with the appellation. He was very silent as to his own early history. He said that his mother was a widow, and that he did not remember his father. He knew that she would not have the means of supporting him, so he wished to come to sea, and with the help of a friend of his own he had, after much exertion, accomplished his object.

"You couldn't have done better—that you couldn't, Harry!" exclaimed True Blue, to whom he had confided thus much of his early history. "I wouldn't have to go and live in smoky cities, or to ride along dirty roads, or to have to look only at sheep, or cows, or horses, not to be the greatest lord in the land. I have never been much on shore, and maybe haven't seen the most beautiful parts of it; but I was heartily glad to get afloat again. There you are on shore stuck in the same place day after day. What does it matter whether it's a calm or a gale, it doesn't make you go faster or slower. And if you want to go away, then you have to get on the outside of a coach, and be covered from truck to kelson with dust, and a precious good chance of a capsize and getting your neck broke. Now, when I was living ashore with Paul Pringle's mother and people, there sprung up one night a gale of wind which blew down the church steeple, I don't know how many big tall trees, and sent a large part of the thatched roof off the cottage, besides scattering the tiles of the houses right and left, and toppling down numbers of chimney-pots. There were half a dozen people killed, I heard, that night, and ever so many hurt."

Harry smiled.

"It is lucky that you think so, and I am quite ready to agree that a sailor's life is one of the best to choose, seeing that we shall have to spend the best part of ours afloat," he answered. "But what I hold is, that we shouldn't think meanly of those who have to live always on shore."

"I don't know as to that, Harry," said Billy quickly. "We shouldn't think ill of them, I'll allow; but who can help pitying them? That's all I say."

The conversation of the two boys was interrupted by an order which True Blue received to go aloft and take a lookout round the horizon. This was a post of honour to which he had been especially appointed, on account of the sharpness of his vision, and the accuracy with which he noted and could describe the various sail which might be in sight. Paul Pringle watched him with pride. Up—up—up he went. The topmast shrouds were reached—topgallant masthead; the royal mast was swarmed up, and then he stood on the main truck, holding on by the staff of the vane, no longer the little child, the pet of the ship's company, but a thorough, fearless young seaman—not the less, however, the darling of the crew.

Chapter Ten.

Day had just broken on the world of waters. It was at that time of the year when there is but little night. The water was smooth, the air soft and balmy. Gradually the grey dawn warmed up as the approaching sun cast some ruddy streaks in the eastern sky. It was True Blue's watch on deck, and he was at his post on the truck at the main-topgallant-mast.

By slow degrees the rich glow increased. He turned his head round to every point of the compass. The Start Point was just in sight, bearing about east by north, distant five or six leagues. When his eye came to the south-east, it rested there steadily for a moment, and then, putting his hand to his mouth, he shouted, "Sail ho!" with a prolonged cadence, pointing in the direction where he saw her. The officer of the watch hailed to know what she was. "A full-rigged ship, sir," was his unhesitating reply, although even from where he stood her topgallant-sails alone could be seen, and to a landsman's eye nothing distinguishable would have been visible.

The Captain soon came on deck. True Blue kept his glance on the stranger, that he might note immediately any change in her course. She was standing across the Channel and drawing nearer.

"I trust that she is one of the frigates of which we are in search, Mr Brine," said the Captain. "We'll soon learn. Make sail on the ship."

"Ay, ay, sir," said the first lieutenant with alacrity. "All hands make sail!"

"All hands make sail!" shouted the boatswain, putting his silver call to his mouth, and sounding a shrill whistle. "All hands make sail!—rouse up there, rouse up!—an enemy in sight, boys!"

The men sprang from their hammocks, and, shaking themselves rapidly into their clothes, were in another instant on deck. Every inch of canvas the frigate could carry was soon got on her, and she bore up in chase.

Another order quickly followed. It was, "Clear ship for action!"

Never was an order obeyed with more alacrity. The stranger appeared also to be standing under a press of sail, and steering to the southward of east.

"She wishes to escape us altogether, or is not quite ready for action," observed the Captain to Mr Brine.

"She seems to be putting her best foot foremost, at all events," answered the first lieutenant, taking a look at the stranger through his glass, for she could now be seen clearly from the deck. "She looks like a frigate of much about our size; and I have little doubt, by the cut of her sails, she is French."

"I have great hopes that she is, and more, that she is one of the very frigates we have been on the lookout for," said the Captain. "What do you think, master?" he added, turning to that officer, Mr Handlead, who stood near.

"A Johnny Crapaud, sir," he answered quickly. "There's no doubt about it; and to my mind the villain is making all sail to be off, because he doesn't like the look of us."

"I trust that we shall overtake her, and take her, too, master," said Captain Garland. "I think that we are already gaining on her. The frigate slips well through the water."

The crew on the forecastle were carrying on a conversation much in the same style. "Bless her heart, she is walking along at a good rate," observed Abel Bush as he looked over the bows. "The old girl's got as pretty a pair of heels of her own as you'd wish to see."

"The faster she goes, the better," answered Peter Ogle. "I never does feel comfortable like when one of those Monsieurs is in sight, till I gets up alongside him and overhauls him one way or the other. You mind how they used to give us the slip in the West Ingies. They'll be trying on the same game now, depend on't."

"But when they do begin, they don't fight badly, you'll allow," observed Paul Pringle.

"Maybe; but while they can lift their heels, they'll run," stoutly maintained Abel.

In this instance the stranger seemed determined to contradict his assertion, for at that very moment she was seen to haul up her foresall, while the topgallant-sails were lowered on the caps, where they hung swelling out and fluttering in the breeze; at the same time the flag of republican France was run up at the peak, and a shot of defiance was fired from one of her after-guns.

The British seamen, led by Paul Pringle, replied to it with a hearty cheer, which, although it could not reach the Frenchmen's ears, served to warm up their own hearts for the fight. Although the crew had not served long together, each man knew his proper station; and there each man now stood bold and fearless, prepared for the contest.

Captain Garland, with Mr Brine near him, walked the quarterdeck, with telescope in hand, watching each movement of the enemy. The marines, commanded by their lieutenant, stood drawn up with muskets, ready to open fire as soon as they could get within range. Added to them were a party of small-arm men prepared for the same object, or ready to board if required, while others were stationed there to fight the quarterdeck guns, or to attend the braces. Here, also, were grouped the mates and midshipmen, not wanted elsewhere, ready to be despatched on any duty which might be required of them. On the maindeck the crew of each gun, with handkerchiefs round their heads, and stripped to the waist, clustered round it, the locks fixed in readiness, and the lanyards coiled around them, the tackles laid along the decks, the captains with their priming-boxes buckled on, the officers with their swords on, standing by their proper divisions; while in long rows were the round-shot and wads, with grape and canister; and at intervals sat the ship's boys,—powder-monkeys they were often called,—each on his proper tub full of powder, which he had brought up from the magazine below. Here in the depths of the ship was the gunner, the presiding genius of destruction, ready to serve out the further supply of powder which might be required, as the boys came tripping down nimbly to receive it, with no more concern than if they had had to carry up baskets of flour or of corn. The carpenter was also below. He and his mates were preparing shot-plugs with tallow and oakum, and were placing them in readiness in the wings to stop any holes which the enemy's round-shot might make in the ship's side; while he was prepared to sound the well occasionally, and to make his report as to the depth of water in the hold. The other warrant-officer, the second in rank, the boatswain, stood on the forecastle with his mates, having especially to look after the masts and spars, and to repair immediately, if possible, any material damage. The purser and Captain's clerks were mostly on the quarterdeck, and, though not fighting officers, ready and willing enough to fight like the rest; while, lastly, the surgeon and his assistants were in the cockpit, with the tables prepared, and the various implements required by them spread out—saws, tourniquets, knives, basins, and sponges, as well as restoratives of different kinds—to repair the damage, and to soothe or alleviate the pain which the chances of cruel war might inflict on frail humanity.

True Blue sat on his tub, with Harry Hartland next to him, and the big Gipples on the other side of Harry. They were stationed on the upper deck. True Blue was wishing that he was bigger, that he might be serving the guns, or might be standing with Abel Bush and other friends, who, with pistols in their belts and cutlasses at their sides, were collected ready to board the enemy, or to repel boarders, should their opponents make the attempt.

Big Gipples was in no way liking the look of things; and only the conviction that he would be sent up again with a rope's end prevented him jumping off his tub and running down to stow himself away in the hold. The other boys, though not aware of the excess of his terror, maliciously wished to frighten him in retaliation for his bullying.

"Who's likely to be best off now?" began Tim Fid, one of the smallest of the set, speaking across Gipples to Harry; "we little chaps or the big ones, when the round-shot comes bowling about us? They'd just as soon take a big chap's head off as a little one's. I'd rather, for my part, be small and weak than big and strong. Wouldn't you, Harry?"

"Certainly," answered Harry, who, having glanced at Gipples' countenance, could not resist the temptation of having a fling at him. "I've heard it said that the big fellows in a sea-fight are generally picked off first, and that that is the reason there are more small sailors than large ones. I wonder what Billy has to say about it?"

True Blue, thus appealed to, was nothing loth to join in trying to increase the evident terror of Gipples. "Oh, as to that, I've heard tell how these powder tubs on which we are made to sit sometimes catches fire and blows the fellows on them like sky-rockets into the air," remarked Billy, laughing. "Mind, it's what I've heard tell of, though I never saw it. But I did see once a ship and a whole ship's company blown up together; and, mates, I hope I may never see the same sight again. I was a little chap then, and I saw some sad things that day, but I remember that one just as clearly as if it happened a week ago."

"Well, I do think it's a shame we small chaps, as have never done anybody any harm, should be made to sit here to be shot at by them Monsieurs out there—that I do," continued Tim Fid. "For my part, I do think that the Captain ought to let us little ones go down and stow ourselves comfortably away in the hold. Don't you, Gipples?"

Gipples, not perceiving that Tim was joking, looked up and said in a half-crying tone:

"Yes, I do; if any on you chaps will come, I'll bolt—that I will."

On this there was a general laugh.

"I'd just like to see you," said Tim, "whether you'd go down or come up the fastest. If every man was to do as you'd do, I should like to know what would become of the ship. The sooner you goes home and learns to hem or sell dog's meat the better."

The wretched Gipples saw that his feelings gained no sympathy. He tried to back out of his proposal, but his tormentors were in no way inclined to let him alone, till at last they made so much noise that they were called to order by the men standing at the guns nearest them.

Presently, too, the deep-toned voice of the Captain was heard.

"Silence there, fore and aft!" he exclaimed. "We have an enemy in sight, of equal if not greater force. We must take her, of course, but the sooner we take her the less loss and the more honour we shall gain. I intend to wait till we are close alongside before we open our fire. I shall take off my hat—wait till I lift it above my head; and then, my lads, I expect you'll give her a right good dose of our shot."

The seamen raised three hearty cheers. British sailors are always ready for that; and directly afterwards the taunt masts and white canvas of the French frigate were seen by those on deck rising above the hammock nettings on the larboard bow. The Captain stepped to the larboard gangway. A voice came from the deck of the Frenchman.

"What do they say?" asked the Captain of the master, who was nearest him.

"I don't know, sir. I never could make out the Frenchmen's lingo, and I doubt that they intend us to understand them," answered Mr Handlead with a tone of contempt in his voice. "They are only mocking at us. It's their way, sir." Mr Brine more briefly said that he could not make out the Frenchman's hail.

"Then keep her as she goes, master," said Captain Garland; and, putting his speaking trumpet to his mouth, he shouted, "This is His Britannic Majesty's ship, the Ruby, and I beg to know the name of yours, and the King you serve?"

"This is La Belle Citoyenne, belonging to the Republican Government of France," was the answer. To which was added by several men in chorus, "We serve no King—no, no!"

"But we do!" cried Paul Pringle. "And right glad we are to serve him. Hurrah, boys, for King George and Old England! Hurrah! hurrah!"

Three hearty cheers burst from the throats of the British tars. Scarcely had they ceased when the French Captain, who was still standing in the gangway, was seen to hold aloft in his hand a bonnet rouge, the red cap of liberty, and briefly to address his crew in terms of considerable animation. "Vive la Nation!" he exclaimed. "Vive la République!" answered the crew.

The French Captain, having finished his speech, handed the red cap to one of the seamen, who ran with it up the rigging and screwed it on to the masthead, where it was evident that a hole was prepared to receive the screw. The marines might easily have picked him off; but no one even thought of attempting to injure the brave fellow.

The Ruby was now well up with her opponent, and the two Captains, taking off their hats, made the politest of bows to each other, the Frenchman, however, beating the English Captain in the vehemence of his flourish. Both then returned to the quarterdeck. The moment to begin the fight had arrived. Captain Garland, who had kept his hat in his hand, raised it to his head. Every eye was on him. All knew the signal he had promised to give. For an instant not a sound was heard; and then there burst forth the loud continued roar of the broadsides of the two frigates as gun after gun of the Ruby, beginning at the foremost, was brought to bear on her antagonist, responded to by the after-guns of the Frenchman. And now the two frigates ran on before the wind, so close together that the combatants could see their opponents' faces, pouring their shot into each other's sides. Fast as the British seamen could run in their guns, they loaded, and, straining every muscle, they were rapidly run out again and fired. While round-shot and grapeshot and canister were sent rattling in through the enemy's ports and across her decks, about her rigging, or tearing open her sides, she gallantly returned the compliment with much the same coin. Many of the bold seamen on board the Ruby were cut down.

A shot struck two men working the gun nearest to where Gipples was sitting on his powder tub in terror unspeakable, not knowing what moment he might be hit. On came the mangled forms of the poor fellows, writhing in their dying agonies, directly against him. He and his tub were upset, and he was sent, covered with their blood, sprawling on the deck.

"Oh, I'm killed! I'm killed!" he shrieked out, and, overcome with terror, did not attempt to rise.

Two of the idlers, whose duty it was to carry the wounded below and throw the dead overboard,—the common custom in those days of disposing of them,—hearing him shriek out, thought that he had also been killed. Having disposed of the first two men who really were dead, they lifted him up and were about to throw him overboard, when, discovering how he was to be treated, he groaned out, "Oh, I ain't dead yet—take me below." The men having been ordered to take all the wounded to the cockpit, immediately carried him below, and, placing him on the surgeon's table, one of them said:

"Here's a poor fellow, gentlemen, as seems very bad; but I don't know whether he wants an arm or a leg cut off most."

"I hope that he may escape without losing either," said the surgeon, lifting up Gipples and preparing to strip him to examine his wound. "Where are you hit, my man?"

"Oh, oh, sir! all over, sir!" answered Gregory.

The surgeon, who had noted Gipples for some time and guessed his character, very quickly ascertained that there was nothing whatever the matter with him. Taking up a splint, he bestowed a few hearty cuts with it on his bare body, and then, telling him to jump up and slip on his clothes, he sent him up on deck to attend to his duty. Poor Gipples would gladly have hid himself away; but he was watched, and started from deck to deck till he had resumed the charge of his powder tub. Meantime Paul Pringle was keeping an anxious eye on True Blue. There he sat as composed and fearless as if nothing unusual was going forward, only jumping up with alacrity and handing out the powder to the crews of the guns he was ordered to serve. Never was his eye brighter. Never had he seemed more full of life and animation.

"Ay, he's of the right sort," said Paul to himself; "I knew he'd be."

The moment his tub was empty, down he ran to the magazine, and speedily again sprang with it on deck. His friend Harry imitated his example as well as he could; but he could not avoid stopping short when a shot crashed in just before him, carrying off the head of a seaman, whose body fell across the deck along where he had to pass.

The cry of "Powder, powder, boy!" from the captain of the gun made him move on, but his knees trembled so that he could scarcely reach his post. After he had delivered the amount of powder required and sat down on his tub, his tranquillity of mind and nerve returned. Another shot came whizzing by; he merely bobbed his head. When the next passed near him, he sat perfectly still. After that he scarcely moved eyelid or muscle, in spite of all the missiles and splinters and fragments flying about

Not so the miserable Gipples. Compelled to stay on deck he was; but nothing could keep his head from bobbing at every shot which struck the ship or passed over her, while his whole body was continually shrinking down on the deck. Several times he lay flat along it, and so confused was he, that, when called on to deliver the powder, he often did not appear to hear, or ran off to the wrong gun; till at last, had there been anybody to supply his place, he would have been kicked below and declared unfit to be even a powder-monkey. Even Tim Fid, when the firing began, was not altogether as steady as usual; but though he bobbed and sprang about with the feeling that he was dodging the shot, which he could not do in reality, it was much in the same way that he would have dodged a big play fellow whom he did not wish to touch him; and as he never for a moment was found wanting at his post, no one complained.

The action began at a quarter-past six that bright summer morning, and for about a quarter of an hour the two frigates ran along parallel to each other, exchanging broadsides with the greatest rapidity of which their respective crews were capable. They were keeping all the time directly before the wind, and within hailing distance of each other. In that short period great had been the carnage on both sides. One of the English lieutenants and two midshipmen, besides a dozen men or more, had been killed, and half as many again had been wounded; while the bulwarks of the lately trim frigate were shattered and torn, her crew begrimed with powder, perspiration, and blood, and her white decks slippery with gore, torn up with shot, and covered with fragments from the yards and the rent woodwork around. The mainmast, too, had been severely wounded; and though some of the carpenter's crew were busy in lashing and otherwise strengthening it, great fears were felt for its safety.

"If that goes," exclaimed Paul Pringle, who saw the accident, "those rascally Monsieurs will get off after all!"

At about half-past six the Belle Citoyenne hauled up about eight points from the wind, thus increasing her distance from the Ruby.

"I thought how it would be!" exclaimed Paul Pringle when he saw the manoeuvre. "The Monsieurs can't stand our fire. Wing him, boys, wing him! Don't let the Frenchman get away from us. Here, Billy, you come here. You all know that there isn't a better eye in the ship. Let him have a shot, boys."

True Blue, thus summoned, sprang with delight to the gun. The mass of smoke which hung round them, and the death of the officer in charge of his division, enabled Paul to accomplish his object without question.

"Now steady, Billy, as you love me, boy!" he exclaimed in his eagerness.

True Blue had not far to stoop as he took the lanyard of the lock in his hand and looked carefully along the gun. The Ruby had herself hauled up a little. For an instant there was a cessation of firing. Billy at that moment pulled the trigger. The Frenchmen were in the very act of bracing up the mizen-topsail-yard when the mizen-mast was seen to bend over to starboard, and, with a crash, to come toppling down overboard, shot away a few feet only above the deck.

"You did it—you did it, Billy, my boy!" exclaimed Paul Pringle, almost beside himself with joy, seizing his godson in his arms and giving him a squeeze which would have pressed the breath out of a slighter body.

"Who fired that last shot?" asked the Captain from aft.

"True Blue, sir—Billy Freeborn!" cried Paul Pringle.

"Hurrah! hurrah!" shouted the men at the gun.

"Bravo! let him fire another, then," answered Captain Garland, not complaining of the irregularity of the proceeding. Not another word could have been heard, for both the Ruby and the French frigate again began pounding away at each other.

True Blue, with the encouragement he had received, stepped boldly up to the gun. The captain was Tom Marline, one of his assistant-guardians, and he was a favourite with all the rest, so that there was no feeling of jealousy excited against him.

Again he looked along it. He waited his time till the smoke had cleared away a little, and then once more he fired. The shot hit—of that both Marline and Paul Pringle were certain, but what damage was done they could not determine.

"I pitched it astern, not far from the wheel," observed True Blue quietly. "Maybe it hit the wheel—maybe not."

Again the firing went on as before, and True Blue modestly returned to his powder tub. More than once he jumped up, anxious to have another pull at the lanyard of his gun. Paul, however, did not encourage this; he wisely considered that he had done enough to establish a reputation, which more shots would not have increased.

Suddenly Paul struck his hands together with delight. "She is steering wildly! she is steering wildly!" he cried out. "True Blue, you did knock her wheel away—you did, boy. See what she's about!"

The French frigate as he spoke paid off right before the wind, and presented her bows directly at the Ruby. In that position she received a raking broadside; but nothing could stop her—she was utterly without guidance, and on she came like a battering-ram directly at the beam of the Ruby. Captain Garland, so sudden was the movement, could accomplish no manoeuvre to avoid the collision. The French ship's jibboom, as she fell on board the English frigate, passed directly between her fore and mainmasts, and there she hung, while it pressed so hard against the already wounded mainmast that there appeared every prospect of the latter being carried away. Just before, a shot had struck the boatswain and brought him mortally wounded to the deck.

Paul Pringle knew of his loss. As he looked at the mast, strained to the utmost, the main and spring stays being also shot away, he thought to himself, "If the mast goes the Frenchman will break clear, and ten to one, after all, escape us."

It was a time for decision, not for much consideration.

"Who'll follow me, lads?" he exclaimed, seizing an axe and springing into the rigging.

Tom Marline and several other bold fellows did follow. They had to ascend and then to descend the tottering mast. Terrific was the danger. Should the mast fall, their death would be almost certain. They thought, however, only of the safety of the ship, or rather, how they might best prevent the escape of the enemy. With right good will they plied their axes on the enemy's jibboom. Bravely they hacked away, in spite of the fire of musketry which was kept up from her decks. Meantime a cry was raised below that the French were about to board.

"Boarders, repel boarders!" cried Captain Garland.

"I'll lead you, my lads!" exclaimed the first lieutenant. "See, they are not coming; but we'll be at them—hurrah!"

True Blue, finding that there was no more work for him to do in getting up powder, and seeing Abel Bush and Peter Ogle, with a few others, following Mr Brine on board the Frenchman, seized the cutlass of a seaman who had just been killed close to him, and, in the impulse of the moment, sprang after them. In vain, however, their gallant leader endeavoured to get on board from the upper deck. Numbers of Frenchmen stood in the head, and, in spite of all the activity of the British seamen, they could not spring into it. On finding this, quick as lightning Mr Brine leaped down, and, followed by a few, reached the maindeck. Then, calling more round him, he sprang through the bow-ports of the enemy's maindeck, with Peter Ogle, True Blue, and a few others, driving all opponents before him. Just at that moment, before all the boarders had time to follow, Paul Pringle had succeeded in cutting through the Frenchman's jibboom, with all the connecting rigging, and, her head coming round, she was once more clear of the Ruby, and drifting helplessly away from her. Even while engaged in his task, Paul's watchful eye had detected True Blue seizing the cutlass, and when he followed Mr Brine he guessed his object. Still he did not suppose that those with him would allow the boy to board the Frenchman; and, at all events, he was not the man to be deterred by any consideration from completing the duty which he had undertaken.

The moment, however, that he had performed it thus effectually, he slid down rapidly on deck and eagerly sought for his godson. He was met with a cry from Harry Hartland and Tim Fid, "Oh yes, Paul, he's gone—True Blue's gone; he's on board the Frenchman, and they'll make mincemeat of him—that they will!"

He observed, also, Abel Bush, Tom Marline, and others standing eyeing the French frigate, the very pictures of anxiety and disappointed rage. He saw too clearly that True Blue must have been one of those who had been carried off in the French ship when she broke adrift from them. To assist in clearing her, the Ruby's helm had been put aport, or to larboard, as was then the expression, and this carried her still farther away from La Belle Citoyenne.

Captain Garland was not aware for some little time that any of his people had gained the enemy's decks. The instant the fact was communicated to him, he became doubly eager to get once more alongside. The minutes, however, appeared like hours to those who knew that their shipmates and friends were surrounded by exasperated foes, who were too likely, in the heat of the moment, to give no quarter. Paul Pringle groaned with anxiety for the fate of his godson. There he stood, his huge beard blackened with smoke and dabbled with a shipmate's blood; his hair, which had escaped from under his handkerchief when he went aloft, streaming in the breeze; his brawny arm bared, and his drawn cutlass in his hand; and looking truly like one of the sea-kings of old, the rovers of the main, prepared for a desperate struggle with his enemies. Just then the sails of the French frigate were taken aback, and the effect of this was to cause her to make a stern board, which drove her right down on the Ruby.

Once more, by slightly shifting his helm, Captain Garland allowed her to drop alongside, the respective bows and sterns of the two ships being in opposite directions.

"And now, my lads, lash her fast!" he shouted. "We must not let her part from us till she is ours."

The very instant the sides of the two frigates ground together, Paul Pringle, who, with a party of boarders, many of them old shipmates, stood ready on the maindeck, sprang through the after-ports, shouting out, "Remember little True Blue, boys! Let us get back our Billy True Blue!"

The clash of steel and the occasional report of pistols saluted their ears, and there stood at bay the gallant little band, the lieutenant and Peter Ogle, with most of the men, bleeding at every pore—one or two, indeed, stretched lifeless at their feet; but True Blue himself was nowhere to be seen. Numbers were pressing round the gallant band, and in another instant it seemed likely that they would have been overwhelmed. With such impetuosity, however, did Paul and his party dash on board, that although numbers of the Frenchmen were thronging the maindeck, they were rapidly driven back. In vain they struggled—in vain they fought. Nothing could stop the fierce onslaught of the British seamen.

High above all other cries, Paul Pringle's voice was heard shouting the name of True Blue. "We must find our True Blue. Huzza for our True Blue, boys!"

Thus timely relieved, Mr Brine was once more able to advance aft, and now on both sides, led by him and by old Handlead, who was among the first of the second party, the British tars swept the Frenchman's maindeck fore and aft, cutting down or driving below all before them.

At length, when near the after-hatchway, the Frenchmen made a bold stand, as if resolved to sell their lives dearly or to drive back their assailants. Just then, Paul caught sight of True Blue himself, struggling to get free from between two of the after-guns, to which place it was evident he had been carried as a prisoner.

"There he is, boys! there is our True Blue!" shouted Paul, and at the same moment he and his companions dashed on with redoubled energy from the check they had received, tumbled all the remaining Frenchmen down into the cockpit, and in another instant Paul had once more grasped his godson by the hand.

"You deserve one thing, Billy, and you shall do it!" he exclaimed. "Follow me quick, though."

He sprang up the ladder to the upper deck. Meantime the officers had placed parties at the hatchways to keep in check those who had taken refuge below, the remaining few who appeared on the maindeck having thrown down their arms and prayed for mercy.

On the upper deck stood a gallant few surrounding their Captain, who lay wounded among them at the foot of the mainmast. They seemed scarcely aware that their companions below had yielded, and that all hope of resistance was vain. The rush of the British seamen who now swarmed on board and swept along the deck undeceived them, and, driven right and left or overboard, the remainder dropped their swords and asked for quarter.

Paul, followed by True Blue, had gained the main-rigging. His quick eye had discovered that the halliards of the Frenchman's flag, that of the new Republic, led into the top.

"There, boy!" exclaimed Paul, "you must haul that down. Quick, aloft!"

True Blue required no second order, but, springing up the ratlines before anybody could overtake him, he had reached the top, when, seizing the halliards, down came gliding the flaunting tricolour, followed quickly by the red cap of liberty, which, unscrewing, he threw among the people on deck; and three hearty cheers from the British crew announced that the well-fought battle was won.

The gallant French Captain opened his dim eyes at the sound, to see the emblem for which he had striven trampled under foot. He had been endeavouring, since he saw that all hope of escape was over, to tear to pieces with his teeth and to swallow a paper which he had drawn from his pocket. Suddenly, while thus engaged, he saw the red cap fall like a flash of fire from aloft. His fingers released their hold of the paper, and with a deep groan he expired.

Mr Brine stooped down by the side of his brave opponent. The paper he had been endeavouring to destroy was his commission; but another paper projected from his pocket. It was a code of private signals, which, with noble patriotism, he had wished to prevent falling into an enemy's hands.

"Well, I suppose there is some good in those Frenchmen after all!" exclaimed old Handlead when he heard of it. "He tried to serve his country to the last, at all events."

No time was now lost in securing the prisoners and removing them to the Ruby as the two ships lay alongside each other. Some of the Frenchmen looked very glum, and evidently, if they could get an opportunity, meant mischief; but they mostly yielded to the fortune of war with a shrug, and by the evening were skipping away right merrily, to the sound of Sam Smatch's fiddle. Indeed, they had little cause for animosity against him, as he had taken no part whatever in their capture, having volunteered to remain below to assist the surgeon. The English, in this gallant action, a type of many which were to follow, had just fifty men killed and wounded, while the French lost between sixty and seventy. Just as the last of the prisoners were removed, and the prize crew of the Belle Citoyenne had got on board, the two ships separated.

When once more the two frigates were in a condition to make sail, and were standing along amicably together, Captain Garland called the crew aft. "My lads," he cried, "all have done well to-day. That fine frigate, now ours, is the best proof of it—won, too, let me tell you, from the moment the first shot was fired till the flag was hauled down, in less than an hour. When all have done their duty like brave British seamen, I can scarcely pick out any in particular to praise; but there is one lad among you who rendered material service in the work of the day."

Paul Pringle brightened, and, his countenance beaming with pleasure, he placed his hand on his godson's shoulder. The Captain went on:

"There was one shot which especially tended to secure us the prize; that shot was fired by the boy Freeborn—True Blue Freeborn. I shall have my eye upon him. If he goes on as he has begun, he will be an honour to the service, and rise in it, too, if I mistake not. Lads, you have all my hearty thanks, and our King and country will thank you too."

Three hearty cheers for their gallant Captain were given by the crew as he finished his address;

and then, however unexpected, and as Paul Pringle expressed himself, "almost dumfoundering," three more were raised for Billy True Blue Freeborn, the pride of the crew. No one shouted louder than Tim Fid and Harry Hartland; but Gipples growled out as he sneaked below, "It'll be all the same some day when a shot takes his head off. They can't keep that on with all their petting."

The next day the frigate reached Portsmouth, where the brave French Captain was buried with all the honours of war; and Captain Garland, and his officers and ship's company, received the praises and rewards which they so well-merited for their gallant achievement.

Chapter Eleven.

The frigate very soon had made good the damages she received in the fight, and once more put to sea, all on board wishing for nothing better than a similar encounter with another enemy, feeling full confidence that the result would be the same.

One morning at daybreak, when True Blue had been sent aloft to take a lookout and report any sail in sight, his keen eye detected a small speck floating in the calm, hazy ocean. He knew that the speck was a boat, and hailed to that effect. There was a light breeze from the eastward, and the frigate, under all plain sail, was standing on a bowline to the southward. She was hauled up a few more points, to fetch the boat, which it was soon seen, instead of attempting to escape, was approaching the frigate. Numerous were the conjectures as to what she was; for although an open boat out in mid-channel was not exactly a novelty, still any incident was of interest in those stirring times, when all knew that apparent trifles often led to something important.

The boat appeared to be that of a merchantman. Six men were in her; four were pulling, and two sat in the sternsheets. One of these was a wrinkled, wiry old man, with a big red nightcap on his head, and a huge green and yellow comforter round his throat, while a thick flushing coat and trousers, and high boots, concealed the rest of his form. The other looked like the master of a merchantman. As soon as they got alongside, the latter begged that the boat might be hoisted up. This was done; and while the other men went forward among the crew, he and his strange-looking companion repaired aft to the Captain's cabin. The information they gave seemed to afford infinite satisfaction to Captain Garland. Several of his officers were breakfasting with him.

"I trust, gentlemen, that, before many days have passed, we shall fall in with another enemy's frigate, a worthy antagonist for the Ruby," he remarked as soon as they were seated. "We have also on board, I am happy to say, one of the most experienced pilots for the Channel Islands and the French coast to the westward—a Guernsey man; and, what is more, I know that he is thoroughly to be trusted. He and his companions were on board a merchant vessel, captured by a French privateer; and as the enemy leaped on the deck on one side, they slipped over the bulwarks on the other, and, favoured by the darkness, effected their escape. I propose to run over to the French coast, and watch off Cherbourg for the return of two French frigates, which, I understand, robber-like, go out every night and return into harbour in the morning."

At first the crew were very much inclined to laugh at the odd appearance of the old pilot; but Paul Pringle soon got into conversation with him, and gave it as his opinion that the little finger of the old Guernsey man knew more than a dozen of their heads put together, both as to seamanship and as to the navigation of the adjacent coasts. It quickly became known that there was something in the wind, and that the Captain hoped to fall in with another enemy before long.

Cape Barfleur, to the westward of Cherbourg, was made during the night. The wind was off shore, and the Ruby was close-hauled on the larboard tack, when, as day dawned, a ship and a cutter were seen from her deck coming in from seaward. All hands were called up, the frigate was cleared for action, and the men went to their quarters. Every glass was turned towards the approaching strangers.

"We shall have another scrimmage—that we shall!" exclaimed Tim Fid to True Blue. "I wonder what Gipples will do this time?"

"It's a pity he ever came to sea again after the last cruise," answered Billy. "He'll never make a sailor, and only bring shame on the name of one."

"He's just fit to sell cat's meat," observed Harry. "Maybe one of the shot he's so afraid of will take his head off, as it might that of a better fellow, and that will settle for him."

With this philosophical remark the boys sat down on their powder tubs to await the commencement of the action; while poor Gipples, who had overheard what was said, sat quaking on his in a most pitiable manner.

The Ruby was kept edging away towards the supposed enemy. As the daylight increased, there was little doubt of her character, and she was pronounced to be a thirty-six-gun frigate.

"A fit opponent for us!" exclaimed the Captain. "We can allow her the cutter's assistance, and we must see how quickly we can take them both."

The cutter, however, seemed to have no inclination to assist her consort, from whom she kept hovering at some distance.

There was not much time for talking or speculation. The Ruby soon ranged up on the weather and larboard side of the Frenchman, at whose peak flew the ensign of Republican France. It would have been throwing away words to have exchanged compliments or interrogations in this case. The Frenchmen, indeed, maintained a surly silence, till it was broken by the rapid interchange of broadsides between the two well-matched combatants. The chances of war seemed, however, in this instance to be going against the Ruby. At the second broadside, down came her fore-topsail-yard, followed soon afterwards by the fore-topmast.

"This will never do!" exclaimed Paul Pringle, beckoning to Billy and sending a man to take charge of his tub. "Come here, boy. You must try and see if you can't do as well as you did when we took the Citoyenne. Give her as good at least as she has given us."

True Blue, nothing loth, began to take a sight along the gun. Just then the Captain had ordered the Ruby's helm to be put hard a-starboard, by which she came suddenly round on the opposite tack, and brought her larboard guns to bear on the enemy.

True Blue, finding the ship going about, knew that no time was to be lost. He fired, and the enemy's foreyard came instantly down. The effect was to throw her up into the wind, in which position she received a raking broadside from the Ruby.

"That's your doing, True Blue. All at the gun saw it—I know they did."

"Yes, that was True Blue's shot, as sure as a gun!" cried Tom Marline. "You shall have as many more as you like, Billy."

Again True Blue fired, and the enemy's mizen-topmast came down. This enabled the Ruby to sail round and round her, giving her numerous raking broadsides. Still the gallant Frenchman held out. All this time not a shot had been fired from the cutter, and, greatly to the annoyance of the British sailors, she was seen making off under all sail for Cherbourg.

At the same time, during a pause in the action, when the smoke cleared off, another sail was descried to the northward, three or four leagues off. The sound of the firing had undoubtedly brought her thus far, and there she lay becalmed, unable to get up and join in the fight. Her presence, however, was not welcomed by the Ruby's crew. She was evidently a frigate. If an enemy, she might prevent the capture of the other Frenchman, and indeed endanger the safety of the Ruby herself. If a friend, they would rather have had the honour of taking their antagonist singlehanded, as they fully expected to do.

As to there being any danger of their being captured, that did not enter the heads of the British tars.

"Come, bear a hand, boys," said Paul. "We must take this here chap first, and then, if the calm holds for a little longer, we may get all ataunto and be ready for the others. One down, the other come on. That's it, boys."

Strange to say, except one man, who had his leg broken by the recoil of a gun he was fighting, not a man on board the Ruby had been hit, though it was evident that numbers of the Frenchmen had been killed, as several were seen thrown overboard. The British began to grow impatient. The French frigate was holding out, probably in expectation of assistance from her consort. The breeze now increased, and the stranger in the offing approached.

"Hurrah!" cried Paul Pringle, "another broadside, lads, and the Monsieurs will haul down their flag."

Paul's assertion proved correct. Down came the Frenchman's colours, after an action which lasted two hours and ten minutes. She proved to be the thirty-eight-gun frigate Réunion, Captain François Adénian.

Numbers of people stood on the French shore watching the combat, and much disappointed they must have been at its termination. The Réunion's consort, the Sémillante, was seen to make an attempt to come out of harbour to her assistance; but there was not wind sufficient for her to stem a contrary and very strong tide.

"I do wish she'd come!" exclaimed Paul Pringle as he eyed her, while he and his companions were repairing damages, again to make sail. "We'd have her too—I know we should."

"I thought that I should bring you good luck, Monsieur le Captain," said the old pilot when the action was over; "I always do."

"I hope you will stay with us and bring us more, then," answered Captain Garland.

"With all my heart," was the answer; and so it was arranged.

Some time after this the Ruby put into Plymouth, from whence she was ordered to proceed to Guernsey in company with the Druid, a thirty-two-gun frigate, and the Eurydice, a twenty-four-gun ship.

A bright lookout was as usual kept. The squadron had got to the distance of about twelve leagues to the northward of the island, when one of the lookouts hailed that two ships were in sight to the westward. Presently two more and a fifth was made out. Whether friends or foes, at first it was difficult to say; but clear glasses were brought to bear on them, and it was declared that they were two fifty-gun ships, two large frigates and a brig, which had crowded all sail in chase.

Many a man might have been daunted by these fearful odds. True British seamen never give in while there is a possibility of escape. Captain Garland called aft the old Guernsey pilot and had a short conversation with him. "Then I'll do it," was his remark, and threw out a signal for the Eurydice to make the best of her way under all sail for Guernsey.

Meantime he and the Druid, under easy sail, waited the approach of the enemy. On they came, exulting in their strength, and confident of making prizes of the two British frigates. The latter, nothing daunted, opened their fire on the enemy in a way which must not a little have astonished them.

"Our Captain knows what he is about," observed Paul Pringle in his usual quiet way, as some of the frigate's shots were seen to strike the headmost of one of the French ships.

"What! Paul, are we going to take all those big ships?" asked True Blue with much animation. "That will be fine work."

"As to taking them, Billy, I can't say," answered Paul. "It won't be bad work if we don't get taken ourselves, do ye see."

Never, however, did two ships appear in greater jeopardy than did the Ruby and her consort. True Blue observed his Captain. There he stood calm and composed, watching every movement of the enemy, with the old pilot by his side. They were now rapidly approaching Guernsey, and could be seen from the shore, all the neighbouring heights of which were crowded with spectators, eager and anxious witnesses of the unequal contest. Although both the English frigates fired well, they had not as yet succeeded in bringing down any of the Frenchmen's spars.

Captain Garland now threw out another signal. It was to order the Druid to crowd all sail and make the best of her way for the harbour. Those on board her could scarcely understand his object. It appeared as if he was about to sacrifice himself for the sake of preserving the other two ships. The Captain of the Druid was too good an officer not to obey orders simply because he could not understand their object, or he would have been inclined rather to have gone to the Ruby's aid, and to have shared her fate, whatever that might have been.

As soon as Captain Garland saw that the Druid was obeying his directions, he boldly hauled up and stood right along the French line, at which the frigate kept up all the time a hot fire. The enemy kept firing away all the while in return; but their gunnery was fortunately none of the best, and but few of their shot had hitherto struck the Ruby.

"Well, what are we going to do now, Paul?" asked True Blue. "Does the Captain intend to try and weather on the Frenchmen, and so get clear?"

"Wait a bit, Billy," answered his godfather. "You'll see presently. The Captain means to proceed to Guernsey, and to Guernsey, it's my opinion, we shall go, in spite of all the Frenchmen may do to try and prevent us."

On stood the gallant Ruby. The two frigates and brig were passed; then came one of the big ships, then the other. The Eurydice was now close in with the harbour and safe. The Druid was so near that, unless becalmed, there appeared no doubt about her getting in.

"Now, my lads," cried Captain Garland, "be sharp in all you do!"

The helm was put up, the yards were squared, and on she stood towards a collection of rocky islands, islets, and shoals, apparently to destruction. The never-quiet ocean was sending dense masses of spray and foam over the rocks. The old pilot stood calm by the Captain's side. The Frenchmen, who had concentrated all their attention on the Ruby and let the other two ships escape, now bore up after them.

On she stood under all sail towards the rocks. The old pilot took his stand in the weather-rigging. The helmsman's eye was upon him, ready to answer each wave of his hand, or deep-toned sound of his voice. The guns were deserted, and all the crew stood by either the tacks or sheets or braces, or crowded the tops aloft, ready with all possible rapidity to make any alteration in the sails which a shift of wind or change of course might require.

Still the enemy kept firing at the frigate, but their shot fell either altogether short or wide of their mark. The wind increased—the frigate flew on. On either side of her there appeared white foaming seas, dancing up fantastically and wildly, without apparent cause, but which the seamen well knew betokened rocks and shoals. They were aware that they were among the most dangerous reefs on that rock-bound coast.

No one in the ship had ever been there except the curious old pilot. There he stood, as cool and collected as if the ship were sailing in the open sea, with a gentle breeze filling her canvas. The Captain stood near the pilot, and they all knew that they could trust him, and so were content if he trusted the old Guernsey man.

"He knows what he's about," observed Paul Pringle to his godson, looking at the pilot. "Mind, Billy, that's what you must always do. Never attempt to do what you don't know how to do; but then what I say is, set to work and learn to do all sorts of things. Never throw a chance away. Note all the landmarks as we go along now, and whenever you go into a harbour mark them in the same way."

"Ay, ay, Paul," answered Billy; "I'll do my best."

"That's all any man can do," remarked his godfather. "Stick to that, boy, and you'll do well. But, I say, I wish those Monsieurs would just try and follow us. We might lead them a dance which would leave them on some of these pretty rocks alongside."

True Blue's interest in what was going forward was so great that he could scarcely reply to Paul's remarks. The sea foamed and roared on either side of the ship. Now the water became smoother over a wider surface, now black rocks rose sheer out of the sea as high as the hammock nettings, and then once more there was a bubbling, and hissing, and frothing, betokening concealed dangers, which none but the most experienced of pilots could hope to avoid. Meantime, many an eye was turned towards the French squadron. It was scarcely to be expected that the enemy should be ignorant of the surrounding dangers; still no one would have been sorry if, in their eagerness, they had run themselves on shore.

Suddenly the leading French ship was seen to haul her wind—so suddenly, indeed, that the next almost ran into her, and, as it was, shot so far beyond her that she must have almost grazed the rocks before her yards were braced up, and she was able to stand off shore. In a few minutes more the Ruby ran triumphantly into Guernsey roads, where the Druid and Eurydice had already arrived in safety, while thousands of spectators were looking down and cheering them from the surrounding heights.

"I knew our Captain would do it!" exclaimed Paul, when, the sails being furled and the ship brought to an anchor, he and his messmates were once again below. "There are few things a brave man can't do when he tries. Our Captain can fight a ship and take care of a ship. What I've been saying to Billy is, that we should never give up, however great the odds against us, because, for what we can tell, even at the last moment something or other may turn up in our favour. Mind, Billy, whatever you may think now, you'll find one of these days that what I tell you is right."

Chapter Twelve.

The frigate did not remain long at Guernsey, but, with the rest of the squadron, put to sea. She soon separated from them, and stood down Channel to extend her cruise to the distance of a couple of hundred leagues or so to the westward of Cape Clear.

As usual, she was very successful and picked up several prizes. Among the prizes were three large merchantmen and two privateers. The latter, especially, required a considerable number of men to take them home. Captain Garland was unwilling thus to weaken his crew, and yet the prizes were too valuable to abandon. These vessels had just been despatched when a brig was descried from the masthead. Chase was given. She was a fast vessel and well handled, but before night she was come up with. When her Captain saw that he had no longer any hope of escape, he, like a wise man, hove to and hauled down his colours.

She proved to be La Sybille, a French letter of marque, carrying eight guns, twenty-five men, and bound for the French West India Islands with a valuable cargo. The prisoners, with the exception of four, three white men and a black, who were left on board to assist in working her, were removed to the frigate; and Captain Garland, who could not spare any more lieutenants or mates, sent a midshipman and prize crew to take charge of her.

The midshipman's name was Nott. He was generally called in the mess Johnny Nott. He was as short as his name, but he was a brave, dashing little fellow; but though he had been some time at sea, being very idle, his navigation, at all events, was not as first-rate as he managed to make it appear that it was when he had the honour of dining with his Captain. Captain Garland sent for him and told him that he would spare him two men and a couple of boys, and he expected that with them and the prisoners he would be able to carry the brig safe into Falmouth or Plymouth.

"I shall send one of the quartermasters with you, Pringle. He is a steady man; and you shall have Marline and Freeborn, who is as good as a man, and the boy Hartland: he is steady."

"May I have Fid, sir, also?" put in Nott, who was always free-spoken and wonderfully at ease with his Captain. "He is such an amusing young dog. He'll keep the rest alive by his jokes, if he does nothing else."

"You may take him, Mr Nott; but take care that they don't get to skylarking and fall overboard," said the Captain.

"Oh no, sir," answered the midshipman; "I'll maintain the strictest discipline, and hope to have the brig safe in harbour in the course of a few days."

Captain Garland smiled at the air with which Johnny Nott spoke, and, shaking him by the hand, sincerely wished him a prosperous passage.

Meantime the first lieutenant had sent for Paul Pringle, and, knowing how thoroughly he could be trusted, had given him his instructions to look after Mr Nott—in other words, to act as his dry-nurse.

"I need not tell you how to behave, Pringle," observed the lieutenant. "You must advise him when to shorten sail, and what to do, indeed, under any emergency; and let him, as much as possible, suppose that he is following his own ideas."

"Ay, ay, sir," answered Paul, not a little flattered. "I know pretty well how to speak to most of the young gentlemen; I always leave them to fancy that they are telling me what to do. Most young gentlemen nowadays are fond of 'teaching their grandmothers to suck eggs,' and I never stop them when they like to do it."

"All right, then, Pringle," answered Mr Brine; "we understand each other clearly. Keep order among the boys, and have an eye on the prisoners."

All arrangements being made, Mr Nott, with his quadrant, book of navigation, and his crew, went on board the prize and took charge of her, instead of the officer who had boarded her when she was captured.

Scarcely had he got on board and made sail than a large ship was seen to the southwest. The frigate signalled the brig to continue on her course, and then stood away in chase of the stranger. Johnny Nott would much have liked to have gone too, for he could not help fancying that the stranger was an enemy, and if so, he knew full well that whatever her size, even should she happen to be a line-of-battle ship, his Captain would very likely bring her to action. Though he dared not follow her, he waited till he guessed that no one on board would be paying him any attention, and then, having persuaded himself that there would be no harm in so doing, hove the brig to, that he might have a better chance of ascertaining what might happen.

He then ordered True Blue to the masthead to watch the proceedings of the stranger. The wind was about north-west; the stranger was steering about east, and had apparently come from the southward. In a little time Billy hailed that she had brailed up her courses.

"Then, sir," observed Paul, "depend on it she is an enemy."

"I wonder what size she is? What do you think, Pringle?" asked the midshipman.

"Freeborn can tell better than any of us," was the reply; and on Billy being hailed, he reported her a heavy frigate or a fifty-gun ship.

"I only hope our bright Ruby won't find that she has caught a Tartar, then," said Johnny Nott. "I don't think that we could be of much use if we were to go and try and help."

"Never fear, sir," observed Paul; "our Captain will know how to tackle with her, whatever she is."

While this conversation was going forward, True Blue hailed that the frigate was again making signals, and on Johnny Nott referring to his book he discovered that it was a reprimand ordering him to make all sail to the eastward. Had he persevered in remaining hove to, he would have been guilty of an act of insubordination, and most reluctantly, therefore, he made sail and stood on his proper course.

When daylight returned the next morning the frigate was nowhere to be seen, and La Sybille continued her solitary course towards England.

The Frenchmen had hitherto behaved in a perfectly orderly, quiet manner, and obeyed cheerfully the orders issued to them. No change, indeed, was exhibited towards their English captors; but they soon began to quarrel among themselves, and were constantly fighting and disputing. If they did not actually proceed to blows, they appeared every instant as if about to do so. Their conduct was reported to Mr Nott.

"No great harm in that," he remarked. "If they are quarrelling among themselves, they are less likely to combine to play us any tricks."

Not many hours had passed before, while he was below, one of the Frenchmen was left at the helm, and True Blue, who was forward, saw another come up on deck, and, with a capstan-bar in his hand, make a blow, so it seemed, at the helmsman's head. He missed it, however, and the bar, descending with full force on the binnacle, smashed it and the compasses within it to pieces. Billy remarked the men. There was a great deal of jabbering, vociferation, and action, but neither of them struck or hurt the other.

As he watched them an idea occurred to him. "I don't think those fellows did that by chance," he said to himself. "I will keep an eye on them."

The noise brought Mr Nott and Paul Pringle on deck.

"A pretty mess you have made, Messieurs," observed the midshipman, who spoke a sufficient amount of bad French to make himself perfectly understood by them, and this was one of the reasons why he had been selected to command the brig. "If I was to give you four dozen each, or put you in irons, or stop your grog, you'd only get what you deserve. Now, go and find another compass and put the binnacle to rights. You Frenchmen are handy at that sort of thing."

The men slunk off as if very much ashamed of themselves, and Paul Pringle took the helm. True Blue, however, watched them, and he was certain that there was a laugh in their eyes, giving evidence that they were well content with what they had done. When they went below also, they seemed to be on perfectly good terms with each other.

On search being made, no compass whatever was to be found.

"I thought that I had observed, when I first came on board, a spare compass and boat compass," observed Mr Nott.

But the Frenchmen, on being interrogated, all declared that they were not aware that there were any others, and said that if there were, they were private property, and that the Captain had taken them with him. The other Frenchmen appeared to be very angry at what their countrymen had done, and did their best to ingratiate themselves with Mr Nott. The difficulty was now to know how to steer. The midshipman's knowledge of navigation was put to a severe test. While the sky was clear, either by night or by day, it was tolerably easy to steer more or less to the eastward; but whether they should hit the chops of the Channel or run on shore on the coast of Ireland or France, or the Scilly Islands, it was impossible to say.

"We must do our best, sir, and trust in Providence," observed Paul Pringle to the young officer. "Only there's one thing I'd do—I'd rather steer to the nor'ard than the south'ard of our course, so as to avoid the chance of running ashore on the Frenchman's coast. Of all the places I should hate most it would be a French prison."

True Blue was certainly not of a suspicious disposition, but he could not help watching the Frenchmen. He whispered his ideas also to Harry and Tim Fid, who agreed to keep a watchful eye on the prisoners. Little did the Frenchmen think how narrowly all their proceedings were noted. Fid soon remarked that when either of the Frenchmen was at the helm, one of the others was constantly going to a chest in the forepeak and looking steadily into it. His curiosity was therefore aroused to ascertain what it was they went to look at. He reflected how he could discover this without being seen.

Some of the crew slept in the bunks or standing bed-places arranged along the sides of the vessel, but others in hammocks. The hammocks were, however, not sent up on deck every day as they are on board of a man-of-war. One of these hung over the Frenchmen's chests, and into it Tim stowed himself away, making the lower surface smooth with the blankets, so that the form of his body should not be observed. A slight slit in the canvas enabled him to breathe and to look down below him. Poor Fid had to watch a considerable time, however, and felt sadly cramped and almost stifled without being the wiser for all the trouble he had taken. The Frenchmen were there; but first Tom Marline came below, and then Hartland, and then the black; and the Frenchmen sat on the lockers cutting out beef bones into various shapes and polishing them.

At last all but one man went on deck, and then he jumped up, and instantly going to the chest opened it; and then Tim saw clearly a compass, and, moreover, that the brig was steering a course considerably to the southward of east. The Frenchman then put his head up through the fore-hatchway, took a look round, and then, again diving into the forepeak, had another glance at the compass.

"That's it," thought Tim; "True Blue is right. The Frenchmen intend to run us near their own coast and then rise on us, or they hope to fall in with one of their own cruisers and be retaken. Small blame to them."

The thread of his soliloquy was interrupted by his observing the Frenchman go to a chest on the opposite side, which, when opened, he saw was full of arms, cutlasses, long knives, and pistols. The man sat down by the side of it, and deliberately began to load one after the other, and then to arrange the knives and dirks, so that they could in an instant be drawn out for use.

"Ho, ho!" thought Tim; "that's your plan, is it? Two can play at that game, we will show you!"

Fid was now very anxious to get out of his hiding-place, and to go and tell True Blue what he had seen. The Frenchman, however, after he had made all his arrangements, put a brace of pistols into his pocket and stuck a dirk into his belt, concealed by his jacket, sat down on a locker, and, with the greatest apparent unconcern, pursued his usual occupation of bone-cutting.

Fid grew more and more impatient. He waited some time longer, then he saw the man prick up his ears and listen eagerly. Presently there was the sound of a scuffle on deck. The Frenchman sprang up the ladder through the fore-hatch-way. As he did so a key fell from his pocket. The moment he was gone, Fid jumped out of his hiding-place, picked up the key, applied it to the chest which contained the arms—the lid flew open. He drew out several brace of pistols and a bundle of dirks. He stuck as many of both into his belt and pockets as he could carry, and hid the others in the hammock in which he had been concealed, while the key he also hid away. All was done as quick as lightning. Then, with a pistol in one hand and a dirk in the other, he followed the Frenchman up the hatchway.

As he did so he chanced to cast his eye aloft, when he saw True Blue in the fore-rigging. He signed to him to come on deck. Billy saw him, and slid down rapidly by the foretop-mast-stay. On looking aft they saw Hartland and Mr Nott stretched on the deck, apparently lifeless, while the three Frenchmen, with the black, were making a furious attack on Tom Marline, who had the helm, while Paul Pringle stood by defending him with a boat's stretcher. Neither Pringle nor Marline had arms, while two of the Frenchmen and the black had dirks, and the third Frenchman, as Fid knew, had pistols. Fid immediately handed a brace of pistols and a dirk to True Blue, and together they rushed aft. Paul saw them coming, but the Frenchmen did not. One of them had cocked his pistol, and was taking a deliberate aim at Paul, when True Blue, who at that instant had reached the quarterdeck, lifted his arm and fired.

The Frenchman staggered a few paces, fired his pistol in the air, and then fell to the deck. To prevent his companions from seizing his weapons, Fid drew them from his pocket and bolted off with them round the deck. Before, however, the smoke of the pistol which True Blue had fired had cleared off, he had sprung to the side of Paul Pringle and handed him the remaining pistol and a dirk. Paul on this sprang on the Frenchmen.

The black was the first to fly. The other two men, finding themselves clearly overmatched, retreated forward and gained the fore-hatchway. It was blowing fresh, so that Marline was afraid if he left the wheel the brig would broach to. Consequently only Paul and True Blue pursued the Frenchmen. One of them leaped down the fore-hatchway. As he did so a pistol-shot was heard, and Fid immediately afterwards appeared at the same place, exclaiming:

"I've done for the fellow—settle the other two!"

Fid held a pistol in his hand. The black saw it, and sprang at the boy to seize it; but True Blue, who saw it also, was too quick for him, and had got hold of it just before the negro reached the spot. Fid sprang out of his way; and so eager had he been, that he pitched head-forward down the hatchway.

The last Frenchman attempted to defend himself; but when he saw Paul and the two lads with arms in their hands approaching him, while his companions were unable to assist him, he knew that resistance was useless and cried out for quarter.

"You don't deserve it, Monsieur Crapaud," answered Paul; "but I'm not the fellow to take a man's life in cold blood. Howsomdever, there's one thing I'll take, and that is, good care you don't attempt to play us such a trick again. Here, Billy, hand me that coil of rope. We'll keep him out of harm for the present."

Saying this, while True Blue stood by presenting a pistol at the prisoner's head, Paul proceeded to lash his arms and legs, and to secure him to one of the guns.

"Well done, mate!" exclaimed Tom Marline from aft. "And now just come and have a look at Mr Nott. I think that he's coming to."

"And I do hope that Harry isn't killed either!" cried Fid. "He's breathing, and that's more than dead men can do."

In a little time both Mr Midshipman Nott and the boy Hartland came to themselves, and sat up rubbing their eyes, as if trying to understand what had occurred. The moment the truth flashed on Mr Nott's mind, he sprang to his feet, and, seizing a stretcher, the nearest weapon he could lay hold of, stood on the defensive, looking about for an enemy.

He was much relieved in his mind when he saw one of the Frenchmen lying not far off dead on the deck, and another sitting bound, where Paul and True Blue had placed him, between the guns.

"What! have we come off victorious in the struggle?" he exclaimed, turning to Marline.

"Yes, sir," answered the seaman, "we've been and drubbed the Monsieurs; but there are still two on 'em below kicking up a bobbery. If you'll take the helm, sir, I'll go and help Pringle to make them fast."

"No, no," answered the midshipman somewhat indignantly, as if his courage or strength had been called in question. "I can do that. You stay at the helm."

When the Frenchman and the black had jumped down into the forepeak, Tim Fid had very wisely clapped the hatch on, so that they were left in darkness, and were also unable to return again on deck. Pringle was on the point of taking off the hatch to secure the two men when the midshipman got forward.

"Very glad, sir, to see you all to rights," said Paul, looking up. "I suppose that you'll wish us to get hold of the two fellows down below?"

"By all means. I'll hail them and advise them to surrender at discretion."

The hatch was taken off, and Mr Nott explained, as well as his limited knowledge of French would allow, that all their chance of success was gone. Only the black man answered. Mr Nott ordered him to come up.

"L'autre est mort," (the other is dead), said he as he made his appearance, looking very much frightened.

"He is as treacherous as the rest; it will not do to let him be at liberty," said Mr Nott. "It was he who knocked me down and began the mutiny."

The black was accordingly lashed to a gun on the opposite side of the deck, facing his companion.

On going below they found that the Frenchman whom Fid had shot was not dead, having only been stunned by the fall. He would, however, very shortly have bled to death had they not bound up his wound. In mercy to the poor wretch, they placed him in a bunk, but did not tell him that either of his companions had escaped.

"Ah, I deserve my fate!" he observed to Mr Nott. "Had we succeeded, we should have thrown you all overboard and carried the vessel into a French port. There is a large sum of money on board stowed away below the after-lockers. It escaped the vigilance of the officers who examined the vessel. We knew of it, and for its sake we intended to get rid of you, that we might obtain possession of the whole."

"Much obliged for your kind intentions," answered Johnny, laughing. "The dollars we'll look after, and you will consider yourself a prisoner in your berth till I give you leave to get out of it. If you put your head above the hatchway, you'll be shot. That is an understood thing between us."

The Frenchman could only make a grimace as a sign of his acquiescence.

"I'm in earnest, remember!" said Mr Nott as he climbed up the ladder on deck.

Fid now reported all that he had done, and he and True Blue received the praise from their young commander which they so fully merited. The compass was got up on deck and shipped in the binnacle, and the arms were carried aft and placed in the cabin. The other chests belonging to the Frenchmen were broken open; but nothing particular was found in them.

When all these arrangements were made, the officer and his small crew assembled on deck to hold a council of war.

"The first thing we had better do, sir, is to shorten sail, seeing how shorthanded we are," observed Paul Pringle. "We couldn't do it in a hurry, and if it comes on to blow, our spars and sails may be carried away before we know where we are."

This advice was too good to be neglected. "Then, sir, as these Frenchmen have been steering to the southward and east whenever they have had the helm, oughtn't we to steer so much to the nor'ard to make up for the distance we have run out of our course?" observed True Blue with much modesty.

"Capital idea, Freeborn!" exclaimed the midshipman with a patronising air. "You've a very good notion of navigation; we'll do it."

Mr Nott now took the helm, while the crew went aloft to furl the lighter canvas and to take a reef in the topsails. While True Blue was on his way up to hand the main-royal, his eye fell on a vessel following directly in the wake of the brig, which might have been seen long before had not they all been so fully occupied. He hailed Mr Nott and pointed her out.

The midshipman, who, from being at the helm, could not at the same time take a steady look at her, inquired what she was like. "A schooner, sir, with a wide spread of canvas," answered True Blue. "She seems to be coming up fast with us."

"All hands come down on deck!" shouted Mr Nott. He then asked Paul what he thought of the stranger.

"She does not look like an English craft, and may be an enemy—a privateer probably," was the answer. "I suppose, sir, you'll think fit to hold on and try and get away from her?" continued Paul. "It will soon be growing dark, and if the weather becomes thick, as it promises to do, we may alter our course without being discovered."

"Yes, exactly—that is just my idea," observed Mr Nott. "We could not have hit upon a better."

The sail was consequently not taken off the brig, which, under other circumstances, it ought to have been; and on she stood, the breeze gradually increasing, and the weather becoming more and more unsettled. Mr Nott watched the schooner. It was very clear that she was gaining on the brig.

"It is very probable that we shall have to fight, after all," he said to himself. "So, as the Captain always makes a speech to the crew before a battle is begun, I think I ought to do so."

Accordingly, calling all hands aft, he cleared his throat and began. "My lads," he said, imitating as well as he could the tone and manner of Captain Garland, "we shall very likely have to fight that fellow astern of us. You'll do your duty like true Britons, I know you will—you always do. We will take her if we can. If not, we'll try to get away from her; but if we cannot do either, we'll blow up the brig and go down with our colours flying. I don't think that it matters much which. Both are equally glorious modes of proceeding."

True Blue was very much taken with the speech, and told Harry Hartland that it was just what he thought they ought to do; but Tim Fid said that he hadn't made up his mind which he should prefer. Blowing up was very fine to look at, but going down must be a very disagreeable sensation.

Paul, meantime, took off his hat to reply. "As you wish it, Mr Nott, we'll fight the brig to the last, and maybe we shall knock away some of her spars and get off. I don't think we shall have much chance of taking her, and as to blowing up or going down with our colours flying, if the enemy send their shot through her sides, between wind and water, and won't take us on board, we can't help ourselves; but perhaps, sir, you'll just think over the matter about blowing up. It would be like throwing our best chance away. I for one don't wish to see the inside of a French prison; but you know, sir, even if we are taken, we may have a chance of being retaken before we get into a French port, or of escaping even when we are there. Now, if we blow ourselves up into the air, we shall have no chance of either."

"Very true, Pringle, very true," answered the midshipman; "I did not think of that. Well, we won't blow ourselves up; and if we find our brig sinking, we'll strike our flag and yield. There'll be no dishonour in doing that, I hope. Several brave officers have been obliged to strike to a superior force at times; so it will be all proper, but it's what the Frenchmen are more accustomed to do than we are."

There was no sun visible, so Mr Nott looked at his watch and found that there would be scarcely more than an hour of daylight.

"If we can but keep ahead, we shall do," he remarked.

Paul agreed with him in this, but suggested that, by cutting away the stern-boat, and by making two temporary ports in her stern, they might fight a couple of long brass guns which they had found on board. This idea was immediately adopted, and all hands set to work to get the guns and tackle ready, while Paul, with an axe, soon made the required ports. He was not very particular as to their appearance. With the aid of the timber-heads, there were already a sufficient number of ringbolts to enable them to work the tackles.

All this time the schooner was gaining on them. Scarcely were these two guns fitted and loaded than the schooner yawed, and a shot came skipping along the water and disappeared close under their counter.

"Not badly aimed," observed True Blue, "but the range is too great. Paul, don't you think that these long guns would carry farther?"

"Wait a bit, Billy," answered Paul; "we haven't much powder or many shot to spare. We won't throw away either till she gets a little nearer. Then you shall have it all your own way."

True Blue, with this promise, was eager for the Frenchman to get nearer. There had been no doubt that such the stranger was. Her own colours could not be seen; but, to make sure, Mr Nott first hoisted a French flag. No notice was taken of this. Then he hoisted the English ensign over the French, and immediately the stranger yawed and fired a bow-chaser.

"You'd think it well to mystify them a little, sir," observed Paul. "We should do that if we hoisted the French flag over the English."

This was done, and for some time no other shot was fired. Still the stranger seemed to be not altogether satisfied. The breeze was freshening all this time, and at length it became evident that the brig was carrying much more canvas than was necessary, unless she was trying to get away from the schooner. The stranger seemed to think so, at all events, and without yawing fired a shot as a signal to the chase to heave-to.

This was what no one but the prisoners had the slightest wish to do; and so, as it was now getting dark, both flags were hauled down and not again hoisted.

"Now, Billy," said Paul, "let us see, my boy, what you can do."

True Blue was in his glory. He had a gun almost entirely to himself. Tim Fid acted the part of powder-monkey; while he and Hartland had charge of one gun, and Mr Nott, helped by Paul, worked the other. Paul, indeed, stepped from gun to gun as his services were required. Now they set to work in right earnest and began to blaze away as hard as they could, while Tom Marline stood at the helm and steered the flying brig. He had no easy work either, for, with the immense press of canvas she had on her and the strong breeze, it was with difficulty he could keep her on her course.

True Blue was delighted to find that his shot, at all events, reached the enemy.

"Paul, Paul, that shot hit her bows—I saw the splinters fly from them!" he exclaimed while he and Harry were again loading.

"All right," answered Paul, who likewise saw the effect of the shot. "Keep on like that, and you'll soon bring down some of the chap's spars."

Meantime, Mr Nott was working away manfully with his gun. He felt rather vexed to think that a ship's boy was a better shot than himself; only just then, as he wished to preserve the brig, he was thankful to any one who could aid in accomplishing that object. Now and then the schooner fired; but as at each time, in order to do so, she had to yaw and then keep away, she fired much less frequently than the brig. The Frenchmen probably also judged that, as they were rapidly coming up with the chase, it was not worth while to throw their shot away. As the darkness increased, the wind got up more and more, and so did the sea, and all around looked very gloomy and threatening.

"We must shorten sail, sir!" exclaimed Tom Marline at last, who had been looking up ever and anon at the bending, quivering spars.

"Never mind, my man," said Johnny Nott with the greatest coolness, "the brig will do that for herself better than we can. We have enough to do just now to try and wing the enemy."

There seemed a fair chance of their doing this. The guns were excellent, and True Blue's gunnery was first-rate. But as the brig tumbled about and pitched more and more, he found greater difficulty in taking aim. Still he persevered, and so did Mr Nott; and as it was far too dark for them to see the effects of their shot, they both hoped that they were doing a great deal of damage. One thing concerned Paul exceedingly. He feared that, the instant they hauled their wind and got out of their previous course, the masts would go over the side.

Still True Blue, regardless of everything else, kept firing away as fast as ever. What did he care what might happen besides just then? There was a fine brass gun he had been ordered to serve, and there was the enemy. The scud was flying rapidly overhead, the wind howled, the thunder roared, and flash after flash burst forth from the sky, mocking the tiny light of the British guns. The whole ocean was of a dark slaty hue, with white, hissing, foaming crests dancing up as far as the eye could reach, while many came hissing up and almost leaped on board. The brig went tearing along, her masts bending and writhing as if they were about to be torn out of her. Suddenly there was a terrific crash, and both the tall masts leant over and went by the board. Fortunately they fell forward and none of the party was hurt.

"Well, we have shortened sail with a vengeance!" cried the midshipman, even at that moment unable to restrain a joke, though he felt in no joking mood. "Never mind the guns now. Let us clear the wreck. Perhaps the Frenchman may pass us in the dark."

This was a wise thought, as it was the best thing that could be done. With axes and knives they set energetically to work to cut the ropes which kept the masts and spars thumping against the vessel's sides like battering-rams.

While thus engaged, True Blue exclaimed:

"See, see!—what is that?"

All hands looked up. The dark outline of the schooner was visible flying by them. Just then a vivid flash of lightning darted from the sky. There was a loud crackling noise heard even amid the raging of the rising tempest; the flame ran down the schooner's mainmast. Shrieks reached their ears; there was a loud roar like a single clap of thunder without an echo; the whole dark mass seemed to rise in the air, and here and there dark spots could be seen, and splashes could be heard close to the vessel, and for a few seconds flames burst forth from where the schooner had been seen; but in an instant they disappeared and not a trace of her could be discovered. The dismantled brig floated alone, surrounded by darkness on the wild tumultuous ocean.

Chapter Thirteen.

The dismasted brig lay tumbling about, utterly helpless. Neither moon nor stars were visible. The seas came roaring up around her, now throwing her on one side, now on the other. Her stern-boat had already been cut adrift.

Not long after the disappearance of the schooner, a sea struck her quarter and carried away one of the boats on that side, and at the next roll the one on the opposite quarter went.

Mr Nott, with Paul and Marline, and the three boys, were clustered aft.

"Paul," observed True Blue, "the Frenchman and black can't play us any tricks now. They run a great chance of being drowned where they are; couldn't we cast them loose and let them come aft here?"

"Right, Billy," answered Paul. "We should be merciful even to our enemies. I had forgotten them."

Mr Nott offering no objection, Paul and True Blue worked their way to the waist, where the two men sat bound. Paul loosened the Frenchman, and True Blue took out his knife and cut the lashings which bound the black; and then, assisting him up on his legs, pointed aft, and by a push in that direction intimated that he had better get there as soon as possible.

Billy then bethought him of the wounded prisoner in the dark damp forepeak, all alone, expecting every instant to be his last. "I shouldn't like to be left thus," he thought; "I'll go and see what I can do for him."

Without, therefore, telling Paul what he was going to do, he worked his way gradually forward, grasping tightly on by the belaying-pins and cleats made fast to the bulwarks.

Just as he got close to the fore-hatch, he saw rolling up, just ahead of the vessel, what looked like a huge black mountain with a snowy top. It was a vast sea appearing still larger in the darkness. On it rolled, roaring above the bows of the brig, and then with a terrific crash down it came on her deck, threatening to swamp her and sweeping everything before it.

True Blue's foot had been pressing against a ringbolt: a rope was made fast to it. He threw himself flat down, grasping the ring with one hand and making several turns with the rope round the other. He felt the breath almost pressed out of his body with the weight of water rushing above him; and then he fancied that the vessel herself was going down and would never rise again.

The rush and the roaring sound of water passed on. He felt the bows of the brig rise once more; he lifted himself up on his knees and looked over his shoulder. The sea had made a clean sweep, and had carried away the caboose, the boats on the booms, and every spar remaining on deck, besides, as it appeared to him, a considerable portion of the larboard bulwarks.

His anxiety was for his shipmates. How had they withstood the rush of waters? He shouted; but though his voice was loud and shrill, the howling of the tempest and the dash of the sea were louder. He tried to penetrate the darkness, but he could distinguish nothing beyond half the length of the ship. His heart sank lower than it had ever done before at the thought that his faithful kind guardian might be torn from him for ever.

Having started to visit the wounded Frenchman, he wished to do so before he tried to find his way aft again to ascertain the state of the case. He lifted the hatch off and dived below. All was dark. There were no means of procuring a light in the place.

"I say, Monsieur Frenchman, how are you?" he began, groping his way towards the bunk where the prisoner lay.

A groan showed that the man was not dead. True Blue remembered that there was some food in one of the lockers. Taking some sausages and biscuit, he put them into the man's hand. "Here, eat; you're hungry, I daresay."

"Merci! merci! de l'eau-de-vie, je vous prie, donnez-moi de l'eau-de-vie."

Billy, on searching about, had found a can with a little water at the bottom of it, and a flask of spirits; so, guessing what the man wanted, he poured some of the spirits into the can and gave it to him.

The draught must have been very refreshing, for the Frenchman's expression of gratitude knew no limits. He made True Blue understand that he had better take something himself. This, as he was very hungry, he was nothing loth to do; but he had not eaten much, and had only taken one pull at the grog can when he recollected his friends. He felt that he could eat nothing more until he had ascertained their fate.

"If they are alive, they'll want to eat," he said to himself. "They can't be gone—no, no; I won't believe it."

So he filled his pockets with as many sausages and as much biscuit as they could carry, and, shaking the Frenchman by the hand to show that he would not be forgotten, he ascended the ladder, closed the fore-hatch behind him, and began his perilous journey towards the stern. The sea on one side, he discovered, had made so complete a wreck, that he knew, should he slip, there would be nothing to prevent his going overboard.

The greatest caution therefore was necessary. He could feel the ringbolts, but he could not see them, or indeed any object by which to secure himself. On hands and knees he crept on, feeling his way. He had got as far as the main hatchway when he saw another sea rising. He clung, as before, to a ringbolt. Over came the water with a furious rush, which would have carried any one unprepared for it away. He felt his arm strained to the utmost; still he had no notion of letting go. When the sea had passed over, the vessel was steadier for an instant than she had been. He took the opportunity to make a bold rush to the nearest part of the bulwarks remaining entire. He now got aft with less difficulty. His heart felt lighter when he saw the group he expected standing there; but Paul didn't come forward to welcome him. Instead, he heard Marline's voice say, "Rouse up, Pringle; rouse up, mate—the boy is safe."

True Blue was in an instant kneeling down by the side of his guardian. "I am here, Paul, I am here; Billy True Blue all right, godfather!" he exclaimed, putting his mouth to Paul's ear.

"What has happened? Is he hurt?" he asked.

"He has hurt his side and ribs, and we are afraid he has broken his leg," answered Marline. "We all thought that you were gone—washed clean away, boy; but he wouldn't believe it, and started off to look for you, when a sea took him and washed him back in the state you now see him. He was nearly carried overboard, and we have had hard work to save him."

True Blue forgot everything else but the state of his friend, till at length Paul came to himself and comprehended what had occurred. The knowledge that his godson was safe seemed to revive him. Billy then remembered the provisions he had got in his pocket, and served them out among his companions, the two prisoners getting an equal share.

Dawn came at last, and presented a fearful scene of wreck and confusion: the dark-green seas were rising up on every side, topped with foam, which came down in showers on the deck, blown off by the fierce wind; while the lately trim brig lay shattered and dismantled, and, too evidently, far deeper in the water than she had been before the gale.

Not a boat remained; there were not even the means of making a raft.

"But what can we do, Paul?" asked True Blue, thinking how sad it was that his fine old friend should thus ingloriously lose his life. Paul smiled as he answered:

"Trust in Providence, boy. That's the best sheet-anchor a seaman can hold to when he's done his duty and can do no more. There are others as badly off as we are, depend on that."

When his godfather had ceased speaking, True Blue cast his eye around in the faint hope that some aid might possibly be at hand. As he did so, he saw that several pieces of wreck were floating round the brig. As the light increased, he thought he saw the form of a man on one of them. He looked again; he pointed the spar out to the rest: they were of the same opinion. The man was alive, too. He saw the wreck, he waved to them, he turned his face with a look imploring assistance.

"Here, Tom, make this rope fast round me; I think that I can reach that poor fellow. The next send of the sea will bring him close alongside."

Though True Blue was a first-rate swimmer for his age, Marline demurred and appealed to Pringle.

"He is only a Frenchman and an enemy, after all," argued Marline.

"He's a fellow-creature, Tom," answered True Blue. "Here, make fast the rope. I am sure I can save him."

"Will you let him go, Paul?" asked Tom as a last resource.

Paul raised himself on his arm.

"If the lad thinks it's his duty to try and save the man, yes," he answered firmly. "If he loses his life, it will be just as a true British sailor should wish to lose it. Go, boy; Heaven preserve you."

There was an unusual tone of solemnity and dignity in the way Paul spoke as he grasped his godson's hand. The rope had by this time been properly adjusted. The piece of wreck with the man on it was drifting nearer and nearer. The man on it again waved his hand. True Blue waved his in return. "He is alive!—he is alive!" he shouted.

"If go you must, now is your time," shouted Tom.

True Blue leaped off the deck into the raging sea. Boldly he struck out. Down came a sea thundering towards him, hurling the spar with it. There was a shriek of horror: all on board thought he was lost. He had only dived to avoid the sea. Then up again he was on the other side, clinging on to the spar, with his knife in his mouth, ready to cut the lashings which secured the stranger to it. It was done in a moment. He had him tight round the waist.

The stranger is now seen to be a boy not bigger than himself. This makes his task easier. The spar drifts away; the two are in the water together.

Tom and Mr Nott, and the other boys, and the Frenchman and the black, haul away, and, with some severe bruises, rescuer and rescued are safely brought on deck.

"It's Sir Henry, I do believe!" shouted Tom, hauling in the rope.

"Why, Elmore, my dear fellow, is it you?" exclaimed Johnny Nott, taking the hand of the lad, who, with True Blue, had been dragged aft and placed in as safe a spot as the deck afforded. "We thought you were a Frenchman."

"I scarcely know who I am. I know that I have to thank Freeborn for my preservation," answered the young baronet.

He took True Blue's hand.

"I do thank you heartily, Freeborn," he said with much emotion.

The excitement of the first minutes of his wonderful preservation over, young Elmore felt the effects of the exposure to which he had been subjected so long, and sank almost helpless on the deck.

"He wants food," said Tom. "I wish that we had some." True Blue instantly volunteered to try and go and get it; but of this the rest would not hear.

Marline said he would go; but he was wanted to look after the rest, and take care of poor Pringle, who was utterly unable to help himself. Neither the Frenchman nor the black volunteered to go. The truth was, they dared not face the danger.

"I'll go if I may!" exclaimed Tim Fid. "If I am not strong, I'm little, and a shrimp can swim where a big fish would be knocked to pieces."

"Stay, though," said True Blue. "Here, make fast the rope round you. If you are washed away, we can haul you in by it. It served me a good turn, it will now serve you one."

"A good thought," said Tim, fastening the rope round his waist, and away he went. He worked his way forward, as, True Blue had done; but just as he was in the middle of the waist, a sea swept the deck, and would have carried him off had it not been for the rope round him.

He was hauled back not a little bruised. Still he insisted on making another attempt. Having kicked off his shoes, away he went. The deck was clearer than usual of water. He ran and leaped along, and before another sea came had reached the fore-hatch. His first care was to make the rope fast to the windlass. Then he slipped off the hatch and descended. He soon again appeared, and succeeded in reaching the after part of the vessel with a good supply of food and a can.

"There," he said, "that's full of honest grog; it will do all hands good. But, I say, we must try and get the poor Frenchman up out of his bunk. He'll be drowned in it if we don't in a short time."

It was agreed that the Frenchman and the black ought to perform the duty; but it was not till they had taken several pulls at the grog can that they seemed to understand what was required of them. Even then Mr Nott had to show a pistol, and hint that they should not remain where they were if they did not go and help the wounded man.

The rope which Fid secured made the task comparatively, easy. Led by the little fellow himself, at last they set off. When they got below, they found so much water that the poor fellow was very nearly washed out of his berth. They managed, however, to get him on deck. To carry him aft, however, was the most difficult part of their task. As it was, the Frenchman, in his anxiety to take care of himself, let go his hold of his wounded countryman; and had it not been for Fid and the black, he would have been washed overboard.

At length they reached the stern in safety. The account Fid gave, however, of the quantity of water below, was truly appalling. They could not hope that the brig could swim many hours longer, and should she go down, they had nothing on which to float; the boats were gone, not a spar remained. There were the hatches, certainly; but there would scarcely be time to construct a raft out of them.

Mr Nott had, during this time, been attending to his messmate. It was some time before young Elmore again revived.

Nott was curious to know how his messmate had come to be on board the schooner which had chased them.

"I will tell you in a few words," said Elmore. "We had not parted company with the frigate many hours before a strange sail hove in sight. As I knew that we could gain but little by fighting should the stranger prove an enemy, we did our best to run away. The prize, however, sailed badly, and the stranger, which turned out to be a large schooner, sailed remarkably well. We had a couple of guns; so we fired away with them as long as we could till she ranged up alongside, when a number of men leaped on our decks and we were obliged to give in. I was carried on board the schooner; but the rest of the men were left on board the brig to work her, so that I hope that their lives may have been preserved. She was a privateer out of Saint Malo. Your determined attempt to escape excited their anger to the highest degree; and at the very moment that the vessel was struck by lightning, from the effects of which she foundered, they were swearing vengeance against you, wherever you might be. Their terrific shrieks and cries, as one after the other they were overwhelmed by the waves, made my heart sink within me. Still I determined not to yield as long as my strength endured, and I struck out for dear life. I soon found myself close to a shattered spar, to which was attached a quantity of rigging. I climbed up and lashed myself securely to it. Thus I passed the night. I more than once thought I saw the dismantled brig; and you may fancy my joy when I caught sight of her at dawn. Still I scarcely expected that anybody on board would be able to render me assistance; and when I saw that all her boats were gone, I almost gave up hope. I have not thanked Freeborn as I wish; but I have those at home who will thank him still more, if we are allowed to reach dry land, and I am sure our Captain will thank him too."

While the lads had been talking, the appearance of the sky gave evident signs that the gale was breaking. Still the sea ran very high, and the waterlogged wreck laboured in a way which made it doubtful whether each plunge she made would not prove her last. She sunk lower and lower, and it was very evident that in a short time no part of her deck would be tenable. Anxiously, therefore, all eyes were looking out for a sail. Each time that the brig rose to the top of a sea, they all looked out on every side, in the hope of catching a glimpse of some approaching vessel; and blank was the feeling when she again sunk down into the deep trough and they knew that no help was near.

Suddenly True Blue shouted out, "A sail! a sail!—she is standing towards us!" He had seen her before, but was uncertain which way she was steering, and he had not forgotten a caution given to him by Paul—never to raise hopes when there is a likelihood of their being disappointed.

The sea had for some time been decreasing; but there was still so much that a boat would run considerable risk in boarding the wreck. It was soon proved that True Blue was right. The stranger was steering towards them. On she came. She was a brig, and showed English colours.

A cheer rose from the deck of the waterlogged vessel. The brig came down in gallant style; but she gave evident signs that she also had been battling with the gale. Her bulwarks were shattered, and not a boat was to be seen on board. Her flag showed her to be a packet. A fine-looking man stood in the main-rigging.

The midshipmen shouted, "We are going down, we fear. Can you render assistance?"

"Ay, ay—that I will!" answered the master of the packet. "I will run alongside you. Stand by to leap on board!"

The least experienced of the party saw the great risk the packet was running by this proceeding; for a send of the sea might easily have driven the wreck against her and stove in her upper works. This consideration did not deter the gallant sailor from his act of mercy. He made a signal as he approached, that he would pass the wreck on the larboard quarter. The Frenchman and the black were told that they must help their wounded shipmate. Tom and True Blue begged that they might take charge of Paul, while the rest were to leap on board the instant the vessels' sides touched. The midshipmen and the two boys wanted to stay and help Paul, but he would not hear of this.

"No, no," he answered; "if we talk about it, no one will be saved; and if I am left on board, I shall be no worse off than we all have been till now."

The packet tacked. Now she stood down towards the wreck. The sides of the two vessels touched. The midshipmen and two boys leaped on board. So did the Frenchman and the black; they made a pretence of helping their comrade, it seemed. They placed him on the bulwarks of the wreck, and then, when safe themselves, they were about to regain their hold of him; but the poor wretch lost his balance, and with a cry of horror fell between the two vessels. The two men looked over the side with stupid dismay, abusing each other; but their unfortunate comrade had sunk for ever from their sight.

Meanwhile Tom and True Blue had made an attempt to lift Paul on board the packet. Had her crew known his condition, they probably would have been ready to render assistance; as it was, his two friends, fearful of letting him slip between the two vessels, lost the moment as the brig glided by, and all three were left on the sinking wreck.

"Why have you done this?" said Paul when he saw that the packet had shot ahead. "You should have left me, boys."

"Left you, Paul!" exclaimed True Blue with an emotion he rarely exhibited. "How can you say that? Please Heaven, we'll save you yet."

There was no necessity for hailing the packet. They knew well that the two midshipmen would make every effort in their power to render them assistance. Once more the brig tacked and stood towards them; but the position of the wreck had changed, and it was impossible to run alongside.

Again and again the gallant Captain of the packet tried the manoeuvre without success. At last, passing close to them, he shouted, "Lads, I will heave you ropes; you must make yourselves fast to them and jump overboard: it's your only chance."

"Tom, you must do it!" said True Blue, turning to Marline. "It would kill Paul; I'll stay by him. We shall be taken off when the weather moderates; and if not, I'm ready to go down with him."

Paul heard this. "True Blue, I'm your guardian, and you must obey me!" he said almost sternly. "The ducking won't hurt me more than others. Maybe it may do me good. So, I say, make the rope fast round me, and help me overboard when you two go, and I shall not be the worse for it."

Thus commanded, True Blue could no longer refuse obedience. Down came the packet towards them. The ropes were hove on board.

"Tom, you can't swim—go by yourself. I'll stay by Paul!" exclaimed True Blue as he was securing the rope. "Help me to launch him first. Away, now!"

Paul was lowered into the water, True Blue keeping tight hold of the rope just at his waist with his left hand, while he struck out with his right. Thus the two together were drawn through the foaming sea towards the packet. Arrived at the vessel's side, True Blue was of the greatest service to Paul in protecting him from the blows he would otherwise have received by the sea driving him against it.

Right hearty was the welcome they received from all hands, especially from the gallant commander, Captain Jones.

Scarcely had the packet got a hundred fathoms from the brig when she was seen to make a plunge forward. The two midshipmen were watching her, expecting to see her rise again. They rubbed their eyes. Another sea rolled over the spot where she had been, but no sign of her was there.

Chapter Fourteen.

The Chesterfield packet was bound from Halifax to Falmouth. Fortunately among the passengers was a surgeon, who was able to attend to Paul's hurts. He set his leg, which was really broken, as were one or more of his ribs.

The passengers, when they heard from Sir Henry Elmore and Johnny Nott of True Blue's gallantry, were very anxious to have him into the cabin to talk to him, and to hear an account of his adventures. The young midshipmen, knowing instinctively that he would not like this, did not back the passengers' frequent messages to him; besides, nothing would induce him to leave the side of his godfather, except when the doctor sent him on deck to take some fresh air.

A strange sail was seen on the starboard bow. In a short time she was pronounced to be a ship, and, from the whiteness and spread of her canvas, a man-of-war. Elmore and Nott hoped that she might be their own frigate. They thought that it was a latitude in which she might very likely be fallen in with. Of course, till the character of the brig had been ascertained, she would bear up in chase. They expressed their hopes to Captain Jones, and begged him to steer for her.

"Were I certain that she is your frigate, I would gladly do so; but as you cannot possibly recognise her at this distance, we shall be wiser to stand clear of her till we find out what she is. I will not alter our course, unless when we get nearer she has the cut of an enemy."

The midshipmen, having borrowed telescopes, were continually going aloft to have a look at the stranger.

"I say, Elmore, it must be she. That's her fore-topsail, I'll declare!" exclaimed Johnny Nott. Elmore was not quite so certain.

After a little time, they were joined by True Blue.

"Paul Pringle, sirs, sent me up to have a look at the stranger," he remarked.

"I am very glad you have come, Freeborn," said Sir Henry. "Your eyes are the best in the ship. What do you make her out to be?"

True Blue looked long and earnestly without speaking. At last he answered, in an unusually serious tone:

"She is not our frigate, sir—that I'm certain of; and I'm more than afraid—I'm very nearly certain—that she is French. By the cut of her sails and her general look, she puts me in mind of one of the squadron which chased us off Guernsey."

True Blue's confidence made the midshipmen look at the stranger in a different light, and they finally both confessed that they were afraid he was right. Captain Jones agreeing with them, all sail was now crowded on the brig to escape.

In spite of all the sail the brig could carry, the frigate was fast coming up with her.

"I wish that we could fight," said Johnny Nott to Elmore. "Don't you think that if we were to get two of the guns aft, we might knock away some of her spars?"

"I fear not," said his brother midshipman, pointing to the popguns which adorned the packet's deck. "These things would not carry half as far as the frigate's guns; and, probably, as soon as we began to fire she would let fly a broadside and sink us."

"Too true, Sir Henry," observed the brave Captain of the packet, who stood on deck surrounded by the passengers, many of them asking all sorts of useless questions His countenance showed how distressed he was. "In this case I fear discretion will form the best part of valour."

Captain Jones cast anxious glances aloft, as well he might, and the midshipmen and True Blue eyed the frigate; and Nott turned to his messmate and said, in a doubting tone, "Elmore, what do you think of it?"

The other answered sadly. "There is no doubt of it. She is coming up hand over hand with us. Freeborn, I am afraid that I am right."

"Yes, sir," answered True Blue, touching his hat. "She is going nearly ten knots to our six."

"Then she will be up with us within a couple of hours at most," said the young midshipman with a deep-drawn sigh.

The breeze kept freshening rapidly. The brig carried on, however, till her royal masts went over the side, and her topgallant-masts would have followed had the sails not been handed in time; and now all expectation of escape was abandoned.

Still Captain Jones held on his course, remarking, "It will be time enough to heave-to when her shot comes aboard us."

The crew went below and put on their clean things and a double allowance of clothing, as well as all their possessions which they could stow away in their pockets. When they returned on deck, they certainly did look, as Johnny Nott observed, "a remarkably stout set of Britons."

Sir Henry borrowed a midshipman's hat and dirk, as he had lost his own; and Nott, who had a few sovereigns in his pocket,—a wonderful sum for a midshipman,—divided them with him. The Captain insisted, as the last act of his authority, that all the passengers should remain below, during which time the ladies, at all events, employed themselves in imitating the example of the sailors.

At last a shot was heard; then another and another followed, and then a whole volley of musketry.

Captain Jones kept calmly walking his deck till the French frigate began to fire. He then looked round: there was no ship in sight, no prospect of escape; so, with a sad heart, hauling down the British ensign, he ordered the topsails to be lowered and the courses brailed up, and thus waited the approach of the enemy. What was the astonishment and rage of all on deck to have a volley of musketry fired right down on them, with the coolest deliberation, from the forecastle of the frigate as she ranged up alongside, and then, passing ahead of the brig, rounded-to near her.

"Ah, bêtes! we will teach you dogs of Englishmen to lead a French ship such a chase as you have done when you have no chance of escape!" shouted some one from the quarterdeck.

A bullet passed through Elmore's hat; another struck Captain Jones on the side, but in the excitement of the moment he did not perceive that he was hurt; while a third grazed True Blue's arm, wounding the skin and making the blood flow rapidly. Without moving from where he stood or saying a word, he took off his handkerchief and began to bind it up, Harry Hartland and Tim Fid hurrying up with expressions of sorrow to help him.

"Never mind this—it's nothing," he said, the tears starting into his eyes. "But it's the French prison for Paul I'm thinking of. It will break his heart. And those brutes may take me from him."

The frigate now lowered all her boats, and sent them, with their crews armed to the teeth, on board the brig. The Frenchmen jumped on her deck as if she had been a pirate captured after a desperate fight and long chase.

Scarcely a word was spoken—not a question asked, but officers and men were indiscriminately seized by the collars and hurled into the boats, some of the French officers striking them with the flat side of their drawn swords, and at the same time showering down the most abusive epithets on their heads.

Captain Jones, whose appearance and bearing might have saved him from insult, was seized by several men and thrust, with kicks, into the nearest boat.

Just as the boats came alongside, True Blue had gone below to remain with Paul Pringle. The Frenchmen soon followed him. He tried to show by signs that his godfather was very much hurt. This was evident, indeed. At first the men who came below were going to let him remain; but the order soon reached them that all the English were immediately to be removed from the brig. Not without difficulty, True Blue got leave to assist in carrying Paul, aided by Tom Marline, who had fought his way down below to his friend, and the black cook. With no help from the Frenchmen, Paul was at last placed in a boat, with True Blue by his side.

The passengers were scarcely better treated than were the seamen. The ladies and gentlemen were bundled out of the vessel together, and were allowed to take only such articles as they could carry in their hands. Some of the gentlemen who spoke French expostulated.

"Very good," answered the Lieutenant. "You have chosen to lighten the vessel of all public property, which would, at all events, have been ours; we must make amends to ourselves by the seizure of what you call private property."

As True Blue sat at Paul's head, his godfather looked up. "Ah, boy!" he said with a deep sigh, "this is the worst thing that I ever thought could happen to us; yet it's a comfort to think that it isn't our own brave frigate that has been taken, and that a number of our shipmates haven't been struck down by the enemy's fire. But it's the thoughts of the French prison tries me. Yet, Billy, I don't mind even that so much as I should have done once. You are now a big strong chap, and you won't let them make a Frenchman of you, as they might have done when you were little, will you?"

"No, Paul; they'll have a very tough job if they try it on—that they will," answered True Blue with a scornful laugh which perfectly satisfied his godfather.

"What are the brutes of Englishmen talking about?" growled out one of the Frenchmen. "Hold your tongues, dogs."

Neither Paul nor True Blue understood these complimentary remarks; but the tone of the speaker's voice showed them that it might be more prudent to be silent.

As soon as Captain Jones and his mates and the two midshipmen appeared above the gangway of the French frigate, they were seized on by a party of seamen, who threw them on the deck, knocked off their hats, out of which they tore the cockades, and, with oaths, trampled them beneath their feet.

In vain Captain Jones in a manly way appealed to the good feelings of his captors. In vain Sir Henry Elmore repeated what he said in French. The Frenchmen were deaf to all expostulations. The second Captain of the frigate stood by, not only superintending, but aiding in inflicting the indignities with which they were treated.

They were next dragged off and brought into the Captain's own cabin. Here they expected to be better treated; but no sooner did the Captain enter, than, walking up and down and showering on them the most abusive epithets, he ordered his men to take away their swords and dirks, and to strip off their coats and waistcoats, exclaiming as he did so:

"No one on board La Ralieuse shall wear the livery of a despot—one of those hateful things, a King. Bah!" The Captain and his second in command, having thus vented their rage and spite, ordered the men to carry off their prisoners. The Captain and the young officers were therefore again unceremoniously dragged out of the cabin and forced down below into a space in the hold, dimly lighted by a single lantern. There they found the greater part of the crew already assembled, bursting with rage and indignation at the way they had been treated.

Meantime the boat which contained Paul Pringle, with Tom Marline, True Blue, and the other two boys, arrived alongside the frigate. The French sailors were going to hoist up Paul with very little consideration for his hurts, when, in spite of their black looks, Tom shoved in his shoulder, vehemently exclaiming:

"Avast, ye lubbers! Can't you see that the man has his ribs stove in? Send down proper slings to lift him on deck, or out of this boat he don't go while I've an arm to strike for him."

True Blue had continued to support Paul's head in his lap. The Frenchmen did not understand this demand, and might have proceeded to force Tom up the side had not Pringle himself interfered.

"Don't fall out with the men, Tom; there's no use grumbling with them. Do you and Billy help me up. I've still some strength left in me."

Aided thus, Paul reached the Frenchman's deck, the first he had ever trod except as a victor. No sooner were they there than Tom was seized on, as had been the other seamen, and was dragged off to be abused and kicked down into the hold with the rest. No sooner, however, did some of the Frenchmen attempt to lay hands on Paul, who had been placed sitting up against a gun, than True Blue threw himself before him, and, with a blow on the chest of the man who was about to drag him along, sent him reeling across the deck. Tim Fid and Harry, who had been left at liberty, on this flew to his support, and, standing on either side, literally kept the rest at bay.

True Blue said not a word, but his lips quivered, and, had he held a sharp cutlass in his hand, he would evidently have proved no contemptible opponent.

At first the Frenchmen were amused, and so were a number of the French boys belonging to the ship, who quickly assembled at the spot, especially devoting their attention to jeering and quizzing Fid and Harry.

Their good humour, however, was rapidly vanishing, and they would have probably proceeded to disagreeable extremities had not the surgeon of the ship appeared on the deck. He was a gentleman and a royalist, and had been most unwillingly compelled to come to sea as the alternative of losing his head. His profession gave him some influence among the crew, which he exerted on the side of humanity. Seeing at a glance Paul's condition, he appealed to his countrymen, remarking that the Englishman must evidently be a good-natured person, or the boys would not be so ready to fight for him.

"Brave little fellows! They deserve to be well treated," he remarked. "And now do some of you help me to carry the old man below. He is not in a state to be left on deck. Any one of us, remember, may speedily be in a worse condition."

This appeal had the desired effect, and, the kind surgeon leading the way, Paul was lifted up and carried below to a side cabin on the orlop-deck. True Blue was allowed to remain with him.

The mode of proceeding on board the frigate seemed to True Blue like that of the very slackest of privateers; indeed, when he described what he saw to his godfather, Paul told him that even pirates could not carry on in a worse way.

Before long several of the crew looked in and attempted to speak English, but very seldom got beyond a few of the ordinary oaths so general in the mouths of seamen. At length a man appeared who had been in England as a prisoner during the last war, and could really speak enough English to explain himself. He asked them a number of questions, which either Paul or True Blue answered truly.

"And so," he said, "I hear from my compatriot that you belonged to the Ruby frigate. Ah! she was a fine ship, and her crew were brave fellows—they fought well. You have heard of her fate, perhaps?"

"No," answered Paul and True Blue in a breath. "What has happened to her?"

"The fortune of war, my friends," answered the Frenchman. "She fell in with our consort, La Nymphe of forty guns, and engaged her bravely for three hours. For which side victory would have declared is doubtful, when we appeared in sight. Just then, awful to relate, whether by design or not I cannot say, she blew up with a loud explosion, wounding and killing many on board La Nymphe. Not one man escaped of all her crew."

"Oh, mate, do you speak the truth?" exclaimed Paul, starting up and seizing the Frenchman by the hand.

"Why should I deceive you, my friend?" answered the republican, putting his other hand on his bosom. "I know how to pity a brave enemy, believe me."

Paul lay back on his bed and placed both his hands before his eyes, while a gasping sob showed how much True Blue felt the sad news.

Chapter Fifteen.

The account of the destruction of the Ruby soon spread among the English prisoners. At first the two midshipmen especially would not credit it; but the date of the alleged occurrence answered exactly with that of the day when Johnny Nott parted with her and saw her standing towards an enemy's ship, and heard the firing at the commencement of the action.

"They do not even boast that they took her, or that she had hauled down her flag before she blew up," he observed. "If they had done so, we might have doubted them. I'm afraid their account is too true."

"I am afraid so, indeed," responded Elmore mournfully; "so many fine fellows lost. Our brave skipper Garland, he is a public loss. They do not say that a single officer was saved."

Thus the midshipmen talked on. They almost forgot their own misfortunes and abominable ill-treatment while thinking of their friends. Some coarse bread and cheese was handed to them in a dirty basket, and water was the only liquid given them to drink; while at night no bedding nor the slightest accommodation was afforded them. In vain the officers pleaded. The men to whom they spoke only laughed and jeered at them, and poor young Elmore only came in for a greater share of abuse when by some means it was discovered that he was what they called an English aristocrat.

"Ah, milord!" exclaimed one fellow with a horrid grin; "if we had you in la belle France, your head would not remain long on your shoulders. We guillotine all such. It's the best way to treat them. They have trampled too long on our rights, to be forgiven."

The next morning the British seamen and officers were ordered up on deck, and, being placed near the gangway, were surrounded by a guard of marines with fixed bayonets. If they attempted to move from the spot, they soon had notice to go back again.

The prize had parted company, and they supposed had been sent into port; but the frigate herself stood away to the westward to continue her cruise. In spite of the general want of discipline, a very bright lookout was kept for any strange sail in sight. In the afternoon watch a vessel was seen to the southward, and the frigate bore up in chase. The stranger, on seeing this, made all sail to escape.

The French seamen pointed her out to the British. "Ah! ah! we shall soon have her!" they exclaimed. "See, the cowards dare not wait our coming up."

Meantime, Paul Pringle lay in his berth, pretty well cared for, and most devotedly watched by True Blue. Billy was advised by the kind doctor to show himself as little as possible, lest he should be ordered to join the rest of the prisoners. He occasionally, however, stole out, that he might ascertain for Paul in what direction the ship was steering, and what was taking place. It was towards the evening that he came quickly back and reported that he had seen all the prisoners hurried below on a sudden, and that the wind being from the westward, all sail had been made on the frigate, and that she had been put dead before it, having abandoned the chase of the vessel of which she had been in pursuit.

"What it means I don't quite know," observed True Blue; "but there's something in the wind, of that I'm pretty certain."

The tramping of feet overhead, the hurried passing of the crew up and down, showed Paul also that such was the case. True Blue was standing at the door of the berth when the surgeon came below, and, as he passed him, whispered, "Keep quiet with your friend, boy. The crew may not be in the humour to bear the sight of you." He did as he was advised for some time; but, peeping out, he saw the powder-boys carrying up powder and shot, and other missiles from the magazine, while the flurry and bustle increased, and he felt sure that the frigate was going into action.

"Paul, I must go and learn what it is all about," he said. "I suppose that we are coming up with the chase."

Paul, not supposing there would be any risk, did not prevent his going. He crept out quietly. Everybody was so busy that no one remarked him. He looked out at one of the bow ports; but nothing was to be seen ahead. He glanced on the other side; not a sail was in sight.

He came back to the berth. "Paul!" he exclaimed joyfully, "it is not that the frigate is chasing, but she is being chased. She seems to be under all sail, and in a desperate hurry to get away."

"We've a chance, then, of not having to see the inside of a French port," observed Paul Pringle. "That's a thing to be thankful for; but, Billy, it's sad news we shall have to take home about Abel, and Peter, and the rest. I must go and break it to Mrs Ogle and Mrs Bush, and their children. It will make my heart bleed—that it will, I know."

Paul and True Blue talked on for some time, as very naturally they often did, about their old ship and shipmates, till their well-practised ears caught the sound of a distant gun.

"That's right aft!" exclaimed Paul. "It comes, I doubt, from the leading ship of the pursuing squadron. I pray that the frigate may not escape them."

"I must go on deck and see how many ships there are," said True Blue. "The Frenchmen can but kick me down again, and I can easily jump out of their way."

He had not gone long when down he came again, panting as if for want of breath. "Oh, Paul!" he exclaimed, "I thought to have seen two or three frigates or a line-of-battle ship at least; but, would you believe it, there is but one frigate, more like the Ruby than any ship I ever saw; and if I didn't know for certain that her keel was at the bottom of the Atlantic, I could have sworn that it was she herself. It quite took away my breath to look at her, and then when the Frenchmen saw me looking at the stranger, they hove their gun-sponges and rammers at me, so I had to run for it to get out of their way."

"Billy, I wish that I could have a look at this stranger the Frenchmen are so afraid of," said Paul. "If she is a frigate I have seen before, I should know her again."

"I don't mind the Frenchmen. I will go and have another look at her," answered True Blue. "We shall soon be within speaking distance of her guns."

As he spoke, he kept moving about the berth like a hyena in its cage; and soon, unable any longer to restrain his impatience, out he darted and unimpeded reached the deck. The pursuing frigate ran up the British colours, and opened her fire with a couple of bow-chasers. She had good reason to do so, for the Frenchman was steering to the southward and land was ahead. One of the shot struck the counter of La Ralieuse, the other passed a little on one side. True Blue gazed earnestly and long at the English frigate. He was recalled in a disagreeable way to a sense of where he was by feeling the point of a cutlass pressed against his back, and, looking round, he saw a seaman with no pleasant looks grinning at him and pointing below.

What the man said he could not make out. He got out of the fellow's way and hurried below. "Paul, I am right!" he exclaimed. "She is either the Ruby or another frigate so like her that you couldn't tell one from the other."

The next ten minutes were passed in a state of great anxiety, and when True Blue again looked out, he reported that the Frenchmen were shortening sail preparatory to commencing action. The crew were all at their stations. An unusual silence reigned on board. The Captain was making a speech. It was about liberty, equality, and fraternity, and the bonnet rouge was displayed.

The cheers were cut very short by a broadside from the English frigate, the shot of which crashed through the Frenchman's sides, tore up the planks, and carried off the heads of two or more of the cheerers.

"That was a right hearty English broadside!" exclaimed Paul. "I could almost fancy I knew the sound of the shot. I wish that you and I were with them, Billy, instead of being cooped up here."

The English had not the game all to themselves. The French almost immediately replied with considerable spirit to the compliment they had received.

"They are having a running fight of it—yardarm to yardarm, as far as I can make out," said Paul. "Well, that's the right way to go about the business. A brave fellow commands the English frigate, whatever she is."

"She's no bigger than the Frenchman," said True Blue.

"Maybe not, Billy," observed Paul, lifting himself up on his elbow. "It isn't the size of the ship—it's the men on board her makes the difference. Depend on't, those in the ship alongside us are of the right sort and properly commanded."

Presently there was a louder noise on deck than usual, and evident confusion. True Blue could contain his curiosity no longer, and before Paul could stop him, he had darted out of the berth.

"Heaven will guard him," said Paul to himself; "but he runs as great a risk as any of these Frenchmen."

True Blue was soon back. "The English frigate has shot away the Frenchman's fore-topmast and foreyard, and she's up in the wind, and the Englishman is ranging ahead to rake her!" he exclaimed enthusiastically. "We shall have it in another half minute. And do you know, Paul, the more I look at the stranger, the more I fancy she is like our brave little Ruby. Here it comes."

True enough, the shot did come, thick and fast—not one seemed to have missed—right into the bows of La Ralieuse. Some seemed to be sweeping her main, others her upper deck, or flying among her masts and spars, while more than one struck between wind and water. At the same moment shrieks, and cries, and groans, arose from all parts of the ship, mingled with shouts and oaths, levelled at the heads of their enemies.

"Keep quiet, Billy," said Paul. "The French, if they saw you, might do you an injury, boy. We shall soon have the flag of England flying over our heads."

As True Blue peeped out as before from the berth, he saw numerous wounded men brought into the cockpit, where the surgeons were already busy at work with their instruments and bandages. More and more were brought down. Further supplies of shot were being carried up, and the rapid passing of the powder-boys to and from the magazine showed that there was no expectation of bringing the contest to a speedy termination.

Nearly all this time the Frenchman's guns kept up an incessant roar. They ceased only now and then, when, as Paul conjectured, the English frigate was passing either ahead or astern of them, so that they could not reach her.

Now La Ralieuse had to stand the effects of another raking broadside. This time it was astern, and came in at the after-ports, tearing away the head of the rudder, and sweeping both decks from one end to the other. Thirty men or more were killed or wounded as they stood at their guns by this one broadside. True Blue ran up on deck to take a look round and saw them stretched on the decks in ghastly rows, pale and still, or writhing in their agony. The mizen-topmast was also gone, and the rigging of the mainmast seemed terribly cut up.

He rapidly again dived below to report what he had seen.

"That's enough, boy!" exclaimed Paul in a voice of triumph. "She cannot get away from the English ship, and sooner or later our brave fellows will have her. Ah, there they are at it again. Hurrah for Old England!"

"Old England for ever!" shouted True Blue. He might have sung out at the top of his voice, for amid the terrific din of battle the Frenchmen could not have heard him.

Presently there was a loud crashing sound, a severe shock, and the frigate heeled over with the blow, which made her quiver in every timber.

"Oh, boy!" cried Paul, seizing True Blue's hand in his eagerness, "they are going to board, and here I lie with my ribs stove in. If I could but handle my cutlass, we could be on deck and join them; but no—stay below by me, Billy. They'll make short work of it. Hark! those are true British cheers. They have the Frenchman fast. There they come! They are swarming over the side and through the ports! There's the sound of the cutlasses! Cold steel will do it! Those are the Frenchmen's pistols; our fellows know what's the best thing to use. They've gained a footing on the deck—they'll not lose it, depend on that. There! they shout again! The sounds are just above our heads. Hurrah for Old England! The Frenchmen are crying out, too. It is—it is for quarter! They'll get that, though they don't deserve it. On come our brave fellows! There's the tramp of their feet—the clash of the cutlasses! Nearer they come! They're overhead! They've gained the main deck! Hark! Shut to the door and hold it tight, boy. Down come the Frenchmen, helter-skelter! They're flying for their lives! They're coming down by dozens, twenties, fifties! They've given way fore and aft! All hands are shouting for quarter! Hurrah, boy! Hurrah, True Blue! That cheer, I know it. The Frenchman's flag is down! Once more we've the glorious British ensign above our heads! Here come our fellows, open the door and hail them!"

True Blue did as he was bid; and at that instant who should appear, cutlass and pistol in hand, but Abel Bush, Peter Ogle, and a dozen or more, whose well-known faces proclaimed them part of the crew of the Ruby. Great was their surprise at finding Paul and True Blue there, and loud and hearty were the greetings which hurriedly passed between them.

"And so you all escaped when the frigate blew up in action with the Frenchman the day we left you?" said Paul after he had explained in a few words how he and his companions had been captured by the Frenchmen.

"Blew up!" exclaimed Abel. "We never blew up; though we had a jolly good blow-out that evening, after we had taken a thundering big French frigate, which we must have begun to engage before you lost sight of our mastheads. We should have taken her consort, too, before the sun went down, if, like a cur, she hadn't turned tail and run for it; when, as it took us some little time to repair damages, we could not follow."

"Hurrah!" exclaimed Paul. "Hurrah! I thought so. This is the very craft herself, depend on it; and that is the reason the hounds have been worrying our poor fellows, as if they had been mere brutes. You'll hear all about it by and by. But I say, Abel, do you go and look after the surgeon of this ship. He's a kind-hearted gentleman. Take care no one hurts him. Billy will try and find him."

Paul Pringle never forgot those who had been kind to him. True Blue was also very glad to show his gratitude to the French doctor, whom they soon found in his cabin, where he had retired during the first rush of the British on board.

Summoning his assistants, the surgeon returned to the cockpit, where he was quickly occupied in endeavouring to mitigate the sufferings of his wounded countrymen, who now, mangled and bleeding, were being collected from all parts of the captured ship.

When True Blue got back to Paul, he found Tom Marline and Harry and Fid with him. The prisoners had been released; but by the particular advice of the officers, they had not yet mentioned the insults they had received, lest, already heated with the excitement of battle, the accounts should exasperate the crew of the Ruby and make them retaliate on the Frenchmen.

Paul, at his earnest request, was now removed back to his own ship while she lay alongside the prize. He and True Blue were warmly received by their shipmates, as were Tom and Fid and Harry. So also were the two midshipmen. The Captain, especially, was delighted at getting back young Elmore, who was an only son, and placed by his mother especially under his care.

"Yes, sir; here I am!" said the middy after the Captain had greeted him. "And, sir, I owe my life to the bravery of Freeborn, who leaped overboard to save me, in a raging sea, when no other means could have been employed."

"A noble, gallant young fellow. I will not overlook him, depend on that, Elmore. You and I must settle what we can best do for his interests," said the Captain warmly. But just then there was so much to be done that he could say no more on the subject.

The Ruby had suffered considerably both in hull and rigging, and in killed and wounded. The Frenchmen had, however, lost between seventy and eighty men in all. The second Captain was killed, and the first desperately wounded. The frigates had got so close in with the French coast that they were obliged to anchor to repair damages, so as to be in a condition to make sail and stand off again. It was a very anxious time for the English, for they were close enough in to be very much annoyed, should guns be brought down to the coast to bear upon them, or should any French ships be warned of their vicinity, and be able to get up and attack them before they were prepared for another engagement.

These considerations made everybody on board work with a will, and all night long the wearied crew of the Ruby were putting their own ship into fighting order, and getting up jury-masts so as to make sail on the prize. A careful lookout was kept, however, so that they might be prepared to meet danger from whatever quarter it might come.

The passengers taken in the packet were among the first removed from the French frigate, and were accommodated as well as circumstances would allow on board the Ruby.

The morning after the battle, the wind came off the shore, and a large concourse of people assembled on the coast had the mortification to see the Ruby and her prize make sail and stand away to the northward.

A few hours afterwards, a fleet of gunboats and two frigates came to look for them; but they were beyond reach of the former, and though the frigates followed, they were driven back by the sight of an English squadron, and both the Ruby and La Ralieuse reached Portsmouth in safety.

Chapter Sixteen.

True Blue's agitation was considerable, when, the day after the ship's arrival in Portsmouth Harbour, he heard his name called along the deck, and found that he was sent for into the Captain's cabin. "I wonder what I can be wanted for," he said to Abel Bush as he was giving his jacket a shake, and seeing that his shoes and handkerchief were tied with nautical propriety.

"About the matter of the jumping overboard," said Abel. "They think a good deal of it, you know!"

"That's more than I do," answered True Blue. "I wish they hadn't found out it was me. Still I must go. Good-bye, Abel. I hope they won't want to be paying me. I'll not touch a shilling—of that I'm determined!"

"Stick to that, boy—don't," said Abel. "You did your duty, and that's all you'd wish to do."

True Blue hurried along the deck till he reached the Captain's cabin, then hat in hand he entered, and, pulling a lock of his hair, stood humbly at the foot of the table. He saw that the Captain and Mr Brine, and the two midshipmen, Sir Henry Elmore and Mr Nott, were there, and two or three strange gentlemen from the shore.

"Sit down, Freeborn," said the Captain, pointing to a chair, which, very much to his surprise, Mr Nott got up and placed near him. "It is now a good many years since we were first shipmates, and during all that time I have only seen and heard good of you, and now I wish to thank you most heartily for the gallant way in which you saved Sir Henry Elmore's life. He and all his family wish also to show what they feel in the way most likely to be acceptable to you."

"Indeed they do. You performed a very gallant, noble action, young man, one to be proud of!" observed one of the gentlemen from the shore, who was an uncle of Sir Henry. "On what have you especially set your heart? What would you like to do? I suppose that you would not wish to leave the navy?"

"No, that I would not, sir," answered True Blue warmly. "But I know, sir, what I would like to do."

"What is it, my man? Speak out frankly at once!" said the gentleman. "I have no doubt that we shall be able to do as you wish."

"Then, sir, it's this," said True Blue, brightening up. "They've carried Paul Pringle to the hospital. Captain Garland knows the man, sir—my godfather. He'll be alone there, nobody particular to look after him; and what I should like, sir, would be to be allowed to go and stay with him till he is well and about again, or till the ship sails, when I don't think godfather would wish me to stay on shore even to be with him."

The gentlemen looked at each other, and then at the Captain and Mr Brine, who did not seem surprised, though Johnny Nott appeared a little inclined to laugh.

"A seaman thinks less of jumping overboard to save the life of a fellow-creature than you would of picking a drunken man up out of the road," said the Captain, addressing the gentleman. "You must propose something to him. He will not suggest anything himself."

"I think, Freeborn, I may easily promise that you will be allowed to remain with your old friend as long as he wishes it," said the Captain, turning to True Blue. "But I am sure Sir Henry's family will not be satisfied without showing some mark of their esteem and gratitude. What should you say now if the way was open to you of becoming an officer—first lieutenant of a ship like this, or perhaps her Captain? There is nothing to prevent it. I am very sure that you would be welcomed by all those among whom you were placed."

"There would be no difficulty as to expense," said the gentleman from the shore.

True Blue looked up at first as if the Captain was joking with him; then he became very grave, and in a voice almost choking with agitation he answered, "Oh, don't ask me, sir; don't ask me. I don't want to be anything but a seaman, such as my father was before me. I couldn't go and leave Paul, and Abel, and Peter, and the rest—men who have bred me up, and taught me all a sailor's duties in a way very few get taught. I couldn't, indeed, I wouldn't, leave them even to be an officer on the quarterdeck."

True Blue was silent, and no one spoke for some time, till the Captain turned aside to the gentleman and said, "I told you that I thought it likely such would be his answer. You must find some means of overcoming his scruples. Perhaps Elmore and Nott will manage him by themselves better than we shall."

The two midshipmen took the hint and invited True Blue to accompany them out of the cabin. They wisely did not take him on the quarterdeck, but got him between two of the after-guns, where they could converse without interruption. The result of the deliberation was that True Blue promised to consult his friends on the subject; and Elmore wound up by saying, "At all events, you must come up with me to see my mother and sisters in London. They will not be content without thanking you, and they cannot come down here to do so."

"With you, Sir Henry!" said True Blue, thinking that the midshipman really now was joking. "They wouldn't know what to do with such as me. I should like to go and see great London town—that I should; but—but—"

"No 'buts,' and so you shall, Freeborn; and that's all settled."

True Blue got leave of absence that afternoon, and Abel Bush accompanied him to the hospital, where he left him with Paul. He had never been more happy in his life, for the hospital servants were very glad to have their labours lightened, and left him to attend all day long on his godfather, and on several other wounded shipmates in the same ward. He told Paul all that had been said to him, and all the offers made him; but his godfather declined giving any advice till a formal consultation had been held by all his sponsors and their mates. Still True Blue thought that he seemed inclined to recommend him to do what he himself wished.

Paul was rapidly getting better, and in less than ten days who should appear at the hospital but Sir Henry Elmore himself. He went round the wards and spoke separately to each of the wounded men belonging to the Ruby, and then he came to Paul Pringle and had a long talk with him. Paul thought that in a few days he should be sufficiently recovered to leave the hospital and get as far as his own home, at the pretty village of Emsworth, and he had proposed that True Blue should accompany him. Abel Bush and Peter Ogle both lived there, and had families, among whom their godson would pass his time pleasantly enough.

"I daresay he might," said the young baronet, to whom Paul had mentioned this; "but I have the first claim on him. I have come now expressly to carry him off, so let him pack up his traps and accompany me."

Paul offered no further opposition to this proposal; so True Blue, having tied up a clean shirt and a thin pair of shoes, with a few other things in a handkerchief, announced that he had his clothes ready and was prepared to accompany the baronet.

The midshipman looked at the bundle, but said nothing. He knew well enough that a ship's boy was not likely to have any large amount of clothing. He had a coach at the door, and he ordered the coachman to drive to the George Hotel at Portsmouth. On the way he asked his companion whether he would not prefer dressing in plain clothes, and that, if so, a suit forthwith should be at his service; but True Blue so earnestly entreated that he might be allowed to wear the dress to which he had always been accustomed, that his friend gave up the point.

They found a capital dinner prepared for them at the George, in a private room; and the gentleman whom True Blue had seen on board the Ruby was there to receive them, and talked so kindly and pleasantly that he soon found himself very much at his ease, and was able and willing to do ample justice to the good things placed before him.

As Mr Leslie, Sir Henry's uncle, was obliged to return to London that night, they set off by the mail. Mr Leslie went inside; but the midshipman and True Blue, who disdained such a mode of proceeding, took their places behind the coachman, the box seat being already occupied by a naval officer. Mail coaches in those days were not the rapidly-moving vehicles they afterwards became. Passengers sat not only in front, but behind, where the guard also had his post—a most important personage, resplendent in red livery, and armed to the teeth with pistols, a heavy blunderbuss, and often a hanger or cutlass; so that he had the means, if he possessed a bold heart, of defending the property confided to him.

True Blue had never before been on the top of a coach, and his remarks as they drove along, till the long summer day came to a close, amused the young baronet very much.

When they reached London, Mr Leslie called a hackney coach, and True Blue found himself rumbling along through the streets of London, towards Portman Square, at an early hour on a bright summer morning.

"Where are all the people, sir?" he asked, looking out of the window. "I thought London was full of people."

"So it is. They are all asleep now, like ants in their nest. When the sun is up by and by, they will be busy enough, you will see," answered Mr Leslie.

It was still very early when they arrived at Lady Elmore's house; and, as they were not expected, no one was up to receive them. They, however, got in quietly; and while his arrival was being made known to his mother, Sir Henry took True Blue to a room and advised him to turn in and get some sleep. He would, however, very much rather have been allowed to go out and see the wonders of the great city; but his friend assuring him that, if he did, he would inevitably lose himself, he reluctantly went to bed.

The moment, however, that his head was on the pillow, he was fast asleep, and, in spite of the bright sun which gleamed in at the window, it was not till nearly the family breakfast-time that he awoke.

He was awakened by a bland voice saying, "It is time to get up, sir. Shall I help you to dress?"

True Blue opened his eyes and saw before him a personage in a very fine coat, with powdered hair, who he thought must be some great lord or other, even though he held a can of hot water in his hand.

The young sailor sat up, and, seeing no one else in the room, said, pulling a front lock of his hair, "Did you speak to me, sir?"

"Sir Henry sent me to ascertain if you wanted anything," answered the footman, somewhat puzzled, as he had not been told who the occupant of the room was.

When, however, he came to examine the clothes by the bedside, he guessed that he was some naval follower of his young master. He was about to carry off the clothes to brush them.

True Blue saw the proceeding with dismay. "Don't take them away, please. I have no others!" he exclaimed. "But, I say, I'm very hungry, and shouldn't mind some bread and cheese if there's any served out yet."

"I can get it for you at once; but breakfast will be ready directly, and you will find better things to eat then," said the footman, smiling.

"Oh, I'll be dressed in a jiffy, then," answered True Blue, jumping out of bed and forthwith commencing his ablutions in sea fashion, and almost before the footman had left the room he was ready to go downstairs.

Sir Henry came for him.

"Come along, Freeborn. My mother and sisters are anxious to see you. They are in the breakfast-room. I am sure that you will like them."

True Blue, looking every inch the sailor, with his rich light curling hair, sunburnt countenance, laughing blue eye, and white strong teeth, followed the midshipman. He felt rather strange when the door opened and a handsome, tall lady came forward, and, taking him by both his hands, said:

"You saved my dear boy's life at the risk of your own. I owe you all the gratitude a mother can offer."

She shook his hands warmly. He made no answer, for he did not know exactly what to say, except, "Oh, marm, it's nothing!"

Two tall girls then followed her example, and he thought that they were going to kiss him; but they did not, which he was glad of, as it would have made him feel very bashful.

Mr Leslie came down, and the party were soon seated round the breakfast-table. True Blue was very hungry, but at first everything seemed so strange about him that he could not eat. However, the ladies spoke in such kind, sweet voices, while they in no way seemed to notice what he was about, that he quickly gained courage and made the beef, and ham, and eggs, and bread and butter, rapidly disappear.

After the meal was over, some time was spent by Sir Henry with his mother and sisters, while Mr Leslie remained with True Blue, talking with him in a friendly way; and then he gave him a number of books with prints to look over, which interested him very much.

At last his host came back. "Come along, Freeborn," he said. "The coach is at the door, and we have numberless sights to see, which, truth to say, I have never seen myself; so my mother will go with us to show them. Is there anything you have heard of you would particularly like to see?"

True Blue thought a little. "Yes, indeed there is, Sir Henry," he answered. "There is one thing I'd rather see than anything else. It is what I have always longed to have a sight of, and that is His Majesty the King we fight for. Paul Pringle says he would go a hundred miles any day to see him; and so would I—two hundred for that matter. Every true sailor is ready enough to shed his blood for him, marm; but we should all of us like to see him just once, at all events."

"I daresay that we shall be able to manage that without difficulty," said Lady Elmore. "His Majesty will probably soon come up to deliver a speech in Parliament, and we shall then have a good opportunity of seeing him."

This promise highly delighted True Blue; and he evidently looked forward to seeing the King with more satisfaction than to any sight he expected to witness during his visit to London.

True Blue was taken one evening to the play, but, unfortunately, what was called a naval drama was acted. Here both he and the midshipman were well qualified to criticise. He certainly was the more severe.

"Does that fellow call himself a sailor, marm?" he asked, turning to Lady Elmore. "Don't believe it. He isn't a bit more like a sailor than that thing they are hauling across the deck is like a ship—that is to say, any ship I ever saw. If she came to be launched, she'd do nothing but go round boxing the compass till she went to the bottom. Would she, Sir Henry?"

The midshipman was highly diverted. "The manager little thought that he had us to criticise his arrangements," he answered, laughing. "The play is only got up for the amusement of landsmen, and to show them how we sailors fight for them."

"But wouldn't they like us to go and do that just now ourselves, Sir Henry?" exclaimed True Blue with eagerness. "If they'd give us a cutlass apiece, and would get those Frenchmen we saw just now to stand up like men, we would show them how we boarded and took the French frigate in our first cruise."

Lady Elmore said she thought some confusion might be created if the proposal was carried out, and persuaded True Blue to give up the idea. When, however, one of the stage sailors came on and volunteered to dance a hornpipe, his indignation knew no bounds. "He's not a true bluejacket—that I'll warrant!" he exclaimed. "If he was, he wouldn't be handling his feet in the way he is doing. I should so like to step down and just show you, my lady, and the rest of the good people here, how we dance aboard. If I had but Sam Smatch and his fiddle, I'll warrant people would say which was the right and which was the wrong way pretty quickly."

Lady Elmore explained to him, much to his surprise, that none but the actors who were paid for it were allowed to appear on the stage, but assured him that she would be very glad if some evening he would give them, at her house, an exhibition of his skill in dancing the hornpipe.

"That I will, my lady, with all my heart!" he exclaimed frankly. "There's nothing I wouldn't do to please you and the young ladies; and I think that you would like to see a right real sailor's hornpipe danced. It does my heart good to dance it, I know. It is rare fun."

On driving home, Lady Elmore asked him how he liked the play altogether.

"Well, my lady," he exclaimed, "much obliged to you for taking me to the place! It was very good sport, but I should have liked it better if I could have lent a hand in the work. When there is a scrimmage, it is natural-like to wish to be in it. And I couldn't bear to see that black pirate fellow carry off the young gal, and all the gold and silver plates and candlesticks, and not be able just to go and rout out his nest of villains."

This visit to the play enabled his friends to understand True Blue's style of thought and manners far better than they had before done, and was in reality of considerable benefit to him. Gentle of heart and right-minded, and brave as a lion, he was still a rough sailor; and only a considerable time spent in the society of polished people could have given him the polish which is looked-for in a gentleman.

The next day the King was to prorogue Parliament. Mr Leslie called in the morning and took his nephew and young guest down towards Westminster to wait for his approach. True Blue was full of excitement at the thought of seeing the King. "I wonder what he can be like? He must be a very grand person to have so many big ships all of his own," he observed to Mr Leslie.

"You would find His Majesty a very affable, kind old gentleman if he were to speak to you at any time," said Mr Leslie. "Here he comes, though. You will see him inside the coach. Take off your hat when he passes."

At a slow and stately pace the carriage of the kind-hearted monarch of Great Britain approached. First came the body of Life Guards, their belts well whitened with pipeclay, and their heads plastered with pomatum and powder; and then followed the royal carriage, as fine as gold and paint and varnish could make it.

"There's King George, Freeborn," said Mr Leslie, pointing out his Majesty, who sat looking very gracious as he bowed now out of one window, now out of the other.

"God bless him, then!" shouted True Blue, almost beside himself with excitement, throwing up his hat and catching it again. "Three cheers for King George, boys! Three cheers for the King! Hurrah! hurrah! hurrah, boys! Hip, hip, hip, hurrah!" True Blue's eye had fallen on several other bluejackets, who happened to be near him in the crowd, come up to London on a spree to get rid of their prize-money. Instantly the shout was taken up by them and echoed by the rest of the crowd, till the air was rent with cries of "Long live the King!" "Long live King George!"

"Hurrah! hurrah! hurrah for King George!" "Hurrah for Old England!" "Old England in arms against the world—Old England for ever!"

Mr Leslie was highly delighted, and he and his nephew joined in the shout as loudly as any one, while the King, looking from the windows, bowed and smiled even more cordially than before.

"Well, I've had a good sight of His Majesty, and I'll not forget his kind face as long as I live!" exclaimed True Blue as the party walked homeward. "It is a pleasure to know the face of the King one is fighting for; and, God bless His Majesty, his kind look would make me more ready than ever to stand up for him!"

All the way home True Blue could talk of nothing but the King, and how glad he was to have seen him. In the evening, however, one of the young ladies began to play a hornpipe, the music of which Sir Henry, not without difficulty, had procured for her. True Blue pricked up his ears, and then, running to the piano, exclaimed, "You play it very well indeed, Miss Julia—that you do; but I wish that you could just hear Sam Smatch with his fiddle—he'd take the shine out of you, I think you'd say. Howsomdever, my lady, if you and the young ladies and Sir Henry please, and Miss Julia will just strike up a bit of a tune, I'll shuffle my feet about and show you what we call a hornpipe at sea. Sir Henry knows, though, right well; but, to say truth, I'd rather have the smooth deck under my feet than this grassy sort of stuff, which wants the right sort of spring in it."

"Never mind, Freeborn," said Sir Henry, laughing. "They are not such severe judges as Ogle and Bush, and Marline and our other shipmates."

"To be sure—to be sure," said True Blue in a compassionate tone. "Now, Miss Julia, please marm, strike up and off I go."

True Blue did go off indeed, and with the greatest spirit performed a hornpipe which deservedly elicited the admiration of all the spectators. Miss Julia's fingers were tired before his feet, and, having made the usual bow round to the company, throwing back his hair, he stood ready to begin again.

The applause which followed having ceased, he laughed, exclaiming, "Oh, it's nothing, ladies—nothing to what I can do, Sir Henry will tell you; but, you see, there's a good deal of difference between the forecastle of a man-of-war, and this here drawing-room in big London City." The tone of his voice showed that he gave the preference to the forecastle.

That evening Lady Elmore and her son had a long discussion.

"But are you certain, Henry, that we are doing the best thing for the brave lad?" she said.

"Oh, he'll polish—he'll polish rapidly!" answered her son. "He has no notion of concealment, or that it is necessary for him to assume shoregoing manners, now that he has got over his bashfulness at finding himself among strangers. He says exactly what he thinks and feels. The outside husk is rough enough, I own, but, depend on it, the jewel within will soon take a polish which will shine brightly through the shell and light up the whole form. Not a bad notion for a midshipman, mother!"

"Oh, you were always poetical and warm-hearted and good and enthusiastic, Henry," said Lady Elmore, pressing him to her heart. "Do as you think best, and I have no doubt our young sailor will turn out a shining character."

Chapter Seventeen.

It had been arranged that True Blue should visit Paul Pringle and his other friends at Emsworth before returning to his ship. The day for his leaving London was fixed. He had seen all the sights and been several times to the play, and though he thought it all very amusing, he was, in truth, beginning to get somewhat tired of the sort of life. As to Lady Elmore and her daughters, he thought them, as he said, next door to angels, and would have gone through fire and water to serve them.

One morning he awoke just as the footman walked in with a jug of hot water, and, leaving it on the washhand stand, retired without saying a word. Sir Henry had directed that he should be waited on exactly as he was himself. True Blue jumped out of bed; but when he came to put on his clothes, they had disappeared. In their stead there was a midshipman's uniform suit, dirk, and hat, and cockade complete, while a chest stood open, containing shirts, and socks, and shoes, and a quadrant, and books—indeed, a most perfect outfit.

"There's a mistake," he said to himself. "They have been and brought Sir Henry's traps in here, and John has carried off my clothes, and forgot to bring them back. I never do like ringing the bell, it seems so fine-gentleman-like. Still, if he doesn't come, it will be the only way to get to him." While waiting, he was looking about, when his eye fell on a paper on the dressing-table. His own name was on it. It was a document from the Admiralty, directing Mr Billy True Blue Freeborn, midshipman of H.M. frigate Ruby, to go down and join her in a week's time. He rubbed his eyes—he read the paper over and over again; he shook himself, for he thought that he must be still in bed and asleep, and then he very nearly burst into tears.

"No, no!" he exclaimed passionately; "it's what I don't want to be. I can't be and won't be. I'll not go and be above Paul, and Abel, and Peter, and Tom, which I should be if I was on the quarterdeck: I shouldn't be one of them any longer. I couldn't mess with them and talk with them, as I have always done. I know my place; I like Sir Henry and many of the other young gentlemen very much, and even Mr Nott, though he does play curious pranks now and then; but I never wished to be one of them, and what's more, I won't, and so my mind is made up."

Just then he saw another document on the table. It was a letter addressed to him. He opened it and found that it came from Paul Pringle. It began:

True Blue read the epistle over several times. Though signed by Pringle, it had partly been written by Abel Bush, and partly by Peter Ogle. It contained a postscript, inviting him to come down to Emsworth, whatever the determination he might come to, as his many friends there were anxious to see him.

The mention of his old friends roused up thoughts and feelings in which, for some time past, he had not indulged. Both Peter Ogle and Abel Bush were married men, with large families. With them he felt how perfectly at home and happy he should be. One of them, too, Mary Ogle, though rather younger than himself, had always been his counsellor and friend, and had also materially assisted in giving him the amount of knowledge he possessed in reading and writing. Had it not been for her, he confessed that he would have remained a sad dunce.

After he had thought over the letter, he exclaimed, "Then again, now, if I was an officer I should have to go with the other officers wherever they went; and when the ship came into port, I should be for starting off for London, and couldn't go and stay comfortably with my old friends. No, I'm thankful to Sir Henry—I am, indeed; but I've made up my mind."

He rang the bell. When John appeared, he asked for his clothes.

"There they are, sir," said John, pointing to the midshipman's uniform.

"I see; but I want the clothes I wore yesterday, John," said True Blue.

"Master said those were for you, sir," explained John.

"I'm not going to put on those clothes, John," said True Blue quietly. "They don't suit me, and I don't suit them."

The footman was astonished.

"But they will make you an officer and a gentleman," said he earnestly.

"That's just what I don't want to be, John," answered True Blue. "They wouldn't do it, either. It isn't the clothes makes the man. You know that. Bring me back my own jacket and trousers. I know Sir Henry won't be angry with you. I'll set it all right. There's a good chap, now—do as I ask you."

John still hesitated.

"Very well," continued True Blue, "if you don't, I'll just jump into bed again, and there I'll stay. The only clothes I'll put on are my own. They were brand new only last week, and I've not done with them."

John, seeing that the young sailor was in earnest, went and brought back his clothes. True Blue was soon dressed, and considerable disappointment was expressed on the countenances of the ladies as they entered the breakfast-room, when, instead of the gay-looking midshipman they expected to see, they found him in his seaman's dress. He looked up frankly, and not in the slightest degree abashed.

"My lady," he said, "I know what you and Sir Henry intended for me, and there isn't a part of my heart that doesn't thank you; but d'ye see, my lady, I was born a true sailor, and a true sailor I wish to be. I have old friends—I can't leave them. I know what I'm fitted for, and I shouldn't be happy in a midshipman's berth. I know, too, that it was all done in great kindness; but it's a thousand times more than I deserve. I shall always love you, my lady, and the young ladies, and Sir Henry; and if ever he gets a ship, it will be my pride to be with him and to be his coxswain. There's only one favour more I have to ask—it is that Sir Henry will set to rights the order about my having a midshipman's rating aboard the Ruby. It's a great favour, I'll allow; but it's one I don't deserve and don't want. I've made up my mind about it, and, my lady, you will let me be as I was—I was very happy, and shall not be happier as an officer."

"I think very likely not," said Lady Elmore, taking his hand. "But, Freeborn, we are all anxious to show our gratitude to you. Can you point out how it may best be done?"

"That's it, my lady!" exclaimed True Blue vehemently. "I have done nothing to speak of, and I do not wish for anything. Let me just think about you all, and how kind you've been to me, and that's all I want. If I serve with Sir Henry, I'll always be by his side, and I'll do my best to keep the Frenchmen's cutlasses off his head."

"Thanks, thanks, my boy. Your love for my son makes me take a double interest in you," said Lady Elmore warmly; and then she added, "still I wish that you would allow us somewhat to lighten the load of obligation we owe you."

As True Blue had not the slightest notion what this meant, he made no reply.

Everybody in the house was sorry to part with the frank-spoken young sailor. Even the butler and footman begged him to accept some token of remembrance; and Mrs Jellybag, the housekeeper, put him up a box containing all sorts of good things, which, she told him, he might share with his friends down at Emsworth. He reached Emsworth in the evening, and right hearty was the welcome he received from all the members of the Ogle and Bush families, though not more kind than that old Mrs Pringle and Paul bestowed on him.

The whole party assembled to tea and supper at Mrs Pringle's, and he had not been many minutes in the house before he unpacked his chest and produced his box of good things for them. He insisted on serving them out himself, and he managed to slip the largest piece of cake into Mary's plate, and somehow to give her a double allowance of jam.

Then there were a couple of pounds of tea,—a rare luxury in those days, except among the richer classes,—and some bottles of homemade wines or cordials, which served still more to cheer the hearts of the guests. The pipes were brought in and fragrant tobacco smoked, and songs were called for. Paul and Abel struck up. True Blue sang some of his best, and, as he every now and then gave Mary a sly kiss, suiting the action to the words of his songs, he never felt so happy in his life.

Supper was scarcely over when there was a rap at the door, and a well-known voice exclaiming, "What cheer, mates, what cheer?"

Billy sprang from his stool, and, lifting the latch, cried out, "Come in, Sam, come in! Hurrah! here's Sam Smatch. We were just wishing for you to help us to shake down our supper, but little thought to see you."

"Why, d'ye see, I wasn't wanted aboard, and so I got leave and just worked my way along here, playing at the publics and taking my time about it," said Sam.

"Not getting drunk, I hope, Sam?" asked Paul.

"Why, as to that, Paul, d'ye see, sometimes more liquor got into my head than went down into my heels; and so, you see, the heels was overballasted-like and kicked up a bit, just as the old Terrible used to do in a heavy sea; but as to being drunk, don't for to go and think such a thing of me, Paul,—I, who was always fit to look after the cook's coppers when no one else could have told whether they had beef and duff or round-shot boiling in them."

The black's countenance and the twinkle of his eyes belied his words, but he was not the less welcome. Paul told him to sit down, and he was soon doing ample justice to the remains of the supper. Without a word the table was cleared away. Mrs Pringle and the older people retired into the wide chimney recess. Sam, taking his fiddle, mounted on a meal-tub, which stood in a corner by the old clock, and then, striking up one of his merriest tunes, he soon had all the lads and lasses capering and frisking about before him, True Blue being the most lively and active of them all. Never did his heart and heels feel so light as he bounded up and down the room with Mary by his side, sometimes grasping her hands, and sometimes whirling round and round, while both were shrieking and laughing in the exuberance of their spirits.

He felt as if a load had been taken off his mind. Once more he was among his old friends and associates, and, without confessing the fact to himself, he infinitely preferred being with them to enjoying all the luxury and refinement which Lady Elmore's house in London had afforded. So the days flew rapidly by till the party of seamen had once more to rejoin their ship.

She was bound for the Mediterranean. The first port they entered was Toulon. The town and the surrounding fortifications were held by the Royalists, aided by British, Spanish, Sardinians, and Neapolitan troops, and strong parties of seamen from the English and Spanish squadron. The Republican troops were besieging the place, vowing vengeance against their countrymen who opposed them. Lord Hood, the British Commander-in-Chief, was expecting a reinforcement of Austrian troops to defend the town. He sent some ships to convey them, but an answer was returned that they could not be spared; and the Republican army having increased rapidly in numbers and gained several posts, a council of war was held to deliberate as to the advisability of longer holding the place. The result was that Toulon must be abandoned. It was the death-knell to thousands of the inhabitants.

Several important objects had to be accomplished. The ships of war must first be carried out of the harbour, the defenders withdrawn from the batteries, the Royalist inhabitants got off, and, finally, all the French ships, magazines, and stores which could not be removed destroyed.

It was an anxious and awful period. Between forty and fifty thousand Republican troops were preparing to storm the works, which, covering a vast extent of ground, were defended by less than eleven thousand. Sir Sydney Smith had volunteered to destroy the magazines and ships.

On the 18th of December, all the troops, having been withdrawn from the forts, were concentrated in the town. Happily the weather was fine and the sea smooth. The enemy had been so severely handled that they advanced cautiously. Among those who volunteered to accompany Sir Sydney Smith was Mr Alston, one of the lieutenants of the Ruby. Mr Nott, too, was of his party, as was Abel Bush, and True Blue got leave to go also.

The Neapolitan troops, by their dastardly desertion of the fort of the Mississi, at which they were stationed, nearly disconcerted all the arrangements. Great numbers of the inhabitants had already gone on board the ships of war.

Sir Sydney Smith had with him the Swallow, a small lateen-rigged vessel, three English and three Spanish gunboats, and the Vulcan fireship, under charge of Captain Charles Hare, with a brigade of boats in attendance.

The ships had got out; the boats of the fleet were waiting to carry off the troops. Already shot and shell from the surrounding heights were beginning to fall thickly into the harbour. The galley slaves in the arsenal, 800 in number, were threatening to interfere, but were kept in check by the gunboats; the Republicans were descending the hill in numbers, and opening fire with musketry and cannon on the British and Spanish.

Night came on; the fireship, towed by the boats, entered the basin. Her well-shotted guns were pointed so as to keep the enemy in check. The Spaniards had undertaken to scuttle the Iris frigate, which contained several thousand barrels of powder, as also another powder vessel, the Montreal frigate.

Hitherto Sir Sydney Smith and his gallant companions had performed all their operations in darkness, the only light being the flashes of the cannon and muskets playing on them. At length ten o'clock struck—a single rocket ascended into the air. In an instant the fireship and all the trains leading to the different magazines and stores were ignited. The boats lay alongside the former, ready to take off the crew. There was a loud explosion—the priming had burst, and the brave Captain Hare narrowly escaped with his life. "To the boats, lads, for your lives!" he shouted.

Mr Nott and True Blue were assisting him. Not a moment was to be lost. Upwards burst the flames with terrific fury, literally scorching them as they ran along the deck to jump into the boats. Abel Bush caught True Blue, or he would have been overboard.

"Bravo, boy!" cried Abel; "you've done it well."

"Yes, we've done it; but where's the Captain?" asked True Blue, about to spring back to look for him.

Just then the Captain appeared, with his clothes almost burnt off his back. The flames of the burning ships, the storehouses and magazines, now clearly exposed to the view of the exasperated Republicans those who were engaged in the work of destruction, and showers of shot and shell soon came rattling down among them. Still the gallant seamen persevered in the work they had undertaken, when suddenly the very air seemed to be rent in two; the masts, rigging, and deck of the Iris rose upwards in a mass of flame, shattering two gunboats which happened to be close to her, and scattering her burning fragments far and wide around her among the boats. The brave fellows in the latter, heedless of the danger, dashed on to assist the crews of the gunboats. Several people in one had been killed; but the whole crew of the other, though she had been blown into the air, were picked up alive.

"That is the ship the lazy Spaniards undertook to scuttle!" exclaimed Mr Alston after they had picked up all the poor fellows they could find. "However, bear a hand; we have plenty of work before us. There are two seventy-fours. We must destroy them by some means or other."

When, however, they reached the seventy-fours, they found them full of French prisoners, who seemed inclined to protect them.

"Very well, gentlemen," shouted Sir Sydney; "it will be a painful necessity to have to burn you in the ships!"

The hint was taken, and the prisoners thankfully allowed themselves to be conveyed to the nearest point of land.

The British ran no little risk in this undertaking, for the French far outnumbered them; but no attempt at rising was made; and now the two ships, Héros and Thémistocle, being cleared of their occupants, were set on fire in every direction, and were soon blazing up brightly.

In every direction similar large bonfires were lighting up the harbour and shores of Toulon, among which the British boats were incessantly plying, carrying off the remaining troops and rescuing the terrified inhabitants.

At length the work of destruction, as far as means would allow, was well-nigh accomplished, when another fearful explosion, even greater than the first, took place, close to where the tender and the boats were at the moment passing.

It was the frigate Montreal. Down came around the boats a complete avalanche of burning timbers, huge guns, masts, spars, and blocks, rattling, and crashing, and hissing into the water. The seamen, already almost exhausted with their exertions, could scarcely attempt even to escape the fiery shower. Many of the poor fellows sank down at their oars, and those in each boat believed that their comrades had been destroyed; but when they drew out of the circle of destruction and mustered once more, not one had been injured.

Although fired on by the Republicans, who had taken possession of Forts Balaguier and Aiguillette, the boats slowly pulled out to join the fleet already outside. A few only, whose crews had strength left, returned to aid the flying inhabitants. The last of the troops had been embarked under the able management of Captain Elphinstone, of the Robust, and other Captains, without the loss of a man, the Robust being the last ship to leave the harbour when the infuriated Republicans, breathing vengeance on the helpless inhabitants, rushed into the city.

The terrible intelligence reached them that even in the suburbs neither age nor sex had been spared. Husbands seized their wives or daughters, mothers their children, and, rushing from their houses, fled towards the water, where their friends had already long ago embarked. Shot and shell were remorselessly fired down on them; numbers were cut in pieces as they fled. Every step they heard behind they thought came from a pursuing foe. Many, unable to reach the boats, preferring instant death to the bayonets of their countrymen, rushed, with their infants in their arms, and perished in the waves.

Daylight approached, and with sorrowful reluctance the brave seamen had to draw off from the scene of destruction to avoid falling into the hands of the enemy.

The boat in which True Blue pulled the bow oar was one of the last to quit the harbour, and for many a day afterwards the shrieks of the hapless Toulonese, murdered by their countrymen, rang in his ears.

Chapter Eighteen.

The frigate was soon after this sent home with dispatches; but scarcely was she clear of the Straits of Gibraltar than the wind fell, a thick fog came on, and she lay becalmed some twenty leagues off the Spanish coast. So dense was the fog, that no object could be seen a quarter of a mile off.

At length a light breeze sprang up from the westward; but though strong enough to fill her sails and send her slowly gliding over the mirror-like surface of the water, it had not the power of blowing away the mist which hung over it.

True Blue was walking the forecastle with Paul Pringle when his quick ear caught the sound of a distant bell. He touched Paul's arm as a sign not to speak, and stood listening; then almost simultaneously another and another sounded, and the ship's bell directly after struck, as if responding to them. The sounds, it was evident, came down with the wind.

"Come aft and report them, in case the officer should not have heard them."

Mr Brine was on deck and listened attentively to what True Blue had to say. "How far off were the bells?" he asked.

"Half a mile, sir," was the prompt answer.

"Large or small, should you say?"

"Large, sir," said True Blue.

"English or French? I take it that there is a difference in the sound."

"And so there is, sir," quickly replied True Blue. "I marked it when we were aboard the Ralieuse; and now, sir, you ask me, I should say they were French."

"Very clear, indeed," remarked the first lieutenant. "Go into the weather-rigging, Freeborn, and keep your eyes about you and your ears open, and report anything more you may discover."

Mr Brine then went into the cabin to consult with the Captain. The sentry was ordered, when his half-hour glass was run out, to turn it, but not to sound the bell; and the word was passed along the decks to keep the ship as quiet as possible.

It was possible that they were in the presence of a greatly superior force of the enemy. The frigate's course, however, was not altered. The breeze was freshening, and any moment the veil might be lifted from the face of the waters, and the vessels floating on it disclosed to each other. Everything on board the frigate was prepared for flight or battle; and, in spite of the probability of having to contend with a superior force, the crew showed by their remarks that they would infinitely prefer the latter to the former alternative.

The only two, probably, on board who wished to avoid a fight were Sam Smatch and Gregory Gipples, who still remained on board. Poor Gregory would gladly have followed some more pacific calling, but his poverty, and not his will, compelled him to be a sailor. Besides, he was now a big, stout, well-fed fellow, and could pull and haul as well as many seamen; and in those days the pressgang took care that once a sailor, a man should remain always a sailor. Big as he was, and inclined to bully all fresh hands, Tim Fid defied him, and never ceased playing him tricks and quizzing him.

"Gipples, my boy, they say that there are three big Frenchmen coming down upon us, and that we are to fight them all!" cried Fid, giving his messmate a dig in the ribs. "One down, t'other come on, I hope it will be; but whether we drub them or not, some of us will be losing the number of our mess."

"Oh, don't talk so, Fid!" answered Gipples, looking very yellow. "What's the use of it? We don't see the enemy."

"No, but we very soon shall," said Fid. "Just let the mist lift, and there they'll be as big as life one on each quarter, so that every shot they fire will rake us pretty nigh fore and aft. Our Captain's not a man to give in, as you well know; so we shall soon have our sticks a-rattling down about our heads, and the round-shot whizzing by us, and splinters flying about, and arms and legs and heads tumbling off. How does yours feel, Gipples? It's odd a shot has never come foul of it yet. Howsomdever, you can't expect that always to be. But never mind, old fellow. I'll tell the old people at home how you died like a true British sailor; and if you have any message to your old chums, just tell me what to say."

Thus, with an ingenious talent at tormenting, Tim Fid ran on, till, from the vivid picture he drew, poor Gipples was fairly frightened out of his senses. Tim was just then called off by the boatswain. When he came back, Gipples was nowhere to be seen. The crew had been sent quietly to their quarters without the usual beat of drum. Gipples ought to have been seated on his powder tub, but he was not. He had been seen to go forward. Fid looked anxiously for him. He did not return.

A considerable time passed. No Gipples appeared, and Fid felt sure that he must have slipped purposely overboard.

Still Fid was not as happy as usual. True Blue asked him what was the matter. He told him of his fears about Gipples. Indeed, the unguarded powder tub was strong evidence that he was right in his surmises. Another boy was ordered to take charge of the tub, and nobody but Tim thought much more about the hapless Gregory.

The wind had gradually been increasing, and at length it gained sufficient strength to sweep before it the banks of heavy mist, when the loud sharp cry of the lookouts announced five sail right astern, and some five or six miles distant. As they could be seen clearly from the deck, numerous glasses were instantly pointed at them, when they were pronounced without doubt to be enemy's ships.

They also saw the frigate, and instantly bore up in chase. Had they all been line-of-battle ships, the swift-footed little Ruby might easily have escaped from them; but two looked very like frigates, and many of that class in those days were superior in speed to the fleetest English frigates.

All sail was made on the Ruby, and she was kept due north. "We may fall in with one of our own squadrons, or we may manage to keep ahead of the enemy till night, and then I shall have no fear of them," observed the Captain as he walked the quarterdeck with his first lieutenant.

"We shall soon see how fast the Frenchmen can walk along after us," answered Mr Brine. "I hope the Ruby won't prove a sluggard on this occasion; she has shown that she can go along when in chase of an enemy."

"Even should the two frigates come up with us, we must manage to keep them at bay," said the Captain. "I know, Brine, that you will never strike as long as a hope of escape remains."

"That I will not, sir!" exclaimed the first lieutenant warmly, and Mr Brine was not the man to neglect such a pledge.

"Never fear, lads," said Paul Pringle; "the Captain carried us clear with about as great odds against us once before, and he'll do it again now if the breeze holds fair."

"But suppose it doesn't, and those thundering big Frenchmen manage to get alongside of us, what are we to do then?" asked a young seaman who had lately been impressed from a merchantman.

"What do, Dunnage?—why, fight them, man!" answered Paul briskly "You don't suppose, do you, that we should do anything else till we have done that? We may knock away their spars, or maybe a shift of wind may come, or a gale spring up, or we may give such hard knocks that the enemy may think us a bad bargain. At all events, the first thing a man-of-war has to do is to fight."

In a short time it was seen that the two frigates took the lead, and that one of them was much ahead of the other. "All right," said Paul when he perceived this, "we shall be able to settle with one before the other comes on."

The officers, however, knew well enough, as in reality did Paul, that a vessel much inferior in size might so far cripple them and impede their progress as to allow the more powerful ships to come up. Still the Ruby was well ahead when the sun went down. As twilight rapidly deepened into the gloom of night, the spirits of all on board increased. A light was now shown at the cabin window. There was no moon, and the night became very dark. Meantime, a cask had been prepared with a bright light on the top of it. The loftier sails were handed, the cask was lowered, and at the same instant the after-ports were closed. The light was seen floating brightly and calmly astern. The helm was then put down, the yards braced up, and the frigate stood away on a bowline close-hauled to the westward.

For some hours she tore on with her hammock nettings almost in the water; but it was a race for freedom, and what Briton would not undergo any risk for that? No one, not even the idlers, thought of turning in. Dawn came at length. Eager and sharp eyes were on the lookout at the mastheads, but not a sign of the enemy was perceived. Once more the helm was put up, and the frigate stood to the north-west.

Never did a ship's company turn to at their breakfast with more hearty goodwill than did that of the Ruby. The only person missing at his mess was Gregory Gipples; and this convinced Tim Fid that he must have thrown himself overboard. True Blue and Harry Hartland, however, differed with him, and argued the point. "If he was such a coward and so afraid of shot, surely he would not deliberately go and destroy himself," said they.

Fid insisted that his great fear of being shot made him dread less the idea of drowning.

"He wasn't quite such a fool as all that," said Harry. "Here comes Sam Smatch. Let's ask him what he thinks about it."

"What do I think about it?" exclaimed Sam, after they had laid the state of the case before him. "I'll tell ye, boys. Big Gipples, him no fool. He's stowed his fat carcase away somewhere down in de hold. Let's you all and me go and look for him, and we soon rouse him up like one great rat with rope's end."

"Set a thief to catch a thief!" whispered Harry to Fid. "I thought he would know where Gipples was likely to be found."

Sam had been known on more than one occasion to stow himself snugly away during action. When discovered, he had boldly avowed the wisdom of his conduct. "For why?" he argued. "Suppose now my arm shot away, ship's company lose fiddler; for how I fiddle without arm? And suppose no fiddler, how anchor got up? how ship go to sea? and how take prize? and how dance and be merry? No, no; you men no signify—go and be shot. I berry important—take care of self."

Accordingly, Sam being the guide, the party set out with proper authority to look for the missing Gipples. They searched in every vacant space in the cable tier, and in every accessible spot in the hold, among the water-casks and more bulky stores not under lock and key; but no Gregory was forthcoming.

Fid began to fear that his forebodings would prove true. One spot, however, had to be visited, commonly called the coal-hole. It was very dark and close, and not a place that any one would willingly pass a day in.

They thought that every corner had been explored, when, just as they were retiring, Fid heard a suppressed groan. He started, and, had he been alone, he felt that he should not have liked it; but he was a brave little fellow, especially in company with others; so he stopped and listened, and called Sam, who held the lantern, to examine the spot whence the groan had proceeded.

There was a loose pile of firewood in one corner; and, on examining it, there was no doubt that it had slipped over during the night. "He or his ghost is under there," said Fid, pointing to it.

"Even if it's his ghost, it's not a pleasant place to be in!" exclaimed True Blue, setting to work to remove the logs.

This was soon accomplished; and there, sure enough, black as a sweep from the coal dust, and bruised with the logs, lay not the ghost of Gipples, but Gipples himself, terribly frightened with the idea that he was looked-for only that he might be drawn forth to be punished.

"Oh, lagged—lagged!" he exclaimed bitterly. "I'll not do it again—indeed I won't, your worship. Just let me off this once. Oh do!"

"What's the fellow singing out about?" exclaimed Sam. "Just you come out. No one's going to hurt you. Just wash yourself and come and have some breakfast. You look pretty near dead already."

The truth was that the poor wretch was already out of his wits with fright, starvation, and sleepiness, and had a very confused idea of where he was or what had happened.

Sam Smatch now acted the part of a good Samaritan towards him. He got him up on the lower-deck, and then went and called the doctor, and said that he had found him bruised all over and apparently out of his wits. The doctor ordered him to be put into a hammock in the sick-bay.

Sam, however, first got him washed and cleaned, and gave him some food, which considerably revived him. After this, when Gipples came to himself, Sam administered a severe lecture to him for his cowardice.

"But you, Sam—you're afraid, I'm sure, Sam," whimpered the culprit.

"No, I not afraid," he answered indignantly; "but why for I go lose my head or arm, when I get noding for it? I am paid to play the fiddle and help the cook. I do my duty and keep out of harm's way. You, Gipples, are paid to be shot—you must stay where the shot comes, or you not do your duty. There all de difference."

"Then I'll try and get a rating where I needn't stop and be shot!" cried Gipples, as if a bright idea had seized him. "If I can't, I'll cut and run. I can't stand it—that I can't."

Had not the doctor reported the boy Gipples as having met with an accident, he would have been severely flogged for not having been at his quarters. As it was, he escaped without further punishment; but he got the name from his messmates of "Gregory Coal-hole."

The ship without further adventure reached Portsmouth. At this time, in spite of the destruction of so many ships and magazines at Toulon, the French Republic was preparing an armament so great that she hoped to be able at once to crush with it the fleets of Old England. The British Government, however, had not been idle; and a superb fleet of thirty-four line-of-battle ships, and numerous frigates, under Lord Howe, lay at Portsmouth ready to sail to meet the enemy.

Besides fighting, the Admiral had, however, two important objects in view. One was to intercept a convoy of some three hundred and fifty merchant vessels coming from the ports of the United States, laden with provisions and the produce of the West India Islands for the supply of the people of France, who were threatened with starvation for the want of them; the other object was to see the British East and West India and Newfoundland convoys clear of the Channel, where they might be intercepted by French cruisers.

The Ruby was attached to Lord Howe's squadron. It was a magnificent sight, when, on the morning of the 2nd of May 1794, a fleet of one hundred and forty-eight sail collected at Saint Helen's, of which forty-nine were ships of war, weighed by signal, and with the wind at north-east, stood out from that well-known anchorage at the east end of the Isle of Wight, from which they were clear by noon. The weather was fine, the crews were in good discipline, the ships kept well together, and the men doubted not that they were able to fight and to conquer any foe they might encounter.

Never had Paul Pringle felt more proud of his country and his profession, as, walking the deck of the frigate, with True Blue at his side, he looked out at the numerous magnificent ships which glided proudly over the blue ocean.

"Look there, Billy—look there, my boy! Isn't that a sight to make a sailor's heart swell high with pride?" he exclaimed as he swept his arm round the horizon.

"It does, godfather—it does!" answered True Blue warmly. "And if I hadn't loved the sea and the life of a sailor better than anything else, I should have loved it now, I think."

"Right, boy—right!" exclaimed Paul. "It's the calling for a man—there's no doubt on't. Look there now at Earl Howe's ship, the Queen Charlotte, called after our own good Queen, with her hundred guns; and then the Royal George, with Admiral Sir Alexander Hood's flag, and the Royal Sovereign, which carries that of Admiral Graves, each with their hundred bulldogs; and the Barfleur, and the Impregnable. And the Queen, and the Glory, each of them not much smaller; and the Gibraltar, and the Caesar, of eighty guns each. And then look at that hoop of seventy-fours. There's the Billy Ruffian, and the Tremendous, and the Ramillies, and the Audacious, and the Leviathan, and Majestic, and the Orion, and Marlborough, and Brunswick, and Culloden—they'll make a noise in the world some day, and perhaps before long too."

"That's it, Paul," said True Blue, looking up at his godfather's face. "I like our ship, as you know right well, and every timber and plank in her; but I should like to be aboard one of those seventy-fours when the day of battle comes. We aboard the frigates shall see what is going on, but the fine fellows belonging to them will have the real work."

Paul glanced down approvingly at True Blue. "Never mind that, boy," he answered. "We have had our turn while the line-of-battle ships were in harbour doing nothing, and we shall have it again, no fear of that. Besides, d'ye see, the enemy have frigates, and we may pick out one of them to lay aboard; or what do you say when the Frenchmen take to flight, we may then go in chase of some of their ships, and, big as they are, make them haul down their colours."

"Ay, that's some consolation," answered True Blue. "Still, it is not like being in the middle of the fight—that you'll allow, godfather."

"No, True Blue, it is not, boy; but in the middle of the fight you see nothing often—only your own gun and the side of the enemy at which you are firing away," remarked Paul. "Now aboard a frigate we are outside of all, and can see all the movements of our ships as well as those of the enemy; and as to fighting, a frigate with a smart Captain gets twice as much of that as any line-of-battle ship; except, perhaps, three or four favourites of fortune, which somehow seem to be in at everything. Look now, there's Lord Howe signalling away, and Admiral Montague answering him."

The fleet was now off the Lizard. The signal was made for the different convoys to part company, and for Admiral Montague, with six seventy-fours and two frigates, to protect them as far as the latitude of Cape Finisterre. Away sailed the rich argosies, many of the Indiamen worth hundreds of thousands of pounds, and almost as large as the line-of-battle ships themselves. Extending far as the eye could reach, they covered the glittering ocean with their white canvas and shining hulls, their flags streaming out gaily to the breeze.

Lord Howe, with the remainder of the men-of-war, steered for Ushant, and, arriving there, sent some frigates to look into Brest, to ascertain if the French fleet was there. The frigates returned with the report that it was in the harbour, a large number of ships having been clearly seen. Lord Howe calculating the time that the expected convoy from America would probably arrive, steered straight on a course to intercept them. The line-of-battle ships had of necessity to keep together, in case of encountering an enemy's squadron; but the frigates were scattered far and wide; and True Blue had no reason to complain of want of employment, as night and day a sharp lookout was kept for a strange sail.

None, however, was seen, and once more the fleet returned to the neighbourhood of Brest. Two frigates, with two line-of-battle ships to support them, were now ordered to look once more into Brest harbour. On going in, they met with an American merchantman coming out, and, on a boat from the Leviathan boarding her, the master informed the officer in command that the French fleet had sailed some days before. This report was found to be correct, and the same evening the reconnoitring detachment rejoined the fleet.

Without loss of time, Lord Howe sailed in search of the French fleet. This consisted of some twenty-five ships of the line, and sixteen frigates or corvettes under the command of Admiral Villaret-Joyeuse, in the Montague, of 120 guns; besides this ship, considered so enormous in those days, there were three of 110 guns, and four eighty-gun ships, all the rest being seventy-fours. The first object of this fleet was to protect the expected convoy of provision ships, while that of the English was to capture it. The French Admiral steered, therefore, a direct course to the point where he hoped to intercept the convoy. His ships, indeed, passed so close to those of the British during a thick fog that they heard the usual fog-signals of the latter, such as the ringing of bells and beating of drums; but as their object was not then to fight, they did their best not to be discovered, and on the following morning, when the fog cleared, they were out of sight of each other.

Lord Howe had, however, determined to overtake and bring the Frenchmen to action; and as the ocean at that time was covered with vessels of all nations, playing somewhat a puss-in-the-corner game as they ran from port to port, he had every reason to expect that he would obtain the required information as to their movements.

On the evening of the 19th of May a frigate appeared, despatched by Admiral Montague, saying that, while cruising in the latitude of Cape Ortegal, he had captured a French twenty-gun ship and a corvette, with ten British sail of the Newfoundland convoy which they had taken; that, from the information he obtained from the prisoners, he found that the squadron protecting the American merchant fleet now consisted of nine line-of-battle ships and several frigates, and requesting, therefore, reinforcements. He was then, he stated, about to proceed along the same meridian of longitude to the latitude of 45 degrees 47 minutes north, in which, according to the information of the prisoners, the Rochefort squadron had been directed to cruise.

On learning this, Lord Howe, believing that Admiral Montague's squadron was in danger of being overpowered by Villaret, made all sail to his rescue.

On the 21st, however, the lookout gave notice of a strange fleet in sight. Chase was made, and ten out of fifteen sail of merchantmen—part of the Lisbon convoy captured by the Brest fleet—were retaken.

The vessels were burnt, as Lord Howe could not weaken his crews by sending them into port. From the prize crews taken in them, he learned that the French had prepared red-hot shot, and that the officers had determined to engage at close quarters. At the first piece of information the British seamen were inclined to laugh; and as to the second, though inclined to doubt it, they only hoped it might be true.

No sooner was the information received that the French fleet was so near, than Lord Howe abandoned his intention of joining Admiral Montague, whom he considered in safety, and stretched away to the northward and westward in daily expectation of coming up with the enemy.

All the information he gleaned confirmed Lord Howe in the opinion that he was but a short distance from the enemy. The morning of the 28th of May found the British fleet, with a strong wind at south by west and a heavy sea, formed in order of sailing, with the lookout frigates stationed around them. The Ruby was to windward, about one hundred and forty leagues west of Ushant, and True Blue was one of the lookouts. Great was his delight when at 6:30 a.m., he discovered a sail to the south-south-east, and scarcely had he hailed the deck with the information than he made out a strange fleet directly to windward.

"Hurrah! there is the enemy!" was the general cry throughout the British fleet.

Intense was the interest on board every English ship. In about two hours the French were seen bearing down in somewhat loose order; but when about ten miles off, they hauled their wind and began to form in order of battle.

The frigates were now for safety recalled, and the main body continued in the order of sailing, except the Bellerophon, Leviathan, Marlborough, Audacious, Russell, and Thunderer, which were a considerable distance in advance to windward, and were coming fast up with the enemy's rear. The ever-exciting signal of the whole fleet to chase and prepare for action was now thrown out from the Queen Charlotte. Every sail the ships could carry was immediately set, and away the whole fleet plunged through the rolling, tumbling sea in chase of the flying enemy. It was not, however, till towards the evening that Admiral Pasley, in the Bellerophon, closed with the rear ship of the enemy's line, a three-decker, on which he commenced a firm and resolute attack, supported occasionally by the ships in his division. The Bellerophon being soon disabled, fell to leeward; and just then the Audacious came up, and for two hours most gallantly engaged the Frenchman, which proved to be the Révolutionnaire of 110 guns. The enemy's mizen-mast falling overboard, and her lower yards and main-topsail-yard having been shot away, she fell athwart hawse of the Audacious. Getting clear, however, she put before the wind; nor was it in the power of the latter, from her own crippled condition, to follow her.

Still the French, though having the weather-gage, and therefore having it entirely in their power to engage, avoided an action. By the persevering efforts of some of the weathermost ships of the British, several of their ships most to leeward were compelled to fight. One of them indeed struck; but, a consort coming up and pouring a broadside into her as a gentle reminder of her duty she again hoisted her colours. The frigates meantime were hovering about, ready to obey any orders they might receive, their Captains and officers, as well as their crews, naturally severely criticising the movements of the two fleets, and jealous that they themselves were not permitted to take part in the now active work going on.

"That's always like them, Abel, isn't it?" exclaimed Paul Pringle as he watched the main body of the French fleet still keeping aloof. "It puts me just in mind of what they used to do in the West Indies. When they numbered twice as strong as we did, they would come down boldly enough; but when we showed our teeth and barked, they'd be about again, thinking that they would wait for a better opportunity."

"Ay, Paul, I mind it well. Even Billy here minds it, too, though he was a little chap then," answered Abel, placing his hand on the lad's shoulder. "And, True Blue, what's more, do you tell it to your children's children. Never mind how big may be the ships of the enemy, or how many guns they may carry, let British seamen when they meet them, as we do nowadays, feel sure that they will conquer, and I am very sure that conquer they will; ay, however the Frenchmen may bluster and boast of their mountain ships, just as the French Admiral does now."

"That's it, mate," chimed in Peter Ogle. "That's the way. Go at them. Show them that you know you are going to thrash them—stick to it. Never mind if you are getting the worst; be sure you'll be getting the better before long, and, as Abel was a-saying, so you will in the end."

"Right, right!" said Abel impressively. "Suppose now they were for to go for to cover up their ships with padding, or thick coats of wood or iron, just as men once had to do their bodies, I've heard tell, when they went to battle,—not that in the matter of ships it could be done on course, ha! ha! ha! but we never knows what vagaries the Monsieurs may try. Well, what should we do? Stand and play at long bowls with them? No, I should think not; but go at them, run them down, or lay them alongside just as we do now, and give them the taste of our cutlasses. They'll never stand them as long as there's muscle and bone in an Englishman's arm."

"Never did you say a truer word, Abel!" exclaimed Paul. "And mind you remember it, True Blue. But I say, mates, what's the Caesar about there? I've been watching her for some hours, and there she is still under treble-reefed topsails; and, instead of boldly standing up along the French line, she has been edging away, and now she's been and tacked as if she was afraid of the enemy. What can she be about? He's making the Frenchmen fancy that there is a British officer in this fleet who fears them. Oh, boys, for my part I would sooner be the cook than the Captain of that ship! But don't let's look at him; it makes my heart turn sick. Look instead at our brave old Admiral! He is a fine fellow. See, see! he has tacked. He doesn't care a rap for the Frenchman's fire. The Queen Charlotte must be getting it pretty warmly, though. There, he's standing right down, and he's going to break the French line. There's a broadside the old lady has poured into the quarter of one of those rear French ships. Now he luffs up right under her stern, and has repeated the dose. The Frenchman will not forget it in a hurry. There go the Billy Ruffian and the Leviathan. They'll cut off a couple of Frenchmen if they manage well. Hurrah! That's the way to go about the work. It cannot be long before our fine old chief makes the Frenchmen fight, whether they will or not."

Several other ships, besides those observed by Paul Pringle and True Blue, were hotly engaged during the course of that 29th of May, and lost a considerable number of officers and men.

Chapter Nineteen.

On the first of June 1794, the British fleet was steering to the westward with a moderate breeze, south by west, and a tolerably smooth sea. All night Lord Howe had carried a press of sail to keep up with the French fleet, which he rightly conjectured would be doing the same; and as he eagerly looked forth at early dawn, great was his satisfaction to descry them, about six miles off, on the starboard or lee bow of his fleet, still steering in line of battle on the larboard tack. His great fear had been that the French Admiral would weather on him and escape; now he felt sure that he had him.

At about 5 a.m. the ships of the British fleet bore up, steering first to the north-west, then to the north; and then again, having closed with the Frenchmen, they hauled their wind once more, and the Admiral, knowing that their crews had heavy work before them, ordered them to heave-to and to pipe to breakfast.

The frigates, the Ruby among them, and the smaller vessels brought up the rear. Exactly at twelve minutes past 8 a.m., Lord Howe made the looked-for signal for the fleet to fill and bear down on the enemy; then came one for each ship to steer for and independently engage the ship opposed to her in the enemy's line.

The British line was to windward, and Lord Howe wished that each ship should cut through the enemy's line astern of her proper opponent, and engage her to leeward.

Soon after 9 a.m. the French ships opened their fire on the advancing British line, which was warmly returned. The gallant old English Admiral set an example of bravery by steering for the stern of the largest French ship, the Montague, and passed between her and the Jacobin, almost running aboard the latter.

So energetically did the men labour at their guns, and so tremendous was the fire that they poured into both their opponents, that in less than an hour the Montague had her stern-frame and starboard quarter shattered to pieces, and a hundred killed and two hundred wounded. In this condition she was still able to make sail, which she did, as did also the Jacobin, the Queen Charlotte being too much disabled in her masts and rigging to follow.

Most of the other British ships were in the meantime hotly engaging those of the enemy. The Queen especially received a tremendous fire from several ships, and became so crippled that the Montague, after she had got clear of the Queen Charlotte, followed by several other ships, bore down to surround her.

Lord Howe, however, having once more made sail on his ship, wore round, followed by several other ships, to her rescue. The Montague, though she had suffered so much in her hull and had lost so many men, had her masts and rigging entire; and this enabled her to make sail ahead, followed by other ships which had in the same way escaped with their rigging uninjured. Twelve French ships, however, were by half-past eleven almost totally dismasted, while eleven of the British were in little better condition; but then the Frenchmen had suffered in addition far more severely in their hulls.

The proceedings of the line-of-battle ships had been viewed at a distance by the eager crew of the Ruby. As one ship after the other was dismasted, their enthusiasm knew no bounds.

"Oh, Paul, I wish I was there!" cried True Blue vehemently. "There!—there!—another Frenchman is getting it! Down comes her foremast!—see!—her mainmast and mizen-mast follow! Oh, what a crash there must be! That's the eighth Frenchman without a lower mast standing. Hurrah! we shall have them all!"

"Not quite so sure of that, boy," observed Peter Ogle, who had come upon the forecastle. "Two of our own ships, you see, are no better off; and several have lost their topmasts and topgallant-masts. Still they are right bravely doing their duty. I've never seen warmer work in my day. Have you, Paul?"

"No. With Lord Rodney we have had hot work enough; but the Frenchmen didn't fight as well as they do to-day, I must say that for them," observed Paul. "See now that Admiral of theirs; he is bearing down once more to help some of his disabled ships. See, his division seems to have four or five of them under their lee; but there are a good many more left to our share."

"Hurrah!" cried True Blue, who had been watching an action briskly carried on in another direction. "There's one more Frenchman will be ours before long. That's a tremendous drubbing the Brunswick has given her."

No ship's company displayed more determined gallantry during that eventful day than did the Brunswick, commanded by the brave Captain Harvey. Being prevented from passing between the Achille and Vengeur, in consequence of the latter shooting ahead and filling up the intervening space, she ran foul of the Vengeur, her own starboard anchors hooking on the Frenchman's larboard foreshrouds and fore-channels.

"Shall we cut away the anchor, sir?" inquired the master, Mr Stewart, of the Captain.

"No, no. We have got her, and we will keep her," replied Captain Harvey.

The two ships on this swung close to each other, and, paying off before the wind with their heads to the northward, with their yards squared, and with a considerable way on them, they speedily ran out of the line, commencing a furious engagement. The British crew, unable to open the eight lower-deck starboard ports from the third abaft, blew them off. The Vengeur's musketry, meantime, and her poop carronades, soon played havoc on the Brunswick's quarterdeck, killing several officers and men, and wounding others, among whom was Captain Harvey, three of his fingers being torn away by a musket-shot, though he refused to leave the deck.

For an hour and a half the gallant Brunswick carried on the desperate strife, the courage of her opponent's crew being equal to that of her own, when, at about 11 a.m., a French ship was discovered through the smoke, with her foremast only standing, bearing down on her larboard quarter, with her gangways and rigging crowded with men, prepared, it was evident, to board her, for the purpose of releasing the Vengeur. Instead of trembling at finding the number of their enemies doubled, the British seamen cheered, and the men stationed at the five aftermost lower-deck guns on the starboard side were turned over to those on the larboard side, on which the fresh enemy appeared. A double-headed shot was added to each of these guns, already loaded with a 32-pounder. The main and upper deck guns were already manned.

"Now, my lads," cried the officer, "fire high, and knock away her remaining mast!"

The stranger, which was the Achille, had now got within musket-shot, and wonderfully surprised were her crew at the hot fire with which they were received. Round after round from the after-guns were discharged in rapid succession, till, in a few minutes, down came the Frenchman's foremast, falling on the starboard side, where the wreck of the main and mizen-masts already lay, and preventing him making the slightest resistance. A few more rounds were given. They were not returned, and down came the Frenchman's colours, which had been hoisted on one of her remaining stumps. The Brunswick, however, was utterly unable to take possession, not having a boat that would swim, and being still hotly engaged with her opponent on the opposite side.

When the Frenchmen discovered this, they once more rehoisted their colours, and, setting a spritsail on the bowsprit, endeavoured to make off. The Brunswick, as they did so, gave them a parting dose; but it had not the effect of making them once more lower their colours. All this time, the crews stationed at the Brunswick's lower and main deck guns were heroically labouring away. Profiting by the rolling of the Vengeur, they frequently drove home the quoins and depressed the muzzles of the guns, which were loaded with two round-shot, and then before the next discharge withdrew the quoins and pointed the muzzles upwards, thus alternately firing into her opponent's bottom and ripping up her decks. While, however, they were hurling destruction into the side of the enemy below, the French musketry was sweeping the quarterdeck, forecastle, and poop, whence, in consequence, it was scarcely possible to work the guns. Several times, also, she had been on fire from the wadding which came blazing on board.

The brave Captain Harvey, on passing along the deck, was knocked down by a splinter; but, though seriously injured, he was quickly on his legs again encouraging his men. Soon afterwards, however, the crown of a double-headed shot, which had split, struck his right arm and shattered it to fragments. He fell into the arms of some of those standing round.

"Stay a moment before you take me below!" he exclaimed, believing that he was mortally wounded. "Persevere, my brave lads, in your duty. Continue the action with spirit, for the honour of our King and country; and remember my last word, 'The colours of the Brunswick shall never be struck!'"

Hearty shouts answered this heroic address, and the crew set to work with renewed energy to compel their opponents to succumb. Never, perhaps, however, were two braver men than the Captains of the Brunswick and Vengeur opposed to each other, and their spirits undoubtedly animated their crews. If the British had resolved to conquer, the French had determined not to yield as long as their ship remained afloat.

Still it appeared doubtful which would come off the victor. At this crisis, for an instant, as the smoke cleared off, another line-of-battle ship was seen approaching the Brunswick. If a Frenchman, all on board saw it would go hard with her. Still they determined not to disappoint their Captain's hopes, and to go down with their colours flying rather than strike.

The command had now devolved on Lieutenant Cracraft. For three hours the two ships had been locked in their fiery embrace, pounding away at each other with the most desperate fury, when, near 1 p.m., the Vengeur, tearing away the three anchors from the Brunswick's bow, rolled herself clear, and the two well-matched combatants separated.

The newcomer was seen to be the Ramillies, with her masts and spars still uninjured. Having, indeed, had but two seamen killed and seven wounded, she was quite a fresh ship. She, however, waited for the French ship to settle farther from the Brunswick, in order to have room to fire at her without injuring the latter. The brave crew of the Brunswick were, however, not idle even yet, and continued their fire so well-directed that they split the Vengeur's rudder and shattered her stern-post, besides making a large hole in her counter, through which they could see the water rushing furiously.

At this spot the Ramillies, now only forty yards distant, pointed her guns, and the Brunswick, still firing, in a few minutes reduced the brave Vengeur to a sinking state. Just then, it being seen from the Ramillies that the Achille was endeavouring to make her escape, all sail was made on her, and away she stood from the two exhausted combatants in chase of the fugitive, which she ultimately secured without opposition. Soon after 1 p.m., the two gallant opponents ceased firing at each other, and at the same time a Union-Jack was displayed over the quarter of the Frenchman as a token of submission and a desire to be relieved.

Not a boat, however, could be sent from the Brunswick, and in a few minutes her mizen-mast went by the board and made her still less able to render assistance. It made the hearts of the brave crew of the Brunswick bleed to think of the sad fate which awaited their late enemies, and which no exertion they had the power of making could avert.

Mr Cracraft now considered what was best to be done. The French Admiral Villaret was leading a fresh line on the starboard tack, to recover as many as he could of his dismasted ships; and the difficulty of the Brunswick was to rejoin her own fleet, without passing dangerously near that of the French, the loss of the mizen-mast and the wounded state of the other masts rendering it impossible to haul on a wind as was necessary. Accordingly, the head of the Brunswick was put to the northward for the purpose of making the best of her way into port, while all possible sail was made on her.

Sad was her state. Her mizen-mast was gone, and her two other masts and bowsprit were desperately wounded; her yards were shattered; all her running and most of her standing rigging was shot away, and her sails were in shreds and tatters. Twenty-three guns lay dismounted; her starboard quarter gallery had been carried away, and her best bower anchor with the starboard cathead was towing under her stem. Her brave Captain was mortally wounded, and she had three officers, eleven marines, and thirty seamen killed, and three officers, nineteen marines and ninety-one seamen wounded. The survivors immediately began to fish the masts, repair the damaged rigging, and to secure the lower-deck ports, through which the water was rushing at every roll. Her adventures were not over, though; for at 3 p.m., on her homeward course, she fell in with the Jemappes, wholly dismasted, and moved only by means of her spritsails. The Brunswick, which had received, early in the day, considerable annoyance from her, luffed up under her lee for the purpose of capturing her; but her crew displayed the Union-Jack over her quarter, and hailed that she had struck to the English Admiral, at the same time pointing at the

Queen, then some distance to the south. The assertion being credited, the Brunswick stood on, and happily reached Plymouth Sound in safety, where, on the 30th, her brave Captain, John Harvey, died.

Her gallant opponent, meantime, the Vengeur, soon after they parted, lost her wounded fore and main masts, the latter in its fall carrying away the head of the mizen-mast. Thus reduced to a complete wreck, she rolled her ports deeply in the water, and the lids of those on the larboard side having been torn or knocked off in her late engagement, she filled faster than ever. Hopeless seemed the fate of all on board. Her officers scarcely expected that she could float many hours, or indeed minutes, longer.

None of her own consorts could come to her assistance. Her boats were knocked to pieces; there was no time to construct a raft, and the sea was too rough to launch one. Her decks were covered with the dead and dying; her cockpit full of desperately wounded men, not less than two hundred in all. Discipline was at end. Many broke into the spirit-room. Many burst forth into wild Republican songs, and insisted on the tricoloured flag being again hoisted.

Their brave Captain looked on with grief and pain at what was going forward, and did his utmost to restore order. He had a young son with him—a gallant little fellow, who had stood unharmed by his side during the hottest of the fight; and was he now thus to perish? Could he save the boy? There seemed no hope.

Captain Garland had been aloft all day with his glass, as had also several of his officers, eagerly watching the proceedings of the two fleets. Never for a moment did he doubt on which side victory would drop her wreath of laurel; still his heart beat with an anxiety unusual for him. He had remarked the two ships remaining hotly engaged, yardarm to yardarm out of the line, and he had never lost sight of them altogether. What their condition would be after so desperate and lengthened an encounter he justly surmised, and he at length bore down to aid a friend in capturing an enemy, or to succour one or the other.

The Ruby had more than one ship to contend with on her way, and her boats were summoned by signal to take possession of a prize; so that the evening was drawing on when she, with another ship, and the Rattler cutter, got down to the sinking Frenchman.

Evidently, from the depth of the shattered seventy-four in the water, and the slow way in which she rolled, she had but a short time longer to float. The guns were secured, and every boat that could swim was instantly lowered from the sides of the British ships. The gallant seamen showed themselves as eager to save life as they had been to destroy it.

"Jump, jump, Jean Crapaud!—jump, jump, friends!" they shouted as they got alongside. "We'll catch you, never fear," they added, holding out their arms.

Numbers of Frenchmen, begrimed with powder and covered with blood, threw themselves headlong into the boats, and had it not been for the English seamen, would have been severely injured. Some refused to come, and looked through the ports, shouting, "Vive la Nation!", "Vive la République!"

"Poor fools!" cried Paul Pringle sadly; "they'll soon be singing a different tune when the water is closing over their heads. That will bring them too late to their senses."

The boats, as fast as their eager crews could urge them, went backwards and forwards between the sinking Frenchman and the English ships. Some hundreds had been taken off; but still the wounded and many of the drunken remained.

Sir Henry Elmore commanded one of the boats, and True Blue was in her. In one of her early trips an officer appeared at one of the ports, dragging forward a young midshipman.

"Monsieur," he said, hearing Sir Henry speak French, "I beg that you will take this brave boy in your boat. He wishes to be one of the last to leave the ship, and, as you see, we know not how soon she may go down, and he may be lost. He is our Captain's son, and where his father is I cannot say."

"Gladly—willingly," answered Sir Henry. "And you, my friend, come with the boy."

The lad showed signs of resistance; but True Blue sprang up into the port, aided by a boathook which he held, and, taking the lad round the waist, leaped with him into the boat. The officer refused to come, saying that he had duties to which he must attend; and the boat being now full, Sir Henry had to return to the frigate.

On hastening back to the ship, the officer again appeared. "I will accompany you now," he said, leaping in and taking his seat in the sternsheets. "But I have been searching in vain for our brave Captain Renaudin. What can have, become of him I do not know. If he is lost, it will break that poor boy's heart, they were so wrapped up in each other."

The boat, as he spoke, was rapidly filling with French seamen.

"Shove off! shove off!" cried Sir Henry energetically.

It was time, indeed. There was a general rush from all the decks and ports of the hapless Vengeur. Some threw themselves into the water, some headlong into the boats; others danced away, shouting as before; while one, more drunken or frantic than the rest, waved over her counter the tricoloured flag under which the ship had been so gallantly fought.

The boats shoved off and pulled away as fast as they could move; there was danger in delay. The men pulled for their lives. The ship gave a heavy lurch, the madmen shouted louder than ever; and then every voice was silent, and down she went like some huge monster beneath the waves, which speedily closed over the spot where she had been, not a human being floating upwards alive from her vast hull, now the tomb of nearly a third of her crew.

There were many other desperate encounters that day, but none so gallantly fought out to the death as that between the Brunswick and the Vengeur. Six line-of-battle ships were secured as prizes. The total loss of the French in killed, wounded, and prisoners was not less than 7000 men, of whom fully 3000 were killed.

The whole loss of the English on the 1st of June, and on the previous days, was 290 killed and 858 wounded. The French having suffered more in their hulls than in their masts and rigging, were able to manoeuvre better than the English; and Admiral Villaret, being content with having secured four of his ships, made no attempt to renew the battle, but under all the sail he could set, with the dismasted ships in tow, stood away to the northward, and by 6 p.m. was completely out of sight, a single frigate only remaining astern to reconnoitre.

Thus ended this celebrated sea-fight, chronicled in the naval annals of England as the glorious

First—1st of June. Its immediate results were in themselves not important; but it showed Englishmen what they were ready enough to believe, that they could thrash the Frenchmen as in days of yore; and it taught the French to dread the dogged resolution and stern courage of the English, and to be prepared to suffer defeat whenever they should meet on equal terms.

The news of the victory reached London on the 10th. So important was it considered, that Lord Chatham carried the account of it to the opera, and just after the second act it was made known to the house. A burst of transport interrupted the opera, and never was any scene of emotion so rapturous as the audience exhibited when the band struck up "Rule Britannia!" The same enthusiasm welcomed the news at the other theatres. The event was celebrated throughout the night by the ringing of bells and firing of cannon, and the next day at noon by the firing of the Park and Tower guns. For three successive evenings also the whole metropolis was illuminated.

A few days afterwards, the King himself, with the Queen and Royal Family, went to Portsmouth to visit the fleet. Lord Howe's flag was shifted to a frigate, and the royal standard was hoisted on board the Queen Charlotte. The whole garrison was under arms, and the concourse of people was immense. The King, with his own hand, carried a valuable diamond-hilted sword from the Commissioner's house down to the boat. As soon as His Majesty arrived on board the Queen Charlotte, with numbers of his ministers and nobles, and the officers of the fleet standing round on the quarterdeck, he presented the sword to Lord Howe, as a mark of his satisfaction and entire approbation of his conduct.

As their Majesties' barges passed, the crews cheered, the ships saluted, the bands played martial symphonies, and every sign of a general enthusiasm was exhibited.

The next day, the King gave audience to the officers of Lord Howe's fleet, and to the officers of the army and navy generally; and after their Majesties had dined at the Commissioner's house, they proceeded up the harbour to view the six French prizes which lay there at their moorings.

The primary object for which the fleet had put to sea was not accomplished; the great American convoy was not fallen in with, nor did Admiral Montague succeed in intercepting it, though he himself met Admiral Villaret's defeated Squadron, and might, had the French shown more courage, have been overpowered by it. He avoided an engagement and returned into port; and a day or two afterwards, the expected convoy appeared off the French coast, and gained a harbour in safety.

The Ruby had arrived with the rest of the fleet at Spithead. The seamen treated their prisoners with the greatest kindness and humanity; and even Paul Pringle declared that the Jean Crapauds were not after all such bad fellows, if you got them by themselves to talk to quietly.

Young Renaudin, the son of the brave Captain of the Vengeur, during their ten days' passage home, became a great pet among the officers and midshipmen. Still his spirits were very low, and he was very despondent, believing that his father was lost to him for ever. He had especially attached himself to Sir Henry Elmore and Johnny Nott, who, remembering their own preservation from foundering, had a fellow-feeling for him, and more especially looked after all his wants, while True Blue was appointed to attend on him.

The day after their arrival, Sir Henry got leave to go on shore and take their young prisoner, as well as Nott and True Blue, with him. Scarcely had they touched the point, than the boy sprang from the boat, and, breathless with excitement, rushed into the arms of a gentleman who had just landed with some English officers.

"Mon père! mon père!" exclaimed the boy.

"Mon fils! mon fils!" cried the gentleman, enclosing him in his arms and bursting into tears.

It was the gallant Captain of the Vengeur.

"Next to winning the battle, I would sooner have seen that meeting between the brave French Captain and his son than anything else I know of!" exclaimed True Blue as he recounted the adventure to Tim Fid, Harry Hartland, and other messmates on board the Ruby.

Chapter Twenty.

A considerable time had passed after that celebrated 1st of June, and the French had learned to suspect who were to be the masters at sea, whatever they might have thought of their own powers on shore, when a fine new corvette of eighteen guns, the Gannet, was standing across the British Channel on a cruise. Her master and commander was Captain Brine, long first lieutenant of the Ruby. Her first lieutenant was a very gallant officer, Mr Digby; and her second was Sir Henry Elmore, who was glad to go to sea again with his old friend Captain Brine. She had a boatswain, who had not long received his warrant for that rank, Paul Pringle by name; her gunner was Peter Ogle, and her carpenter Abel Bush; while one of her youngest though most active A,B,s was Billy True Blue Freeborn. She had a black cook too. He was not a very good one; but he played the fiddle, and that was considered to make amends for his want of skill.

"For why," he used to remark, "if my duff hard, I fiddle much; you dance de more, and den de duff go down—what more you want?"

True Blue's three godfathers had resolved to become warrant-officers if they could, and all had studied hard to pass their examinations, which they did in a very satisfactory way.

Their example was not lost upon True Blue. "I have never been sorry that I am not on the quarterdeck," said he one day to Paul. "But, godfather, I shall be if I cannot become a boatswain. That's what I am fitted for, and that's what my father would have wished me to be, I'm sure."

"That he would, Billy," answered Paul. "You see a boatswain's an officer and wears a uniform; and he's a seaman, too, so to speak, and that's what your father wished you to be; and I'll tell you what, godson, if some of these days, when you're old enough, you becomes a boatswain, and when the war's over you goes on shore and marries Mary Ogle, so that you'll have a home of your own when I am under hatches, that's all I wishes for you. It's the happiest lot for any man—a good wife, a snug little cottage, a garden to dig in, with a summer-house to smoke your pipe in, and maybe a berth in the dockyard, just to keep you employed and your legs going, is all a man like you or me can want for, and that is what I hope you may get."

Some young men would have turned the matter off with a laugh, but True Blue replied, "Ay, godfather, there isn't such a girl between the North Foreland and the Land's End so good and so pretty to my mind as Mary Ogle; and that I'll maintain, let others say what they will."

"True, boy, true!" cried Paul, slapping him affectionately on the shoulder. "You are right about Mary; and when a lad does like a girl, it's pleasant to see that he really does like her right heartily and honestly, and isn't ashamed of saying so."

The Gannet had altogether a picked crew, and Captain Brine was on the lookout to give them every opportunity of distinguishing themselves. There were, to be sure, some not quite equal to the rest. Tim Fid and Harry Hartland had joined with True Blue, and poor Gregory Gipples had managed still to hang on in the service, though, as his messmates observed, he was more suited to sweep the decks than to set the Thames on fire.

As yet the saucy little Gannet, as her crew delighted to call her, had done nothing particularly to boast of, except capturing and burning a few chasse-marées, looking into various holes and corners of the French coast, exchanging shots with small batteries here and there, and keeping the French coastguard in a very lively and active condition, never knowing when they might receive a nine-pound round-shot in the middle of one of their lookout towers, or be otherwise disturbed in their nocturnal slumbers.

Captain Brine was up the coast and down the coast in every direction; and if he could manage to appear at a point where the wind was least likely to allow him to be, by dint of slashing at it in the offing against a head wind, or by creeping in shore with short tacks, he was always more pleased and satisfied, and so were his crew.

The wind was north-east, the ship's head was south; it was in the month of March, and the weather not over balmy.

"A sail on the weather bow!" cried the lookout from the masthead.

"What is she like?" asked the second lieutenant, who had charge of the deck.

"She looms large, sir," was the answer.

The information was notified to the Captain, who was on deck in an instant.

Whether the stranger was friend or foe was the next question to be ascertained. Doubts were expressed as to that point both fore and aft. She was a frigate, that was very certain; still, without trying her with the private signal, Captain Brine did not like to haul his wind and make sail away from her. The nearer she drew, the more French she looked. Eighteen guns to thirty-eight or forty, which probably the stranger carried, was a greater disproportion than even the gallant Brine was inclined to encounter. All hands stood ready to make sail at an instant's notice.

At length the two ships drew almost near enough to exchange signals. "That ship is French, depend on it, sir!" exclaimed the first lieutenant to the Captain.

"I am not quite so certain of that, Digby," answered Captain Brine. "But if she is not an enemy, she is the Diamond frigate, commanded by Sir Sydney Smith. He has a wonderful knack of disguising his ship. I have known him to deceive the French themselves, and quietly to sail under a battery, look into a port, and be out again before he was suspected. He delights in such sort of work, and is not over bashful in describing afterwards what he has done. We shall soon, however, ascertain the truth. Try the stranger now with our private signals."

The flags were run up, and in a short time Sir Henry exclaimed, "You are right, sir! She replies, and makes the Diamond's number. There is another signal now. Sir Sydney orders us to close with him."

"I felt almost certain that it was the Diamond," said the Captain. "Well, gentlemen, I have no doubt that we shall soon have some work to do."

As soon as the corvette got within a short distance of the frigate, she hove to; and a boat being lowered, Captain Brine went on board to pay his respects to his superior officer. He, however, speedily returned.

"Sir Sydney proposes a cruise round the French coast together, which accords with our instructions," he said, addressing his two lieutenants, and the news soon spread through the ship.

Away the frigate and corvette sailed together, and soon fell in with a large lugger, to which they gave chase; but she turned out to be the Aristocrat, a hired vessel, fitted out by Government, and commanded by Lieutenant Gossett. Sir Sydney rubbed his hands.

"We could not be better off!" he exclaimed. "The Lion, Wolf, and Jackal all hunting in company."

Not many days had passed before a fleet of vessels was espied under the land, and evidently French. One was made out to be a corvette, and the others brigs, schooners, and luggers, which she was apparently convoying. Chase was instantly given, and the strangers made all sail to escape.

Away they went, close in with the shore, just as a herd of oxen run along a hedge looking for an opening into which to escape. At length the water shoaled so much that the frigate had to haul off. The corvette stood on a little longer, and had to do the same; while the lugger, running on still farther, signalled that all the enemy had run into a harbour under some high land which appeared to be surmounted with batteries.

Sir Sydney on this called the other two vessels near to him, and informed their commanders that he knew the place, and that he intended surveying the entrance, which he believed was deep enough for the frigate herself. The frigate and her consorts then stood off till the approach of evening, as if giving up the pursuit. As soon, however as it was dark, they once more approached the land.

All the night Sir Sydney and his lieutenants, and Captain Brine and his, were busily sounding the channel; but before daybreak the little squadron was too far from the land to seen from it. A favourable breeze carried them back, and without hesitating, they stood boldly on towards the mouth of the port. The entrance to it was guarded by two batteries one beyond the other, on the left hand, and by several guns posted on a commanding point which it was necessary to round before the harbour could be entered. For the forts Sir Sydney was prepared, as he knew of their existence; and he had directed four of his own boats, with three from the corvette and one from the lugger, to attack and carry them in succession.

Mr Digby, from a wound in his right arm, which prevented him from using it, was unable to go; and so Sir Henry Elmore had command of the Gannet's boats, and True Blue went in his boat as his coxswain, Mr Nott, now a mate, accompanying him. Paul Pringle, the boatswain, had command of another boat, and a mate and midshipman of the Gannet had charge of the other two. The whole expedition was under the command of the first lieutenant of the frigate, who was accompanied by a lieutenant and the marines of the two ships. As soon as the frigate and corvette got within range of the guns on the point, the latter opened a hot fire on them; but so well did the ships ply theirs in return as they passed that the gunners were speedily driven from them.

On rounding the point, however, the vessels became exposed to a severe fire from the two batteries. A considerable tide was running out, and Sir Sydney saw, as he expected, that the ships might suffer a severe loss before they could be passed, unless the batteries could be silenced. The order was therefore given for the boats to be lowered, and instantly to shove off. Away they dashed with loud cheers. The French troops, not expecting such a mode of attack, hurried down from their batteries to oppose them on the beach. This was just what Sir Sydney wished, as it enabled the ships to creep up without being fired at.

The boats, as they advanced, were so warmly received by the troops on the beach that they could not effect a landing at the spot proposed. True Blue's quick eye, however, observed what he thought looked like a landing-place, close under the nearest fort. He pointed it out to Sir Henry, who, calling the boats nearest to him to follow, dashed on towards it. The first lieutenant of the Diamond meantime so entirely kept the troops on the beach employed, that no one saw what was occurring.

In another minute Sir Henry and his followers were on shore. True Blue was next to him, carrying the flag. A rocky height, almost a precipice, had to be climbed to reach the fort. Up they all went at once, like goats, making violent springs, or climbing up with hands and knees. True Blue was one of the first, helping up Sir Henry, whose strength was often not equal to his spirit.

When the English were half way up, the French caught sight of them, and now the whole body hurried along the road to regain the fort. It was a desperate race between the two parties. The English had a short but rugged height to scale, the French a longer but smoother path to traverse. The frigate's boats however, by a well-directed fire, assisted to impede their progress, and to thin their numbers as they went. On sprang the daring seamen. True Blue was the first over the parapet and into the fort. Sir Henry followed close to him. The French were almost at the gate, which was left open.

"Here, Freeborn!" he exclaimed; "this gun, slew it round and give it to them. It is loaded and primed—see!"

The gun which Sir Henry touched was a field-piece, evidently brought for the occasion into the fort. Several seamen assembling, the gun was instantly got round, and as the leading body of French appeared, True Blue pointing it, fired it directly in their faces; then with a loud shout drawing his cutlass, he and Sir Henry rushed furiously at them, followed by most of the men. So unexpected was the assault that the leading files gave way, and, pressing on the others, hurried down the narrow path. Sir Henry calling back his companions, they re-entered the fort.

The gate was then shut, lest the enemy should return, and all the guns were immediately spiked. The commander of the expedition, and the lieutenant of marines and his men, had in the meantime come round and gained the height, in spite of a heavy flank fire from the French. Several of the guns were now, besides being spiked, tumbled down the precipice, and a considerable amount of destruction effected in the fort.

The French, however, were now collecting in stronger force, and the work on which the party were sent being accomplished, a return to the ships became necessary. The officer in command, seeing that, if they attempted to return by the steep way they ascended, they might be shot down in detail, resolved to make a bold dash and cut his way back to the boats, which had been compelled to return under shelter of the ships. The plan suited the spirits of the men. The gate was thrown open. Out of the fort they dashed, and down the hill at a double quick march. They had not got far before they encountered a large body of French, who attempted to oppose them; but the enemy, though double their number, could no more withstand their headlong charge than does the wooden village the force of the avalanche. Down before them went the Frenchmen, scattered right and left; but some got up, and others came on, and the English found themselves nearly surrounded, while a considerable body, remaining at a distance, kept up a hot and galling fire, which brought down several of the bold invaders.

Pistols were flashing, cutlasses were clashing, and the marines were charging here and there with their bayonets, keeping the French back while they retired towards the water, when another large body of French was seen coming over the hill. Their friends below saw them also, and now all uniting made a furious onslaught on the French.

"Charge them, my lads, and drive them back, or they will not let us embark quietly!" shouted the Diamond's lieutenant.

Sir Henry Elmore with a number of followers, carried on by his ardour, went farther than was necessary, when a shot from a distance brought him to the ground.

At that moment the retreat was sounded, for the fresh body of French was coming on. True Blue had two stout Frenchmen to attend to, and had just disabled one and driven the other back when he saw what had occurred. Sir Henry's followers were almost overpowered and retreating. True Blue saw that he would be made prisoner or killed, and that not a moment should be lost if he was to be rescued. "Back lads, and help our officer!" he shouted, springing desperately onward.

Several of the corvette's crew, headed by Tom Marline, followed him, Tom shouting, "Hurrah, lads, hurrah! We mustn't let our True Blue be made prisoner."

The French, who had already had a sufficient taste of the English seamen's quality, hurriedly retreated for a few yards, keeping up, however, a galling fire. They then waited till the reinforcement came up, and left Elmore unmolested. This gave time to True Blue to spring forward and lift him in his arms, and to run back with him through showers of bullets among his shipmates before the enemy could recover their prisoner.

Sir Henry, though suffering great pain, was perfectly conscious. "Thanks, my brave friend— thanks Freeborn!" he exclaimed; "you've again saved me from worse than death. But now, my lads, back to our boats; we shall do nothing now, I fear."

The boats only just then reached the beach, and True Blue had but bare time to spring with his charge into the first, which proved to be their own, when the French troops came charging down upon them. The last man to leave the beach was the officer of marines, who, like a true soldier, retreated with his face to the foe amidst thick showers of bullets. He had just stepped into one of the boats, when he fell back into the arms of the Captain with a cry, shot through the body. He was lifted up and placed in the sternsheets.

"Shove off! shove off!" cried the officer.

The sailors shoved away with their oars, while the marines stood up with their muskets, returning the fire of the enemy, desirous to punish them for the loss of their officer. One marine and two seamen had fallen, and several men were wounded. In another minute they would with difficulty have got off, for, in the rear of the reinforcement, there came rattling along two small field-pieces.

The boats were afloat, the men pulled away with all their might and were soon on board the ships. True Blue would allow no one but himself to carry the young lieutenant below to his cabin. Of course he had to return to his duty on deck, for there was hot work going on; but he stood anxiously waiting till he could hear the surgeon's report.

"Ah, mates!" he said to Fid and Hartland, and other friends stationed near him, "if you had seen, as I have, young Sir Henry at home, and how her ladyship, his mother, and sisters loved him and made much of him, you would understand what a killing blow it would be to them if they heard that he was dead or even hurt. I'd rather lose my own right arm any day, and my life too, than have them hear such a tale."

As soon as the boats returned, the fire from the frigate and corvette knocked over the two field-pieces and several of the men who served them, and the ships then proceeded up the harbour. The French troops, as they did so, followed them along the shore, keeping, however, as well as they could, concealed behind the inequalities of the ground, and only occasionally halting and firing rapid volleys at them.

The corvette, and several brigs and schooners, and three armed luggers, were soon seen either at anchor close to the beach or on shore. The frigate could not venture to close with them, but the gallant little Gannet, with the lead going, stood on till she had scarcely a foot of water under her keel, and then, dropping an anchor with a spring to the cable, so as to keep her broadside to the corvette, opened her fire.

The Frenchmen replied briskly enough at first; but as they occasionally got a dose from the frigate's long guns, they gradually slackened in their efforts to defend their ships, and finally were seen taking to their boats and escaping on shore. Mr Nott instantly volunteered to board and set fire to the corvette. He beckoned to True Blue, who flew to the boats, which had been kept ready on the side of the ship away from the shore. Within a minute, two boats were pulling under a hot fire towards the French ship. True Blue and his companions speedily climbed through her ports both fore and aft. They had brought abundance of combustibles. These were instantly carried below, and, the most inflammable materials being thrown together in piles along her lower deck, were set on fire. The thick wreaths of smoke which ascended assisted to conceal the party in their rapid retreat, the more rapid as they could not tell at what moment a spark might enter the magazine and blow them all into the air.

Back they pulled, and were on board the Gannet once more, within five minutes after they had left her side, not a man having been hurt, and the work so thoroughly accomplished that the corvette was in a furious blaze fore and aft, the flames already licking the heels of her topmasts in their upward ascent.

All this time, the frigate astern and the lugger ahead of the Gannet were keeping up a warm fire on the shore, to hold the troops in check. They wisely concealed themselves when no boats appeared; but as the various merchantmen, one after the other, were attacked by the boats of the squadron, they sallied bravely out, and endeavoured to drive back their assailants. In vain, however, they made the attempt; the British seamen persevered, and before the evening every vessel in the harbour was destroyed.

Not a moment had honest True Blue been idle, from the time that the boats had been first sent away till dark; nor had he had an opportunity of inquiring after the second lieutenant. At length the surgeon came on deck to take a breath of fresh air. True Blue stepped up to him, and, touching his hat, inquired after Sir Henry.

"Hurt very badly, my lad," answered the surgeon, "and, I am very much afraid, will slip through our fingers; but do not let that vex you. He has told me of the gallant way in which you brought him off from the enemy; and his great anxiety seems to be, that your interest should be cared for—that you should be rewarded."

"Rewarded, sir!" exclaimed True Blue in a tone of indignation and sorrow. "Oh, sir, I don't want any reward. Sir Henry knows that I would go through fire and water to serve him, that I would sooner have lost my own right arm or my life than that he should be hurt. Do tell him, sir, that I am unhappy when I hear about a reward. I shall be joyful, indeed, if he gets round again, and be able to go to his duty."

"All right, my lad, I will tell him; and I hope he may recover, and settle the matter with you in your own way."

"I hope so, sir—I hope so," said True Blue; but he felt very sad about what he had heard.

This conversation took place during a short cessation of firing, when, for some reason not ascertained, the French troops retreated. They now came back with more field-pieces, and opened on the ships. Happily the ebb just then made, and a light breeze sprang up and blew down the harbour. A fire was kept up from the ships, however, all the time, while their anchors were weighed, and their topsails being sheeted home, they stood out of the harbour. Still the shot followed them. They had got some way when True Blue felt himself struck to the deck. He lay some little time before being observed in the dark, and then he was carried below. He knew no more, till he heard a voice in a tone of deep grief saying, "Oh, doctor, is he killed?"

It was that of Paul Pringle.

"I hope not, boatswain," was the answer. "I have extracted the bullet, which was pretty deep in; and I trust he may do well."

Chapter Twenty One.

As True Blue lay wounded in his hammock, he made daily, almost hourly, inquiries after Sir Henry; and nothing seemed to expedite his own recovery so much as hearing that the lieutenant was considered out of danger.

The Gannet still continued in company with the Diamond, and True Blue's chief unhappiness arose at not being allowed to join the various cutting-out expeditions in which the crews of the two ships were engaged.

At length, by the time that they once more stood up channel, both Sir Henry and True Blue were sufficiently recovered to go on deck, the lieutenant being almost fit to do some duty, though the latter was not allowed to exert himself.

Sir Sydney had invited the young lieutenant to spend a day or two on board the frigate, as he said, for change of air; and Sir Henry got leave for True Blue to accompany him, for the purpose, in reality, of making him known to one who, brave himself, could so well appreciate bravery in others, and who, if he had the will, would probably have the means of forwarding the young seaman's interests.

Soon after this, in a thick fog, the frigate parted company with the corvette. The Diamond had taken a number of prizes, and sent them away under the command of various officers, so that she had very few left. Sir Sydney had intended to go the next day into Portsmouth to pick them up, when he fell in with a schooner making for the French coast, which turned out to be a prize to a French privateer lugger, the Vengeur, known to have taken a number of prizes.

From the prisoners, Sir Sydney learned that she had the character of being very fast, that she was armed with ten nine-pounders, that her commander was a very enterprising character himself, and that she had been in vain chased on several occasions by British cruisers.

"Then we must put a stop to this gentleman's proceedings!" exclaimed Sir Sydney. "We may not gain much glory, but we shall be doing good service to the commerce of our country; and that, after all, is our duty, and I take it we could not be engaged in more honourable work than in the performance of our duty."

"Certainly not, sir," warmly responded the young lieutenant, his guest; "and, if you will give me leave, I will accompany you. I am quite able to endure fatigue, and will take my young shipmate, True Blue Freeborn, with me, of whom I spoke to you—a gallant fellow, who has twice saved my life."

Sir Sydney, who delighted in the sort of spirit exhibited by the young lieutenant, at once acceded to his wishes, and arranged that he should have charge of one of the boats. The frigate stood in, and soon discovered the lugger at anchor in the outer roads. The first lieutenant was on shore in England, the second was very ill, and the third lay in his berth severely wounded; so Sir Sydney gave notice that he himself would take command of the expedition.

The information was received with infinite satisfaction on board, because, in the first place, it seemed certain that there was some dashing work to be done; and, in the second, it was believed that, in whatever the Captain engaged, he succeeded. The necessary preparations were rapidly carried out. An eighteen-pounder carronade was mounted in the frigate launch, and her crew were also armed with muskets; three other boats were armed with smaller guns on swivels, and muskets; and one with muskets only—a wherry, pulling two oars.

Everything was ready by ten o'clock at night, when Sir Sydney Smith pushed off from the frigate, taking the lead of the other boats in his wherry. In perfect silence they pulled away, till through the darkness they perceived the lugger ahead of them. The crews now lay on their oars, while their Captain, in a clear, distinct voice, issued his definite orders.

"Understand, my lads, we must not alarm the enemy sooner than we can help. Give her a wide berth, therefore, and get between her and the shore, so that those on board, if they see us, may fancy that we are fishing-boats dropping out of the harbour. Then pull directly for the lugger, and be on board her as soon as possible."

No further words were spoken. When they had got to the position indicated, no apparent notice was taken of them, and they hoped to get close alongside undiscovered.

"Pass the word along to the men to reserve their fire till the Frenchmen open theirs," said the Captain, who continued ahead. "Now, my lads, pull straight for her."

Away dashed the boats as fast as their crews could urge them. The Frenchmen were all asleep, or the watch on deck had not made them out. When, however, about a musket-shot off, lights were seen, and there was a considerable bustle on deck, and hallooing and shouting. On they dashed; they had got within half pistol-shot of the lugger, when a volley was let fly amongst them. As usual, the dose, instead of checking their progress, only stimulated them to greater exertions. The marines and small-arm men returned the fire in right good earnest, while the boats advanced more rapidly than before.

The Frenchmen had been taken by surprise: they had barely time to load their guns. As they had not pointed them precisely, most of their shot flew over the heads of their opponents, and there had been no time to trice up the boarding nettings. The British were therefore soon alongside; a fierce hand-to-hand conflict commenced with pistols, boarding-pikes, and cutlasses, and the gallant assailants began to climb over her low bulwarks and furiously to attack the enemy with cutlass and pistol. The French crew, though far outnumbering the British, could not withstand the desperate onslaught.

Sir Sydney Smith was one of the first on board. True Blue, cutlass in hand, leaped over the bulwarks at the same moment from another boat, with Sir Henry Elmore. There was a rapid mingling of shouts and cheers and cries, and rattling of musketry, and the crack of pistols and clashing of cutlasses and then the privateer's men gave way, leaped down below, and cried for quarter. It was given, and the prisoners were at once secured.

Scarcely was this done, when True Blue, who was forward, discovered that the cable was cut, and that the vessel was drifting with the tide, now making strong up the river, rapidly towards the shore. He reported this to Sir Sydney, who instantly ordered the boats to go ahead and tow her away. Meantime, search was made for an anchor to hold the vessel against the tide making up the Seine, every instant apparently increasing in strength.

"Here's a small kedge, sir!" cried True Blue, who, one of the most active, was searching away in the forehold. "It will be of little service, I fear, though."

"Get it bent on. We will try what our canvas will do first," answered the Captain.

Every stitch of sail the lugger could carry was set on her; but still the breeze refused to blow with sufficient strength to enable her to stem the tide, even with all the boats towing ahead. The kedge was therefore let go, but though it somewhat stopped her way, still she dragged it rapidly on. Higher and higher she drifted up the Seine, till at length she brought up off Harfleur, on the northern bank of the river, two miles above Havre.

It seemed as if nothing more could now be done.

"I ought to return to the frigate," said the Captain, "Sir Henry, you will accompany me. Mr Wright, you will get under weigh the instant the tide slackens or a breeze springs up, and run out to us."

Sir Henry begged that he might remain on board the lugger and share the risk with the rest, though it was not without considerable reluctance that Sir Sydney consented to leave him. Sir Sydney then pulled off in his small boat for the frigate.

Daylight was now coming on, and by its means several boats were seen coming down the Seine, evidently with the intention of trying to recapture the Vengeur. At the same time, however, a small boat was observed approaching from the frigate, and soon afterwards Sir Sydney Smith himself stepped on board.

"My lads," he said, "I believe that we shall have to fight for our prize, and I have returned to lend a hand in defending her. However, we have more boats and people than are required. Sir Henry Elmore, I must beg you to undertake the charge of landing the prisoners at Honfleur, on the southern bank of the river, in the launch and pinnace, and then return to the Diamond. These are my orders. We must first, however, make the Frenchmen give us their parole not in any way to interfere in whatever takes place. I propose fighting the lugger under weigh, till the breeze and ebb tide enable us to carry her out. The tide will soon make, and I hope to be alongside the frigate in an hour or little more."

Very unwillingly Sir Henry quitted his gallant chief and friend, taking, of course, True Blue with him.

It was now broad daylight, and all the glasses of the frigate were turned towards the Vengeur. Another large lugger as big as herself was seen approaching her. She got under weigh, and a warm action began.

"She is giving it her!—she is giving it her!" shouted True Blue. "Sir Sydney will beat him, I am certain."

So it seemed probable by the gallant way in which the Vengeur met her approach. The latter was soon seen to sheer off and drop up the river again, evidently having had fighting enough. Most anxiously a breeze was looked-for.

Though victorious in this instance, the prize was even in a more perilous position than before, having drifted still more up the river, and numerous boats being seen in the distance approaching her. Down they came, their numbers rapidly increasing. Now she opened her fire right and left upon them. They returned it with heavy discharges of musketry, till she was completely surrounded by smoke, an evidence also that she had no breeze to assist her in manoeuvring.

Farther and farther off she drifted, till, with hearts foreboding evil, the spectators on board the Diamond lost sight of her in the distance, surrounded by smoke. In vain they waited. The day wore on; there was not a sign of their gallant Captain and his brave followers, and at length it became too certain that they must have been taken prisoners by the French.

A strong breeze now sprang up. After waiting off the port all the night, the Diamond ran across the Channel, and anchored at Spithead, with the intelligence of Sir Sydney Smith's capture. The Gannet had not yet appeared, and True Blue, as well as Sir Henry, began to be anxious, fearing that some mishap might have befallen her.

Two days passed by. On the third, True Blue was looking out to the south-east, when he espied two ships standing in towards the anchorage. He looked and looked again. One was, he thought, and yet doubted, the Gannet, so different did she look to the trim and gallant little ship she had but lately been; the other was a craft much of her size, with the English ensign flying over the tricolour of France. The first soon made her number, and left no doubt as to her being the Gannet.

An action, and a well-fought one, had evidently taken place, and the corvette had brought in her captured prize; but then came the question, who among shipmates and friends had suffered? True Blue could not help thinking of Paul Pringle, whom he loved with an affection which could not have been surpassed had Paul been his father, and Peter Ogle, and Abel Bush, and his own messmates. Had any of them been killed or hurt?

He knew that Sir Henry, who had remained doing duty on board the Diamond, would feel somewhat as he did; so he went to him, and Sir Henry gratified him by saying that he would at once make arrangements for returning to the corvette the instant she anchored. A boat was got ready, and away they pulled for her. They were on board almost as soon as the anchor was dropped.

True Blue glanced eagerly forward. Paul Pringle was on the forecastle, call in mouth, issuing the necessary orders for furling sails. Peter Ogle was not to be seen, nor was Abel Bush, but they might be about some duty below; nor were Tim Fid nor Gregory Gipples visible, though they ought to have been on deck.

Having reported himself as come on board with Sir Henry to the first lieutenant, who was near the gangway, he dived below. Numerous hammocks slung up forward showed that there were many sick or wounded, while groups of Frenchmen, with sentries over them, proved that a prize had been taken.

He first hurried to the gunner's cabin. The door was closed—he knocked—there was no answer—his heart sank within him—his thoughts flew to Mary and her mother. Could Peter Ogle be among the killed in the late action? He dared not ask; he opened the door and looked in. The cabin was empty. He went next to that of Abel Bush.

"Come in," said the carpenter in a weak voice, very unlike his usual sturdy bass. "True Blue, is it you, my lad? Right glad to see you!" he exclaimed in a more cheerful tone. "Well, we have had a warm brush. Only sorry you were not with us; but we took her, as you see, though we had a hard struggle for it. Do you know, Billy, these Frenchmen do fight well sometimes. They've given me an ugly knock in the ribs; but the doctor says I shall be all to rights soon, so no matter. I don't want to be laid up in ordinary yet. Time enough when I am as old as Lord Howe. He keeps afloat; so may I for twenty years to come yet, I hope."

Thus he ran on. He was evidently feverish from his wound.

"But oh, Abel, where is Peter Ogle?" exclaimed True Blue, interrupting him at length.

"Peter?—oh, aboard the prize!" answered Abel. "Where did you think he was?"

"All right," replied True Blue.

In the evening, both ships went into the harbour to be refitted, an operation which, from the battered condition of the corvette and her prize, would evidently take some time.

Scarcely was the ship moored, when Sir Henry sent for True Blue, and told him that, on account of his having been wounded, he had obtained leave for him to have a run on shore, and that if he liked he would take him up to London with him, and let him see more of the wonders of the great metropolis.

The colour came to the young sailor's cheeks. "Thank you, Sir Henry—thank you," he answered; "but to be honest, I'd as lief go to my friends at Emsworth, you see, sir. They know me, and I know them; and though I should like to see her ladyship and the young ladies,—indeed I should,—there's Mary Ogle, Peter Ogle's daughter; and the truth is, we've come to understand each other, and talk of splicing one of these days, when I'm a bo'sun perhaps, or maybe before that. If you saw Mary, sir, I'm sure you wouldn't be offended at my wishing to go down there rather than go up to big London with you, sir. But you'll give, I hope, my dutiful respect to your mother, sir, and the young ladies, and tell them it's not for want of love and duty to them that I don't come."

"I am sure that they will think everything right of you, Freeborn," answered the young baronet, struck by True Blue's truthful frankness. "But instead of being a boatswain, why not aim at being placed, as I long ago wished, on the quarterdeck? Surely it would please your Mary more, and I daresay my friends would accomplish it for you."

"Thank you, Sir Henry—thank you. I've thought the matter over scores of times, and never thought differently," answered True Blue with a thoughtful look. "And do you know, sir, I'm sure that Mary wouldn't love me a bit the more because I was a Captain, than she does now, or than she will when I am a bo'sun. She isn't a lady, and doesn't set up for a lady; and why should she? I couldn't love her a bit the more than I now do if she did. You see, Sir Henry, she's a right true honest good girl, and what more can a man like me want in the world to make him happy?"

"You are right, Freeborn—you are right!" exclaimed the young baronet, springing up and taking his friend's hand; "and I wish you every happiness your Mary can give you. Remember, too, if I am in England, invite me to your wedding, and I'll do my utmost to come to it. I have not often been at a wedding, and never thought of marrying; but I am very sure that somehow or other you will set me on the right course, by the pleasure I shall experience on that occasion."

The next day, while Sir Henry went up to London, True Blue started off by himself to Emsworth, his godfather having too much to do in refitting the ship to be spared away from her.

He had not given notice that he was coming, and the cry of pleasure with which he was received when his smiling countenance appeared at Peter Ogle's cottage door showed him that he might depend on a hearty welcome.

A fair girl, with the sweetest of faces, rose from her seat, and, running towards him, put out both her hands, and did not seem overwhelmed with astonishment when he threw an arm round her waist and kissed her heartily.

"Hillo, Master True Blue, are those the manners you have learned at sea?" exclaimed Mrs Ogle, not very angrily, though.

"Yes, mother," answered Billy, laughing, and still holding Mary by the hand and looking into her face. "It's the way I behaved scores of times whenever I've thought of the only girl I ever loved; and now, though I didn't intend to do it, I couldn't help it—indeed I couldn't. I hope you'll forgive me, Mrs Ogle, if Mary does."

"Well, Billy, as my goodman has known you since you were a baby, and I've known you nearly as long, I suppose I must overlook it this time," answered Mrs Ogle. "And now tell me, how is my husband, and Pringle, and the rest?"

"Ogle and Pringle are very well; but Abel Bush has had an ugly knock on his side. It will grieve poor Mrs Bush, I know, when I tell her. He'll be here as soon as he is out of hospital; but he wants to be aboard again when the ship is ready for sea."

Good Mrs Ogle, on hearing this, said that she would go in and prepare her neighbour for the news of Abel being wounded; and after she had done so, True Blue went and told her all the particulars, and comforted her to the best of his power; and then he hurried off to see old Mrs Pringle, who forgave him for not coming first to her, which he ought to have done.

The hours of True Blue's short stay flew quickly by—quicker by far than he wished. Never had the country to his eyes looked so beautiful, the meadows so green, the woods so fresh, and the flowers so bright; never had the birds seemed to sing so sweetly; and never had he watched with so much pleasure the sheep feeding on the distant downs, or the cattle come trooping in to their homesteads in the evening.

"After all, Mary," he said, "I really do think there are more things on shore worth looking at than I once fancied. Once I used to think that the sea was the only place fit for a man to live on, and now, though I don't like it less than I did, I do love the look of this place at all events."

Mary smiled. They were sitting on a mossy bank on the hillside, with green fields before them and a wood on the right, in which the leaves were bursting forth fresh and bright, and a wide piece of water some hundred yards below, in which several wild fowl were dipping their wings; while beyond rose a range of smooth downs, the intermediate space being sprinkled over with neat farmhouses and labourers' cottages; and rising above the trees appeared the grey, ivy-covered tower of the parish church, with the taper spire pointing upwards to the clear blue sky—not more clear or bright, though, than his Mary's eyes; so True Blue thought, whether he said it or not.

"Yes," said Mary; "I am sure, True Blue, when you come to know more of dear Old England, you'll love it as I do."

"I love it now, Mary—that I do, and everything in it for your sake, Mary, and its own sake!" exclaimed True Blue enthusiastically. "I used to think only of fighting for the King, God bless him; but now, though I won't fight the less for him than I did, I'll fight for Old England, and for you too, Mary; and not the worse either, because I shall be thinking of you, and of how I shall hope some day to come and live on shore with you, and perhaps go no more to sea."

Mary returned the pressure of his honest hand, and in the wide realms of England no two people were happier than they were; for they were faithful, guileless, and true, honest and virtuous, and no shadow cast by a thought of future misfortune crossed their path.

Thus the days sped on. Then a letter came from Sir Henry, saying that he had obtained another fortnight's leave for True Blue; and the different families looked forward to a visit from the three warrant-officers of the Gannet, and felt how proud they should be at seeing them in their uniforms. Abel Bush was so far recovered that he was expected in a day or two.

Such was the state of affairs, when one evening True Blue heard that an old shipmate of his in the Ruby was ill at a little public-house about three miles off, nearer the sea; so he at once set off to visit him, intending to bring him up to Mrs Pringle's, if he was able to be removed, for he was a favourite and friend of Paul's.

When he got there, he found a good many men in the house, mostly seamen, drinking and smoking in the bar. However, he passed on, and went up into the room where his old shipmate was in bed. He sat talking to him for some time, and then he gave him Mrs Pringle's message, and told him that, as she had a spare room, he must come up there and stay till he was well. He had arranged to return with a cart the next morning, and had bid his friend good-bye, when, as he was on his way down the dark narrow stairs, he heard the door burst open, and a tremendous scuffle, and shouts, and oaths, and cries, and tables and chairs and benches upset, and blows rapidly dealt.

He had little doubt that a pressgang had broken into the house, and, though they lawfully couldn't touch him, he instinctively hurried back into his friend's room, knowing how unscrupulous many people, when thus engaged, were, and that if they got hold of him he would have no little difficulty in escaping from their clutches.

His friend, Ned Archer, thought the same. "Here, Billy," he exclaimed, "jump out of the window! I will shut it after you, and you will be free of these fellows."

There was not a moment to be lost. True Blue threw open the casement, and dropped to the ground. It was a good height; but to an active lad like him the fall was nothing, and he would have made no noise had not a tin pan been set up against the wall. He kicked it over, and, as he was running off, he found himself collared by three stout fellows, drawn to the spot by the clatter it made.

"You'll have to serve His Majesty, my lad—that's all; so be quiet," said one of the men, for True Blue very naturally could not help trying to escape.

"I have served His Majesty long and faithfully, and hope before long to be serving him again afloat," answered True Blue. "But just hands off, mates. You've got hold of a wrong bird. I belong to a sloop of war, the Gannet, and am away from her on leave."

"A likely story, my lad," said the officer commanding the pressgang, who just then came up. "You are fair-spoken enough; but men with protections don't jump out of windows and try to make off at the sight of a pressgang. Whether you've served His Majesty or not, you'll come along with us and serve him now—that's all I've to say on the subject."

The officer would not listen to a word True Blue had to plead, but with eight or nine other men, captured at the same time, he was forthwith marched down in the direction of the Hamble river.

It was a long tramp, and True Blue often looked round for an opportunity of escaping; but his captors were vigilant, and there seemed but little chance of his getting away. Never had he felt so anxious, and, as he expressed his feelings, downhearted, not for himself,—he believed that all would come right at last, as far as he was concerned,—but for those he left behind him. He thought how anxious and grieved Mary would be when he did not return; and though he was aware that ultimately she would ascertain that he had been carried off by a pressgang, he knew that that would not mend matters much.

A boat was waiting for them in the Hamble creek; and the party pulled on, till at daybreak they found themselves at the mouth of the Southampton Water, on board an eighteen-gun brig. The pressed men looked very sulky and angry, and eyed the shore as if even then they longed to jump overboard and swim for it; but the sentry, with his musket, at the gangway was a strong hint that they would have other dangers besides drowning to contend with should they attempt it.

True Blue, who disdained to shirk duty on any pretence, performed as rapidly and well as he could what he was ordered to do; but at the same time his heart was heavier, probably, than that of any one on board. The officer who had captured him might or might not believe his assertion that he belonged to another ship. He had not his papers with him, and he had been caught trying to escape from the pressgang. The Captain of the brig was on shore, and was to be taken on board at Plymouth, where she was to call in for him.

"Where are we bound for?" asked True Blue of one of his new shipmates.

"Don't you know, lad?" answered the man with a laugh which sounded harsh and cruel in his ears. "Why, out to the East Indies, to be sure—that's the land, I've heard, of gold and silver and jewels. We shall all come back with our pockets well lined with the rhino. Lots of prize-money, lad—that's the stuff we want. No wonder our skipper is in a hurry to be off. We shan't drop anchor even in Plymouth Sound, but he'll post down from London; and as soon as he sees us he'll be aboard, for I know well that he will be eager to be off. He's in as great a hurry to finger the ingots as any of us."

This was very unpleasant information for True Blue. He had no reason, either, to doubt it. As soon as the tide made, the brig got under weigh, and, standing out of the river, ran down the Solent towards the Needle Passage.

Had True Blue been on board his own ship, he would have been contented enough, even though he had been bound for the East Indies; but to be carried off among strangers, without an opportunity of communicating with those he loved, was hard indeed to bear. The brig had got down as far as Berryhead, when it fell very nearly calm, and a thick fog came on. All night long the fog continued, and though it was not dark, all objects beyond ten or twenty fathoms at most of the brig were rendered invisible. Her head, therefore, was put off shore, to avoid the risk of running on it, and sail was reduced, so as merely to allow her to have steerage way.

The breeze, however, got up a little with the sun, which was seen endeavouring to pierce the mist; but for a long time the sun appeared to strive in vain to accomplish that object.

At last the silvery mist was, as it were, torn asunder; and then, running under all sail, and about to pass between the brig and the land, appeared a large lugger. The brig under reduced sail, seen through the fog, looked probably more like a merchantman than a man-of-war. The lugger ran up the tricolour and fired a round-shot at the brig.

The first lieutenant, springing on deck with his trousers in one hand and his coat in the other, ordered the brig to be put about, and then all hands to make sail, and the guns to be cast loose and run out. The Frenchmen, before they discovered their mistake, had also tacked,—the wind was from the southward,—and were standing back towards the brig; but what was their astonishment, when, instead, of the thumping big merchantman they had expected to make their easy prize, they saw a trim man-of-war with nine guns looking down on them!

They at the same time had the full taste of the nine guns, and of a volley of musketry also, to which they, however, in another minute, responded in gallant style. The brig was to windward. The object of her commanding officer was to jam the lugger up between her and the land, so that she could not possibly escape.

The lugger's Captain, unwilling to be thus caught, hauled his tacks aboard, and made a gallant attempt to cross the bows of the brig. Her helm, however, at that moment was put down, and a broadside fired right into the lugger, one shot bringing down her mainyard, and another knocking the mizen-mast over her side. The escape of the Frenchmen was now hopeless—they must either conquer or be captured. They made a bold attempt to win, by immediately running aboard the brig, before the lugger had lost her way, and securing her with grappling-irons.

"Boarders, repel boarders!" shouted the first lieutenant of the brig.

Among the first to answer the call was True Blue. Seizing a cutlass from a heap brought on deck,—for there had been no time to buckle them on,—he sprang to the spot where he Frenchmen were swarming on board.

"Drive them back, for the sake of Old England, our King, and the homes we love!" he shouted, a dozen arming themselves as he had done, and following him.

The officers in the same way seized what weapons they could lay hands on, and met their desperate assailants. In boarding, those who board, if they can take their opponents by surprise, have greatly the advantage. The Frenchmen reckoned on this, and were not disappointed. A strong party had made good their footing on the brig's deck, when the first lieutenant, who was a powerful man, seizing a cutlass, with some of the best of the crew, threw himself upon them. So desperate was the onslaught he made that none could withstand it. The Frenchmen fired their pistols, by which several of the English, who had not one loaded, fell; and the gallant lieutenant was among others hit. Still his wound did not stop his progress.

The Frenchmen retreated inch by inch, throwing themselves over the brig's bulwarks into their own vessel. True Blue and his party had been equally successful forward, and now not a

Frenchman remained on the brig's deck. In another moment, he with his companions had leaped down on that of the lugger, and, though the French far outnumbered the British, drove them all abaft the foremast, where they found themselves attacked by another portion of the brig's crew, headed by two of her officers.

The first lieutenant had carried her aft, and the French, seeing that all was lost, threw down their arms and cried out for quarter. It was instantly given, and in ten minutes from the time the first shot was fired, the capture of the lugger was complete.

As True Blue looked along her decks, he thought he recognised her appearance. "Hurrah!" he shouted. "Why, she's the very craft, the Vengeur, we took in the Seine."

So she proved. From one of the prisoners, who spoke English, True Blue learned that, soon after the boats had left her for the frigate, the Vengeur had been attacked by a large armed lugger, which, however, she beat off; that then a number of boats with soldiers in them surrounded her, and that, after a furious action had been carried on for some time, chiefly with musketry, and numbers of the British had been killed or wounded, Sir Sydney had yielded.

Between twenty or thirty officers and men only had been landed at Rouen, the rest having fallen. The greater number were imprisoned at Rouen; but the French Government had considered Sir Sydney as a prisoner of state, and, with his secretary and servant, he had been placed in the tower of the Temple at Paris.

In the afternoon, the brig and her prize ran up Plymouth Sound; and as she had killed and wounded and prisoners to land, and repairs to make good, instead of sailing at once, as had been intended, she had to wait several days.

True Blue's gallant conduct had been observed both by the first lieutenant and the master, and when the Captain came on board it was reported to him.

"I think I must know the man," he observed. "A fine young fellow—an old shipmate of mine in the Ruby."

True Blue was sent for. The recognition was mutual. He told his story, and described also how he had been at the former capture of the Vengeur.

"I do not doubt a word you say," said the Captain. "Still, here you are. I am unwilling to lose you, and am not compelled to release you. I will give you any rating you like to select in the ship."

"Thank you, sir, heartily," answered True Blue; "but I belong to the Gannet, and have no right to desert her, and have all my best friends aboard her. I would rather be put ashore to join her as soon as I can."

"But I cannot take any man's word for such a statement," answered the Captain. "If it were known, I should have all the pressed men coming to me with long yarns, which it might be difficult to disprove."

"Then, sir, perhaps you will take Sir Henry Elmore's word for it. You know his handwriting, I daresay. I got this letter from him a few days ago;" and True Blue handed in the note, somewhat crumpled, which the young baronet had sent, saying that he had obtained longer leave for him.

"That is sufficient warrant to me in allowing you to leave me, if we fall in with the Gannet," observed the Captain, who was a man never inclined, whether right or wrong, to yield a point.

True Blue felt that he was cruelly wronged; still he hated the notion of running from the ship. Others put it into his head, but he would not accept it. "No, I have been unfairly taken, and I will be properly released," he said to himself. "I'll do what is right, whatever comes of it."

The brig's repairs did not take long; but the arrangements respecting the prize occupied the Captain some time, so that nearly ten days passed before the brig was standing once more down the Sound.

Poor True Blue's application for a release had been ignored, and he now felt certain that he should have to go out to India. As they reached the entrance of the Sound, a corvette was seen standing in. She exchanged colours with the brig, and proved to be the Gannet. Captain Brine, who was superior officer, directed the brig to heave-to A boat shoved off from her, and, coming alongside, who should jump on the deck of the brig but Paul Pringle, who, touching his hat, said in a stern voice that he had been sent to bring back to his own ship Billy True Blue Freeborn.

Chapter Twenty Two.

The Gannet was bound to the West Indies. All True Blue's friends were on board. The indignation they felt at the way he had first been captured, and then kept on board, was very great. He had contrived to get off a letter to Mary, who of course told her father and Abel Bush what had occurred; and they at once told the Captain, who, finding that the brig was still at Plymouth, hoped to get there in time to recover him.

"Ah, True Blue, my lad, you did right to stick to your ship, and not to run," observed Paul Pringle, when his godson told him how much he had been tempted to do so. "Look here, now; if you had run, you see, you would have found the Gannet sailed, and lost your ship altogether. There's no doubt about the matter."

Sir Henry Elmore was still on board as second lieutenant, and appeared very glad to see him. Captain Brine called him aft, and spoke very kindly to him. Moreover, he told him that he had given him the rating of captain of the foretop, which was a great honour for so young a seaman, and that when another vacancy occurred, he should have the highest which his age would allow.

The ship had a quick passage to the West Indies, without meeting with an enemy or even making a prize of a merchantman. When there, however, plenty of work appeared cut out for her.

Before long, when cruising off Porto Rico, a sail was descried from the masthead. The stranger at once bore down on the corvette. She was soon made out to be a large ship. No thought of flight entered the heads of any one. If Spanish, they would take her; if French, they might hope to beat her off. All hands were rather disappointed when she made the signal of H.M. frigate Trent; and when she came up she hove to, and Captain Brine, ordering his boat, went on board.

The two ships made sail and stood in for the land. As they skirted along the coast, as near in as they could venture, several vessels were seen at anchor in a bay, under the protection of a fort. Some were large and apparently armed. The frigate and corvette now stood off shore again, and the senior Captain informed Captain Brine that he proposed cutting them out at night, when they would be less prepared for an attack. Before the evening, the two ships had run to a sufficient distance not to be seen from the shore.

As soon as it was dark, they once more beat up towards the bay. Every preparation was made for the intended cutting-out expedition. There were six boats, all of which were placed under the command of the first lieutenant of the frigate, and Sir Henry Elmore went as second in command, with True Blue as his coxswain.

The ships hove to, and the boats shoved off about midnight. In two of them the marines of the frigate, with their officer, were embarked, to act on shore if necessary. The plan was, that they were together to board each vessel in succession, beginning at the largest. With muffled oars and in dead silence away they pulled. The night was dark; but the phosphoric sparkle of the water as the boats clove their way through it, and the oars lifted it in their upward stroke, might have betrayed them as they drew near, had the Spaniards been vigilant.

The frigate's boats, it was settled, should board aft, while the corvette's boarded forward of each vessel.

The outline of the hills rose in a clear line ahead, while the fort appeared directly above their heads, looking down on the anchorage, where the vessels lay clustered together. Not a light appeared; there was not a movement of any sort: the Dons were evidently fast asleep.

They were close alongside one of the largest ships—a heavy merchantman, she seemed—when the loud barking of a dog was heard. Still no one was aroused. It increased in fury as they approached. At last one of the watch must have seen the strange boats, for he shouted to his shipmates. They did not understand their danger till the British seamen were climbing up the ship's sides. The deck was won, and every Spaniard who came up from below was unceremoniously knocked down again. The prize was armed and the crew were numerous; so, as soon as they were secured below hatches, a mate with a boat's crew was ordered to cut the cable, make sail, and carry her out to the ships outside.

This first victory had been bloodless and easy; but now all the crews of the vessels were on the alert, as were the garrison of the fort, though in the darkness they were unable to ascertain in which direction to point their guns. However, they soon opened their fire on the outer ship, when she began to move; but their range was not correct, and their shot fell among friends and foes alike. The shot fell rapidly among the boats; and at the same moment a warm fire of musketry was opened on them from the decks of the vessels, proving that there must be a considerable number of men among them, and that some were well armed.

To silence the fort, the marines were ordered to land; and while they gallantly rushed up the heights to storm it, the bluejackets pulled on towards the next vessel. As they got alongside, she seemed like a man-of-war or a privateer; but there was no time for deliberation. Up her sides they were bound to go. As Sir Henry and his boat's crew made the attempt, they were received with boarding-pikes and pistol-shots in their faces. The bow-gun in the boat was in return pointed up and loaded to the muzzle with musket balls and all sorts of langrage. It cleared a space on the deck, and before it was again occupied the English had possession of it.

Two vessels were thus taken, both armed; but the strength of the cutting-out party was gradually decreasing, while the number of the enemy appeared as large as ever.

The cable of the vessel, a schooner, was cut; and the night wind blowing off shore, headsail was got on her, and she stood out after the first captured. The boats pulled on to attack a third vessel, while the fire of the marines as they stormed the fort, smartly returned by its defenders, lighted up the ground above them.

The next vessel was also a schooner. She looked long but low, and it seemed as if there would be but little difficulty in boarding her; but it was found as they got up to her that stout boarding nettings were triced up all round, though no one was to be seen on her decks.

Sir Henry Elmore's division was the first which reached, her, and True Blue was the first man up her side, the young lieutenant being close behind him. True Blue was hacking away at the netting, as were the other boarders, several of whom had leaped down on deck, when True Blue sprang through the opening he had made, and, grasping Sir Henry, literally forced him back into the boat. Before a word could be spoken there was a loud roar, the deck of the vessel lifted, fierce flames burst out from her sides, and all on board were blown into the air. True Blue's quick eye had detected the first glare of the flame as it appeared through the hatchway, and instantly he sprang back, or he would have been too late. As it was, he was very much scorched, as was Sir Henry in a less degree, though somewhat hurt by his fall.

"You have again saved my life, Freeborn!" he exclaimed as soon as he had recovered his senses and saw what had occurred.

"All right, sir," answered Billy; "but we will punish the next craft. I suppose they don't all intend to blow up. Hurrah, lads, we've not done with the Dons yet!"

Even while he was speaking, the mast, spars, and rigging of the vessel which had blown up kept thickly falling around them. Some of the English seamen were hurt, and one or more killed by them, besides three or four killed by the actual explosion on board; still the commander of the expedition was not a man to give up any work on account of losses. On they went, therefore, towards the next vessel—a large brig. The Spanish crew were prepared to receive them, and opened a hot fire from several guns. However, from being pointed too high, the shot passed over their heads.

The boats were the next instant alongside. Sir Henry, with True Blue, gained the forecastle. Scarcely for a minute did the Spaniards withstand their onslaught; their boats were on the opposite side, and, rapidly retreating, they leaped into them.

"Elmore, you and your boat's crew keep possession of the vessel, and carry her out," said the first lieutenant. "I will take a couple more, and, if possible, come back for the rest."

Having hurriedly given these directions, he with his men leaped into their boats, while Sir Henry gave the necessary orders for getting the brig under weigh; the jib was hoisted, and two hands were sent aloft to lower the fore-topsail.

True Blue, however, without waiting for orders, acted on the impulse which seized him, and hurried below. It was more than an impulse; his mind was full of the dreadful fate he and his companions had just escaped, and it occurred to him that the Spaniards might again be guilty of a similar act of barbarity.

All was quiet below, but a stream of light issued from a chink in one of the side cabins. He hastily opened the door; a taper was burning on the top of a cask. The cask was full of gunpowder! Several similar casks stood around. The slightest heeling over of the brig, as her sails felt the wind, might make her share the fate of her consort, or, in another minute or two, the candle itself would burn down and ignite the powder.

There was not a moment for deliberation, and yet the slightest act of carelessness would destroy him and his friends. A single spark falling from the long wick would be ruin. A firm hand and a brave heart were required to do that apparently simple act—to withdraw the taper from the cask. It must be done at that moment! He heard Sir Henry calling him to take the helm. Planting his feet one on each side of the cask, to steady himself, he stooped down, and, bringing his hands round the taper, enclosed it tightly within them, withdrawing them quickly, and at the same time pressing out every particle of fire. When it was done, his heart beat more freely. He hurried round to ascertain that no similar mine existed, ready to destroy them, and then, returning on deck, went calmly to the helm.

The gallant marines had in the meantime bravely done the work on which they had been sent, as was evident from the cessation of the fire from the fort, and the cries of the Spaniards who had been driven out of it. Having spiked the guns, they came down to the shore, when the boats went in and re-embarked them.

A large merchant ship was brought off, and another schooner. The rest of the vessels were either scuttled or had driven on shore. The latter were set on fire, and the whole expedition then sailed away with their well-won prizes.

"I called to you some time before you came to the helm. Where were you, Freeborn?" said Sir Henry as the brig they had captured had got some way out of the harbour.

True Blue only then told his superior officer of the providential escape they had had.

"But we ought to have drowned the casks. Should any careless fellow be prowling about with a light, we might all be blown up as it is."

"The people were too busy on deck, I know, Sir Henry," answered True Blue. "I shut the door, and think there is no risk."

Sir Henry, however, did not feel comfortable till he had taken precautions against the risk they were running. Sending Tom Marline, now a quartermaster, to the helm, he got a lantern, and he and True Blue, going below, brought on deck all the casks of powder they could find. True Blue then suggested that they might search further; and in the hold of the vessel they discovered a considerable quantity more, while the magazine, the door of which had been left open, was full. Had, therefore, the first explosion merely set her on fire, the remainder of the powder would have blown her and all on board to fragments.

"Had you been an officer, Freeborn, you would have been able to have command of the prize," observed Sir Henry. "I wish you were from my heart, for you deserve it richly."

"Very happy as I am, Sir Henry, thank you," was True Blue's answer. "Maybe when I'm a bo'sun I may have charge of some craft or other; but I've no wish now to command this or any other vessel."

All Sir Henry could say would not rouse True Blue's ambition. He got, however, very great commendation from Captain Brine for his conduct in the cutting-out expedition. The prizes were officered and manned from the frigate and corvette, and the two ships shortly after this parted company. The Gannet took two or three more prizes, and sent them into Jamaica. Some little time had passed when, as the Gannet was standing to the southward of Guadaloupe, having gone through the passage between that island and Dominique, just as day broke, the land was seen in the far distance; and much nearer, on the weather beam, a sail, which no one doubted was an enemy's frigate.

There she lay, with fully twenty guns grinning through each of her sides, opposed to the Gannet's nine in her broadside. Some short time elapsed after the two ships had discovered each other. The midshipman of the watch had gone down to summon Captain Brine.

"I wonder what our skipper will do?" observed Tom Marline to True Blue. "Shall we fight the Frenchman, or up stick and run? or give in if we find that he has a faster pair of heels than we have, which is likely enough?"

"Run! Give in!" ejaculated True Blue. "I hope not, indeed. I know you too well, Tom, to fancy that you'd be for doing either one or the other without a hard tussle for it. It's my idea the Captain won't give in as long as we have a stick standing or the ship will float. If we are taken, depend on it, he will sell the Frenchmen a hard bargain."

"Right, lad—right!" exclaimed Tom Marline. "I knowed, Billy, that you'd think as I do; and if the Captain proposes to do what I think he will, we must stick by him, for I know some of the people don't quite like the look of things, and fancy it's hopeless to contend with such odds."

Captain Brine, however, when he came on deck and took a survey of the state of affairs, did not seem to hold quite to the opinion of Tom and True Blue. His heart did not quail more than theirs; but he reflected that he had no right to hazard the lives of his people and the loss of his ship in a contest against odds so great, if it could be avoided. He gave a seaman's glance round as he came on deck, and then instantly ordered all sail to be made, and the ship's head to be kept north-west. The stranger, which then hoisted French colours, leaving no doubt of her character, made all sail in chase. Anxiously she was watched by all hands.

"I thought how it would be, Billy!" exclaimed Tom Marline; "she is coming up fast with us. The Monsieurs build fast ships—there's no doubt on't; we shall have to fight her."

Meantime, all the crew were not so satisfied. Gipples and several others like him looked at their overpowering enemy, and some went below to fetch out their bags, for the sake of putting on their best clothing.

"I don't see why we should go for to have our heads shot away, or get our legs and arms knocked off, just for the sake of what the Captain calls honour and glory," observed Gipples in a low voice to those standing near him. "We are certain to lose the ship and be made prisoners when a quarter of us, or it maybe half, are killed and wounded, and I for one don't see the fun of that."

"No more don't I," observed Sam Smatch, who had come up on deck to have a look round. "I've been fiddler of a seventy-four, and now I'm cook of this here little craft, all for the sake of old friends, and I've larned a thing or two; but I haven't larned that there's any use knocking your head against a stone wall, or trying to fight an enemy just three times your size, and that's the real difference between us and that big Frenchman. Mind you, mates, though, I don't want to be made a prisoner by the Frenchmen, but it can't be helped—that I see."

Such was the tone of the remarks made by a considerable number of the crew as they watched the gradual approach of the frigate. It was not surprising, when they considered that they had, with their diminished numbers, not a hundred men to oppose, probably, three hundred. Mr Digby, the first lieutenant, as he passed along the decks, observed their temper and reported it to the Captain.

"Never mind what some of them just now feel," he answered; "we have plenty of good men and true, who will stand by me to the last. I intend to fight the Frenchman, and beat him off, too. Send the men aft; I will speak to them."

The crew, both the discontented and the staunch, came crowding aft.

"My lads," cried Captain Brine, "you have served with me now for some time, and on numerous occasions showed yourselves to be gallant and true British sailors. We have been in several actions when the enemy has been fully equal to us in force, and we have never failed to come off victorious; and not only victorious, but for every man we have lost, the enemy has lost five or six. As I have ever before been successful, so I hope to be now. You see that French frigate coming up astern? I intend to engage her, as I am sure you will all stand by me to the last. Never mind that she has got twice as many guns as we have; if we handle our bulldogs twice as well as she does hers, we shall be a match for her. So, my lads, go to your quarters. Fight as bravely as you ever have done for our good King and dear Old England; and let us uphold the honour of our flag, and thoroughly drub the Frenchmen."

"That we will, sir—that we will!" shouted True Blue, several others joining him. "Hurrah for Old England! Hurrah! hurrah!"

"The sooner, then, we begin the better, my lads," continued Captain Brine. "Wait till I give the word to fire; and when I do give it, don't throw your shot away."

After another hearty cheer, set off by True Blue, the men went steadily to their quarters. Royals and topgallant-sails were handed, the courses were clewed up, and the corvette under her three topsails stood calmly on, waiting the approach of the enemy. Undoubtedly the Frenchmen fancied that some desperate trick was going to be played them.

On came the frigate. "Remember, lads, do not fire till every shot will tell!" cried Captain Brine. "Wait till I give the word."

The frigate, under all sail, approached on the starboard and weather beam of the corvette. As the former found that her small antagonist was within range of her guns, she opened her fire; but the guns, being pointed high, either passed over the British ship or merely injured some of her rigging.

When the Frenchman got within hail, some one on board, seeing the small size of the corvette, and believing that she would instantly give in, sang out, "Strike! strike, you English!"

"Ay, that we will, and pretty hard, too," answered Captain Brine through his speaking trumpet. "Give it them, my lads!"

The loud cheer which the crew gave on hearing this reply had not died away before every shot from the corvette's broadside had found its way across the frigate's decks, or through her side. Again the heavy carronades were run in and loaded.

"Remember, lads, we have to make our nine guns of a side do more work than the Frenchman's twenty!" cried True Blue as he hauled in on the gun-tackle, every muscle strained to the utmost. "Hurrah, boys! we've already sent twice as many shot aboard him as he has given us."

With similar cries and exclamations, True Blue and others of the best seamen encouraged the rest, while the commissioned and warrant-officers kept their eyes on any who seemed to despair of success, and urged them to persevere.

Captain Brine seldom for a moment took his eyes off the French ship, and kept his own just at sufficient distance to let his carronades have their full effect, and yet not near enough to run the risk of being suddenly boarded, should any of his masts or spars be shot away. This seemed to be the aim of the Frenchman, for but very few of her shot had struck the hull of the corvette, though they had considerably damaged her rigging.

At length the frigate put up her helm to close. Captain Brine, who had been watching for this manoeuvre, shouted to his men to cease firing for an instant, till her head came round.

"Now rake her, my boys!" he cried; and the shot and various missiles with which the guns were loaded went crashing in through the frigate's bow-ports and along her main deck.

He then put his own helm down, and, hauling the tacks aboard, would have shot ahead of the Frenchman, had not the latter done the same to prevent her opponent obtaining the weather-gage. Just as she was doing so, she received the larger portion of another broadside. Thus the two ships ran on. Nothing could exceed the rapidity with which the Gannet's crew kept up their fire. For nearly two hours they had fought on. One man only had been wounded. What the casualties of the enemy were, they could not tell; but they had every reason to believe them severe. Suddenly the frigate ceased firing; she was seen to haul her tacks aboard, and away she stood to the northward, under a press of sail, the corvette being too much cut up in rigging and sails to follow.

Right hearty were the cheers which burst from the throats of the seamen when they found that their Captain had fulfilled his promise and beat off the Frenchmen. No one cheered more loudly than Gregory Gipples, whether or not at pleasure at having escaped without harm, or at the honour of having beaten the enemy, may be doubted.

"Well shouted, old Gipples!" cried Tim Fid. "One would suppose you'd been and done it all yourself."

Just then a puff of smoke was seen to proceed from one of the retreating frigate's after-ports, and the next instant poor Gipples was spinning along the deck, shrieking out with terror and pain. Out of all the crew, in spite of the heavy fire to which the corvette had been exposed, he and another poor fellow were the only men hit. This shot seemed a parting one of revenge. As Captain Brine watched the receding frigate, he could scarcely persuade himself that she would not again bear down upon him. On she stood—farther and farther off she got, till her hull sank beneath the horizon, and her courses, and then her topsails, and finally her topgallant-sails and royals, were hid from sight.

Fid, Hartland, and others carried poor Gipples below. Wonderful to relate, when the surgeon came to examine him, he pronounced his wound, though bad, not of necessity mortal, and thought that under favourable circumstances he might possibly do well. No one could have tended him more carefully and kindly than True Blue and his other old messmates; and he showed more gratitude for their attention than might have been expected.

Scarcely had the enemy disappeared, when the lookout at the masthead reported a large ship on the lee beam. Every exertion that could be made was applied to get the Gannet into a condition to chase, and in an hour's time, under a wide spread of canvas she was standing after the stranger.

The latter appeared not to be a man-of-war, as she made off towards the Island of Guadaloupe, then dead to leeward. As she had so far the start, it became a question whether she could be brought to before she ran herself on shore. Still the Gannet, it was soon seen, sailed faster than she did, and Guadaloupe was scarcely visible on the horizon.

The breeze freshened, the corvette tore with foam-covered bows through the blue glittering ocean. At 11 a.m. she had made sail. By 3 p.m. she had got the stranger within range of her long guns.

"She is remarkably like an English ship, and from the way she is handled, I think she must be a prize, with a small crew on board," observed the first to the second lieutenant.

After a few shots, the stranger's main-topsail-yard was shot away, when she brought to, and proved to be the Swift, a British merchant ship, bound to Barbadoes, a prize to the frigate the Gannet had just beaten off. Mr Nott, with ten men, including True Blue and Tim Fid, were sent on board to work her; and as, instead of deserving the name of the Swift, she was more worthy of that of the Tub, the Gannet took her in tow, hoping to carry her to Barbadoes. All night long she towed her.

At daybreak next day, Captain Brine found that the misnamed Swift had drifted close in towards the land, while within her lay a frigate, and to all appearance the very frigate he had beaten off the day before.

Not a breath of wind ruffled the calm surface of that tropical sea. It was evident that the Gannet herself could do nothing to assist her prize. The Captain therefore called his officers round him, and asked their opinion as to the possibility of successfully defending her with the boats. They were against the advisability of making such an attempt.

As the daylight increased, the French frigate discovered the character of the two ships outside her.

"I wonder whether she will attempt to retake the Swift," said Captain Brine. "If so, Nott will be unable to defend her, and I must recall him. Let the lookout aloft give us notice the instant any boats are seen to leave her side."

No long time had elapsed before the French, supposing that the calm was going to continue, put off from the frigate with four boats.

"I believe Nott and his men would defend the prize to the last; but I must not expose them to such a risk," observed the Captain.

"I am sure our True Blue won't give in if he has a word in the matter," observed Paul Pringle to Peter Ogle. "Mr Nott is staunch, too. They'll do their best to beat the Frenchmen off."

This was very well; but though possible, it was not probable that they would succeed; so the Captain ordered the signal, "Escape in your boats," to be made.

It had been made some time, and yet it was not answered, probably because it was not seen. The French were getting very near.

"It's my belief that they intend to try and defend the ship," observed Paul Pringle. "I wish I was with them if they do—that's all."

"Fire a gun to call their attention to the signal!" cried the Captain.

Immediately the signal was answered, and two boats put off from the ship's side. In two minutes afterwards the French were up to the prize; but they seemed inclined to have the crew as well, and, instead of boarding her, pulled on in chase. Captain Brine, on seeing this, ordered three boats to be lowered and manned on the opposite side, hoping that they might venture near enough to be caught themselves. They now began firing at the two English boats, with which they were fast coming up. The Frenchmen must have seen that there was a great chance of their prey escaping them, unless they captured them at once. The crews uttered loud cries, the boats dashed on. In another minute they would have been up to them, when the corvette's three boats appeared from under her counter, and pulled rapidly towards them.

They saw that their chance of success was over, and, pulling round, went back to the prize as fast as they came.

"We should have fought them, sir, if we had not been recalled," observed Mr Nott, when reporting what had occurred to the Captain.

There appeared every probability of the corvette having to contend with two frigates instead of one, for the masts of another were made out in the harbour just abreast of them. The crew also knew of this. There was a good deal of talking among them, when they all came aft in a body. True Blue stepped out from among them, and spoke in a clear, firm voice:

"You called on us, sir, to fight the last time; we hope, sir, that you will allow us to ask you to fight this time, and we'll stick by you."

"Thank you, my lads—thank you; I am sure that you will," answered the Captain. "Whatever we do, we will not disgrace our flag."

The crew gave three loud cheers and retired. Cat's-paws were now seen playing on the water; the sails of the French frigate filled, but her head was not turned towards the corvette. Soon the latter also felt the force of the breeze. Captain Brine ordered the sails to be trimmed, and the corvette stood away from the land. As she did so, her crew could clearly make out another frigate coming out of harbour to join her consort, but what the enemy's two ships were about, it was impossible to say, as in a short time, with the freshening breeze, they were both run out of sight.

Chapter Twenty Three.

The Gannet had now been some time on the station, and had performed a number of deeds worthy of note, taken several prizes, and injured the enemy in a variety of ways, when one morning, just at daybreak, as she lay not far from Porto Rico, a schooner was seen creeping out from under the land towards her.

Captain Brine had done his best to make his ship look as much as possible like a merchantman. She was now slowly yawed about as if badly steered, with sails ill trimmed, and her sides brown and dirty and long unacquainted with fresh paint, a screen of canvas concealing her ports. The schooner came on boldly, her crew evidently fancying that they had got a rich prize before them.

"Are those Spaniards or French, Paul?" inquired True Blue of his godfather.

"Anything you please, probably," was the answer. "They have, I doubt not, as many flags on board as there are months in the year. She looks at this distance just like a craft of that sort—a regular hornet; I hope we may stop her buzzing."

While Paul was speaking, the wind fell, and the schooner, now about six miles off, was seen to get out her sweeps and pull away from the corvette.

"We must get that fellow!" exclaimed the boatswain. "If the Captain will let me, I'll volunteer to pull after him. True Blue, you'll come?"

"I should think so," answered True Blue, looking into Paul's face. "If none of the quarterdeck officers have thought of going, he'll not refuse."

"I'll go too!" cried Abel Bush. "The superior officers have had their share lately, and the Captain will be glad to give us our turn."

Without further parley, the two warrant-officers went to the quarterdeck, where the Captain was standing. The lieutenant and master gave up their right, as did the master's mates; and, accordingly, the pinnace and launch were ordered to be lowered and manned immediately, ready for service.

Paul went in the pinnace with True Blue, while Abel Bush had charge of the launch. Away the boats glided in gallant style through the smooth water. The men had taken a hurried breakfast before leaving the ship, for they saw that they had a long pull before them.

The crew of the schooner seemed determined to give them as long a pull as possible, and with their sweeps kept well ahead, not going less than three or four knots an hour. This, however, in no way daunted the boatswain and his companions. "Hurrah, my lads, we'll soon be aboard!" he shouted. Give way—give way! In two minutes we may open fire on her. We've distanced the launch. The schooner must be ours before she comes up.

Even while he was speaking, the shot from the chase came falling pretty thickly around them. That only made them pull the faster. The schooner appeared to be full of men, with several guns on each side, and boarding nettings fixed up. Paul might have been excused if he had waited for the coming up of the other boat, but that was not his way of doing things—on he pulled.

The schooner swept round so as to present her broadside to the approaching boats; but he, altering his course a little, steered directly for her quarter. Led by True Blue, the crew gave a loud cheer as they dashed on under her counter, and then, pushing round to her quarter, hooked on. In a moment, cutting the tricing lines of her boarding nettings, they sprang up her side and threw themselves on the deck. They were received with a shower of musket and pistol bullets, and the points of a row of pikes.

The bullets struck down two of the daring boarders; but the remainder pushed on, striking down the pikes with their cutlasses, and playing havoc among the heads of the men who held them.

The Frenchmen stoutly defended themselves for some time with swords and axes, but in vain did they attempt to withstand the fierce onslaught of the British seamen. They began to give way; some were cut down, others in their terror sprang overboard. Paul received a wound in his side which prevented him from moving; but True Blue, heading his companions, with his sharp cutlass whirling away in front, swept along the deck, driving the Frenchmen before him.

A desperate stand was made by the officers of the vessel on the forecastle, and from the small number of their assailants they might even then have hoped, with some reason, still to gain the victory; but while they were discussing what was to be done, the British seamen were making good use of their cutlasses, and in another moment they found themselves hurled down the hatchway, knocked overboard, or, if alive, on their knees asking for quarter.

All opposition had ceased, and the schooner's flag was hauled down, when Abel, in his heavy-pulling launch, came alongside.

"Well, mates, you've made quick work of the Monsieurs, and have had the honour and glory, too, while we've only had the hot pull!" cried the crew of the latter boat.

"And what's more, mates," answered the boatswain, "you'll have to pull hard to get us back again; for there are few of us who have not got touched up by the enemy."

Of this, the appearance of the survivors of the gallant crew of the pinnace gave evidence. Paul himself was pretty severely wounded; and True Blue, Hartland, Fid, and all the rest were more or less hurt. One seaman had been killed, and one marine knocked overboard by the French.

The enemy's loss had, however, been much more severe. Out of a crew of nearly fifty men, four lay killed on her deck, fully eight had jumped or been knocked overboard, and a dozen or more were badly wounded.

After the remainder had been mustered and secured, a watchful eye was kept on them; but they showed no disposition to mutiny, even though compelled to work the sweeps, to enable the schooner to close with the corvette.

Captain Brine highly applauded the gallant way in which the schooner had been taken.

"Ay, sir, and I wish you could have seen my godson as his cutlass cleared the Frenchman's decks!" exclaimed Paul.

"I have no doubt about it," answered the Captain. "It is no fault of his friends that he is not on the quarterdeck. But for yourself, Mr Pringle, I wish to know what reward you would like, that I may do my best to secure it for you."

"I have not thought about that, sir; but if you could spare me, I should be glad to have charge of the prize to take her to Jamaica. I should just like to find out how I feel acting as Captain."

Captain Brine was amused at Paul's notion.

"But how will the Gannet get on without her boatswain, Mr Pringle?" asked the Captain. "She can ill spare him, I should think."

"Why, sir, I thought about that, and wouldn't have asked leave if I didn't know my place would be well filled while I was away," replied Paul. "There's my first mate, Dick Marlowe, a very steady man, who hopes to pass as boatswain when he gets to England; and I'll engage the duty is properly done while he is acting for me."

"But you and the rest are wounded. How can you do without a surgeon?" said Captain Brine.

"Mere fleabites, sir—nothing to signify. The doctor has patched up my side, and says I shall do well; and the lads I wish to take with me are only slightly hurt, and don't want doctoring."

The Captain, on sending for the surgeon and hearing his report, made no further objections, but promised compliance with Paul's wishes, the more readily that the Gannet herself was to go to Jamaica in a week or two.

The prisoners were soon removed from the prize, with the exception of a Dane and a Dutchman, who volunteered to remain in her; while Paul took with him True Blue, Tom Marline, Harry Hartland, Tim Fid, and three other hands.

Paul had, since he became a warrant-officer, been studying navigation, and was able to take an observation, and to do a day's work very correctly. All his knowledge he imparted to True Blue, who, however, quickly surpassed him, in consequence of Sir Henry frequently sending for him aft, and giving him regular instruction. By this time, therefore, True Blue, by directing his attention entirely to the work, had become really as good a navigator as any of the midshipmen, and a better one than those who were content to fudge their day's work, and never attempted to understand the principle of the science.

Of navigation, Tom Marline, like most seamen not officers, was profoundly ignorant. Paul, therefore, told him that he was very sorry he could not bestow on him the rating of lieutenant, which he must give to True Blue, but that he would make him sailing-master. Harry Hartland should be a midshipman, on account of his general steadiness and intelligence; the Dutchman should be cook, and the other four men crew; while Tim Fid, who was little less a pickle than when he was a boy, must do duty as gunroom and purser's steward, besides doing his work as part of the crew.

At this arrangement no one grumbled; indeed, all hands liked the boatswain. It was arranged that his gunroom officers should mess with him, Harry also being invited as a regular guest. Paul took one watch with four of the men. True Blue, with Tom, Harry, Fid, the Dane, and the Dutchman, had the other.

These various arrangements occupied some time after the schooner lost sight of the corvette. In the next day, the wind being very light, she made but little progress. The day following, the weather, which had long been fine, gave signs of changing; and instead of the clear blue sky and glass-like sea, which for many weeks had surrounded the ship, dark clouds gathered overhead, sudden gusts of winds began to blow, and the water began to undulate, and every now and then to hiss and foam as the blast passed over it. Then down came the rain in right earnest, and continued for some hours, the watery veil obscuring every object beyond a mile or so. Suddenly, as the rain ceased, about two miles off, a schooner was seen, apparently the size of the prize, if not larger, and dead to windward.

Paul instantly hoisted French colours, and the other vessel did the same. On looking at her through a telescope, she appeared to have on board a numerous crew. Paul, however, determined at all events not to be taken, and, following the example of Captain Brine, he called his crew aft and made them a speech.

"Lads," he began, "you know what we did in the corvette. We beat off a frigate twice our size; we took this craft with twelve men, for, no blame to him, my brother officer, Mr Bush, and his companions did not come up till the day was gained. And I need not tell you, lads, we ourselves and other British seamen have dared and done a thousand things much more desperate than our attempting to beat off such a craft as that one out there, though she may have five times as many hands aboard as we have, and twice as many guns."

"Hurrah, that's just like him!" cried True Blue, turning to his shipmates; "and I say, Mynheer, you'll fight, won't you?" he added, seizing the Dutchman's hand and wringing it heartily.

"Ya, va! I'll stick by you brave Anglish lads," answered the Dutchman.

The Dane made a similar reply, though somewhat less cordial, to Tom's appeal, and then all the crew, having given three hearty cheers, set about getting their prize ready for action.

All the firearms were brought on deck and carefully loaded, and so were the guns, and each man girded a trusty cutlass to his side and stuck his belt full of pistols; and then Paul had all the hammocks brought on deck, and lashed upright inside the bulwarks, so as to serve as a screen to the men working the guns.

The prize had all this time been kept running on under full sail to the westward, and as the stranger was steering the same course, the distance between the two had not been decreased, the latter evidently being under the impression that the prize was a friend.

Suddenly, though it was blowing fresh, she made more sail, put up her helm, and bore down on the prize. Paul stood steadily on with the French flag flying, till the enemy was within musket range; then down came the tricolour and the British ensign flew out at the peak.

"Now, lads, as we've got the flag we all love to fight under aloft, give it them!" he shouted, and, putting his helm down, he brought his broadside to bear on the bows of the advancing stranger. Every one of the raking shot told among the crowd of men who clustered on her deck. Wild shrieks and cries arose; and now her helm being put down, she ranged up on the beam of the prize, with the intention of boarding.

Paul, however, who saw their intention, told Harry Hartland, who was at the helm, to keep away a little, so as to avoid actual contact; and in the meantime all the guns were again fired, within ten yards' distance, directly at the schooner. Hitherto, strange as it may appear, not an Englishman had been hit, while some dozen or more of the enemy had been struck down. Still the privateer had greatly the advantage in point of numbers, besides being a larger and more heavily-armed vessel.

She now steered on alongside the prize for a few seconds, while her guns were reloaded; and then, firing her broadside once more, she kept suddenly away to run aboard her opponent.

The wind had been increasing, and the sea getting rapidly up. This was now much to the advantage of the British, as they could fight their weather guns far more easily than the enemy could their lee ones, the muzzles of which were almost buried in the foam.

The stranger had got so close that Harry was not able to keep away in time to avoid her running her bows right into the prize's quarter.

"Now we've got you, we'll keep you until we have given you more than you bargained for!" cried True Blue, lashing the stranger's bowsprit to their own mainmast, where she was kept in such a position that three of their guns could be continually firing into her, while her crew could not reach the prize's deck without taking a dangerous leap from their bowsprit. Many attempted it; but as they reached the vessel's bulwarks, they had to encounter the cutlasses of True Blue, Paul Pringle, and Tim Fid, while Tom Marline and the other men kept the forward guns in active work.

Frenchmen, negroes, Spaniards, mulattoes, and other mongrels were hurled one after the other into the water; while numbers were jerked overboard by the violent working of the vessels. At length, as the enemy, in greater numbers than ever, were making a furious rush forward, fully expecting to overwhelm the English, the bowsprit with a loud crash gave way, carrying, as it did so, the foremast, just before wounded by a shot, with it.

Wild shrieks and cries and imprecations rose from the savage crew—from some as they fell into the boiling ocean below their feet, now swarming with sharks, called around by the scent of human blood; from the rest at their disappointment in missing their prey.

Glad as Paul would have been to make a prize, he saw that his opponent would prove worse than a barren trophy.

"Up with the helm, Harry!" he cried. "Cut, my lads—cut everything! Clear the wreck!"

The crew needed no second order. True Blue, axe in hand, had already cut away the lashings of the bowsprit. A few more cuts cleared the bowsprit shrouds and other ropes, by which the enemy still hung on, and in another instant the prize was going off before the gale, while her disabled opponent luffed up into the wind's eye.

Down came the squall, darker and more furious than before. Not another shot was fired. Paul and his people had enough to do in shortening sail and getting their craft into a condition to meet the rising gale. Their strength, too, had been reduced in the action. The poor Dutchman was severely wounded, though, like a brave fellow, he insisted on keeping the deck, and so was one of the Gannet's men.

With the next squall down came a thick pour of rain.

"Where is the enemy?" suddenly exclaimed True Blue, looking aft.

Paul turned his eyes in the same direction. "We cannot have run her out of sight in so short a time," he answered gravely; "it's my belief that she this instant has foundered, and all on board have become food for the sharks."

"But ought we not to go about and see if any are afloat?" asked True Blue. "We might pick up some of the poor wretches."

"Not the smallest use," answered Paul firmly. "If she foundered, she went down too quickly to give any one a chance of escaping. We must just now look after ourselves; this craft is very cranky, I see."

No one would have been more ready than Paul to help his fellow-creatures, whatever the risk to himself, had he seen that there was the slightest prospect of doing so effectually.

For the remainder of the day the prize stood on close-hauled, nearly up to her proper course; but as the evening advanced, she fell off more to the westward, while the sea increased more and more, as did the violence of the squalls, while the thunder rolled, and vivid flashes of lightning darted from the dark skies.

The night drew on. True Blue, with Tom, Harry, Tim, and the Dane, had the first watch; Paul, with the rest of the crew, was to keep the middle watch. Though tough enough, he was pretty well worn out with the exertions he had gone through; so he went below, charging True Blue to call him should anything particular occur. His cabin was on the starboard side; and in the main cabin was a table with a swing light above it, and also a compass light in the cabin binnacle.

True Blue with Tom walked the deck for some time, watching each change of the weather; Fid had the helm, Harry was on the lookout forward, while the Dane sat silent on a gun under the weather bulwarks. The rest of the crew were asleep below forward.

The weather, as the night advanced, grew worse and worse.

"Tom, I think we ought to bring the schooner to," said True Blue at last; "she'll do no good keeping at it, and a sudden squall may carry away our masts."

Accordingly the schooner was at once brought to under her close-reefed foresail; and then she lay riding with tolerable ease over the seas, which foamed and hissed as they rushed past her.

Everything having been made secure, True Blue went below to report what had been done. He found Paul sleeping more soundly than usual. Perhaps some of the medicine the surgeon had given him, on account of his wound, had affected him, True Blue thought. He had to speak two or three times before he could make him comprehend what he had to say.

"All right," he answered at length; "if the weather gets worse, call me again."

Scarcely had he uttered the words when he was thrown out of his bed-place, and True Blue was sent with great violence against the bulkhead of the cabin.

"On deck! on deck!" they both shouted; but as they made for the companion-ladder, they were driven back by a tremendous rush of water: the lights were extinguished, and they were left in total darkness. Paul had scarcely recovered his senses, and neither he nor True Blue could find their way to the companion-ladder.

The water continued rushing furiously into the cabin, and one thing only was certain, that the schooner had upset. How the accident had happened, it was difficult to say; in all probability, too, she was sinking. The cabin was now more than three-quarters full of water, and the only places where they could escape being instantly drowned were in the berths on the starboard side. In vain they shouted to their friends on deck to come and help them out of the cabin. No one answered to their cries.

"They are all gone, I fear," said Paul. "It's the fate of many brave seamen; it will be more than likely our fate before many minutes are over. Still, godson, as I have always told you, it's our duty to struggle for life to the last, like men; so climb up into these starboard berths. We shall be free of the water there for a little time longer."

True Blue followed Paul's advice; and there they clung, while the water rose higher and higher. It got up to their waists, then up to their armpits, and by degrees it almost covered their shoulders, though their heads were pressed against the starboard side of the vessel, which lay on her larboard beam-ends. Both were silent; they could not but expect that their last moments were come, and that the vessel must shortly go down.

Time passed on. The water did not further increase; but they felt almost suffocated, and, indeed, the only air they breathed found its way through the seams in the deck above their heads. There they hung, in total darkness: the roar and rush of waters above their heads; the air so close and oppressive that they could scarcely draw breath or find strength to hold themselves in the only position in which they could prolong their lives, while they had the saddest apprehensions for the fate of their companions, as they could scarcely hope, even should they succeed in regaining the deck, that they would find any of them alive.

Hour after hour passed away, when suddenly the vessel righted with a violent jerk, which sent them out of their berths into the centre cabin, where they found themselves swimming and floundering about, sometimes with their heads under water, sometimes above it, among boxes, and bales, and furniture, and articles of all sorts.

They were now fully aroused. True Blue exerted himself to help Paul, who, wounded as he had been, and now sore and bruised, was less able than usual to endure the hardships he was undergoing.

They were still in total darkness, and had to speak to let each other know where they were. True Blue had worked his way close to the companion hatch, and thought that Paul was following. He spoke, but there was no answer. His heart sank within him. He swam and waded back, feeling about in every direction with frantic eagerness.

"Paul Pringle—godfather—where are you?" he shouted.

Suddenly he felt an arm; it was Paul's. He lifted him up, and, with a strength few could have exerted, dragged him under the companion hatch. The ladder had been unshipped; but True Blue having righted it, dragged Paul up a few steps, where, in a short time recovering his breath, and Paul regaining his consciousness, they together made an effort to reach the deck.

Chapter Twenty Four.

When True Blue went below to tell Paul how bad the weather had become, he left the schooner hove to under her foresail, which, being stretched out completely in the body of the vessel, is the best adapted for that object under all circumstances but two—one, is, that being low down, it is apt to get becalmed when the waves run high; the other is, that should a heavy sea strike the vessel, it is likely to hold a dangerous quantity of water. The foreyard had been sprung, or True Blue would have brought the vessel to under her fore-topsail. True Blue had not long left the deck when a tremendous sea, like a huge black hill, was observed rolling up on the weather bow.

"Hold on, lads—hold on!" shouted Tom Marline.

Harry, who was at the helm, in an instant passed a rope round his waist and stood at his post, hoping to luff the vessel up so as to receive the blow on her bows; but the roaring sea came on too rapidly—down it broke on board the vessel, driving against the foresail like a battering-ram. Over it passed, and the schooner in an instant lay on her beam-ends, the water rushing in at each hatchway. The boats, guns, caboose, hencoops—all the things, in short, on deck were swept away, with a great part of her bulwarks.

Tom and the rest secured themselves under the weather bulwarks. They had not been there many seconds before they recollected their companions below. While Harry tried to reach the after cabin, Tom did his best to get to the men in the forepeak. Letting go his hold, he was working his way forward, when another sea struck the vessel.

"Oh, Tom is gone!" cried Fid.

No one could help him. Away the relentless sea washed him; but, just as he was being hurled to destruction, he grasped the fore-rigging hanging overboard, and hauled himself again on deck. Tim and the Dane dragged him up to the weather side, where they were joined by Harry, who reported that the cabin was full of water; and he added, "Oh, mates, it will break my heart—the boatswain and True Blue must both be drowned!"

"Ay, and we shall be drowned too!" cried the Dane, who had been for some time complaining of pain. "Our officers are gone, and we may as well go too. There is no use living on in misery longer than can be helped. Good-bye, mates!"

"Avast there, mate!" exclaimed Tom; "be a man. Don't give in till the last! Let us hope as long as there is life. The day will come back, and the sun will shine out, and a vessel may heave in sight!"

"No, no! I can't stand it!" cried the poor unhappy Dane. "I have no hope—none! Good-bye!"

On this, before Tom could prevent him, he cast off the lashings by which he was secured to the bulwarks, and, sliding down into the water, a roaring sea, as if exulting in its prize, carried him far away out of their sight.

"Oh, mates, this is very sad!" exclaimed Tom to his two younger companions.

"True, true," said Harry. "Don't you think, now, we could do something to try and save the vessel? If we were to cut away the starboard rigging, she might be freed from her masts and right herself."

The suggestion was of a practical nature, and pleased Tom; and all three setting to work with their knives, with considerable labour cut through the shrouds. Scarcely were the last strands severed than the masts with a loud crack went by the board, and with a violent jerk the vessel righted.

"There, lads!" said Tom; "I told you things would mend, if we would but trust in Providence."

Tom wished to encourage his companions, for the state of the vessel was only apparently a degree improved.

"Ah, now, if we had had the bo'sun and True Blue with us, and the poor fellows for'ard, we might have still done well. Howsomdever, daylight will come at last, and then we shall see better what to do."

As he ceased speaking, Tim Fid uttered a loud cry. "Why, oh, mercy!—there be their ghosts!" he exclaimed. "Paul and Billy! It can't be them! They've been drowned this many an hour."

"It's them, though!" cried Harry. "Heaven be praised! They are beckoning to us; let us go aft and help them."

He and his friends were soon grasping each other's hands, and describing what had occurred. Tom soon followed, and poor Tim, having recovered his wits, and being convinced that they were alive, joined them.

Their condition was sad indeed. There lay the vessel rolling and tumbling about in the stormy ocean, the seas constantly making a clear breach over her, the mainmast gone altogether, but the wreck of the foremast still hanging on by the bowsprit and violently striking her bows.

It was found that the best place for safety was inside the companion hatch, where they all collected; and being there partially free from the seas, they endeavoured to get a little rest, to prepare for whatever they might have to do in the morning.

At length daylight broke; but it did little else than reveal more clearly their forlorn condition.

True Blue having been preserved himself, was anxious to ascertain whether his companions might have escaped in a similar way. Tom assured him that there was no hope; but he insisted on going forward to see. The rest of the party watched him as he performed the dangerous passage, for the seas kept continually beating over the vessel, and might easily have washed him away. He reached the fore-hatch, and, stooping down, called to the men. No answer was given. The water was much too high in the cabin to have allowed them to escape, and he returned aft convinced of their death.

For some hours no one had thought of eating, but hunger now reminded them that it was necessary to try and obtain food. There was enough in the vessel, if it could be got at; but the difficulty was to fish it up from beneath the water.

In vain they watched—nothing appeared. True Blue, who was the most active, made several unsuccessful dives; but returned at length so exhausted that Paul would not let him go again.

At last a flag floated up. It seemed to come to remind them that it would be wise to make a signal of distress. A small spar had got jammed in the bulwarks. The flag, which proved to be a French tricolour, was secured to it, and it was stuck in one of the pumps.

"I would rather see any ensign but that flying overhead," said Paul; "but it will help to make us be seen, anyhow."

The night again returned, and during the whole of it they remained in the same miserable condition that they had been in all day, the sea raging as furiously, and the wind blowing as high as before.

The first thing in the morning, True Blue volunteered with Harry to go and cut the foremast adrift. An axe had been found. Together the two worked their way forward. Having secured themselves by ropes, they set to work, True Blue with his axe, Harry with his knife. Now they were completely covered with the seas which broke over the bows; again they rose and drew breath, and made a few more desperate hacks, again to be impeded by the next roaring surge. Several shrouds, however, had been severed. Another sea, fiercer than ever, came rushing on.

A cry from Harry made True Blue turn round. The greedy wave was whirling him away, when True Blue grasped him by the arm and drew him once more on board, when he more firmly secured himself.

"We must not give in, though!" cried True Blue, and went on hacking at the ropes.

Again Harry joined him, and at length the heavy mast went floating away free of the schooner. Successful in their bold attempt, they returned aft. Hunger was now an enemy much to be feared; for among all the articles which kept continually appearing and disappearing from the cabin, nothing fit for food had been discovered. At last two or three roots appeared. Fid, who was on the watch, made a dart at them, and, fishing them up, declared them to be onions; so they were. Several others followed, and, being divided equally, were eagerly devoured. How delicious they tasted!

"Never fear, lads, but what assistance will be sent us in some way or other which we don't expect, if we trust in God," said Paul. "We didn't expect to get these onions a minute ago, and we shall have more before long, I daresay."

Nothing else, however, was found to eat during the rest of the day, and another tempestuous night closed in on them.

Even in the darkness a gleam of hope burst on them; the wind sensibly fell, and the clouds opening, exhibited a bright star above their heads. Again the morning came.

"Lads, we must try and pump the vessel out!" cried Paul, rousing himself with the first gleam of light.

The pumps without another word were manned; all hands set to work, and in an hour a sensible diminution of the water in the vessel had taken place. This encouraged them to persevere; but at length, overcome with fatigue, they had to throw themselves on their backs on the deck, to regain their strength. True Blue was the last to give in; but even he had more than once to stop. By and by they divided into two gangs, one relieving the other at the pumps, while they alternately bailed with buckets. From sheer exhaustion they were compelled, after a time, to knock off altogether; but they had so far rid the vessel of water that there was no immediate fear of her sinking.

Before even they made a search for food, with considerable difficulty they got up from below the bodies of their late shipmates, and, with a sigh for their fate, launched them overboard. Already they were no longer to be distinguished by their features.

While getting up the dead bodies, a prize had been discovered. It was a small keg of water; it seemed to give, new life to all the party. This encouraged them to hunt for other things. Some more onions and some shaddocks were discovered, and in a tureen with the top on, a piece of boiled beef. They had now no fear of dying of starvation or thirst for some time, at all events

True Blue's chief anxiety was about Paul, who suffered far more than the rest, on account of his wound; still nothing would induce him not to exert himself as far as his strength would possibly allow. The next day after these occurrences, the sea went down so much that Paul determined to get some sail on the vessel.

"How is it to be done, though?" asked Tom. "We've no spars, sails, or rigging."

"Hunt about, and let us see if we cannot find what will do," was Paul's answer.

True Blue dived below, and soon discovered some rope, a large coil of strong spun yarn, a fore-royal, and the bonnet of the jib, a palm, sail needles and twine, and many other useful articles; and beside these, one of the ship's compasses, True Blue's quadrant, given him by Sir Henry; and also the larger part of a long sweep, and two small spars. Curiously enough, also, a page of an old navigation book, with the sun's declination for that very year.

The first thing to be done was to get sail on the craft. Paul thoroughly understood sail-making, and Tom was a good hand at it. A mast was formed out of the sweep and one of the spars, which was secured to the stump of the foremast. The canvas they had found was cut into a gaff-sail, while the other spar served as the gaff. It was but a small sail, little larger than that of a frigate's launch; yet, with the wind free, it served to give steerage way to the schooner, and to send her along at the rate of three knots an hour.

All on board had reason to be thankful when once more they found their vessel, which had so long seemed on the point of foundering, almost free from water, and gliding smoothly over the sea. Paul determined to endeavour to reach Jamaica without touching at any other place.

All night they ran on. Sometimes, however, the wind fell so much that they only made a knot an hour; but still, as True Blue remarked, that was something if it was in the right direction.

The want of food was a serious affair, and they resolved the next day to have a grand hunt to try and discover some. Both forward and aft there was a great variety of casks, and bales, and packages, apparently taken out of different vessels which had been captured. As soon as the sun rose, the search was commenced. Another keg of water, found in the forepeak, first rewarded their labours. Some pine apples and other West India fruits were discovered; but a sack of potatoes or a cask of biscuits would have been more acceptable.

Though fitted for fighting, the schooner had also a hold for the stowage of cargo, and here was discovered a considerable number of casks of French wine. Such a discovery as this wine among a set of unsteady men would have been fatal, but to the present crew of the prize it was a most valuable acquisition. A bundle of salt fish and a cask of pork were next hauled out; a cask of bread was also discovered, though much damaged by salt water. Altogether they were well satisfied with the provisions they had discovered.

At noon an observation True Blue took showed that they had drifted a considerable way to the southward, and that it might still take them a long time to reach Jamaica. The rudder also was found to be much injured, the rudder-head being split through the centre, as low down as the upper pintle. It was with the greatest difficulty that it could be kept together, or the tiller held in its place. It was therefore very evident that it would be necessary to husband the provisions and water with the greatest care, as they could not expect to avoid having a long voyage, and might be reduced to very short commons before the end of it.

For three days the weather was fine. On the second day a spar floated alongside, which they secured, and forthwith fitted as a mainmast; a storm-jib which had been discovered was hoisted on it as a sail. It stood pretty well; and now, as the schooner moved with some liveliness through the water, the spirits of all on board revived.

"Ah, now, if that poor Dane had borne up like a man and clung to the ship, he might have been as well and happy as any of us," observed Tom to Fid as they were together setting up the fore-rigging. "Remember, Tim, whatever happens, never despair. It's wicked and unmanly—not like a true British sailor; and that's what I hope you will consider yourself all the days of your life."

Tom was, as it proved, over sanguine. The following day, once more the wind got up, as did the sea, and the helpless schooner lay battered and knocked about by its fury. The fractured rudder-head continually gave way, and, it being impossible to keep the helm properly down, the vessel fell off before the wind, and several heavy seas broke on board, reducing her almost to the same condition in which she had been before.

For two whole days she lay tossed and buffeted; more of her bulwarks were stove in, and the companion hatch received so tremendous a blow from a sea that it was nearly carried away. Had this occurred, the only place of shelter in the vessel would have been destroyed.

During all this trying time, True Blue was the life and soul of the little band. Though others gave way, he kept up his spirits, and cheered and endeavoured to animate them. Even Paul desponded; but True Blue was ever ready to offer some encouraging suggestion. The gale soon must cease—deliverance could not be far off. This was the hurricane season, when bad weather must be expected; and these gales were much better than a regular hurricane, which would too probably send the schooner to the bottom.

The gale came at last to an end, and comparatively fine weather returned. In spite of all their care, their provisions had by this time sadly diminished, and the fruits and roots were entirely destroyed and unfit for food. They still had a supply of salt fish and abundance of wine, and therefore they had no cause to fear dying of actual starvation; but such food was anything but wholesome, and they would gladly have exchanged the finest claret for half the quantity of pure water and a supply of bread—even the hardest of sea biscuits.

Still, True Blue setting them the example, they made the best of everything; and Paul took care that, as soon as the weather allowed again of their moving about the deck, no one should be idle. The French ensign was still flying at the head of the foremast. A lookout was always kept for any sail which might heave in sight, that they might steer so as to try and cut her off if possible.

One morning True Blue descried two sail on the weather bow. They appeared, when the sun rose, to be standing towards the vessel. The hopes of all on board rose high. The strangers were pronounced to be English merchantmen by the cut of their sails and general appearance. They bore down till within the distance of three miles or so, and then suddenly hauled their wind, and stood off again under all sail.

Of course this unaccountable conduct met with no small amount of complaint, if not of abuse. Even Paul Pringle could not help saying, "If the fellows had no intention of helping us, why did they not stand on their proper course, without bearing down to disappoint us?"

Some hours afterwards, he suddenly struck his forehead with the palm of his hand, and exclaimed, "Why didn't I think of that before! Of course it's that Frenchman's flag. I ought to have known that it could never have brought us good. The masters of these vessels evidently thought that the craft was still a French privateer, and that the Monsieurs were playing them off some trick in the hope of catching them. We'll not carry the flag any longer. Haul it down, True Blue."

More anxiously even than at first, all on board kept a lookout for a sail. Several more days passed, and on each they were doomed to disappointment. Tim Fid had the lookout one morning at daybreak. Those asleep were roused up by his voice shouting, "A sail! a sail!—not three miles to windward of us. We must be seen. Hurrah!"

Paul crawled on deck and took a look at the stranger, a large brig with taut masts and square yards. "Yes, Tim, there is a sail," he said slowly. "She is either a man-of-war or a privateer; but from the cut of her sails, she is French. For my part, I would sooner remain on the wreck than be shut up in a French prison."

All hands expressed the same opinion; but how to avoid being compelled to go on board the brig was the question. The stranger soon espied the schooner and bore down upon her. Paul eyed the approaching brig with anything but looks of affection, when, as she drew near, who should be seen on the poop but Sir Henry Elmore and Mr Nott, while forward were several of the Gannet's crew.

She hove to; a boat was sent on board, which conveyed Paul to the brig. All that had occurred was soon explained. The brig was a privateer, captured after a smart action, and Sir Henry had been put in charge to carry her to Jamaica. He now took the prize in tow, and sent some fresh hands on board to relieve those who had suffered so much in her.

In four days they arrived at Port Royal; and Paul and his companions obtained the greatest credit for the way in which they had fought one privateer and preserved their own prize from destruction.

Chapter Twenty Five.

The brig which had been captured by the Gannet was a fine new vessel, mounting sixteen guns, and almost a match for the Gannet herself. Mr Digby, the first lieutenant of the corvette, had been so severely wounded that he was compelled to go home invalided. Sir Henry Elmore had much distinguished himself; and the Admiral on the Jamaica station, who wished to promote him, gave him an acting order as commander of the prize, which, under the name of the Rover was added to the Navy. As soon as Sir Henry had commissioned the brig, he sent for True Blue.

"Freeborn," he said, "I think that I can at once obtain an appointment for you which will suit your wishes. If you will accept it, I will get the Admiral to give you an acting order as boatswain of the Rover, and you can then take out your warrant as soon as you reach England for a still higher rate. What do you say?"

The look of intense satisfaction which lighted up True Blue's countenance assured Sir Henry that his offer would be accepted, and made him shrewdly suspect that an object beyond the rank of boatswain depended on it.

"Thank you, Sir Henry, thank you," he answered. "If Paul Pringle says yes, so do I; and if Peter Ogle doesn't say no, I think that it will be all right."

"But what has Peter Ogle to do with the matter?" inquired Sir Henry, trying to be grave.

"Why, you see, Sir Henry, he's Mary's father, and it wouldn't be right or shipshape to marry without his leave."

"Oh, I see," replied Sir Henry, who had suspected all along how matters stood. "You have agreed with Mary Ogle to marry her as soon as you are a boatswain; and as you did not expect to become one for some time to come, you do not think it would be right 'to steal a march,' as the soldiers say, on her father, and accept the appointment without consulting him."

"That's just it, Sir Henry," answered True Blue with his usual frankness. "Peter knows I want to marry his daughter, and that Mary is ready to marry me; and of course Paul knows it too, and, moreover, says that I might search the world around and not find a better wife; and that I know right well. But then, you see, Sir Henry, I expected, and so did they, that I should have to go out to the East Indies, or round the world maybe, before I should be able to get my warrant; and so I am taken all aback, as it were, with joy and pleasure, and I do thank you from my heart—that I do."

"All right, Freeborn!" exclaimed Sir Henry with evident pleasure, and putting out his hand. "I wish you all happiness from my heart. We must take care to pick up a good supply of prize-money, to help you to set up housekeeping; and all I bargain for is, that you invite me to the wedding."

"Ay, that I will, Sir Henry, and a right hearty welcome we'll give you," was the answer.

Paul Pringle and Peter Ogle yielded their very willing consent to True Blue's acceptance of the offer made him, and he came, highly delighted, to tell Sir Henry, who did not suppose that there would be any doubt about the matter.

"I thought it would be so," he said, handing the newly made boatswain a handsome silver call and chain. "You will wear this, Freeborn, for my sake; and, not to lose time, I have already got your appointment. Mr Nott has also got an acting order as second lieutenant, and Captain Brine has spared me Tom Marline, Hartland, and Fid, so that you will have several old shipmates with you. The rest of the crew we must make up as best we can. Marline will be a quartermaster; are either of the others fit for petty officers?"

"Well, sir, Hartland is fit for anything, I'll say that of him; and so would Fid be, if he was more steady and had some education; but though there is not a fellow I would more trust to in a scrimmage, or to have at my back when boarding an enemy, he can't depend on himself, if there's any mischief under weigh, and that's the worst of him."

"Well, then, I'll make Fid boatswain's mate, and then you can have an eye on him, and keep him in order. As to Hartland, he has been very steady ever since I have known him, some six years or more. What say you, if we get him an appointment as acting gunner? He is as well fitted for the duties as any man I can put my hand on."

"That he is, Sir Henry!" exclaimed True Blue warmly. "There isn't a man in the service you can more depend on in every way than Harry Hartland, and there isn't one I would rather have as a brother officer, for we have, as it were, been brothers ever since he came to sea."

So it was arranged; and Harry Hartland found himself, beyond his most sanguine expectations, appointed as acting gunner of the Rover.

The refitting of the Rover progressed rapidly, while, by degrees, a number of very fair seamen were picked up. She still wanted more than a third of her number, when the Gannet received orders to return to England, and Captain Brine allowed those of his crew who wished to do so to volunteer for the brig. Here would be evidence whether or not Sir Henry Elmore and his second lieutenant, and especially his two young warrant-officers, were popular with their late shipmates.

On the offer being made them, nearly every man on board volunteered for the Rover. Only thirty, however, were allowed to go; but they were all prime hands, with the exception of Sam Smatch, whose love for True Blue overcame every other consideration.

"Ah, Mr Freeborn, I come wid you, you see," he said, stepping on board the brig. "I no call you Billy now, 'cause you great officer, and right glad to see you; but so I officer very great too. Ship's cook. If the crew not eat, what become of dem?"

Sam, who was a sheet or two in the wind,—that is to say, not as sober as he should have been,—was winking and smiling all the time he was speaking, as if he wished True Blue to understand that though he was fully aware of the change in their relative positions, his feelings of affection towards him were in no way altered. One volunteer most of his old shipmates would willingly have seen return home; but, like a bad shilling, he turned up when least wanted. When the Gannet sailed, Gregory Gipples had by some mischance been left on shore, and, meeting Sir Henry, he begged so strenuously to be taken on board the Rover, and promised so earnestly to reform in all respects, that the young commander undertook to give him a trial.

This was the first time in his life that True Blue had been parted, beyond a few days, from Paul Pringle. They both felt the separation more than they ventured to express or exhibit to their shipmates; but, as they knew that it was inevitable, they bore it like brave men, each confident that absence would not diminish the affection which reigned in their hearts.

Away sailed the Rover for a cruise on the Spanish main, famed in days of yore as the locality where the richest prizes were to be picked up. Even Sir Henry Elmore, whose income was, for his rank, somewhat limited, had no objection to the chance offered of obtaining a stock of prize-money; and his officers and crew, including True Blue, looked forward to the prospect with infinite satisfaction.

The brig had been out of Port Royal about a week, when six sail were discovered to leeward, and proved to be a ship, with four brigs and a schooner. They continued their course till the Rover got near enough to allow her commander to see that the schooner and one of the brigs each carried sixteen guns, and that another carried six.

They, on discovering that the Rover was English, showed French colours, and drew close together, as if prepared to engage.

"I know, my lads, that you'll wish to take some of these vessels," said the commander, as he gave the order to bear down upon the enemy.

The schooner, on this, immediately made the signal to all the vessels to disperse in different directions, while she herself stood away under all the sail she could carry.

The Rover made chase, and after three hours came up with the ship and the largest brig, both of which struck without firing a shot. They proved to be prizes to the schooner, a French privateer, said to be one of the fastest vessels in those seas, and, from the number of prizes she had taken, one of the most successful cruisers.

"Fast as she may be," exclaimed Sir Henry, "we will do our best to take her!"

From the prisoners he learned, also, that she not only carried sixteen guns, full as heavy as those of the Rover, but a crew of not less than a hundred and fifty men. The ship and brig having prize crews put on board them, were sent back to Jamaica, and the Rover continued her chase of the schooner. She kept her in sight, running to the southward, till Sir Henry felt satisfied that the vessels he had recaptured were safe, and then, night coming on, she was hid from sight.

When morning broke not a sail was to be seen. Soon after noon, however, land was discovered ahead, and in an hour afterwards a schooner hove in sight. As the Rover drew near, she hoisted Spanish colours, and, evidently soon suspecting the brig's character, put up her helm, and ran before the wind towards the coast.

It was soon seen that she was not the privateer they were in search of. On she went, till she ran right on shore. The Rover on this, shortening sail, hauled her wind, and two boats being lowered, under command of Mr Nott, True Blue having charge of one of them, pulled in to ascertain whether she could be got off. The Spaniards, as they approached, fired a volley at them, and then, abandoning the vessel, pulled through the surf on shore. The schooner was immediately boarded, set on fire in every direction; and the English, driving the Spaniards from the boat, waited till she burned to the water's edge, and the sea, breaking over her, extinguished the flames.

This necessary though unsatisfactory work having been accomplished, the Rover made sail along the coast.

Two days afterwards, as she lay becalmed under the land, a schooner, having long sweeps at work, and three gunboats, were seen making for the Rover. The schooner was large, full of men, and carried a number of guns, and with the aid of the gunboats, should the calm continue, would, it was very evident, prove a formidable opponent to the English brig. Still, as usual, her crew were eager for battle; and as they went to their guns, they laughed and cut their jokes as heartily as ever. Of course, Gipples came in for his ordinary share of quizzing. Fid was the chief quizzer; but he had got several others to join him in making a butt of Gregory.

"I say, mates, did you ever hear what the savages on that shore out there do when they take any prisoners?" he began, winking to some of his shipmates. "They cuts them up just like sheep, and eats them I've heard say, that as you walks the streets, you'll see dozens of fellows sometimes, tarry breeches and all, hanging up in the butchers' shops. There was the whole crew of the Harpy sloop, taken off here, treated in that way—that I know of to a certainty. The Captain was a very fat man, so his flesh fetched twice as much a pound as the others; and when they served him up at dinner, they ornamented the dish with his epaulets and the gold lace off his coat."

Gipples opened his eyes very wide, and did not at all like the description.

Fid continued, "I hope, if they take us, they won't serve us in the same way; but there's no saying. We'll fight to the last; but all these gunboats and that big schooner are great odds against our little brig. Maybe Sir Henry would rather blow up the brig and all on board. I hope as how he will, and so we will disappoint the cannibals."

While Tim Fid and his companions were running on with this sort of nonsense, poor Gipples wishing that he was anywhere but on board the Rover, the enemy were gradually stealing out towards her.

True Blue saw that the contest, if carried on in a calm, would be a very severe one, and anxiously looked out for the signs of a breeze. As the schooner drew near, it was clear that she was the French privateer of which they were in search.

"We must take her somehow or other, there's no doubt about that," thought True Blue. "We have got some long sweeps; we'll get these all ready to rig out as soon as she comes near to lay her on board. I'll hear what the Captain has to say to the idea."

The boatswain on this went as near aft as etiquette would allow, knowing that the Captain would call him up and talk to him about the approaching conflict. Sir Henry had himself intended to board the enemy, but feared, from their being so close in under the land, that before the contest was over the vessels might drift on shore.

The sweeps were, however, got ready. Just then a light air from off the land sprang up, and the brig, making all sail, stood away from it—much, probably, to the satisfaction of her enemies, who fancied that her crew were afraid of fighting, and that, should they come up with her, she would prove an easy conquest. They began, therefore, briskly firing their bow-guns at the Rover, a compliment which she as warmly returned with her after-guns.

The breeze dying away, the sweeps were got out, and the Rover still kept ahead of her pursuers. All her guns were loaded with round and small shot; and a warm fire was kept up from her deck with muskets and pistols at the schooner which followed in her wake, her stern being kept, by means of the sweeps, directly towards the enemy. One of the gunboats had dropped astern, but the other two kept close to her.

A Spanish officer on board the schooner now ordered the gunboats to board the brig, the schooner herself giving signs that she was about to do the same. Sir Henry watched carefully to ascertain in what way they were about to attack the brig. The schooner kept off a little, and then showed that she was about to board on the starboard quarter, while the gunboats pulled for her larboard quarter and bow.

Sir Henry waited till the schooner and gunboats had got within about fifteen yards of the brig; then, with the sweeps on the larboard side, he rapidly pulled her round, so as to bring her starboard broadside to bear athwart the schooner's bow.

"Now, lads, give it them!" he shouted, and the whole broadside of the brig, with round and grape shot, was poured into the schooner's bows, now crowded with men ready to board, raking her fore and aft, and killing numbers of them. The Rover's crew instantly rushed over to the other side and swept her round; then, manning the larboard guns, raked both the gunboats in the same manner.

The shrieks and cries of the wounded showed the damage which had been done, the Spanish boats backing their oars, as if not wishing to renew the contest.

A voice from the schooner, however, ordered them to come on, while she kept firing away, though with somewhat abated energy. The crews of the Spanish boats having somewhat recovered their courage, once more returned to the attack; but the Rover's guns kept them from again attempting to board. Now and then they retired, and whenever they did so she pulled round, and again brought her broadside to bear on the bows of the schooner.

Thus for nearly an hour and a half was the contest carried on, when a light breeze sprang up, which placed the schooner to windward.

True Blue hurried aft. "If we back our headsails, Sir Henry, we shall run stern on the enemy, and may then carry her by boarding!" he exclaimed.

"Right, boatswain," was the answer. "Boarders, away!—follow me!"

The manoeuvre was quickly performed. With a crash the brig's stern ran against the schooner's side, and before the enemy knew what the English seamen were about, they, led by their gallant young Captain, who was closely followed by True Blue, had leaped on her deck and were driving all before them.

A tall French officer, evidently a first-rate swordsman, stood his ground, and rallied a party round him. He encountered Sir Henry, who, attacked by another Frenchman, was on the point of being cut down, when True Blue with his trusty cutlass came to his aid, and turned the fury of the Frenchman against himself.

There was science against strength and pluck. True Blue saw that all ordinary rules of defence and attack must be let aside; so, throwing up the Frenchman's sword with a back stroke of his cutlass, he sprang in on him, seized him by the throat, and, as he pushed him back, with another cut brought him to the deck.

The loss of their champion still more disheartened the French, who now gave way fore and aft.

Numbers had been cut down—some jumped overboard, but the greater portion ran below and sang out lustily for quarter.

Strange to say, not a man of the Rover was hurt, while nearly fifty Frenchmen and Spaniards were killed and wounded.

The moment the schooner's flag was hauled down, the Spanish boats made off; nor did they stop till they had disappeared within some harbour on the coast.

"I suppose," said Gipples, looking at the swarthy Spanish soldiers with no friendly eye, "though these chaps may have liked to eat us if they had caught us, we ain't obliged to eat them."

"That will be as the Captain likes," answered Tim Fid. "Perhaps he'll not think them wholesome at this time of the year, and let them go."

A very few days were sufficient to refit the Rover, and to store and provision her ready for sea. This time, however, she was ordered to cruise along the coasts of San Domingo and Porto Rico, towards the Leeward Islands.

At length she ran farther south, and came off the harbour of Point-à-Pitre, in the Island of Guadaloupe.

The time allowed for the cruise was very nearly expired, and Sir Henry was naturally desirous of doing something more than had yet been accomplished. The saucy little English brig poked her nose close into the French harbour one morning, and there discovered several vessels at anchor close under a strong fort.

"We must be on the watch for some of these gentlemen when they come out, and capture them," thought Sir Henry as the brig steered away again from the land.

True Blue had, however, fixed his eye on a French gun-brig which lay the outermost of all the vessels, and which he thought, by a bold dash, might be carried off.

"It can be done—I know it can, and I will ask the Captain," he said to himself. "Harry will join me, and I will have Tim Fid and a good set of staunch men. With two boats and thirty men, we could do it; but if Sir Henry will give us another boat, so much the better."

Sir Henry, consenting to his proposal, allowed him three boats, and promised to run in that very night, should the weather prove favourable, that he might carry out his object.

The boatswain had no difficulty in obtaining all the volunteers he required for his enterprise, and the rest of the day was spent in making the necessary preparations.

Towards evening the brig once more stood back in the direction of Point-à-Pitre. She reached the mouth of the harbour about midnight, when True Blue and his bold followers shoved off. He had an eight-oared cutter, carrying sixteen men in all; the remainder were in two boats—one under command of the gunner, the other of Tom Marline. Tim Fid was with True Blue.

The night was pitch dark, but a light in the harbour showed them in what direction to steer. The cutter soon got ahead of the other boats, and, as True Blue was anxious to get on board before he was discovered by the French, he kept on without waiting for them.

True Blue was well aware of the dangerous character of the enterprise on which he was engaged. The brig would not have been placed where she was unless she had been well armed and manned; and as the Rover had been perceived in the morning, in all probability her crew would be on the alert and ready to receive them. Still he knew well what daring courage could effect, and he had every hope of success.

The mouth of the harbour was reached, and up it the boats rapidly but silently pulled. There were two or three lights seen glimmering in the forts, and a few in the town farther off; but none were shown on board any of the vessels, and True Blue began to hope that the enemy were not expecting an attack.

True Blue stood up and peered earnestly through the obscurity.

"There she is, lads!" he exclaimed in a low voice. "Starboard a little—that will do; we will board under her quarter. Stand by to hook on. Second division, do not leave the boat till we have gained a footing on the deck. Now, lads, follow me."

True Blue expected when he leaped down to find himself on the deck, with his arms free to use his cutlass with advantage. Instead of that, he discovered that he had fallen into a net spread out over the quarter to dry. Here he could neither stand nor use his weapon, and in this position a Frenchman thrust a pike towards him, which wounded him in the thigh. Happily he got his cutlass sufficiently at liberty to cut the net. Then he dropped once more into the boat, into which he found that Tim Fid and the rest of the men had been thrust back, several severely wounded.

It would never do, however, thus to give up the enterprise; so, in a low voice telling the men to haul the boat farther ahead, he once more sprang up over the brig's bulwarks. Most of the Frenchmen, fancying that the attacking boat was still there, had rushed aft.

The clash of British cutlasses, and the flash of pistols in the waist, quickly brought them back again. True Blue, Fid, and two or three more stood on the bulwarks, bravely attempting to make good their footing; but one after the other, and as many more as came up, were hurled back headlong, some into the water, and others into the boat, till True Blue stood by himself, opposed to the whole French crew.

Undaunted even then he kept them at bay with his rapidly whirling cutlass, till those who had fallen overboard had had time to climb into the boat; then he shouted, "All hands aboard the French brig!"

"Ay, ay," was the answer, "we'll be with you, bo'sun. True Blue for ever! Hurrah!"

Once more the undaunted seamen, in spite of cuts and slashes, and broken heads, were climbing up the brig's sides. Fid was the first who joined True Blue, in time to save him from an awkward thrust of a boarding-pike; and, dragging it out of the hands of the Frenchman who held it, he leaped with it down on the deck. A few sweeps of True Blue's cutlass cleared a space sufficient to enable more of his party to join him; and these driving the Frenchmen still farther back, all the boat's crew at last gained the brig's deck. The Frenchmen now fought more fiercely than before, and muskets and pistols and pikes were opposed to the British cutlasses; but the weapons of cold steel proved the most effective.

On the British went. Some of the enemy jumped overboard, the rest leaped into the cabins, or threw down their weapons and cried for quarter. The after part of the vessel was gained. A group on the forecastle still held out. Another furious charge was made. Just then loud huzzas announced the arrival of the other two boats, and Harry Hartland and Tom Marline, with their followers, climbing up the sides, quickly cleared the forecastle.

The Frenchmen who had escaped below were ordered to be quiet, and sentries, with muskets pointed down, were stationed to keep them so.

The boats were once more manned and sent ahead, the cables were cut, and, amid a shower of shot from the forts, the gallantly-won brig was towed out of the harbour. Several other vessels were seen to be slipping their cables to come in chase; but just then a light air came down the harbour, which those nearer the shore did not feel. Hands were sent aloft to loosen the brig's sails. On she glided, increasing her speed; the boats towed rapidly ahead, but the work became lighter and lighter every instant.

"Hurrah! we have gained her, and shall keep her!" was the cry on board the prize.

However, they were not yet quite out of the enemy's harbour. The shot from the forts came whizzing along after the prize; and though, as not a light was shown on board her, the gunners could not aim very correctly, the missiles reached as far or farther than she then was,—now on one side, now on the other, and sometimes nearly over her.

True Blue occasionally looked aft. Through the darkness he now distinguished two vessels standing after him. The breeze had increased. He called the boats alongside, and ordered the crews on board. Pointing out the vessels astern, "Lads," he said, "we may still have to fight for our prize: but I am sure that you will defend her to the last."

"That we will, bo'sun—that we will, never fear," was the cheerful answer.

The guns were found to be loaded, and the Frenchmen had got up a supply of powder and shot to defend their vessel when True Blue and his companions so unceremoniously cut short their proceedings. In case an action should be fought, it was necessary to secure both the French officers and seamen. Harry Hartland was charged with this duty. On going below, he found that not an officer had escaped without a wound; some had been hurt very severely. Fortunately an assistant-surgeon was on board, able to look after them. Harry placed a sentry in the gunroom, with orders to shoot the first man who made the slightest sign of revolting; while he stationed a couple more over the crew, with directions to treat them in the same way.

The two vessels were getting very near; so was the mouth of the harbour. Not far outside True Blue knew that he should find the Rover. On they came. He luffed across the bows of one, and poured in a broadside; then he treated the other in the same way, and directly afterwards, with a slashing breeze, dashed out of the harbour. In a quarter of an hour he was up to the Rover, and right hearty were the cheers with which he was received; for the constant firing had made Sir Henry fear that the boats were pursued, and that the enterprise had failed.

The two vessels now stood away under all sail from the land.

"I have known many brave actions," said Sir Henry, when on the next day True Blue presented himself before his Captain, "but I assure you, Freeborn, none exceeds the one you have just performed in dash or gallantry. You have still, I am certain, the road to the higher ranks of our noble profession open to you, if you will but accept the first step."

"Thank you, Sir Henry," answered True Blue modestly; "I have just done my duty. My mind is made up about the matter. I wished to take the craft, just to show that I deserved your good opinion of me; and perhaps it may help somewhat to confirm me in my rank as bo'sun, and if it does, I shall be well content."

Chapter Twenty Six.

Peace—known as the Peace of Amiens—was concluded in 1801; and though England called in her cruisers, prohibiting them any longer to burn, sink, and destroy those of her enemies, she wisely declined drawing her own teeth or cutting her claws, by dismantling her ships and disbanding her crews, but, like a good-natured lion, crouched down, wagging her tail and sucking her paws, while, turning her eyes round and round, she carefully watched the turn affairs were likely to take.

Never had more ships been seen arriving day after day at Spithead, and never had Portsmouth Harbour been fuller of others fitting and refitting for sea, or its streets more crowded with seamen laughing, dancing, singing, and committing all sorts of extravagances, and flinging their well-earned money about with the most reckless prodigality.

About this time, while Portsmouth was in the heyday of its uproarious prosperity, and prize-money was as plentiful as blackberries in summer, a man-of-war's eight-oared cutter was seen pulling in from Spithead, and then, entering the harbour, making for the Gosport shore. There was nothing unusual in this, or rather it was an event not only of daily but of hourly occurrence.

There were two officers in the sternsheets; but their simple uniform showed that they were not of any high rank, though the crew paid them the most profound respect. They were young men, though beards, pigtails, and lovelocks, with thoroughly weatherbeaten, sunburnt countenances, made them look somewhat older. One had a silver chain round his neck, with a call or whistle attached to it, which showed that he was a boatswain.

As they stepped on shore, the crew threw up their oars, and with one voice shouted, "We wish you every happiness—that we do, sir, from our hearts! Three cheer for the boatswain! Hip! hip! hip! hurrah!"

"Thank you, lads," said the young boatswain, turning round with a pleasant smile on his countenance. "We have served long and happily together, and done some things to be proud of; and I tell you that I would rather be boatswain of such a crew as you are, than Captain of many I have fallen in with. Come up here and have a parting glass! I know that I can trust you to go back to the ship, as you promised; for it's one of many things to be proud of, to be able to say that we never knew a man to run from our ship."

The two warrant-officers were accompanied by an old black man with a wooden leg, who stumped along, aided by a stick, as fast as they could walk; while a couple of seamen followed with huge painted canvas bags on their shoulders, and various foreign-looking things hung about outside. They themselves carried a couple of birdcages and two parrots; and a mischievous-looking monkey sat on the black's shoulder, another parrot being perched on the top of his hat, and a fiddle-case hung over his neck. They soon got out of Gosport into the country.

"Stay, Harry!" said the elder of the officers; "Paul wrote that we were to steer west by north, and that if we stood on under easy sail for half a glass, we should just fetch Paradise Row. Now here we are, with the sun right astern; let's have the proper bearings of the place."

True Blue—for he was the young boatswain who had been speaking—looked at the sun, and then, turning himself round, in a few seconds seemed to make up his mind that they were proceeding in the right direction.

"I feel uncommonly inclined to set more canvas; and yet we mustn't quit our convoy," he remarked as he moved on.

"No, that wouldn't do," answered his friend, Harry Hartland. "Come, heave ahead, my hearties!" he added, looking back at the seamen carrying the bags; "and you, Sam, shall we lend you a leg, old boy?"

"Tank'ee, gunner—a grand new cork one, if you like!" answered Sam, grinning and chuckling at his joke; "but ye see my timber one will serve me, I tink, till I'm laid under hatches. But I no wonder Billy in a hurry to go along—ha! ha! ha! I call de fine grand bo'sun Billy now again, jes as I did when he was one little chap aboard de old Terrible. We off service, you know! I once more free man! Out-door Greenwich pensioner! What more I want?—plenty to eat, nothing to do! I go wid you and play at your wedding, True Blue—ha! ha! ha! Fancy I, Sam Smatch, play at Billy True's wedding—once little chap born aboard de Terrible, and often nurse in de old nigger's arms."

"And right glad I am to have you by me, Sam," answered True Blue, looking kindly at the negro. "You took good care of me—that I'm sure of—when I was a baby, and we've weathered many a storm together since in all parts of the world. There's scarcely a friend I should be more sorry to miss at my wedding than you, if wedding there is to be; but it is so long since I heard from home, that who can tell what has happened?"

"Ah, yes—Mary Ogle gone and married some oder sailor maybe! Dat is what dey petticoat women often do," said Sam with a wink, sticking his thumb towards the boatswain's ribs.

"No, no. No fear of that, at all events!" exclaimed True Blue vehemently. "You didn't suppose that I meant that. But how can we tell that all our friends are alive and well?" he said gravely, and was silent for a minute. "However," he added in a cheerful tone, "I have no fears that all will be right, and that, before many evenings are over, we shall have you fingering your fiddlestick as merrily as ever."

So they went on, cheerfully talking as they proceeded towards Paradise Row, which, in truth, True Blue hoped would prove a Paradise to him; for there, since Paul, and Abel, and Peter, had become warrant-officers, their respective families had come to reside, to be near them when they came into port.

They, however, had now charge of different ships in ordinary; and as they had all gone through a great deal of service, they did not expect to be again sent to sea.

Old Mrs Pringle was still alive and well when True Blue had last heard from home, and to her house he and his shipmates were now bound. Still, as they went along, True Blue could not help looking into all the windows of the various cottages they passed, just to ascertain if that was the one inhabited by his dear old granny or not.

At last he turned to Harry. "I think, mate, we have run our distance," he observed; "we ought to be in the latitude of Paradise Row by this time. I'll just step up to that pretty little cottage there and ask. Here, Harry, just hold Chatterbox, please."

Suiting the action to the word, having given his parrot to his friend, up to the cottage he went. It had a porch in front of it, covered with jasmine, and a neat verandah, and was altogether a very tasty though unpretending little abode. He rapped at the door with a strangely-carved shark's tooth which he held in his hand. After waiting a little time, the door was opened, and, without looking directly at the person who opened it, he began, "Please, marm, does Mrs Pringle live hereabouts?" Then, suddenly he was heard to exclaim, "What—it is—Mary, Mary!"

What more he said his friends did not hear, for the door was nearly closed as he sprang into the house. However, both Harry and Sam were very discreet people, and they had heard enough to show them that their presence could easily be dispensed with; so, as there was a nice grassy bank under a widespreading tree, they, with the two seamen carrying the bags, and the monkey and the parrots, went and sat down there to wait till the boatswain might recollect that there were such beings in existence.

Harry felt very glad that his friend was likely to be so happy, and old Sam amused himself with scratching the monkey's head, making him hang by his tail, and jump over his own wooden leg, while the seamen went to sleep with their heads on the bags. Sam was the first to grow tired of his amusement, and, getting up, he stumped up towards the cottage and peeped over the neat white blind of the front window.

He came back grinning and chuckling. "All right," he said. "Him bery happy—no tink of us yet, I guess."

Whether or not the apparition of Sam's black visage had been seen does not appear; but in a short time True Blue came to the door of the cottage, looking as happy and lighthearted as a fellow could look, and, hailing his friends, asked them to step in.

Mrs Ogle was there, and Mary, and a younger sister very like her; but Peter was aboard his ship, a seventy-four, in Portsmouth Harbour; and Mary and her sister, and their mother, shook hands heartily with Sam, because he was an old acquaintance, and with Harry, because he was True Blue's brother officer. And then True Blue told Harry that Mrs Ogle could put him up, and would be right glad to do so; and then that he could take Sam to Mrs Pringle's, so that they should have him always to play to them; which were very pleasant arrangements, and seemed to give infinite satisfaction to all parties concerned. It was extraordinary how long it took to get under weigh again; but at last True Blue, with his bags and some of his treasures, did find his way to his adopted grandmother's, and a warm welcome did the dear old lady give him, and did not scold him in the least for inquiring first at Mrs Ogle's where she lived, seeing that he did not know when he went to the door that it was Mrs Ogle's.

Sam and the monkey, and two of the parrots, with the cage birds, took up their residence at Mrs Pringle's. True Blue, accompanied by Harry, paid a visit to Mrs Bush and her family; and the whole party assembled, as they had done several years before, at Mrs Ogle's, which had certainly the handsomest room in it, and Sam Smatch brought his fiddle; and a very merry evening they had, the only drawback being that the three elder warrant-officers were unable to be present, as their duties kept them on board their ships.

They had tea and cakes, and bread and butter, and preserves, and water-cresses; and then Sam screwed up his fiddle, and to work went his bow, his head nodding and his timber toe beating time, while he played the merriest of all merry country-dances and the most vehement of hornpipes.

True Blue had not danced a hornpipe for many a long year,—it would not have been dignified while he was a boatswain,—but he had not forgotten how to do so. That he very soon showed, to the satisfaction of all present, especially to that of Mary, and not a little to that of Sam Smatch, who, in defiance of all the rules of etiquette, kept shouting, "Bravo, Billy—well done, Billy—keep at it, boy! I taught him, dat I did—dat's it. I played de first tune to him he ever danced to. Bravo, Billy! You do my heart good—dat you do. Hurray! hurray! Billy True Blue for ever in dancing a hornpipe!"

As the dancing could not last all the evening, the parrots and the monkey and a considerable portion of the contents of the bags were brought in to be exhibited, and, as it proved, to be distributed among the owner's old friends.

True Blue had given his cage full of birds to Mrs Pringle, as he knew she would prize it; he had, however, gifts especially brought for Mrs Bush and all her family, as well as for Mrs Ogle, and for several other friends not so intimately related to him as they were; and he found that they were the means of affording infinite satisfaction to all parties.

The first thing the next morning, after breakfast, the young warrant-officers set off to pay their respects to the three old warrant-officers in Portsmouth Harbour, on board the Jupiter, Lion, and Portland, seventy-fours.

Paul Pringle was, of course, the first visited. His pipe was shrilly sounding as ponderous yards and coils of rope and casks and guns and gun-carriages and other innumerable fittings and gear of a ship were being hoisted up and lowered into lighters alongside, to convey them to the dockyard. His delight at seeing True Blue as he stepped on deck was so great that he forgot to pipe "Belay," and a twenty-four pounder would have been run up to the yardarm had not his godson instinctively supplied the omission with his own pipe, though, when Harry afterwards informed him of the fact, he was not in the slightest degree aware that he had done so.

As Paul was then so very busy, they promised to return at dinner time, and went on to see Peter Ogle. It was remarked, however, that Paul did not for the remainder of the forenoon carry on his duties with his usual exactness, and seemed far more elated and excitable than was his wont.

Peter Ogle's pleasure at seeing True Blue was only surpassed by that of Paul. He received his old friends in his cabin, which, as True Blue glanced round it, showed that a considerable amount of feminine taste had been exercised in its adornment.

"Make yourselves at home, my lads—brother officers, I should say, though," he said, glancing at their uniforms, "It is a pleasure to see you, Billy, my dear boy, and you too, Harry, though I haven't known you by some fifteen years or more so long as True Blue. Boy, bring glasses. Here's some real honest schiedam, taken out of a Dutch prize. Help yourselves. You neither of you are topers, I know; so much the better. And now let's hear what you've been about since I last clapped eyes on you."

True Blue on this gave a rapid account of their doings in the Rover after the Gannet had sailed for England, and of numerous adventures which had subsequently befallen them before they once more returned home.

After a visit paid to Abel Bush, who welcomed them home as cordially as their other old friends had done, they returned to dine with Paul Pringle.

"And, True Blue, my boy, how soon is it to come off?" inquired Paul when dinner was over. "Have you asked Mary to fix the day yet?"

"No, godfather; I thought she might rather wish to wait a bit, and so I wasn't going to ask her for a day or two," answered True Blue ingenuously.

"Don't put it off, lad," said Paul. "When a sailor meets a girl to love, the shorter the wooing and the sooner he weds the better. How does he know what moment he may have to heave up his anchor and make sail round the world again?"

True Blue very willingly promised to follow his godfather's advice; and Harry, who was listening attentively, thought it excellent. As may be supposed, before the evening was over, the day was settled for True Blue's wedding with Mary Ogle; and before a week had passed, Harry announced that her sister Susan had fixed the same day to marry him.

Close to Mrs Ogle's residence was a barn of large dimensions; it was not a picturesque building, but the floor was smooth, and that was all they required. In a wonderfully short space of time, with the aid of flags innumerable, wreaths of flowers, and painted canvas, it was converted into a most elegant edifice, fit for a ball or supper room. The morning of True Blue's wedding day arrived, and up to Dame Pringle's door drove a postchaise with four horses, out of which stepped Sir Henry Elmore, now, as his full-dress uniform showed, a Post-Captain. He shook hands right cordially with True Blue and all his friends, and the bells of the parish church at that moment set up so merry and joyous a peal that it was evident the ringers believed that it was an occasion of much happiness.

Carriages sufficient to carry all the party now began to collect in the neighbourhood of Paradise Row; and Sam Smatch and Tom Marline, both of whom had got leave to come on shore, were very busy in fastening huge white favours and bunches of flowers to the coats of the party.

"Come, Freeborn, with me in my carriage," said Sir Henry. "I have fulfilled my promise in being present at your marriage, and must beg to stand as your best man, and see that you behave properly; but boarding a Frenchman at the head of a dozen daring fellows, though opposed to a hundred or more, is a very different matter to standing before the altar, about to take a wife for better or for worse to the end of life."

"So I was thinking, Sir Henry," answered True Blue, smiling. "And do you know, that if it wasn't Mary Ogle I was going to marry, I shouldn't like it at all."

"All right, then, my friend; you'll do," said the baronet. "Step into the carriage."

The favours being distributed, Tom Marline mounted the coach-box of the first carriage, in which were Mary Ogle and her father and mother, carrying in his hands a long pole with a huge flag, on which was inscribed, "True Blue for ever! Hurrah for our own Billy True Blue!"

Tim Fid mounted, as he said, the fo'castle of the next carriage, in which came Mrs Bush and

Susan, with Harry, who declared that he didn't fancy the custom of following in different vehicles, as great folks did.

On Fid's banner was the device of a ship, with "Hurrah for the Navy of Old England! Hurrah for her Gunners, Past, Present, and Future!"

On the box of the third carriage sat Sam Smatch, fiddle in hand, playing away most lustily, and occasionally firing off a bow or stern-chaser of jokes at the other carriages with a peculiar loud cackling laugh which none but negroes can produce.

Nobody could have behaved better than did the brides and bridegrooms; and when the ceremony was over, the bells set up a peal even more joyous than before. Instead of driving back to Paradise Row, the carriages proceeded to the harbour; and then at the Hard appeared half a dozen man-of-war's boats, rigged gaily with flags. Sir Henry handed Mrs Billy True Blue Freeborn into one boat, and Mrs Harry Hartland into another, and of course their husbands stepped in after them; and then he performed the same office to all the elder matrons and their younger daughters; and then wishing them all health, happiness, and prosperity, he entered his own boat and pulled across to Portsmouth.

The three godfathers and their mates stepped into another boat, and Sam Smatch and the younger men into the sixth; and thus arranged, away the boats pulled, Sam playing right lustily his merriest tunes. True Blue's boat led, steering up the harbour, where lay Paul's and Abel's and Peter's ships. As they passed, the people on board came to the side, and cheered over and over again with all their might and main, making up by the vehemence and multiplicity of their vociferations for the paucity of their numbers.

True Blue and Harry got up and cheered too, and so did the matrons in the third boat; and the godfathers made the seventy-fours a speech—it sounded as if addressed to the ships rather than to the people on board. Of course the men in the other boats cheered, and Sam almost sprang his bow with the vehemence of his playing; but all this was as nothing compared to the reception the bridal party met with as they reached True Blue's and Harry's own ship.

Up and down the harbour pulled the bridal squadron; and the crews of every ship, as they passed, took up the cheer and welcomed the bridegroom, for True Blue and his deeds were now well-known throughout the British fleet. He had not aimed high, in one sense of the word, and yet he had in another sense always aimed high and nobly—to do his duty.

Right well that duty he had done; he had gained all he desired, and never was there a happier or more contented man.

No pen can do adequate justice to the ball in the barn in the evening. Never were so many warrant-officers collected together with their wives and their families; and never, certainly, had such an amount of gilt buttons and gold lace, and silk and satins and feathers, been seen in such a place. A crashing band overwhelmed Sam Smatch's fiddle; but he, for his consolation, was requested to play frequent solos; and he far out-eclipsed himself when he struck up "Bill's own special hornpipe," as he called it, which, nolens volens, True Blue was compelled to dance.

If the bridegrooms made a tour, it must have been a very short one, as their leave could not have extended to many days. For a short time they lived on shore, when their ship was paid off;

but war soon called them afloat.

True Blue had a numerous family of sons, every one of whom served his country afloat, all becoming warrant-officers; while their sons again, from their intelligence and steady conduct, although they entered before the mast, obtained the same rank.

True Blue himself, who lived to enjoy a hearty and hale old age, gave the same advice to his grandchildren which he received from Paul Pringle.

"Lads," he used to say, "be content with your lot. Do your duty in whatever station you are placed, on the quarterdeck or fo'castle, in the tops aloft or at the guns on the main or lower-deck, and leave the rest to God. Depend on it, if you obey His standing orders, if you steer your course by the chart and compass He has provided for you, and fight your ship manfully, He will give you the victory."